ANT FARM

THE SEAMUS MCCREE SERIES
BY JAMES M. JACKSON

Ant Farm (#0)
Bad Policy (#1)
Cabin Fever (#2)

NON-FICTION
BY JIM JACKSON

One Trick at a Time:
How to Start Winning at Bridge

ANT FARM

A SEAMUS MCCREE MYSTERY

James M. Jackson

Wolf's
Echo
Press

First Edition
Trade Paperback Edition: May 2015

Cover Design by Karen Phillips

Wolf's Echo Press
PO Box 54
Amasa, MI 49903
www.WolfsEchoPress.com

This is a work of fiction. Any references to real places, real people, real organizations, or historical events are used fictitiously. Other names, characters, organizations, places, or events are the product of the author's imagination.

ISBN-13 Trade Paperback: 978-1-943166-00-8
Library of Congress Control Number: 2015908178

Printed in the United States of America
10987654321

DEDICATION

To the Cincinnati Writers Project,
for all you've done and continue to do to advance writing.

ONE

I FLICKED ON THE PORCH light and discovered grief standing in front of my door. In a dead-flat voice my visitor said, "Seamus, I'm glad I caught you." Skyler Weaver's hollow eyes sucked me into her pain and silenced my response.

"I was at church," she continued. "A music committee meeting—and figured since you were on my way home, I'd see if you were in." Her gaze flicked down to her hands clasped at her waist and then back to my face. The corners of her lips curled in an attempted smile that died. "Well, you're not exactly on my way home, but . . ." She shrugged.

I ushered her through the foyer and into my library. She walked with leaden steps to the fireplace and examined the cherry mantel and Rookwood tile. "It's beautiful. Does it still work?"

She turned around. Now that she was in better light, I was struck by the creases that etched her face. She was a shell of the woman who, at the Sunday service following her fiancé's murder, had leaned heavily on the minister as the two stood on the chancel. Gripping the microphone, tears streaking her face, she'd asked us to keep her and Samuel Presser's family in our thoughts after the senseless tragedy. During the summer I had let the memory slip away, and in her presence I felt guilty.

"All six fireplaces were designed for coal," I said, "but none work. Would you like a tour?" I remembered belatedly my duties as host. "Or something to drink?"

"I love these big old Cincinnati Victorians." She slid into the rocking chair, her back to the stained glass window. "But it's late . . ."

I moved the antique Hitchcock chair to face her and sat down. I didn't know Skyler well. She sang soprano in the St. John's Unitarian Universalist Church choir and sat in front of me at rehearsals. I'd seen her at church functions and choir parties, but since I was old enough to be her father, our social paths didn't otherwise cross. Was she an emissary to ask me to join the music committee? I lined up my excuses.

"I can see you're wondering why I'm here." Deep breath. "I'm not satisfied with the police investigation. I want to hire you to investigate Samuel's murder. You come highly recommended."

My stomach clenched knowing I would have to disappoint her. "Oh, Skyler, I am so sorry for your loss, but I'm afraid someone's misinformed you about what I do."

Her gunmetal-gray eyes locked onto mine. "I've talked to a number of people this week. I know you can help."

With each word she spoke, my distress increased. "Skyler, you need a licensed private investigator. I'm just an analyst for Criminal Investigation Group. Besides, that's not how CIG works. I wish I could help, but you have to find someone qualified."

She rocked hard, causing a fault in the ancient rocker to click in protest. Several seconds later, she stopped and leaned toward me. "Look at me, Seamus. I'm a wreck. I can't sleep. I've lost twenty pounds, and I jump at the slightest noise."

I plucked a tissue from the box on the side table and handed it to her. Now that she mentioned it, I noticed that her print blouse with flowers in the Georgia O'Keefe style hung off her shoulders, and she'd cinched in her black dress slacks so tightly their fabric gathered at her waist. She dabbed away the tears welling in her eyes.

"It's been two months since Samuel was murdered. The police say they haven't given up, but I know they have. They've got new killings every week." She sprang from the chair and paced. "They're overworked and can only do so much. I know that. I need a miracle, and people tell me you and your CIG sometimes find them. Even the head of homicide, Lieutenant Hastings, confirmed that your work last year unraveled a frame-up where they had charged the wrong person. I know you can do it . . . if you *want* to help me . . ."

Hoping to ease my discomfort, I stood. No help. "Skyler, it's not my CIG. I work for them. I don't do independent work." I caught myself pressing on my forehead with both hands, trying to smooth the furrow lines. I dropped my hands to my sides.

She bunched the tissue in her hand. "You've got pull. You can get CIG to help—if you want to."

"It's just not that simple. Maybe Lieutenant Hastings failed to mention that CIG only works on cases where we've been invited by the local police. That's our whole modus operandi: we provide additional resources to police departments who don't have the expertise or are understaffed or—"

Her breath erupted in short steam-engine bursts. Feeling trapped in the midst of a lecture, I bumbled on. "They're often cold cases—years after the crime. We—"

She whirled to face me, hands turning white on her hips. "Shay-mus Mac-Cree," she pronounced each syllable with emphasis. "You remind me of Samuel, and not just because you both have dark, curly hair. You spew mountains of information—all accurate—but you don't answer the question. So, I'll rephrase it. How much would it cost to hire you and CIG to investigate Samuel's death? I don't care whether the police cooperate or not. I need to know why he was murdered."

Her mournful eyes reminded me of the confusion, and pain, and searing need I had felt to bring meaning to my father's death. Besides, if the police were stumped—*because* the police were stumped—I was intrigued.

"Let me do this," I said. "I'll call Lieutenant Hastings tomorrow and see if I can find out anything."

"And you'll talk with CIG?"

I tried once more to smooth my brow with the heels of my hands. Why hadn't I just said no? "Unless the Cincinnati police invite CIG to assist, there's nothing I can do. They're not my rules, they're CIG's rules. I promise I'll call Hastings. But you need to promise me you'll look for a licensed investigator. Maybe Hastings can recommend one."

We closed by shaking hands as proper dealmakers do. I should have read the small print.

Two

THE NEXT MORNING I WOKE at six o'clock, as usual. Before I lost courage, I called Lt. Hastings and left a voice message: nothing urgent, but would she give me a call? The gray overcast sky and smell of humidity convinced me to run early, before the sun converted all outdoors into a sauna. I still had a month and a half before a planned marathon, which meant three more weeks of hard work before I began tapering off.

My route around the Clifton Gaslight District took me past areas of historic late-nineteenth-century mansions, turn-of-the-century Victorians like mine, 1920s bungalows, and a scattering of more modern houses. Robins whistled the day in from shade trees and dewed lawns. Running time was thinking time—in this case about Skyler and her fiancé, Samuel Presser.

Why had someone killed him? Skyler had inserted that question under my skin and, like a splinter, it shot a brief twinge up my nerves each time I touched it. Why had I offered to talk to the Cincinnati police? I wasn't sure of my motives, but the mix certainly included not wanting to disappoint Skyler, innate curiosity, the challenge of figuring out something no one else had—and I wouldn't mind seeing Lt. Hastings again. If I hadn't been running already, the thought of her would have increased my heart rate.

The whoop of a police siren startled me into the air.

"Don't you know you're supposed to run on the left side of the road?"

Speak of the devil. Even with my back to her, I recognized Lt. Hastings' voice. I trotted to the passenger side of the unmarked police car. "You scared the bejesus out of me," I said. "I run on the right because it's better for my broken foot."

"Come again?"

Between pants I responded. "Broke my arch playing soccer. Years ago. Killed my pro career in the first year. Never completely healed. It's more comfortable to run on the right." *Why was I telling her all this stuff?*

"You say so. I've been following you for several blocks. Even though I know you're only six foot two, your head was way up in the clouds. You left a message?"

"And you drove all over Clifton to find me?"

"I was heading to Northside and stopped by your house. I happened to see you crossing Ludlow and followed. What'd you want?"

"Long story." I had no clue how to approach this, so I delayed. "How about I buy you lunch sometime in the next few days?"

"That's big of you. Why do I sense an ulterior motive?"

"Me? Ulterior motive? My calendar says in big red letters that it's Law Enforcement Appreciation Week. I want to do my civic duty."

"Just a minute while I put my waders on." A grin crept over her face. "I've got a meeting at city hall later this morning. Would ten till noon at the Rock Bottom on Fountain Square do?"

"Sure you don't want to make it eleven fifty-two to give yourself extra time?"

"What's this crap? I thought it was cop appreciation week."

◊◊◊

MY GARAGE DOOR STUCK PARTWAY up. A hip check rattled it loose. I needed to do something about that track, but no one had ever accused me of being handy. I chose my 1992 Infiniti G20 and parked in a downtown underground lot.

Fountain Square was busy despite August's broiling sun. Young male office workers with rolled-up sleeves and opened collars roosted around the fountain like a flock of pigeons. I walked to the upper section and found a shady spot where I could observe the lower level while waiting for Hastings.

Considering Cincinnati is six hundred miles from the nearest ocean, the girl-watching was excellent. A wash of ponytails, taut bodies in tank tops, and long exposed legs in short skirts flooded the plaza, swirling around the preening males. If I concentrated, I could smell the massed pheromones.

Lt. Hastings appeared on schedule, her own long legs eating up the distance. I hustled to the Rock Bottom in time to hold the door open for her. A blast of air-conditioning hit me like a cold compress, raising goosebumps along my arms. We joined the line waiting for booths.

"Did you take a time management course?" I asked. "And that's why we're meeting at an odd time? Do people keep appointments better?"

"Interesting theory, but no. The captain must have decided I needed to do penance for something and gave me the marvelous opportunity to join Councilman Braun and some of his supporters and listen to their wonderful ideas on how to reduce murder in Cincinnati. The meeting was supposed to end at eleven thirty. I gave them ten minutes' grace, so that's eleven forty. Good thing. They were going strong on time, but not so much on content when I had to excuse myself to meet you. It takes ten minutes to walk here from city hall, so that meant meeting at eleven fifty."

The hostess grabbed menus and motioned us to follow her through the noise by the bar and past the redolent smells of the kitchen before showing us a table. It really was law enforcement appreciation week, at least concerning my appreciation of the swing of Hastings' hips as I followed her. The hostess handed us menus and took our drink orders— soda for the on-duty Hastings and a draft beer for me.

"You've got me here," Hastings said. "What do you want?"

"Presser murder." As though my words had pulled an electrical plug, her eyes went from sparkling to flat. "Can you tell me how it's going?"

She leaned back in the booth, studying me. "You know I'm not supposed to say anything more than what we release to the media, but I figure I can trust you." The sparkle in her eyes reappeared. "Although, since I know you're a sneaky bastard, I just added you to the list of suspects. Where were you on the night of—?"

The waitress interrupted, bringing beverages and taking orders.

"I read about it at the time," I said. "It's been a while and I don't remember many details."

"Our release said Presser was stabbed. We didn't say there were two wounds. First in the back, second, the fatal one, in his chest."

"Who discovered the body?"

"His assistant at TransOhio Life couldn't reach him all day. One of his friends, Matthew Yeung, swung by Presser's apartment on his way home to make sure everything was okay. It wasn't. Presser's car was parked outside, but no one answered when Yeung tried the bell. Side door was locked, but the basement door was ajar. According to dispatch, he called 911 at exactly eighteen twenty-three on the seventh of June, 2007. Stayed outside until a unit got there. They found Presser on the kitchen floor—killed the night before."

She took a long pull on the soda straw. "Forensics has been useless. The murder weapon is a stiletto—a pro's weapon. Amateurs go for macho pig stickers. Far as we can tell, Presser was one clean kid."

"Possible motives?"

"Not a one. Zip. Nada. No drugs. No gambling. No kiddie porn. No debt. Nothing interesting at all. Nothing stolen from his place. You looking to collect the ten grand Presser's employer put up? Got a lead?"

"Sorry. With the cost of my kid's college, I wish I could. So you got nothing?"

"We've interviewed everyone. All we get is, 'How could this happen to such a nice guy?'"

The waitress brought our burgers and fries.

"Smells delicious," I said. "Speaking of which, do I detect a new fragrance you're wearing? Lilac?"

She finished doctoring her burger with ketchup. "Interesting you should notice." She reached over and patted my hand. "Thanks. It is."

Her eyes seemed to smile and my heart went into pitter-patter mode. I quickly took a large bite of my burger and savored the juices. What was I thinking, flirting with Lt. Hastings? Well, I knew what I was thinking, but it was hardly wise. I finished chewing and plunged in. "Presser's fiancée, Skyler Weaver, sings with me in church choir. She wants CIG to investigate the murder."

Hastings motioned like a traffic cop for me to proceed.

"She needs closure. Not knowing why her fiancé was killed is eating her up. I know that pain. I told her I'd ask if CPD would consider having us help."

She leaned back into the bench, absentmindedly shoving french fries into her mouth.

"I told her how unlikely it was you guys would want to use us."

Before leaning forward, she deliberately took a bite of the burger, ate more fries, slurped her cola. "First I get Braun telling me how to prevent murders. Now I have you telling me how to solve them. Pretty bold move, Seamus, inviting me to lunch to tell me I'm not doing my job. If this were two years ago, I'd thank you for the lunch and take this story to the guys and they'd all laugh their rocks off at the joke. No bleeping way we'd let you guys take over."

I choked on my food. "Bleeping?"

Hastings shrugged. "My nephew is two. Couple weeks ago he and a neighbor kid were playing with his toy cars. The other kid's car is blocking his and he yells, 'Hey, you fuckin' asshole, get outta my way.' My sister gave me one of those *significant* looks."

"Oops."

"So I'm trying to clean up my act. Anyway, we're getting more than a murder a week and the backlog keeps growing. We've got so much darn work. No way we can get it all done. If you guys are interested in helping out with a case, and if it were just me, I'd say darn straight, let's do it."

I tried to look neutral. "But?"

"Yeah, but I got the captain and he has the lieutenant colonel and he has the chief and he has the city manager and she has the city council. You hear what I'm saying?"

"Thanks for asking, but no thanks?"

Eyes a-twinkle, she said, "You know what the captain gave me for Christmas last year?"

"Didn't know he was so generous."

"Only for special people, I guess. He hand-delivered an exquisitely wrapped box. Had high-class silver paper with ribbon so tight I had to cut it off. Inside, written in calligraphy on parchment, was the word 'Think.'"

Her sly smile worked at the corners of her mouth and I burst out laughing. Three preppies in the next booth glanced over. "He wants you to think *inside* the box. I didn't realize the captain had such ingenuity."

"Yes sir, he's a bright boy, and the message came through loud and clear. If I want to remain in homicide and not join the motor pool, I need to be a little more conventional."

At least I can tell Skyler I tried.

"But they're never going to keep me inside any old box, no matter how fancy the wrapping." She flashed a wide smile. "I will have to start with the captain. Maybe I lay it off as one of Braun's suggestions—nah, he'd never believe anything half-sane came from him. Has Rand already approved this?"

"Really? You'll ask?" I matched her smile, felt tension release from my shoulders, and raised my beer in salute. Then I thought about her question. I hadn't even contemplated asking Robert Rand, the founder and boss of CIG. Neck tension returned in spades.

"I doubt the captain'll say yes," she said. "Let alone the big bosses. It's a good experiment—why *not* bring in some assistance? We use the feds, and hell, Councilman Braun wants to privatize all the city services—this could be just the beginning." Her eyes sparkled with mischief.

She hadn't waited for my answer about notifying Rand, meaning I didn't have to fess up or lie. I wasn't sure whether she was pursuing this because she thought it was the right thing, or because it gave her a chance to yank on the donkey's tail, even if she did get kicked in the teeth.

"But don't hold your breath. Even assuming the captain agrees, you know how decisions go. If God had had to work with city bureaucracy to create the world, it still wouldn't be finished."

Hastings left while I settled the check. I felt good that I had something positive to tell Skyler and left a generous tip. Walking to the parking garage, I checked my cell phone for messages. One—from my son, who never calls.

"Hey, Dad," the message said. "Call my cell phone STAT. I tried you at home first. Call ASAP."

I hit the "Return Call" button and listened to a computer voice. The party at this number is not available. Please leave a message after the beep.

"Paddy, everything okay? You've got me a bit worried. I'm heading home, but I'll keep my cell phone on."

What's going on with Paddy?

Three

THE AUGUST SUN WAS BAKING bricks from the clay in my front yard. Only the weeds were green, but my lawn had plenty of them. The month-old asphalt patches in my driveway smelled fresh and grabbed my shoes with each step, letting go with soft sucking sounds.

On the wraparound front porch, I kicked off my shoes to avoid tracking in tar. I hurried inside to escape the heat, feeling good about my decision to run early. I checked the bottoms of the shoes—clean. After dropping my keys on the kitchen counter, I hit the "Play" button on the answering machine, wondering what Paddy had been calling about.

You have one message. First message.

"Seamus McCree, this is Robert Rand. Please call me at your convenience concerning a situation of which I have recently become aware. Thank you."

Good grief. Hastings must have called Rand to see if the offer was legitimate before talking to her captain. Why hadn't I thought to call Rand and get his approval? *Stupid. Stupid. Stupid.* I grabbed pen and paper and dialed my boss's number. "Robert, this is Seamus. I'm sorry I didn't call you earlier."

"Perfectly all right." He spoke in tones I associated with private northeastern schools and Ivy League colleges. "Are you cognizant of the Memorial Day picnic disaster in Chillicothe?"

With relief I crumpled into a chair, my execution stayed. I smiled at *cognizant* and wondered if he knew about the pool among CIG employees for the first person to catch him using a contraction. Probably.

"I recall the story on NPR."

Thirty-seven had died in Chillicothe. Roughly a hundred and fifty hospitalized. The picnic, in a park overlooking the Scioto River, was the annual outing of union retirees of Chillicothe Machine Company.

"The public story," Rand said, "is that the botulism came from the green beans. They did not report that the potato salad was also contaminated."

"So murder," I said.

"Correct. According to Ross County's Sheriff Lyons, the picnic occurred outside the Chillicothe city limits, which is why the sheriff's department is leading the investigation. They know what was done, but not why or by whom. They have requested our assistance in trying to determine a financial motive. I know you have been hankering to get into the field. I thought this might be a good match to test whether you like it. Interested?"

"Sounds like a puzzler, and Chillicothe isn't far from here."

"Do I understand that as agreement to undertake this assignment? Your contact at the sheriff's office will be Detective Albert Wright. Once you two talk, let me know what resources you will require. Questions?"

"Our standard contract, I assume? Have we ever worked with them?"

"This is our debut. The sheriff is an elected official, which may be the impetus. Wright heads their task force on corporate crime. That is the mechanism they are using to contract with us." A short pause. "Anything else?"

"See any land mines?"

A quick laugh. "No, I do not anticipate any, but who knows what you might find on your path. Remember, our function is to assist. You will be deputized, but that has more to do with liability than anything else. I look forward to your report. And Seamus? Thank you."

"Before we finish," I said, "there's something else I need to talk with you about."

"Pray tell?"

In a one-breath burst, I told him about Skyler Weaver and how Lt. Hastings had surprised me by agreeing to meet before I had a chance to pass it by him. When I came up for air, his only comment was that he would await contact from the Cincinnati Police Department before considering the issue further. I figured he thought the chances were too small to waste his time over. I apologized again, thanked him, and signed off.

Because I was one of two people in the world without call waiting—I never understood the reason to put on hold someone I wanted to talk with in order to answer a call from someone I might not want to talk with—I checked to make sure Paddy hadn't called while I was on the phone with Rand. He hadn't. I considered calling him again, but that wouldn't accomplish anything. Paddy knew how to check his voicemail. Instead I called Wright.

"Detective Wright." His voice rumbled, low and gravelly. Abraded vocal cords from twenty years of cigarette smoke? I introduced myself.

"Shay-mus?" he said. "That's how you pronounce it?"

"I thought about changing it to Bob, but I never got around to it."

I had hoped for a chuckle. Instead I sensed anger in his statement: "Tell me what you're gonna do to help me."

Having CIG's help was clearly not Wright's idea. "Until we talk," I said, "I honestly don't know. How about I drive up from Cincinnati tomorrow? Whenever's good. We can discuss your case and how CIG might assist."

He gave me directions to a diner called Sue's Home Cooking, where he agreed to meet me for breakfast. He wanted to "get it out of the way" before he started his workday.

I had between now and tomorrow morning to worry about how I could disarm land mine number one without blowing up myself or CIG in the process.

I checked voicemail: still nothing from Paddy.

◊◊◊

THE UNIQUE CLATTER OF PADDY'S Civic pulling into my driveway clued me in that my nineteen-year-old son was visiting from New Jersey, where he was spending the summer with his mother. Once out of the car, he closed his eyes and rolled his shoulders, stretching muscles and showing off his well-developed pecs. We're the same height and had weighed the same 185 pounds until he traded soccer for crew. Rowing added fifteen pounds and filled out his lithe frame with muscle.

"This is a surprise," I said, rushing out to meet him. "You look great." We embraced in a quick squeeze with multiple back slaps. Slapping his back was like patting a pommel horse. Never had my muscles felt that strong.

"You don't look bad yourself . . . for a relic from the Mesozoic era."

"So now you think I lived with the dinosaurs? I returned your call. I assume it was to tell me you were coming? How long are you here for?"

He shrugged. "Probably until school starts."

"Really? I don't have food for you and—we have stores. I can get some. It's been a while since we've had much time together." I blathered away to cover my concern about why he was here instead of at his mother's.

Paddy grabbed two plastic bins containing his clothes and personal items. Two kittens tumbled out of the car and followed their pied piper into the house. I brought up the rear with a litter box, food dish, and cat food. In our second trip, we emptied the trunk of his laptop, color printer, scanner, and four speakers—better quality than those in my stereo system—and settled everything into his bedroom on the second floor.

"Who are the kittens? I haven't heard about them."

"Just got them. Strays I rescued. Cheech and Chong, although they're sisters, but what the hey. They're hilarious. You'll see." He stretched, opening his chest and pulling his shoulder blades together. "Anyhow, I wasn't getting along with Mom, so I figured a change in venue would be better for everyone. I guess I should let her know what I'm doing."

"She doesn't know?" My voice reached tenor range.

He shot me a dirty look. "Fine. I'll call her now." He stomped up the stairs and into his room.

I poured a glass of merlot, parked in the recliner in the library, and listened to Copland's "Quiet City." Paddy and I had graduated from the "What did you do?"—"Nothing," "Where did you go?"—"Nowhere," "Who were you with?"—"No one" stage of parenting. The library had been our neutral room then: the room with two chairs facing the same direction; the room where we sought resolution of confrontations caused by teenage angst and a single father's attempts to cope with it. I hoped it still was.

Cheech or Chong, I didn't yet know who was who, jumped onto my lap, grabbing my leg with sharp kitten claws to gain purchase. My yelp elicited a lovable purr. Her sandpaper tongue licked my hand. She circled twice before settling on my lap and promptly fell asleep while I ran my hand through her silken black and white fur. Paddy clomped down the stairs fifteen minutes later, grabbed a soda from the refrigerator, and plunked into the other chair.

"Mom says hello and good luck."

"Will I need the luck?"

"Don't we all?" Silence.

I've found most people loathe even a five-second pause in conversation. I never had that problem and could usually get people to talk using my silence. Paddy knew that trick. I figured he was in charge of this discussion. It might happen today or tonight. It might not happen until tomorrow. I sure hoped he wouldn't wait until it was too late, as I had with my father.

Over the years, Paddy and I had sized each other up. We knew who could arm wrestle better (him), who had the faster reflexes for slap hands (me), and who was likely to win which card and board games (overall, about even). We knew the exterior traits. We didn't know much else.

He cleared his throat. "I suppose you're wondering what's going on?"

"The question had crossed my mind, but since I have no short-term memory anymore, it didn't leave tracks." I sipped the wine and raised my eyebrows to elicit a laugh.

He smiled. "I needed space. Mom's acting like I'm still a kid."

"Meaning what? I haven't spoken to her in a while."

"She doesn't like me holing up in my room working on computers. She thinks I should be getting out more, being sociable."

"Oh?"

"I lose track of time when I'm doing something interesting. I have a whole community I interact with. People I know from school or here or I've met on the Internet. Anyway, Mom didn't like me becoming nocturnal on her."

"I thought you had a day job."

"They pay me to write computer code. They don't care jack when I do it, as long as I meet my deadlines. I only went to the office to pick up my check. Everything else I did online. You know, I submit work, they send review comments back, we trade test plans, all that stuff. They agreed I didn't have to come in anymore, and I started working at night. You still have decent Internet, right?"

"Yep."

"Pay's great for a summer job. No future in it, though. Only way you make money in tech is to start a company. Anyway . . ." He finished his Pepsi and ran his fingers through curly locks in a gesture I knew well. "That's not the real issue. Mom's seeing some guy and he's a jerk."

We sat there, the Jerk perched on the table between us. I spent the silence wondering if Paddy still harbored hope his mom and I would get back together. I'd told him more than once that would never happen.

"You okay, Dad? You look tired."

"Sorry, thinking. The guy's a jerk?"

"Yeah. So, what are you working on these days? Anything interesting?"

"Last week I would've said not much. Now I have a couple of possibilities." He had heard about the botulism murders in Chillicothe. I also told him about the outside chance of working on the Presser murder.

He rolled his neck. "I should get the computer set up and get some work done before I crash. Tomorrow I'll get a gym membership and pick up what I need for cooking at the grocery store."

I was about to tell him to take it easy. He had driven ten hours from Jersey and should have dinner and get some rest. Fortunately, I remembered how well I took the same advice at his age, and he'd already told me he was a night owl.

After a rice and veggie dinner, I planned to spend the rest of the evening scouring the Internet for information about the Chillicothe picnic in preparation for meeting Detective Wright. First, I called Skyler Weaver and filled her in on my lunch with Lt. Hastings. She was jubilant and I unsuccessfully tried to convince her that the odds CPD would approve the idea were one in a million.

Paddy joined me in my third-floor study and decided entering "Chillicothe murder" into a browser and reading *Chillicothe Gazette* archives was more fun than writing code.

Again, I found myself biting my tongue.

In addition to the thirty-seven dead, three people were still critical. Paddy and I read silently about botulism, a neuroparalytic disease induced by the organism *Clostridium botulinum*.

"Why botulism?" Paddy asked. "Why not arsenic or rat poison? Seems like they'd be more effective."

We read about death rates. Before 1950, about 60 percent of those with food-borne botulism died. Now only 5 to 10 percent did, although because of the advanced age of the victims, the rate had been higher in Chillicothe.

"Got to be a reason," I said.

"Jeez, that's enlightening."

I let it pass. The victims ranged from seventeen, a kid who had worked for the caterer, to eighty-seven, the oldest person at the picnic. The kid was younger than Paddy. I couldn't imagine how his parents must feel.

"Hey, Dad. Looks like you're second string on this. Feds took this puppy over for a while, but they decided it wasn't terrorism and dropped it two weeks ago."

"I prefer to think they finally decided to play the first string. You know when the going gets tough, the—"

"Tough get going. I heard that somewhere. Doesn't look like much else's here. I should too—get going on work, that is." He walked out the door, calling over his shoulder, "Why would someone want to kill a bunch of old people?"

FOUR

IN GEORGIA, THE MOONLESS NIGHT painted the landscape a uniform dark. With night-vision goggles, he had little need for moon or stars. The landscaped evergreens provided ample protection to scout the grounds. For more than two hours he had perched in the pine nearest the main building, observing so quietly a screech owl joined him in the tree. No security guards patrolled outside. How many penguins were in there? A hundred? Probably more. At ten grand a head, he was well into seven digits.

The last light in the building had blinked out shortly past midnight, leaving only the faint red glow of exit signs leaking from stairwell windows. Thirty minutes earlier, a doe had grazed on bushes close to the main building and hadn't triggered any motion sensor lights. Time to explore.

He slipped through the night to the back door. Using his body as a shield, he illuminated the lock with a penlight. A simple cylinder. He extinguished the light and selected a pick from his case. The nearby air-conditioning units running full blast drowned out any sound he made entering the basement.

As the cooler interior air with its hint of mold hit him, he realized how uncomfortable it had been outside in the heat. While waiting and watching, he had ignored the sweat trickling between his shoulder blades. The full-body camouflage was a useful safeguard, but hot. He surveyed the basement and found the furnace room ahead and on the left— precisely matching the building permit records. Besides the special apparatus and a few tools, all he would need on the big night was a stepladder to reach the ductwork.

His reconnoiter in the main building accomplished, he slipped out the door and explored the garage and toolshed until he found where they stored ladders. His smile shone from beneath the brown, green, and black face paint. Softly whistling "Nearer, My God, to Thee," he melded with the night.

FIVE

BOLTING UPRIGHT, I GREETED THE day with an expletive before slamming the "Off" button of the clock radio I had incorrectly set to its piercing alarm rather than to the blather of a local NPR station. Not an omen, I hoped.

I showered and dressed in jeans, sandals, and a golf shirt proclaiming the virtues of last year's Memorial Tournament in Columbus. The sun was hardly up and already the temperature was seventy-five degrees, projected to reach the midnineties with afternoon thunderstorms. The short time it took me to retrieve the newspaper from the lily of the valley by the front stoop was enough to cause my shirt to stick to me. It smelled like rain and my training calendar called for me to run a ten-miler.

Paddy beat me to the kitchen. "You're up early," I said.

"Haven't gone to bed yet. You're going to a business meeting dressed like that?"

"I decided against shorts. Thought they might be a bit too casual."

"Is this the same father who harps, 'You only have one chance to make a good first impression'?"

"Guilty, but this is different. In a world where everyone wears business casual, if I dress down, people either think I'm not bright or absolutely brilliant—both false but useful impressions."

"That's a crock if I ever heard one."

"Thanks for sharing your uplifting commentary. Maybe you'll find your nice gene after you've slept?"

"Whatever. I need to drop my car at the service station for an oil change, and I want to go shopping and hit the gym. Can you leave me keys for the Infiniti? I hate driving your Expedition in city traffic. It's ginormous and I'm not used to it."

I pulled the Infiniti key off the ring and handed it to him.

"And money for food?" He held out his hand.

I retrieved my ATM card from my wallet.

He mimed Snidely Whiplash, twirling his mustache and rubbing his hands. "What's your daily limit and where's the nearest casino?"

"Funny. Very funny." At least I hoped it was.

◊◊◊

WRIGHT'S DIRECTIONS FROM CINCINNATI brought me on a straight shot out US 50 to Chillicothe. Much of the central part of Ohio is flat; for the fifty miles east from Milford to Hillsboro I tried to forget my worries about Paddy and the nagging tension about Wright's . . . what, distrust? Singing along with a Chanticleer CD helped me zone out.

Hillsboro marked the start of the Appalachian foothills as the ground lifted, the twang became more prevalent, the houses a bit shabbier, and the flowered dress no longer hid the slip of poverty. The last forty miles to Chillicothe wandered through the valley carved by Paint Creek.

Some cities have impressive entrances. Cincinnati, for instance, is majestic when approached from the south on I-71/75. You round a hill and find the cityscape laid out before you.

Had I blinked, I would have missed the sign announcing Chillicothe.

Sue's Home Cooking sat on the north side of the road not far past the welcome sign. Because I had allowed more time than I needed for the trip, I continued on the main drag into the historic district. After a quick tour, I returned to the squat single-story building with parking on three sides and Dumpsters in the rear. The lot was filled—a good sign.

I opened the restaurant's door and my glasses steamed. A waitress met me with a wave and a "Wherever you want, hon."

At the counter straight ahead, the dozen stools were mostly filled. Waitresses bustled into and out of the kitchen through twin swinging doors. Red naugahyde booths sprawled to the right and left of the entry. The restaurant hummed. I checked for someone sitting alone who looked like a detective.

The only suit in the place faced the door drinking coffee. A cropped regulation army—not marine—haircut topped his midthirties football-player frame. I guessed him for six eight, probably around 280, and solid. His brown suit and too-wide tie gaping at the neck were hardly fashionable.

"Detective Wright?"

"Yeah. You must be McCree. Have a seat. I noticed you arrived from the wrong direction."

The guy wore some kind of heavy aftershave lotion. "Your directions were perfect. I'm a bit of a history buff and checked out the historic district. I'd forgotten Chillicothe was the capital of the Northwest Territories." I slid into the booth, the seat cool. "Smells good in here. Suggestions?"

Wright's eyes and his cheap suit both shone with angry use. "History buff. Did you also forget Chillicothe was the state capital until they moved it to Columbus?"

"That, I remembered." *Why the heck am I bothering?* I plastered a smile on my face and tried again. "Thanks for meeting me today. I'm interested in understanding how you think CIG might be able to help."

He dropped his stare to his coffee and took a sip. Eyes back up, then locked onto mine. "Look McCree, let's understand each other. I don't want your help, but I wasn't given a choice. I'm here because I was told to be here. You're here because someone told you to be here." His left hand gripped and released the mug.

I waited for more. His hand continued kneading the ceramic. Apparently he was done. "I'm sorry you don't want to be here. I sure don't want to waste your time or mine. I have to eat breakfast anyway. Let's order and take it from there."

Before Detective Wright could respond, the waitress arrived, coffeepot in one hand, a set of silverware and a mug in the other. She slapped down the knife and fork. "Coffee?"

"No thanks," I said. "A large OJ would be great."

She swung to face the detective. "Bear, you want more?" In profile, she was a tight package topped with frizzy bleached hair tucked into a red bandanna. All five foot five of her buzzed with energy. Attached to her belt was a pedometer.

"Thanks, Charlene," he said without making eye contact.

She pulled a pen from behind her ear, releasing a strand of hair. "Have you decided what you want?"

"Give us a couple of minutes," Wright replied.

"You boys holler when you're ready." She bustled over to a booth of newcomers wearing identical kelly-green shirts.

Wright still gripped the mug, but his knuckles had regained their normal pink. I relaxed, put myself back into the peace of a Chanticleer Gregorian *Kyrie* so my voice didn't reflect the anger I felt. "I want to say a couple of things. Afterward, you can decide whether we have breakfast and never see each other again or whether we work together."

His eyes bored into mine.

"You've been ordered to work with us and are none too happy about it."

He shrugged concurrence.

"Sorry. Unlike you, I'm here because I want to be. I have a choice. Now here's the part you might like. If I tell my boss this isn't a good fit for CIG, we'll figure a way to inform Sheriff Lyons we can't do it—we're stretched too thin to help, or some other bullshit excuse. Lyons will never know it had anything to do with our breakfast today. Trust me. If at the end of breakfast you don't want to see my sorry ass again, no problem. Okay?"

I opened the menu and pretended to concentrate. I snuck a glance over the top. His left hand had frozen, a Rodin sculpture.

He expelled a boilerful of air and released the cup. "Okay," he said. "I'm in a vinegar-piss lousy mood today. Sorry."

Charlene brought my orange juice. I ordered french toast; Wright asked for three eggs over easy, hash browns, and a side of Canadian bacon. She hustled off, tucking the pen and an errant strand of hair behind her ear.

"I guess I'm pissed the sheriff decided to call you guys. He sure as hell wouldn't have done that to my predecessor."

I waited him out.

"Okay, McCree. I'm under orders. What can you do?"

I told him the basics of how CIG works: It was a private, nonprofit that assisted police departments by supplementing their investigative resources. It worked pro bono. I would be his conduit to all of CIG's research capabilities. In this case, we anticipated those would mostly involve forensic accounting and the like. The sheriff had already agreed to give us complete access to files. We wanted to unobtrusively help, not garner publicity. I would be deputized, but they, not I, determined when to make arrests.

Charlene interrupted with breakfast. We dug in. Wright's eye contact modified from glare to periodic conversational acknowledgment.

He crossed his fork over the cleaned plate. "If what you say is true, I guess I could use you guys because I'm up against a wall. It isn't my nature to ask for help, and I don't appreciate anyone else requesting it for me."

I nodded.

"The state lab boys pinned down what happened. What we can't figure is a motive. Who benefited? We've come up with a blank. If someone was angry or jealous, why at the whole group? And even if it's a lunatic, botulism isn't sitting in everyone's cupboard. This took serious planning. I'm totally frustrated, and people are scared 'cause we haven't made an arrest."

"I understand you're head of the corporate crime task force," I said. "That your current angle?"

"That's a fucking joke. To get some federal grant money, we had to have a task force on corporate crime, and you're looking at it. Well, me and Mary Lou, one of the clerks in the department. I guess Lyons used the same bull on you guys."

I laughed and offered my congratulations.

He cracked a tentative smile. "We've talked to most everyone in the county by now. We found out lots of stuff, but nothing to make sense of the poisoning. By the way, early this morning another one died. We're up to thirty-eight dead with two still critical."

"I take it you're thinking if it's not an act against an individual, it's somehow connected to the company they had worked for?"

"Yeah, it's the only thing they have in common, besides being union members. We poked around Chillicothe Machine, but hell, we don't have a clue what we're looking for, especially since they're now a subsidiary of a huge Japanese conglomerate. We got a couple of guys on the force with business degrees—I got one myself—but we don't have any CPAs. We understand embezzlement, but that doesn't seem to be it. We're not even sure what questions to ask. I guess that's what your forensic accountants do?"

"Exactly," I said. "Have you tried to check out the company?"

"We talked with the CEO, who's been there for years, and with the Japanese guy brought in to oversee operations after they were bought. Needed to have an interpreter for him. We also talked with their public accountants, who said there was no sign of problems." He shrugged, extending his arms and huge paws in the universal "what can you do" gesture.

Charlene stepped around Wright's outstretched arm. "Whoa. Almost got me that time, Bear. Anything else?"

"Does everyone call him Bear, or just you?" I mimicked his outstretched arms and spread my fingers wide to imitate claws.

She laughed at my gesture. "Everyone. Well, Sheriff Lyons calls him Detective Wright, and I think his mother still calls him Al. Doesn't she?"

"Yeah, sure, you can call me Bear."

To justify sitting longer I asked, "Have any Bengal Spice tea?"

She stifled her laugh. "Sorry, hon. Lipton's it. Want some?"

What was I thinking? I nodded acceptance. She picked up plates and hurried off.

"I can see you've put a lot of work into this," I said. "From what you've told me, it sounds like you've done all the right things. Here's how I think CIG might help. Our network includes CPAs, former accountants, and controllers of major corporations. These guys specialize in forensic accounting and have a lot more experience than the local branch of any accounting firm. If anything funny's going on at Chillicothe Machine, they can find it.

"Or," I continued, "tell me to get lost. Your choice, Bear." I waited. In the pause, Charlene came back with a little pot of hot water and a tea bag. I drowned the bag while Charlene cleared the remaining dishes.

"Look. I really want to tell you to get the fuck out of here and leave me alone. But I can't. If it's just some crazy person getting their kicks, I'm afraid he'll do something else. The feds are gone. Sheriff Lyons is getting heat from all sides. We need help. I guess maybe you're it. Let's finish up here and go to headquarters. I'll show you what we got."

◊◊◊

I FOLLOWED BEAR TO THE sheriff's headquarters on North Paint Street. We parked in front of the two-story building, red brick capped by a green roof. Attached in the rear, a three-story jail with giveaway tiny windows continued the redbrick motif. Walking through a small plaza toward the front door, he stopped and pointed to one of the plaques.

"Since you're into history you might like this. Nine Congressional Medal of Honor winners came from Ross County: seven from the Civil War, one from the Philippine Insurrection, and one from World War Two."

I leaned down and read the plaque. "Weber and Carson were musicians?"

"Yep. And those two," he said pointing to Dorsey and Robertson, the two 1862 Civil War honorees, "received theirs from Andrews' Raid—more commonly known as the Great Locomotive Chase. Not being much into history, I watched the movie."

A receptionist buzzed us into the Ross County Sheriff's Office. Our progress toward Bear's cubicle halted at a "Detective Wright!" from behind us. We reversed and faced a man in his late forties in full uniform.

"Mr. McCree, this is Sheriff Lyons."

I shook hands with the sheriff, who was several inches shorter than I. He too was surrounded by the smell of aftershave—must be department regulation to keep the public from getting too close to the officers. I forced myself not to rub my nose as it twitched at the heavy scent.

"Great to meet you, Mr. McCree. We sure appreciate CIG helping us. I was going to talk to our web manager about adding a little something to the website announcing your assistance." Behind me, Wright was taking short, choppy breaths, and all my hard work at breakfast was about to go down the drain.

"Sheriff, there a place we can talk for a couple of minutes?" I asked.

"Sure, sure . . . my office is back this way."

I craned my neck to look Wright straight in the eye and said, "You come too, Detective." We followed the sheriff into his large office. United States and Ohio flags flanked an oversized oak desk in the center of the room. Three walls were covered with "see how important I am" pictures of the beaming sheriff shaking hands with politicians and assorted others. From a quick glance I recognized Ronald Reagan, the current governor, both Ohio senators, and Ken Griffey Jr.

The sheriff walked behind his weathered desk and pointed to the chairs in front. He looked a little surprised to see Detective Wright, but he didn't say anything.

Seated, a combination of low visitor chairs and an elevated desk forced me to look up at the sheriff. He was about to launch into a speech, so I interrupted the thought before he could voice it.

"Sheriff, I've seen your website and I think it's great. Especially people emailing tips. I don't think posting anything about CIG is a good idea, though. We're most useful when people consider us an adjunct to the police department. It's your case. You get any needed subpoenas. It's your bust if we're successful."

The sheriff's eyes shifted right and left like a squirrel caught crossing the road. He didn't immediately say anything, so I continued.

"We know we can't be kept secret, but experience has shown it's better to keep everything low-key. Provision eleven in the contract. I'm sure you just forgot."

The squirrel finally found his way across the street. "You're absolutely right, Mr. McCree. I let my enthusiasm get a little ahead of me. I'm glad we bumped into each other so I didn't go spoiling things. By the way, I did ask Mary Lou to make copies of all the files. Will you be looking at them here or . . .?"

"Thanks, Sheriff," I said. "Normally we like to check the files first to determine which ones might be worth copying, but since you've jumped the gun, I guess I can take them with me." I caught Bear's eye and rolled mine in silent commiseration.

The sheriff read my shirt and launched into a soliloquy on various Memorial Tournaments he'd seen and how many times he'd met Jack Nicklaus. He prattled on until Bear saved us by suggesting I needed to be formally deputized and get the files from Mary Lou.

Once out of the sheriff's hearing, Bear said in a low voice, "You handled him well. I think we can work together. Lyons' heart is in the right place, and he's done well with the department. He's under a lot of pressure to solve these murders. The election's in November."

Bear introduced me to Mary Lou, who handed me an index for each box. Good thing I brought the Expedition. I had to lower the rear seat to accommodate the files and belt in the last two boxes on the front passenger seat. A roll of thunder sounded in the distance.

"I'll give you a call once I'm through these. In the meantime, I'll start our financial types looking at Chillicothe Machine."

On my return to Cincinnati, I had planned to pull off on a side road, slip on my running shorts and shoes, and get ten miles in. It was a good thing I didn't dare leave the Expedition unattended with all the evidence boxes; the skies opened up and dumped water by the bucketful. I'd have to change my running schedule to account for the unplanned rest day.

Instead of enjoying a tension-reducing run, I gripped the steering wheel tight and peered through the windshield. Once the rain let up enough to switch the wipers from high to normal, I worried whether I was qualified to handle the botulism assignment, and then whether Sheriff Lyons would control his mouth. I patted myself on the back for how I'd handled Bear—I figured I had him on my side for the time being, but it was a fragile truce. I tried listening to some New Age music to ease my tension. All I accomplished was to exchange my work concerns for worry about Paddy, his mother, and her jerk. I arrived home with a pounding headache.

Paddy's room was quiet, so I lugged the boxes up two flights of stairs to my study, cursing the extra steps my ten-foot ceilings entailed. By the time I finished, I decided it would have been easier to move the study to the first floor. At least it was a decent aerobic workout.

I contacted two members of CIG's financial crimes team who had experience with manufacturing and Japanese holding companies and asked them to start looking into Chillicothe Machine. Finally, I called Rand and told him about my visit.

The ringing doorbell interrupted my trip to the kitchen to pour a celebratory glass of wine. Shading her eyes, Lt. Tanya Hastings peered in the side window.

Six

THE LIEUTENANT ENTERED MY FOYER accompanied by her lilac scent. My heart rate accelerated. I wasn't sure if it was because I found her attractive, which I certainly did, or because I would soon have to call Skyler Weaver and tell her the CPD had refused.

I tried a comedic approach to calm my nerves. "You finally dumped your football player and want to move in?" I clasped my hands over my heart.

"It's baseball. Even in the twenty-first century, I believe the order is still first date, copulate, and then shack up. Besides, I gather from the cats wandering around the house that you have company?"

"My son decided I was the less evil parent. Showed up yesterday."

Her smile lit her entire face and I drowned in her dark chocolate eyes. "Good luck with that."

I motioned toward the library. "Want to sit?"

"Won't be that long. Would CIG agree to the same contract we used for the Mitchell case, with an evaluation after two months?"

Stunned, I managed to respond, "I'm sure that would be fine."

"Good. That allows us to avoid the solicitor's office. Fax the contract to the chief by early Monday morning. He'll have the city manager sign it at their lunch."

If it had been physically possible, my jaw would have hit the floor. "What happened to the city's glacial process?"

"Murder's up, budget's cut, and I happened to catch all the approvals in one room. It sold itself." Her sweet voice belied her hard eyes. "I stuck my neck out to get this approved. Don't screw it up." She gave my arm a squeeze and patted my cheek. "I'll keep your offer in mind if I'm ever homeless."

"Let me call Rand and see whom he wants to assign."

"Don't bother. It's you, sugar. That's how I sold it. We get your 'brilliant mind.'" She demonstrated my level of brilliance with air quotes.

"Skyler Weaver gets what she wants, you and CIG on her boyfriend's case. Everybody's happy."

I had a feeling there was at least one hidden agenda I had better figure out before I stepped into the cow pasture.

Before leaving, she gave me the chief's fax number, and we agreed to meet at Presser's place for a walk-through. She would take care of getting a key from the landlord, and once I had visited the murder scene, she would provide access to the case files.

I wandered into the kitchen and finally poured a glass of merlot, called Rand, and related my conversation with Lt. Hastings.

"This is the first time we have ever instigated a case," Rand said. "I am surprised it has not happened sooner. Have you overloaded your plate?"

"I might be pressed a bit for a few days. Better than bored. I'll holler if I need help."

"I will hold you to that. We will fax the contract today. And Seamus? Everyone will be watching to see how this experiment goes."

◊◊◊

EACH TIME I CAME TO a good breaking point in my review of the Chillicothe files, I pulled up the weather radar in hopes I could sneak in a run. Every time, the mass of green, yellow, and orange extended well into Indiana. A grumbling stomach reminded me that a glass of wine had been my lunch. It was five o'clock and my eyes were weary. One last check of the radar convinced me I was not going to run today.

Paddy had finally arisen and picked up his car from the oil change. Years ago, he and I had allocated kitchen responsibilities to our mutual satisfaction and benefit. He cooks and I clean up. He made vegetarian lasagna served with fresh ciabatta bread dipped in herb-infused olive oil.

When I commented on how fresh the lasagna tasted, he reminded me that spices don't last forever and that he had replenished my supply.

"You know, Paddy, I eat to live rather than live to eat."

"I'm the same way," he said. "But that does *not* mean you have to eat poorly when you do eat."

"Agreed," I said. "But it's a matter of priorities, and cooking is not in my top ten."

"Ten thousand, more like it."

He seemed to be in a good mood, so I tried to gently probe his reasons for being here. That killed our conversation in a hurry and we ate in silence. After that blunder I figured I'd let him make the next move.

He did as I cleaned up after dinner. "Do you miss being a stock analyst? If you hadn't quit, you could afford a cook."

I turned, oblivious as soapy drips from the nylon scrubby I had been using on the lasagna pan splattered the wood floor. "Give me some context. Where did that come from?"

"Mom says you walked away for no good reason."

"She and I may not have the same perspective. Yeah, I do miss parts. Like being able to figure out stuff about companies that no one else knows. Like when a stock's overvalued and everyone's still buying or when a company's about to turn around and no one's buying." I noticed the drips and cleaned my mess.

"And the other parts?"

"You have to prostitute your knowledge to the investment bankers. If something was a turkey, I couldn't stomach having to say XYZ was a 'buy' or 'hold' just so they could make a deal." Reacting to my tightening neck, I sat at the table. Like a snapping turtle, my shoulders rose in a futile attempt to cover my head. I thought feeling pissed about my old job was behind me. *Think again, Seamus.*

"I probably would have continued to choke it down if they'd allowed my complete analyses in the reports. Which they did for a while. If you read what I wrote, you could tell what I really thought and ignore the rating. Then they changed a report without telling me, and I quit."

"They did?"

"Less than a month before bonuses were paid—and bonus was eighty-five to ninety percent of total pay." A crackling neck roll partially relieved my tension. I forced my shoulders down. "I didn't wait for the payment, which is what really pissed your mother off. I confirmed the change was intentional and messengered in my resignation the next day."

"Jeez, Dad, I never heard that story. Did they try to get you back?"

"Yeah. And offered a lot more than thirty pieces of silver. I wasn't interested. They made fifty million bucks off that deal. They would have sold their mothers to make fifty million. That's Wall Street."

"Sucky."

"I'm no hero. I'd made plenty of money already. I could afford to quit, although your mother disagreed. Other firms wanted me, but I wasn't interested. They're all the same. I still do some merger and acquisition work now and then. I like the challenge, but feel like I need to take a monthlong bath when I'm done working with Wall Street types."

"How did you hook up with CIG?" He seemed genuinely interested in a part of my life we had rarely discussed.

"Rand saw an article about my resignation in the *Wall Street Journal*. He eventually decided I wasn't planning to return to Wall Street and lured me to dinner with promises of an interesting proposition."

"And that, as they say, was that?"

"Pretty much. Law enforcement agencies had people with forensic and scientific backgrounds, but had realized they were lost when it came to financial chicanery. Rand asked me to build a network of financial analysts, CPAs, and bankers who could sort through the legal and accounting mazes."

"But that's not what you're doing now, is it?"

"Nominally, I still run that part of the practice. Mostly it runs itself, and I was curious about how CIG really worked with police agencies. If I could become involved in a case, it might help me tweak my new network. He assigned me to a team investigating an international child pornography ring."

"Did you get them?"

"We figured out how they were transferring money from place to place through a series of dummy companies. The crime was appalling and the profits huge. I was hooked. It felt good to see brainpower bring them down, and it seems I have a sixth sense about how people cook their books or try to hide money."

Paddy grabbed a dishtowel and dried. "But you already made your pile on Wall Street. Without that you couldn't have afforded to take that job."

"CIG would have paid enough if I had wanted to work full-time." I ruffled his hair. "But I wanted to have more time to spend with you, so part-time was fine with me. Honestly? At your age I wasn't mature enough to realize I didn't need to be in the top one percent of incomes. If one of my friends had taken a job like this right out of college, I'd have considered him a waste. Why the sudden interest? You thinking about heading to Wall Street?"

A twitch crossed his face. "Oh, nothing."

He dropped the towel on the counter, claimed pressing work, and left me with the dishes and my questions about what was really going on.

◊◊◊

MY SATURDAY DISAPPEARED UNDER THE avalanche of reports the Ross County Sheriff's Office and the state police had prepared on the botulism murders. I worked through them for four hours, then broke for the twenty-miler required by my training schedule. After four more hours working, I had dinner with Paddy, and then worked a third four-hour stint. I still had a few files to go when my eyes glazed. I wasn't used to twelve-hour days any longer. I'd make Sunday a rest day.

Sunday broke a bit cooler. I cooked my five-minute oatmeal, mixed in fresh blueberries Paddy had bought, and breakfasted on the deck accompanied by the sweet scent of the still-blooming honeysuckle and the buzz of bees drawn to its nectar. The fresh berries had me reminiscing about the blueberry pancake socials at the parish hall where we boys vied for group recognition as the one who ate the most.

A neighbor's lawnmower roared to life. When I grew up in South Boston, no one would have mowed their lawn on Sunday morning. I bolted down the rest of my food, including one tart blueberry I should have avoided, and returned inside.

My restful day went downhill from there.

As I was crossing Middleton on the way to church, a car ran a stop sign and barely missed me. At church, I spotted Skyler Weaver already in the sanctuary. While I almost certainly had good news for her, I didn't want to jinx the CPD contract by telling her about it before its official signing. I slunk into a chair near the exit to allow easy escape after the benediction. Instead of gaining spiritual sustenance from the service, I spent the time rehashing the botulism case files, making me forget to avoid Skyler and allowing her questioning to pin me to the wall like a prized butterfly. I fessed up to the unexpected good news, withholding information about my scheduled meeting with Lt. Hastings. I sent a quick prayer requesting that nothing would go wrong with the contract.

I walked home through the angry buzz of more lawnmowers. Since heat and humidity had returned, I decided to spend the afternoon in my library reading a book and listening to Marty Brennaman call the Reds game on the radio. The overhead fan pushed enough air around to tickle my skin without the need of the A/C. The S. J. Rozan novel in one hand was good, the beer in the other hand was refreshing, and the Reds had a one-to-nothing lead.

And then the doorbell rang. I opened the door to an unfamiliar young man dressed in crisp shorts, print short-sleeve shirt, and leather sandals.

"I'm Matthew Yeung. Skyler asked me to come over and talk to you about Samuel. I've been his best friend forever and we worked together at TransOhio. I think she hoped I could tell you something that might help. I couldn't say no."

My mother would be proud of my good manners. We shook hands—his grip was light—and I invited him in, gave him a beer, and kissed away my last hopes for the day.

Samuel and Matthew had met in junior high. They were both Fellows of the Society of Actuaries, trained in the mathematics and probabilities of life insurance and annuities, and worked for the same company. They'd even shared an apartment before they could afford separate places.

Matthew had trouble making eye contact, and he periodically fiddled with the bottom hem of his shorts. He droned on about Samuel's college, work, and friends, filling his soliloquy with platitudes. He made no mention of the murder.

"I know this isn't politically correct for me to ask," I said, "but if we're going to crack this case, I need to know." I gestured to include the two of us as the "we." "Did Samuel have a spot of tarnish on his halo? Some behavior that could have brought him in contact with unsavory people?"

Matthew slid a glance in my direction. "He wasn't Simon Pure. But unsavory? No."

"Gambling?"

Matthew cracked a smile. "Not at all. Once our group went to an Indiana riverboat casino. I had to show him how to play craps. He spent a little time at the least expensive blackjack tables. He never went back."

"Drinking? Drugs?"

"Friday nights a group of us had a couple of beers. Skyler often joined us. They were one of the earliest couples to leave. The only time I saw him drunk was to celebrate his fellowship—it's sort of a rite of passage. Samuel never did drugs."

No one is this nice. "Chase women?"

He responded with a headshake and a shrug. "Naw. There's been no one else since he started dating Skyler. Even before, he dated one girl at a time. With studying for the exams, about all we had time for were our occasional bull sessions at somebody's place. We'd play some cards or board games. Stuff like that."

"Chase men?"

"No way."

I mentally slammed my head against the wall. "Was he really that boring?"

Matthew chuckled and finally looked me in the eye. "Do you know the difference between an actuary and an accountant?"

"I'm afraid to ask."

"An actuary is someone who wanted to be an accountant, but didn't have enough personality."

"That's pretty bad."

"The exams are a grind. After that, it really is a good job, even if people don't know what we do. Actuary has been rated the number one job in the country bunches of times. It's always in the top ten."

He had nothing more to offer. I kept frustration from my voice when I thanked him for his valuable information.

The Reds were now losing seven to one. The universe obviously did not want me to have a day of rest. I retreated to my study and completed reading the botulism murder files. Paddy chose to spend his evening with friends rather than his old man—who could blame him? I ended up with a late dinner of leftovers and took the mystery to bed.

Questions from my conversation with Matthew Yeung chased around my brain. What did Skyler hope I would get from Matthew that she couldn't tell me herself? No one was as perfect as Samuel Presser appeared to be. Was Matthew hiding something about Presser? Or something about himself? Or both?

SEVEN

HE LAY IN THE PARCHED arroyo behind the eighteenth house on a street of suburban sprawl. From one hot place to another, but at least Arizona's heat was dry. Ravel's "Boléro" played in his head, beginning to crescendo.

The two people in the house had followed the same pattern this night as during the three previous nights of reconnaissance. At 2130, the living room lights went off. Lights popped on in her front bedroom and the kitchen. In less than ten minutes, the kitchen light extinguished and the back bedroom light flowed into the desert. Both bedrooms went dark by 2230. If their behaviors held, then between 0200 and 0300, his light would briefly come on—nature's nighttime call. She would not have to pee until early morning. Except tonight he wouldn't need to get up.

The adults-only development shut down by 2300, as did the wind, leaving a soundscape of insect chirps broken by the occasional chatter of coyotes. In the still air he sensed a bat's wingbeats overhead. He would wait one more hour for the crescent moon to set. The household would be asleep and nobody's bladder would yet require attention. What more could a Happy Reaper want?

At the stroke of midnight he moved along the swale, gently lifting brittle leaves aside to remain silent in his approach. With no one else outside, it didn't matter, but that was no reason to be sloppy. Once he reached the spot closest to the house, he rose and, like a giant raccoon, scuttled across the backyard to the house corner. The entire complex used the same plan as the model he had toured. He stuck the end of the micro flashlight into his mouth and edged around the house. Picking the patio lock in seconds, he entered the kitchen and waited a count of ten.

For days, he had visualized this moment. His mental "Boléro," with its insistent rhythm, waves of sound piling on each other, peaked and ended in its final dissonance. Preparations complete; time for action. The craft was killing the one without the other knowing. Their separate bedrooms helped. No payment accrued for killing the second, and he didn't give freebies.

He stowed the no-longer-needed flashlight. Ambient light from digital clocks and bathroom nightlights was more than sufficient. He drew his knife and gently held it in his right hand. Muffled snoring emanated from the rear room. He slipped into the hallway between the two bedrooms and moved toward the back. The air conditioner kicked on, briefly freezing him in his tracks. Perfect timing: the A/C would be on for at least five minutes, and its noise would camouflage the execution of his assignment.

He eased the bedroom door open, took two strides, and clapped his left hand over the target's mouth. His right plunged the knife through the sheet, through the powder-blue pajamas, deep into racing heart muscle.

The victim's eyes flew open; his body arched. The killer watched the ancient eyes change from shock, to resignation, to a preternatural brightness, to nothing. The knife stopped pulsing. The killer removed it and assiduously wiped the blade until no more blood transferred onto the golden silk sheet covering the target's legs. His nose curled in disgust as the acrid scent of the urine-stained bed reached him. It reminded him of waking to his "accidents" years ago and the strap stinging his legs to teach him big boys didn't pee their beds. Avoiding that smell was the main advantage a gun had over a blade.

Where to place his calling card? He spotted a Bible on the nightstand and stuck the card so it underlined Matthew 10:28. *That'll give them something to ponder.*

Locking the patio door on his way out, he retraced his steps to the drainage ditch and then to his rental car. This job behind him, he switched his thoughts toward the east.

EIGHT

I WAS SUPPOSED TO MEET Lt. Hastings at Presser's place, 489 Milton Street, at 10:07 Monday morning. Given the emphasis on the exact minute, I did not want to be late. I left home early and approached Presser's Prospect Hill neighborhood from downtown with a tourist's eyes. A rapid rise brought me from the Ohio River to Third Street, where the first office buildings are located with their long views of the river and Kentucky. The street continued climbing to Fourth Street, where the route pancaked for fifteen stop-and-go blocks until I reached Prospect Hill, whose south face provided great city views.

A blue sign proclaiming the Prospect Hill National Register Historic District greeted me. Founded in 1788 with the moniker of Losantiville, Cincinnati had expanded to Prospect Hill before the Civil War. Much had changed in the city since, but the neighborhood's main advantages remained the same: close to downtown, great views, and not outrageously priced.

I parked off Milton on the stub of Young Street that provided four extra parking spaces. Young was a discontinuous street starting at Liberty Hill Road and running up Prospect Hill. Because of the steep incline, stairways connected the brief smear of asphalt I was on with Corporation Alley below and Boal Street above.

Standing outside Presser's place, I noticed a cooling breeze rising up the hill, following the gap in the houses caused by Young Street and its stairways. A squadron of chimney swifts plied the skies, wheeling overhead, chittering after insects. From the tangle of plants next to the stairway down to Corporation Alley came the raspy buzz of a rufous-sided towhee requesting me to "drink your tea."

I pulled my attention from the birds and examined the outside of Presser's apartment. It occupied the first floor and basement of an Italianate row house perched on the southeast corner of the intersection of Milton and Young. A second apartment occupied the upper floor. The green-painted brick façade was in good condition and retained its original six-over-six windows in the front. Milton's upward slant resulted in roof-formed mountain peaks, each one higher than the last. A stone retaining wall in the rear prevented Milton from joining Corporation Alley below in one mad slide down the hill.

I could understand why the couple had planned to live in his place once they married. The topography, despite being in the heart of the city, provided excellent views and a fair amount of privacy. Only one neighbor had a limited view of its side door. No one could see its back door. Between Milton and Corporation Alley was considerable vegetation. It wouldn't have surprised me if it harbored a deer trail or maybe a route used by urban coyotes.

Lt. Hastings pulled up in a cruiser at the appointed time. I wondered if she had parked at the end of the street and waited so she could bust my chops with her exactitude. She motioned me to follow her into the house.

"Responding officers found him there." She pointed to a spot past a half wall at the entrance to the freshly painted kitchen. "Clutching mail in his left hand. Presser left work and picked up Chinese on his way to the young men's discussion group at his church. Before the meeting, he ate in the church kitchen with a couple of guys—brought home leftovers. Several people saw him leave alone in his car. Apparently, he went straight home. Parked in the spot you're in now."

She returned to the door and demonstrated Presser's actions while talking through them. "He unlocked the door. Came in carrying mail, his bag of food, briefcase, and keys. He walked up the steps, dumped stuff on this half wall, and moved toward the kitchen. He never made it."

She pointed behind me. "The killer probably hid in the hall leading to the bathroom and bedroom. The first stab wound, a downward thrust in the back, slipped between vertebrae and severed Presser's spinal cord. Not fatal, but it paralyzed him."

She sprawled on the floor. "Presser lay there looking up at the killer, unable to move. He probably watched the killer slam the knife under his ribs and up into his heart. That one was fatal."

I swallowed hard to hold down an explosion of bile that burned my throat. Perhaps my visceral reaction to Hastings lying "dead" occurred because this was my first physical murder scene. Or maybe the smell of Pine-Sol mixed with paint fumes got to me. I swallowed again.

"Helpless," she said. "He couldn't do anything. The fucker even wiped off his knife on Presser's pant legs." Hastings pushed off the floor and stood next to me looking at where Presser had died. "You want to see the rest of this floor before I take you to the basement?"

"Sure," I said, wondering what I would see besides nail holes in the walls and scrapes on the wooden floors.

Our footsteps echoed in the high-ceilinged rooms. Our survey of the apartment—bedroom, bath, coat closet, and kitchen—provided another sanitized view of Presser as useless as Matthew Yeung's description of his friend. Hastings led me down the narrow stairs into a cavernous basement with seemingly outsized twelve-foot ceilings.

"A lot of these houses have high basements because of the sharp slope of the hill," the mind reader said.

Nondescript gray indoor/outdoor carpeting covered the floor. A solitary window of glass bricks let in a wash of dirty light. Hastings continued to a door on the far wall.

"Here's where the killer entered. Presser never used this door." She leaned on the door with her shoulder, releasing the deadbolt with a loud click.

I pointed to the new hardware. "What—"

"New lock. The original is evidence. We found it drilled out."

We exited into the backyard, much of which was underneath the deck. In the uncovered area, shrubs and weeds fought with old building materials and bald tires for dominance.

"The murderer crossed the yard there." She pointed toward a still visible path of trampled mustard garlic and broken honeysuckle. "The ground is packed hard and we couldn't get any footprints. Our dogs followed the killer's scent from the house over the hedge and down the steps to the street below. The trail went cold about a hundred feet past the foot of the steps. Two neighbors saw a car they didn't recognize parked on Corporation that night. Got your choice. Dark blue Honda or burgundy Camry. You'll be delighted to know they agreed on Kentucky plates. Neither witness came up with even a partial, and no one saw who parked the car or drove it away."

Pointing to a well-worn trail crossing the property from the left and continuing to the hedge, I asked, "What's that?"

"That," she said, "is the route a neighborhood opossum takes each night."

"Did you pick up any fingerprints?"

"No, the opossum didn't leave any."

I groaned.

"Nothing on the door. Inside, we got Presser, his girlfriend, several friends who'd visited the previous weekend, and a cleaning lady who came alternate Wednesdays. No unknowns. A partial sneaker print on the stairs from the basement was too big for Presser, and the housekeeper swears she vacuumed those stairs the preceding Wednesday. The track was from a practically virgin New Balance."

"One of Presser's friends told me he was pretty straight."

"He wasn't rich either, if you're wondering. About fifteen thousand bucks in a mutual fund and a few pieces of upscale furniture. Still had outstanding student loans. Work provided a life insurance policy and decent 401(k) balance. Everything went to his fiancée. She had a tight alibi."

"Any other valuable information you want to share?"

"Do I detect a note of sarcasm? I'll get you access to the files. Might take a day or two. Anything else you want here?"

"Do you surmise the killer either knew the neighborhood or had scouted it out to find a parking spot away from prying eyes and convenient to the steps?"

"If we had a sense of motive I could *surmise*. We don't. Frankly, I'm hoping you can figure out a reason for this killing."

"I assume you don't have other unsolved murders with the same MO."

"Correct. This appears professional. As far as we can tell, nothing was taken except Presser's life. Presser was five ten. From the angle of the first wound, the killer was at least as tall. The knife thrusts were powerful. Probably a male, although some women are as big and plenty strong enough. From the partial footprint, they figure the shoe size is men's eleven or twelve, medium width. No clue on weight since the ground was too hard for any impressions." She checked her watch. "Anything else?"

"Off the record—guesses, feelings?"

She looked at me with steady, hard eyes. "I haven't a clue, which is why I'm glad you're working on this and I can do something more productive. Either Presser was into something he shouldn't have been—

and we can't get even a whiff of what that might have been—or . . ." She paused several seconds before continuing. "Or it was a mistake, which we may figure out only after someone else goes dead."

"A mistake?"

"A major lowlife lives across the street at four-ninety-eight. Maybe he was the target."

"Terrific—a dyslexic hitter."

Her lips formed a straight line, her brow pulled down toward her eyebrows. Her unblinking eyes stared into mine.

"That's it, isn't it?" I said. "You think it was a mistake."

"Doesn't matter what I think." She climbed into her cruiser and lowered the window. "Your problem now. I'll call you about the files."

She pulled away from the curb, leaving me with a bad taste in my mouth.

◊◊◊

I NO SOONER RETURNED HOME from my meeting with Lt. Hastings than Detective Bear called, summoning me to meet him for an interview with Chillicothe Machine's CEO. I followed directions to the company's newly resurfaced parking lot, and in a little over two hours, I tucked my G20 next to a Ross County sheriff's car. Ancient maples and ash trees swayed in the breeze, dwarfing the weathered brick building. The air smelled heavy, as though it would soon rain, but I didn't see it in the scattered clouds.

Bear waited for me beyond the security doors in a large open area. He nodded at my approach and asked the receptionist sporting a kelly-green polo shirt for Mr. Elkin. I wandered the lobby, reading quality awards, perusing Chamber of Commerce plaques, and looking at product displays and pictures of the parent company's Japanese facilities. Mainly I wondered why we were here, but figured I'd soon find out.

Elkin's administrative assistant escorted us down several corridors, past an employee lunchroom, and through a set of double glass doors labeled "Administration." The steady factory thrum stopped once the doors clicked behind us. She pointed to two visitor chairs next to her desk, the ensemble guarding the entrance to the corner office labeled by a brass plate as belonging to Burton G. Elkin. "He'll be right with you."

The door opened and Elkin, equine thin, wearing the ubiquitous green polo, introduced us to two men who were leaving. The older gentleman,

Edward Olson, wore a summer-weight wool suit that must have cost a bundle. It hid his excessive girth by draping flawlessly from his shoulders. He had dark half-moons under his eyes, and his right eye exhibited a pronounced twitch—maybe from fatigue, maybe too much caffeine. His handshake left me wanting to wipe my hand on my leg.

Before I could, the younger guy, Chip Kincaid, grabbed my hand, squeezing my knuckles. Chillicothe Machine's insurance agent looked the part: tasseled loafers, pressed chinos, oxford shirt, and blue blazer with a coat of arms on the pocket. His hair was precision trimmed, his fingernails polished, and his tan earned on a golf course or bought at a salon. He made sure to give me his card before Olson hauled him from the area.

Elkin ushered us to leather chairs in front of his antique walnut desk. Bear pulled out his notepad.

Elkin remained standing. "Who's he?"

Bear explained that because of a particular expertise, I had been deputized to work on the botulism murders. He didn't explain what my expertise was, and Elkin didn't ask. Too bad. I would have been interested in the answer.

Elkin plopped into his chair as though his legs could no longer support him. "Gentlemen, I have terrible news. Glen Framington, our former CEO, was murdered last night."

I glanced at Bear. He seemed taken aback. I concluded this was not what he'd expected.

Elkin pressed on, "He retired ten years ago and moved to Arizona with his wife. The climate helped her arthritis."

Bear scribbled on his pad.

Elkin tightened his quivering lips into a hard line. "Somebody's out to get us. That's why I wanted to meet you in person. I didn't want to risk someone listening in."

Bear straightened. "You think someone is tapping your phones?"

Elkin's eyes opened wide. "Maybe. Maybe they are. All I know is that if word of this leaks to the local press, there'll be panic around here. We can't have that."

We promised we wouldn't contact the media, and left unsaid that someone else surely would. Patiently, Bear extracted what little information Elkin had: Framington's address in Phoenix, that the victim was stabbed in bed, and not much more. Bear's cell phone interrupted his questioning. He muttered a couple of *uh-huhs* and *yeahs* and disconnected.

"Sheriff Lyons needs me on another matter. You two continue. Mr. Elkin, I'll follow up on the . . ."

He checked his notes and I filled in the blank: "Framington murder."

"With the Phoenix police. I can find my way out."

While the two of them shook hands I conjured a way to continue the conversation. "I'm sure you're in shock from this news, Mr. Elkin," I said. "It would help if I could go over some old ground."

I took his nod as permission.

"Do you have any idea why someone wanted to kill your retirees? Or your former CEO?"

"I've asked myself that question every night since Memorial Day and I've drawn a blank. And now, with Glen's death . . ."

He pushed out of his chair and paced with nervous energy, rubbing the back of his neck.

I hoped a business question might calm him by allowing him to focus. "How was your business affected by the picnic?"

"Other than down time while we attended funerals and a predictable temporary drop in productivity, it hasn't had an effect." He poured water from a cut-glass pitcher. "Want some?"

I declined.

He drained the glass, poured another, and resumed prowling the room. "Sorry, dry mouth. Today I found out our insurance carrier plans to jack up our medical rates because of the costs for treating everyone. Chip brought Mr. Olson along to convince me to switch to Olson's company. According to them, the current carrier would be stuck with the past costs with no way to recoup them. I'd still have a small rate increase, but not nearly as bad."

"Who are your competitors?"

"A competitor? Preposterous. Going after our retirees? And why Glen? Why not me?" He took a long drink of water. "The recession pinched, but we've been okay because we diversified over the last few years. We're profitable, but below target." He looked at the glass shaking in his hand. "I'm sorry. What did you ask?"

"Are there changes since you were acquired?"

"Lots." He sat down and unsuccessfully tried to smile. "For starters we all have to wear these green shirts."

I sensed he needed to talk and let him. Our conversation rambled for more than forty-five minutes, covering the takeover, the change from offices to cubicles, Japanese "consensus-driven" management, and his plans to retire in three years.

"You don't sound happy with the changes," I said.

"Sorry I vented. I appreciate your listening. I'm stunned by Glen's death. I don't know what to do."

"Any ideas who could be behind all this? I'll take even wild or crazy ones."

"They say 'follow the money.' The only ones I can see who made any money from this are the funeral directors. I guess Chip Kincaid's commission will be higher this year on the medical premium. I'm sorry I sound bitter, Mr. McCree, but I keep wondering why this happened to us, to me. Frankly, I'm scared of what will happen next, especially if word of Glen's death gets out."

"Understandable. I'd like to talk to someone from the union. Suggestions?"

"Deb Holt, the secretary-treasurer. You'll find her to be . . . direct. The best time to catch her is after work. She usually stops by Lefty's before heading home." He checked his watch. "Shift ends at four."

NINE

WITH HALF AN HOUR BEFORE the shift ended, I could get a head start at the bar, or try something else. I retrieved Chip Kincaid's card from my pocket and used my cell phone to call him.

A cheerful voice answered, "Kincaid Agency." Yes, Chip was in and would wait for me. I found the agency at the far end of a strip mall. Inside I introduced myself to the receptionist, whose smile was as broad as her voice was cheerful. Chip appeared from the rear and again applied his overly strong handshake.

Two can play at being the alpha male. I didn't squeeze; I held his hand and didn't let go until he struggled to disengage.

He ushered me into a spartan office. His desk was bare, except for a beige executive phone and a stargazer lily perfuming the room. Three chairs and a gazillion certificates on the wall completed the decor.

"You're with the police?" he asked. "I thought I knew everyone in the sheriff's department."

"My organization's assisting them on the botulism murders. Do you do a lot of business with Chillicothe Machine?"

His face beamed. "You bet! They're a great client. I represent them for almost everything. I'm independent and get the very best deals regardless of the carrier. Why?"

"How long have you been working with them?"

"I've saved them a ton of money from the get-go. They've been a client since I set up shop. Why?"

"Someone suggested the murders were connected with Chillicothe Machine's business. Have you noticed any recent changes?"

"Really? They're an ideal firm. Absolutely super! Pay their premiums on time. Reasonable to work with. Easy to present to carriers. Have a good credit rating. I place their health insurance, actives and retirees, property and casualty, product liability, worker's comp, and I even bid out annuity contracts last year. I did their directors' liability until the acquisition—that's done in Japan now. The Japanese are a little slower making decisions, which is why you saw me there today. Normally, I'd wait until September before starting discussions about next year's changes."

He removed a rubber ball from his desk drawer and squeezed it, each squeeze producing a soft squeak. "Burt Elkin didn't seem himself today—kinda distracted. Don't get me wrong here, they're still wonderful to work with."

No mystery why Elkin was distracted. In retrospect, I was surprised he hadn't canceled his meeting with Kincaid. "Why would someone target their retirees?"

"I think it's some nutcase. Anything else? I need to meet a client for nine holes at the club."

He promised to call if he thought of anything and we shook—no contests this time. Something with Kincaid didn't feel right, but I couldn't put my finger on it.

◊◊◊

I HELD MY BREATH RUNNING the gauntlet of smokers standing outside Lefty's. Once my eyes adjusted to the relative darkness inside, the place reminded me of the Irish pubs of my youth with their generations of stale cigarette smoke permeating the atmosphere, masking the sweat of hard work or sports teams who came straight from the game to the bar. The place didn't waste money on amenities, except for two dartboards encased in polished wood. People came to talk, drink, and smoke—now in clots outside.

I claimed a stool at the far end of the bar. From there I could watch the door without craning my neck. I ordered a draft beer and placed a ten-spot in front of me. The brass railing felt cool. Next to me sat a morose guy with a shirt front proclaiming, "Bricklayers—it ain't just bricks. Inquire within." An arrow pointed down. I wondered whether the advertising worked. Maybe a third of the barstools had patrons or markers reserving the seat, presumably the smokers outside. Three guys by the jukebox argued how to spend their buck.

Halfway through my beer, a sea of kelly green foamed through the door. The decibel level drowned out Tom Petty lamenting on the jukebox. The group included only two women. Assuming Deb Holt had come, I had a fifty-fifty shot of guessing right.

I waited until they ordered and moseyed over to the pixie with a bouffant hairdo. Once in range I asked, "Deb Holt?"

She pointed toward the redhead. I excused and pardoned my way through the crowd.

The redhead eyed me head to toe to head. "Yeah, what do ya want?"

"I'm Seamus McCree and I'm investigating the Memorial Day picnic. Can we talk for a few minutes?"

She nodded assent and strutted to a vacant spot away from the crowd. "Who sent you?"

"Ross County Sheriff's Office asked my firm to check a few things out." I handed her my card with the CIG logo.

"Cub must be feeling heat in the kitchen."

"Cub?"

"Yeah, Sheriff *Lyons.* Thinks he's king of the jungle, but he's just another weenie politician. Everyone wants this solved and Cub's ass is on the line. What do you wanna know?"

"My question's speculative. Why would someone kill your retirees?"

"What's this speculative crap? It warn't no mistake, mister. Fresh food can't get botulism. Only our people got killed. No other picnics had problems that day. Someone hadda do that on purpose."

She took a slug of beer and continued. "Only the Japs have anything to gain. It's part of their plan to bust the union."

"Bust the union?" Elkin had warned me she was direct.

"We're the only ones standing in the way of them cutting our benefits. They ain't interested in the workers. Only in profits. They bought Chillicothe Machine to make more money. We was making plenty to feed employees and shareholders alike, but they want more."

Some of the green shirts caught the gist of our conversation and leaned in to hear better.

"We might've won World War Two, but heaven knows they're winning this one—buying up all our good companies and making them concentration camps to bring profits to the motherland. And now they show their real selves. When they can't get what they want, they poison us. That's what I think." She took another slug of beer. "Can't prove a damned thing."

Her face had flushed from the speech. Several voices chimed in with "You tell 'em, Debbie," and "God's truth." Others, like me, were quiet, but I sensed she had expressed the sentiment of the majority, even if they wouldn't have used the same words.

I maintained a calm demeanor. "Clearly, it hasn't undermined the union. Why murder? Couldn't they try to decertify—"

She pitched her voice so everyone could hear. "Damn straight it hasn't worked, and it ain't never going to. Right, boys?" They all agreed: she was right. "They found a loophole and killed our pension plan. Put in a damned 401(k) instead. Oh sure, it's got a company match and some profit sharing, but you watch that profit sharing. Each year it'll be smaller and smaller since there ain't no guarantees or requirements that they make it. How'd they do it?"

She made eye contact throughout the room. "We trusted the bastards, that's how. The contract only required them to give us the same pension benefits as nonbargained get. Well, they did that all right. Never asked us or nothin'. First thing the union knows is we get a letter telling us benefits had stopped and they was putting in a 401(k) plan. Would be good for the workers and good for the company, they said. Well, they're half-right. It's been damn good for the company."

She paused to drain her beer. Someone grabbed her mug and handed her a fresh one. She inhaled half and continued.

"I burned Elkin's ear over that. He said the Japs wouldn't let him tell us ahead of time. They also want to cut our retiree medical, but they cain't do that 'cause we got that written tight in the contract." She paused again. Not even the jukebox dared make a sound. "They can, if they ain't got a union to deal with. And it don't cost them nothin' if there's no retirees. When they murdered our retirees, they killed two birds with one stone."

"You're accusing Japanese management of deliberately poisoning your retirees in order to save money on their medical? I just spoke to your insurance agent, and it's going to cost *more*."

A guy with a mermaid's tail showing below his shirtsleeve and a scowl torturing his face said, "Deb Holt, that's a crock. You're making up some far-fetched tale to cover your ass for losing our pension plan."

Deb's flush deepened. "Far-fetched, you say? Ain't they the same Japs who sent our brave soldiers on a death march in Bataan? Ain't they the same ones as had kamikaze pilots? They don't value life like we do."

"What?" I said. "They don't value life as we did when we dropped the atomic bombs on Hiroshima and Nagasaki?"

Her face became purple. "That . . . that was to save lives so we didn't have to invade the place and kill more of them. You asked, mister, and I'm telling you where to look. Look at them Japanese. They're the ones benefiting from this, and them Japs got the morals of a rattlesnake." She drained her second beer and, showing me her back, she headed to the bar. The crowd surged after her.

I looked around for the guy with the mermaid's tail. No sign. I deserted my ten spot and hoped to catch him outside.

I pushed through the ring of smokers and scanned the parking lot. No mermaid's tail. I had no desire to reenter the poisoned atmosphere of the bar. I slid behind the steering wheel of my car. The virulence of her hate of the Japanese left a caustic aftertaste mouthwash could never eliminate. She was good at stirring up the troops, even if she confused the Germans and the Japanese of World War II.

Her kind of hate needs to be challenged and I had wanted to, but I'd retreated when I remembered I was there representing the sheriff's office. I'd bet she was like the many Americans who believe they have no culpability for our treatment of Native Americans or Nisei in World War II internment camps, whereas our enemies' evil character is the root cause of crimes against us. What bullshit. I slammed my hands against the steering wheel and recoiled at the pain.

Maybe I wasn't cut out for fieldwork.

◊◊◊

THE COMBINATION OF NONSTOP GREGORIAN chants on the car's CD player and a fine fast food repast had calmed me by the time I got home. Paddy met me at the front door with the news, "Skyler Weaver is waiting for you in the library."

She popped out of the chair and gave me a hug. I wasn't sure what the hug was for, but I returned it and realized she had no meat on her bones. Her shoulder blades stuck out like sharp elephant ears. She plucked an envelope from the Oklahoma State Department of Health, Division of Vital Records off the mantel. It was addressed to Samuel Presser. "Look at this."

I pulled out a receipt for ten dollars and a slightly blurred copy of a death certificate for George F. Proudt stating that he had died of congestive heart failure in Oklahoma City on February 26, 2002.

"Okay," I said. "You've got my attention. Why did Samuel send away for this death certificate?"

"After Skyler caught me up on what's been happening with my friends from church," Paddy said, "she showed the stuff to me. I wondered about a genealogy link. Skyler just finished talking with one of Samuel's uncles who's into it. No Proudts. No relatives have ever lived in Oklahoma."

Skyler's sniffle yanked my attention to her. She pulled a hankie from her blouse sleeve and dabbed at fresh tears. "I'm sorry. You'd think I'd be over this by now. I guess seeing that Samuel made this request only a week before he died . . ."

She seemed so frail, a breeze could blow her away. I was afraid what would happen if we couldn't find answers. I asked, "Where did you get this?"

"The post office forwards Samuel's mail to his parents. They eventually send it to me. This is the first unusual thing I've received."

"Tomorrow morning," I said, "I'm supposed to look over the Cincinnati Police Department's case file and evidence. Did the police take Samuel's computer or make a copy of the hard drive?"

Skyler's eyes grew wide. I offered her the tissue box, but she waved it off. "Oh my gosh," she said. "I didn't even think of it when they asked if I had anything of Samuel's. We both owned ancient desktops and wouldn't have space when we moved in together. Our solution was two new laptops. A good one for our home computer and a crappy one to use when we both needed to be on at the same time. The police have that one because it was at Samuel's place. I totally forgot mine has some of his stuff. Do you want it, or should I give it to the police?"

Paddy said, "Bring it here. I'll make two copies of the hard drive, one for us and one for the police. That should take care of it without you losing your computer. Could this Proudt stuff be for work?"

"Doubtful," I said, ignoring the conscience twinge suggesting Skyler's laptop should go directly to the police. "He used his own money and they sent it to his home. I'll keep Proudt in mind when I review the CPD files tomorrow. Can I have this?"

We batted around ideas for a few more minutes, but nothing useful came of it. Skyler agreed to drop her computer at my house on her way to work the next morning.

I was anxious for tomorrow to arrive. I would fill Bear in by phone about the rest of my day in Chillicothe, and debrief him regarding what he had learned about the former Chillicothe Machine CEO's death. I had a feeling that death would be critical in helping us understand motivation for the botulism murders, which would then point toward suspects.

I planned to spend most of the day on the Presser case. I'd visit the police to review the evidence and case files. Then when I returned home, I'd spend time looking at Skyler's laptop, unless Paddy had already done that while I was gone. The Proudt death certificate was the first abnormality I had kicked up. Maybe understanding it was a path toward enlightenment—and toward the miracle Skyler said we needed.

TEN

TUESDAY MORNING, I PASSED PADDY'S silent room on the way to the kitchen. A pile of papers decorated the breakfast table. The envelope from Oklahoma capped the pile. Underneath were Proudt's credit history (fine); a listing of places he had lived in the last ten years (house to assisted living to nursing home, illustrating the decline of his health); information about his employer, wife, and ex-wife; the names of his children, where they lived, and for whom they worked. Proudt's *Daily Oklahoman* obit and copies of his hospital bills were at the bottom. Following his last heart attack, Proudt had spent his final two days running up sixty-seven thousand dollars in medical expenses.

It told a lot about George Proudt. It didn't tell me why Samuel Presser had sent away for the death certificate, or why Paddy had done all this work.

◊◊◊

BEFORE I WAS ALLOWED TO review any of the Presser files or evidence, I met with the young officer Lt. Hastings had enlisted to teach me how the CPD kept files, rules of evidence, evidence tracking, and so forth. They allowed me to bring my laptop into the room to take notes, but I could remove nothing. As a visual person I paid particular attention to the pictures, a full-color spread of Presser's home with concentration on his kitchen.

Where I had seen nail holes, now I looked at nature photos. State magnets covered his refrigerator, holding lists and snapshots and appointment cards. The furniture was utilitarian and sparse—awaiting Skyler's additions to fill in the empty spaces. I viewed each picture several times in the hopes of spotting an anomaly—something off—a missing piece or wrong interpretation.

I was doing fine as Mr. Objective Detective until I came to the death pictures, which made me gag. I soldiered on. Viewing the autopsy photos,

I found a place to bury the knowledge that I had known the living, breathing Samuel Presser. I didn't bother reading the report—it could not contain the why of his death.

Next came evidence bags. I peered through the plastic looking for anything strange, anything that didn't fit the picture of a solid, if somewhat boring, young man. The last evidence bag included his clothing. I had expected more blood, forgetting the bleeding had been mostly internal. I had not expected the stench of urine to leach through the plastic.

It was the final straw and I embarrassed myself by puking into the wastebasket. My acking brought the young officer running.

"That," she said, "we'll allow you to remove from the room."

◊◊◊

BY THE TIME I FINISHED reading the Presser interview files, morning had slipped into afternoon. I had filled my laptop with myriad notes and my brain with disgust at humanity. Once home I brushed my teeth and gargled with mouthwash, relishing the cleansing sting. I chose not to challenge myself by eating a late lunch.

Skyler's computer remained where I had left it for Paddy, sitting atop two legal-sized paper cartons of Presser's belongings. Matthew Yeung had transported them from TransOhio, but Skyler hadn't had the heart to open them. She hoped I would let her know what they contained.

I was curious about their contents, but my more responsible self—the superego nag, if you prefer—told me to first touch base with Detective Wright. Since I had nothing useful to report from either CEO Elkin or union firebrand Deb Holt, I figured I'd try to gather some worthwhile information before calling him. I set up a conference call including everyone at CIG who was looking into Chillicothe Machine's finances.

The company remained profitable; had sufficient cash reserves, satisfied customers, and a large, untouched bank line of credit; and was making investments in upgrading its equipment. CIG's verification process had matched actual and reported orders for a number of Chillicothe Machine's larger clients. Conclusion: a strong company, and its income was real.

The analysts had also researched its Japanese parent, Kobe Heavy Metal. Because of the interlocking stock ownership between Japanese companies and their banks, they cautioned that it would take longer to firm up the conclusion. For now, that X-ray was also negative.

I thanked them for their work. Based on nothing more than a too-strong handshake and a feeling he didn't want me snooping around, I asked them to check on Chip Kincaid's insurance agency.

Paddy arose while I was on the phone and took Skyler's laptop to his room. From behind his door, music pumped out at a moderate volume. The sound returned me to his high school years, when he often used the stereo to let me know he was pissed, the decibel level matching a chain saw cutting two-inch pipe.

I prepared myself for a protracted conversation with Bear, except he was unavailable when I called. "I'm sure he'll get back to you when he can," his assistant said.

Paddy had not emerged from his room, so I carted the two boxes of Presser's effects into the library. One box was much heavier than the other. From the lighter one I removed the top layer containing pens and pencils and an appointment book. Next I unearthed two five-by-seven pictures in light oak frames wrapped in paper towels: Skyler and two older people I decided based on facial similarities were probably Presser's parents.

Next came an HP financial calculator and two framed certificates. One indicated Samuel William Presser met all the requirements to become a Fellow of the Society of Actuaries; the other stated Presser was a Member of the American Academy of Actuaries. The bottom layer of this archaeological dig contained a well-used American Heritage dictionary, Paul Hoffman's *Archimedes' Revenge*, and a "famous quotes" daily calendar showing June 6, his last day in the office.

I made a contents list for Skyler and taped it on top of the repacked box.

A spiral-bound TransOhio Life phone directory and summary plan descriptions for TransOhio's pension and 401(k) plans were on top of the heavier box. Volumes containing the Actuarial Standards of Practice composed the penultimate layer. At the bottom lay an unlabeled accordion folder.

I unwound the string holding the flap over the red folder and looked inside. The first pocket contained a computer-generated package labeled "Annual Statement Exhibits for the Fiscal Year Ending 3/31/07."

Stamped in large red letters on the upper left corner of each page was the word *DRAFT*. A background watermark on each page also said *DRAFT*. Subsequent sections, each one labeled with an exhibit number, contained work papers, computer printouts, and handwritten notes.

This appeared to be a work project. Why had Matthew Yeung packed this folder for Skyler? With the possible exception of the TransOhio phone list, everything else was Presser's personal property.

Might as well ask Matthew. I could have bothered him at work, since I had the TransOhio phone list, but it wasn't urgent. His home answering machine responded, "This is Matthew. Leave a message at the beep." I asked about the red folder.

I repacked everything else and thumbed through the appointment book. The Sierra Club engagement calendar contained scattered penciled notations starting in January and running through mid-August. Most of the appointments consisted of a time and a person's name or initials. Was that Presser's habit—to use a personal code—or was he hiding something, something that got him killed? I would put the question to Matthew when he called.

Still no Paddy and it was getting on toward dinner. I knocked on his door.

From inside, over the music, came *"Entré, s'il te plaît."*

I opened the door. "When did you learn French?"

He didn't look up from his computer screen, but decreased the music volume. "Never took it. One of my roommates did." He held up a finger, and I waited until he finished typing something. He looked up. "Debugging someone else's program and it's a killer."

"Does this mean you're blowing me off for dinner?"

He squinted at his monitor. "Wow, that late? Time goes quickly when you're having fun. Maybe tonight you should take me out? Half hour, forty-five minutes?"

My stomach grumbled, perhaps reacting to a delayed dinner when I had already upchucked breakfast and skipped lunch. I knew Paddy's "half hour, forty-five minutes" stuff. It might be ten o'clock before he was done.

"I'll make salad and heat soup. Grab it when you want. Did you get a chance to copy the files from Skyler's laptop?"

He tapped several more keys and shook his head at the computer. Eventually, he said, "I mirrored the drive. It'll be just like we're running her computer, but you'll need my help getting it going. This will go faster if I can concentrate."

"Message received." I pulled the door closed behind me.

◊◊◊

ABOUT THREE THIRTY, I AWOKE to a game of kitty chase. The kittens didn't provide me a rulebook, but evidently each loop around the room had to involve the bed, and they scored extra points for running over my head.

I caught Chong, the calico, and received a scratch in the process. Her claws were little but sharp, and got my attention. *Ouch.* I brought her, howling at the indignity, to Paddy's room. His light was on. I shut the door behind me and let the cat go. She padded to his unmade bed, hopped up, and curled onto the pillow.

"They like your hours better than mine. I'm not a fan of kitty Olympics. You still working on the same problem?"

"Licked it. I'm back to regular coding. You want to look at Samuel Presser's files?"

Are you crazy? It's flipping three thirty in the morning. I spoke my second reaction, "Why not? I won't sleep for a while."

He plugged an external hard drive into an old laptop he had built in high school and executed a series of keystrokes that generated the familiar beep of a boot program starting up. The hard drive's mosquito buzz ended with the message ENTER PASSWORD, followed by a blinking cursor.

"I didn't consider that," I said. "Is there a way around it, or are we screwed? We have Skyler's permission, so you can hack it if you need to."

Paddy laughed. "Now you approve of my hacking? You weren't as enthusiastic when the FBI showed up."

I waved it away. "And this won't contain the Defense Department's expense reports, either. If we were a TV show, we'd guess the password before the next commercial break."

"But we aren't. We get to do the smart thing." He rebooted the computer, pressed a couple of keys as it restarted, and entered the administration module behind the system. Navigating through several tabs, he snapped his fingers once and rebooted. "There you go."

"You reset the password?"

"Killed it." He pointed to the start menu. "*Voilà!* Now, let's see what we have." Paddy's cursor scampered from file to file, checking out who knew what. I sat and stared. I'd started using computers in high school and wasn't a novice, but I was still a kindergartner compared to him.

After about five minutes he said, "We have complete access. I changed settings to allow us to see hidden and password-protected files in addition to the normal ones. Any clue what you're looking for?"

From the door came scratching, followed by a kitty paw sliding underneath it. "Looks like Cheech wants to join the party." I let her in. She rubbed against my leg, as though to let me know I was forgiven for taking away her sister. "Before I forget, thanks for the information on Proudt. How come you're so interested in this case?"

"It's a fun break from writing code." He picked Cheech up and tossed her on the bed.

I pointed at the computer. "He hid files? I have no idea what we're looking for, but if he intentionally hid something, let's find out what."

Paddy sat cross-legged on the floor, computer on his lap. The maestro directed the cursor with his index finger on the touch pad: movement interspersed with quick bursts of typing. I held my tongue and waited. I was sure I would have eventually figured this all out, but Paddy had taken me off the two-lane bumpy country road I would have traveled and put me on the expressway.

"Okay," he said. "Besides the normal systems files that Microsoft hides to prevent you from screwing them up, I found three areas with hidden files. The largest contains pictures and AVI clips—short movies. From the file names, they're porn."

There goes Matthew's halo. "Unless we have to, let's not mention that to Skyler."

"Why, you think she doesn't know? She might have some on her portion of the machine. We can check. I suspect the files were copied over all at one time since they have the same date. Probably came from Samuel's computer. Finances are the second folder. Last is named Actuarial Audit, containing Excel and Word documents."

He had the cursor roaming again before I could respond, and the screen changed to a picture of a gorgeous redhead sucking someone off.

"Yep, porn it is." Paddy had a cat-that-ate-the-canary grin. "Let's see what else he has."

Before he could embarrass me more, not by the pictures but by his sharing them with me, I said, "I want to see his finances." I was interested in Presser's pornographic collection to determine if it contained child pornography or bestiality or fetishes or something to provide a lead, but I planned to do that work privately, without Paddy running the controls.

He shrugged, let out a melodramatic sigh, and opened the financial folder, which consisted of a Quicken program with five years of history, and Excel files with Presser's balance sheets at the end of the last four years. A separate tab held backup for his taxes. According to a sermon I once heard, with access to someone's checkbook and calendar, you can tell what the person really valued. What would I find with Presser?

"Bo-ring," Paddy said in a singsong voice. "You can look at this crap on your own." He opened the Actuarial Audit folder. It contained about forty different spreadsheets, mostly labeled with exhibit numbers. I retrieved the expandable red folder and pulled the material relating to Exhibit XVII from it. It matched the computer file.

"I'll bite. What is it?" Paddy asked. He started exploring the hard drive again.

"I have no clue. I need to talk to Matthew Yeung. He hasn't called me back."

"Look. He's got a bunch of computer games. I wonder where his disks are."

"Okay Patrick, the computer's here for work. Time to shut it down. I'll catch a few more Zs and look again with fresh eyes. Do me a favor and keep Cheech and Chong here."

"Uh-oh, it's Patrick now. I guess I'd better pay attention."

We laughed. I had often related how I could tell the severity of my mother's anger at me by how many parts of my name I heard: Seamus (I was in for a minor rebuke), Seamus McCree (the water was uncomfortably warm), Seamus Anselm McCree (boiling). Here I was channeling my mother and Paddy caught me.

"Yeah, and no sneaking up to my study to look at porn either. This is evidence in a murder. I don't know why he was murdered, and I'm not about to risk setting you up to be victim number two."

"All right, all right, *I get the message.*" He shut down the computer. "Want to fill me in on what you learned today?"

"No, I want to go back to sleep."

I carted the laptop and the red file to my office. The movement woke me up. I might as well work. Pornography was on the docket. An hour later, I concluded Presser was not a pervert. His hard drive contained no pictures of children, sex with animals, fetishes, or sadomasochist material. Presser had collected a smattering of smutty pictures and movie clips. Maybe he used them for self-stimulation when Skyler wasn't around or if he was bored studying for his FSA. They'd made me horny and doubly frustrated since I was still without a reason for Presser's murder.

It was too early for my daily run, an eight-miler this time. I tackled the financial folder next. Presser kept transparent records. His biggest expenses were taxes, rent, church, and savings, in that order. His job explained all his income and I didn't find any mysterious expenses. Even with his little fling of porn, he still appeared as boring as everyone said he was. Hastings' tragic accident theory of the dyslexic killer was gaining strength by default.

I was looking forward to my run, but my enthusiasm dampened as soon as I stepped out the door. The wind blew from the factories lining Mill Creek. One had discharged a peppermint scent, spoiling any chance I could smell what was blooming along the run. Because I was ticked off at the smell, I didn't pay attention to where I was running and stepped on a loose chunk of pavement right on my damaged arch. I should have stopped, but I didn't want to mess up the training schedule. By the time I finished the run, my foot ached.

Before showering, I iced the foot. During breakfast I iced the arch another twenty minutes. Finally back in my office, I decided to tackle the Actuarial Audit information, whatever that was. My Internet search on the term "Actuarial Audit" proved less than satisfactory. The definitions ran the gamut from an audit of actuarial services to a risk management exercise to purportedly determining the "real value of a share of stock." As a former Wall Street stock analyst, I knew the last definition was a massive overreach. Nothing to do but look at the individual files.

Most related to the financial statement of some insurance company, the name of which was scrupulously concealed by inserting the name "Client Company" everywhere the real name should have been. Was this a case study for one of those actuarial exams Matthew Yeung had told me about? Could this information have anything to do with Presser's death? I needed Matthew to point me in the right direction, but he still hadn't returned my call. So much for his being helpful.

I no longer had the patience to avoid disturbing Matthew at work. I called the number listed in the TransOhio phone directory and heard, "You've reached the desk of Matthew Yeung. I will be on vacation until Monday. Please leave a message and I will get back to you when I return. If you need immediate assistance, please dial extension three-two-eight-seven."

His assistant informed me Matthew did not call in for messages while he was on vacation, and she'd only contact him in an emergency. Despite my desire to figure this out, even I wouldn't classify a two-month-old murder as an emergency. I told her I'd try next week.

I hated the idea of waiting until Monday for answers and left a more urgent message on Yeung's home answering machine. When in doubt, plunge in. At worst I was only wasting time and burning up some gray matter between my ears.

The only additional information I gleaned from several hours' work was that everything in the red folder was on the computer, but not vice versa. The computer had additional files, including several massive Excel spreadsheets, some running to over 8,500 lines with what looked like individual policy data. Why? And why did Presser have this material on his personal computer? What exactly was this actuarial audit? For whom?

And, switching gears, why had Bear not called me back?

ELEVEN

PADDY CALLED ME TO "BRINNER": breakfast for him, dinner for me. He'd been up for only three or four hours; I'd been up for thirteen. He sat down, unfolded his napkin, placed it on his lap, and squared the corners. "Do you miss living on the East Coast?"

When had he decided on this non sequitur to start our conversation? Or had I forgotten an earlier conversation from the previous night? "I miss some people . . . and some things. Like Carnegie Hall. The Circle in the Square Theater. The Jersey Shore in fall without all the summer people. Overall, though, I like it better here."

"How come?"

I drowned my pancakes in maple syrup—the real thing from Vermont. Years ago Paddy had insisted I ditch the supermarket plastic-bottle stuff. He claimed maple syrup was the one sweetener that didn't impede mineral absorption, or some such. I admired his eating habits, but usually didn't want to emulate them. He'd live longer than I, but I was unwilling to give up meat to gain a few years of life expectancy. In this case, I didn't care what his reasons were; real tasted better.

I finished a bite. "I don't know. The slower pace? When I arrived here I walked up everyone's heels. Even downtown, they practically crawled. It's indicative. Everything's a push in the East. I like the people here better. They have more balance between work and family, friends and church."

"If that's the case, how come I've gotten more phone calls from friends since I arrived than you have?"

I shoveled in a forkful of pancakes and stalled. "I like the people better here, but I'm still an outsider."

"You've been here forever."

"The fault's mine, not theirs. I haven't spent enough time nurturing friendships. You've seen me. Work comes first. Since I'm an introvert, I'd rather read than go to a party. If I need a real break, I go to our cabin."

He seemed to consider my excuse while he chewed. "I've seen you at church, though. Everyone knows you. You're not standing in a corner like a real introvert."

"They know me because I sing in the choir, I work on church finances, and I'm a past president. But I haven't done anything to let them into my life, really get to know me. You need to open up if you want to develop strong friendships. It's work, like marriage."

"Is that why you and Mom got divorced?"

I was beginning to yearn for the days when we'd argue about whether the Reds had made good off-season trades, or even the birds-and-bees discussion. "First we disagreed about money. Eventually, we disagreed about everything. Why the twenty questions? Does this relate to your mom and her boyfriend?"

I sure know how to change conversation into silent meditation. After a too-long silence, I tried, "How about you? Who are your closest friends now?"

"I'll have to give it some thought," he said.

I refused to give up. "Want to hear about what I found on Presser's computer?"

At his agreement I told him what I'd discovered and that I was on hold until I heard from Matthew Yeung.

"What I'm hearing," Paddy said, "is that after three days, all you have is a death certificate for some guy from Oklahoma that you have no real reason to think has anything to do with Samuel's murder. I like my work better. At least I know when I'm wasting my time."

◊◊◊

I JERKED AWAKE AT HALF past three, ready to imprison the cats. Nails scrabbled against the hardwood floor to get purchase. Once they finally did, the cats skittered out the door. Realizing my startle response had scared them, I whispered apologies to the night and lay waiting for whatever had roused me to reappear. The moon cast the shadow of the blue ash through the window and onto the opposite wall, where the dresser mirror reflected it. Without my glasses, the pattern morphed, as though I looked through a blurred black-and-white kaleidoscope.

Finally the question reappeared. Had Presser used that computer for personal email?

I put on my glasses, flicked on the light, and jotted a complete note on a notepad from the top drawer of the nightstand. Experience had taught me to avoid short, brilliant phrases, which were clear when written under moonlight, but when viewed in harsh daylight became undecipherable spy transmissions.

Normally after hacking up a mental hairball like this I could go directly back to sleep. Not that night. Busy brain about Presser's murder, combined with the feeling I was getting nowhere quickly, continued to afflict me. I tuned to WVXU to listen to the BBC news, but gave up when they started announcing the worldwide cricket scores. Wide awake, I was working in my study before five.

I needed upbeat music to combat my drugged feeling and threw a *Beach Boys Live* CD on the player. *Boy, do they look dorky in those striped shirts—so clean-cut.* The Beach Boys had their secrets; what about Presser?

His email inbox contained six subfolders: *Family, Friends, Misc., Wedding, Skyler,* and *Work.*

The folders presented the minutiae of Presser's still-boring life. I struck pay dirt in Misc. Several messages from mcollier@appcl.com with subject lines like "Annuity Data" and "Life Data" had attachments I recognized. Nothing identified "appcl."

Using my computer, I typed www.appcl.com in the browser address bar. A message flashed: *We can't find "www.appcl.com."* I searched for the term "appcl" and got a ton of hits, but nothing referring to a company.

Rereading those emails, one from jnadler@appcl.com dated June 4 held promise: Meeting confirmed June 11 8:00 a.m. in our offices. Ask for me at the front desk.

Presser's appointment book had the entry: *June 11—8:00 Nadler.* I flipped through previous pages for other references to Nadler or Collier or appcl. Only Nadler showed up, with an eight o'clock notation for the third Monday in March.

What had happened when Presser missed the June meeting? Had he received emails after his June 6 death?

The last email he received on this computer was from June 4, two days before. I made a note to ask Skyler if she had received phone calls from anyone she didn't know. Then I made a second note to ask her about Nadler, Collier, and appcl.

Having to leave myself the notes convinced me I was mentally exhausted and not doing my best work. Today was a cross-training day. I rode my bicycle outside for a couple of hours, during which time Robert Rand left a message for me to "Call regarding the Chillicothe assignment."

"Tell me about Deb Holt," Rand said following the opening phone call pleasantries.

"What's this about?" Who had told him about Holt? And why? I had a feeling I now knew why Detective Wright hadn't called me back.

"In due time, Seamus. Please humor me and tell me about your encounter with her."

I related my conversation with CEO Elkin: how he had suggested I talk with Holt and where I might find her. Then I tried to re-create a verbatim transcript of my conversation with her.

"She called to complain about you," Rand said.

I flushed with embarrassment and nerves, having resurrected a vision of standing in front of the misnamed Sister Angelica, the high school principal, waiting to discuss some infraction I had allegedly committed. "Oh?" I wanted him to show some cards.

"And Detective Wright reports you have not returned his phone calls."

"Bullsh—*baloney*. I called him two days ago. I left *him* a message. With his assistant. *He's* the one who hasn't returned *my* call. You realize he was none too enthusiastic about having to work with us. Is he trying to undermine us with Sheriff Lyons?"

"I do not believe that to be the case," Rand said. "When I spoke with him about the Holt situation, he brushed it off and indicated some of her views were 'out there.' He had been busy on another investigation and happened to mention that he was waiting to hear from you."

"Something's gone wrong somewhere, since we're both waiting for the other one. I'll give him a call. Now what about Deb Holt? Do you need to assign someone else? Maybe I'm not cut out to be talking to people."

"I do not see a need to make a personnel change. Thank you for your time, Seamus."

I heard a beep and then the light buzz of white noise in one ear. My rapid heartbeat sounded in the other. I touched my neck and felt the artery pulse under my fingertips. My heart was working double time.

I could analyze the conversation with Rand later. Right now I needed to call Detective Wright and get our communication difficulties squared away. We connected and I apologized for not getting his messages. He read off the number he'd dialed.

"Oh dear," I said. "The fault's mine. I'm terrible with my cell phone. Either I leave it off, or I don't check messages, or I leave it in my car—which is what I did this time. I pretty much only think of it when I need to use it." I apologized once again and related all my information. His occasional grunts let me know he was still on the line.

I completed my report and asked, "Any additional news on the former CEO killed in Phoenix?"

"Nothing useful," he said. "I'll let you know, and thanks for CIG's information on Chillicothe Machine. I wouldn't have been able to do that—not that it helps much, but at least I can show Sheriff Lyons we're trying. Talk to you soon. Bye."

More civil anyway; I supposed that was progress.

At least I had the Presser case to work on. After a quick stretch and shower, I searched the internet for "J Nadler," "M Collier," and any insurance company that might be "appcl." Late afternoon I gave up and realized that although I had been drinking fluids all day, I had skipped breakfast, missed lunch, and now had a headache.

As though giving amplification to my stomach, a low roll of thunder rattled the window. A front of purple and gray cumulus clouds approached from Indiana. I unplugged the computers and remained at the window to watch a light show.

The pyrotechnics with booming accompaniment drove Paddy from his bed to the third floor to watch the storm with me. I'm not crazy enough to start chasing tornadoes, but I can watch lightning etch the heavens for hours. Even without a light show, I'll gladly listen as thunder's kettledrum booms shake windows, and I'll exalt when the wind causes oaks and maples to pretend they're weeping willows.

The worst of the storm lasted thirty minutes and in the process dumped two and a half inches of rain, overwhelming Cincinnati's storm sewers. A lightning strike fried the transformer at the end of our street.

Paddy and I walked out of the six-block blackout to Ludlow Avenue for Thai food. Paddy asked how my work had gone today. I described my email finds and the fruitless hours searching for Collier, Nadler, and appcl. I left out the conversation with Rand and Detective Wright's unwillingness to share information with me.

"Must be frustrating," Paddy said.

"Not really." I stopped. "Well, that's a lie. I wonder if a gene switches on in parents that tells them they're not supposed to admit work isn't all fun. This has been very frustrating because I feel like I'm *this* close"—I illustrated a small distance between my thumb and index finger—"and I want to know. But the time has been flying and, like you, that's when I know I really am having fun. Even if it is frustrating, I do love figuring stuff out."

"To each his own."

"I'm not sure what I'll do next." I slapped my forehead. "I didn't look at Presser's sent email folder."

Paddy gave me a patronizing smile and, using his most sarcastic tone, pronounced his verdict: "Well, *duh.*"

◊◊◊

ON THE WAY HOME, PADDY dumped me for some acquaintances he spotted standing in line at the Esquire Theater.

With power restored, in no time I found interesting communications in Presser's sent email. Presser called "mcollier" Mimi. The earliest message to her was in late March. The most recent was May 29, in which he thanked Mimi for confirming the dates of death for some annuitants.

My Internet search for "Mimi Collier" produced 4,700 hits. "Mimi Collier" plus "appcl" produced none. I wasted a good while sifting through the results, but nothing jumped off the screen yelling, "Me! Me! I'm the one!"

Three emails were for jnadler, referred to as Mr. Nadler by Presser. Searches on "Nadler" plus "appcl" and "Nadler" plus "Collier" proved similarly useless.

I concentrated on the emails themselves. One referred to a contract. If I could find a copy, I would learn the company's name and maybe who Nadler was. An email sent only four days before Presser's death got me twitchy-excited.

In the process of performing the audit, I have uncovered certain irregularities you should be aware of. I want to present the information in person rather than over the phone. Here are three alternative dates.

Irregularities. I was so close I could taste it.

TWELVE

MY ATTEMPT TO SLEEP ON the problem resulted in lousy sleep and no insight. Nor did my morning run accomplish more than allowing me to put a checkmark next to that day's training schedule. At least my arch didn't hurt. I had one more trick up my sleeve for incubating an "aha" moment without trying to push it.

I called Mrs. Keenan, my neighbor to the right, to see if Alice could come out and play. A four-year-old golden retriever, Alice delighted in wandering around county parks and wildlife refuges with me. Mrs. Keenan had passed the three-quarter-century mark and still took the dog for twice-daily walks around the block, but long romps were beyond her. Alice replaced Mr. Keenan, who had died about five years ago. He had been allergic to dogs and cats, forcing Mrs. Keenan to forgo them during her forty-five-year marriage. Unused to being alone, she'd found Alice at the local pound.

Alice bounded into the car. Mrs. Keenan handed me both a leather leash and a thirty-foot retractable lead for our jaunt. What Alice knew, and Mrs. Keenan didn't, was that once we got to a part of the park where few people go, I let Alice run to her heart's content.

We went to Mt. Airy, one of the largest parks in Hamilton County and only a few miles from home. For midday in the heat of August, the ramble was perfect. Alice looped around me checking a squirrel here, a chattering chipmunk there, and once she sniffed out the trail of a cottontail. Nose to the ground, tail wagging, she followed the rabbit I could see hopping up ahead. I whistled to Alice once she had wandered farther away from me than I was comfortable with. She came trotting up, jingling her rabies and address tags.

From my unconscious came the realization that I needed to check Presser's email contacts list. Maybe he had added an address or other identifying information to his entries for Mimi Collier and J. Nadler.

I patted Alice's head and ruffled her ears. Mrs. Keenan's constant attention kept the dog's fur soft and free of knots. "What a good girl you are." Her tail swished in agreement and she flopped on her back for a well-deserved belly rub.

Although I was excited to pursue the line of inquiry, I did not want to cheat Alice of her full outing. My decision nearly proved disastrous. She spotted a skunk hunting bugs at the edge of a field and pranced toward it, her tail wagging a greeting.

"Alice, down!"

In midstride she flopped to the ground, looking over her shoulder to see what was up.

"Alice, come."

She stood and looked between the skunk and me. *Please, oh please choose me.* I patted my leg and after a last long glance at the skunk, she came to me. We went through the "good dog" routine and, while she was enjoying another belly rub, I gave her a neck massage. She closed her eyes, tilted her head back until her snout was parallel to the ground, and moaned her pleasure.

I bought Alice a pig's ear on the way home. Once there, I rinsed her off with an outside hose, dried her with a designated "Alice" towel, and brought her to Mrs. Keenan. The perfect little lady walked beside me in heel position, carrying her pig's ear reward in her mouth to show her momma.

"You two were gone for a good long while. Was Alice a good girl? Did she pull on her lead?"

I handed Alice off. "She never gives me a bit of trouble about her lead." I ruffled Alice's fur one last time. The dog was grinning around her pig's ear. I waved goodbye to both of them, anxious to find out what "appcl" was.

◊◊◊

A FEW KEYSTROKES IN PRESSER'S contacts list and my answers appeared: "jnadler" was James Nadler, executive VP operations, Appalachian Casualty and Life, and "mcollier" was his operations assistant, Mimi Collier.

A warm glow embraced me when the insurance company's lines of business described on their website corresponded exactly to what I had seen in Presser's files. What surprised me was that Appalachian was headquartered outside Chillicothe, not far from the park where the botulism murders had taken place. Established in 1867 as a mutual insurance company, Appalachian had demutualized, meaning stockholders, instead of policyholders, owned the company. It had been a continuing trend in the industry as insurance companies figured out how to better tap the capital markets and compete with the banks I had followed as an analyst.

I tamped down my excitement and waited to call Skyler until she was home from work. "Did Samuel ever mention anything about Appalachian Casualty and Life?"

"Uh . . ."

Her silence lasted so long I wondered if I'd lost the connection.

"Nope. Doesn't ring any bells. Why?"

I told her what I'd discovered.

"It sounds like the side job he took to pay for our honeymoon. He moonlighted for a small insurance company that doesn't have its own actuaries. They hire people like him to certify their annual report. Maybe Matthew can tell you more."

"Did Samuel work alone?"

"I can hear the excitement in your voice," she said. "You think this is tied to his murder, yes?"

Dial it back, Seamus. Do not falsely get her hopes up. "Can't tell yet. Since nothing about Appalachian was in the police files, it's at least something new. Samuel found a problem and made an appointment to see an executive vice president there. He was killed before the meeting happened."

"So, you *do* think they're connected."

I consciously pitched my voice lower, like a stern father figure. "We can't jump to conclusions. I'm looking for Samuel's contract with Appalachian. Any ideas?"

"Sorry," she said in a deflated voice.

"You mentioned Matthew. I know he's on vacation, but I still expected him to return my calls."

"He's rafting in Idaho," she said. "That's why I wanted him to talk to you before he left. He returns Sunday." We wished each other a good weekend and rang off.

I ran a search on Presser's computer—well, I ran it on the copied image, but I thought of it as Presser's computer. Appalachian Casualty and Life showed up in several spots, one of which was a PDF of the signed contract. James Nadler had signed for Appalachian.

The contract called for Presser to act as "Reviewing Actuary" to give his opinion on portions of Appalachian Casualty and Life's annual statement. He'd be paid six thousand dollars and the work was due by the end of June.

Had he died because of a six-thousand-dollar assignment to pay for a honeymoon?

I needed to get more information on Appalachian and in a hurry. Robert Rand had given me permission to "utilize" my financial crimes network. I called Ingstram Ravel.

"Seamus McCree, always a pleasure to hear your voice. I'd enjoy it more if you called either six hours earlier or later."

Oh, crap. "Sorry Ingstram, my enthusiasm overcame me and I didn't take into account the time in England. Shall I call in the morning?"

"I'm awake now. What's up?"

He agreed to assemble the team over the weekend to perform an analysis of Appalachian and have preliminary results emailed by noon Monday—my time.

I figured I'd have a relaxed weekend with Paddy, but Bear's phone call Saturday morning did unto me as I had done to Ingstram.

◊◊◊

WITH LIGHT SATURDAY TRAFFIC I arrived at the Adena Regional Medical Center emergency room entrance a few minutes earlier than I had expected. Bear was there. "She just got out of emergency. They're taking her to a room. I sent a deputy with them."

"Thanks for calling and having me join you." I meant it. Maybe we could reboot our working relationship. "I don't recall anything particularly outstanding about Janis Abbey from your initial interviews. She was a college kid working the summer for the caterer, right?"

"Nothing pointed to her. If she hadn't tried to commit suicide and left a note, we'd never have looked at her twice."

The deputy guarding the room at the end of a corridor sat in an orange plastic chair tipped against the wall. He and Bear exchanged greetings and we went in to see Miss Abbey. I expected the room to smell like a hospital, but the only whiff of anything I noticed was of air freshener.

She was supine with an IV in her right arm. Bandages covered her left arm from her wrist to her elbow. She looked pale and forlorn. Someone had tried to remove her makeup but left streaks of mascara at the corners of both eyes. She adjusted her head at our entrance and grimaced.

"Are you here to arrest me?"

"We don't usually arrest people for attempted suicide," Bear said.

"For killing all those people. I couldn't have that on my conscience anymore. I guess I botched it." She caressed her bandaged arm.

Bear told her she was not under arrest, but read her the Miranda warning.

"Why would I want an attorney if I don't even want to live?" she said. "Yes, I understand my rights. I'm happy to talk. I made the green beans. I killed them all. I can't face myself in the mirror anymore."

"How did you get botulism in the green beans, Miss Abbey?" Bear asked.

"I screwed up. I must have, otherwise it wouldn't have happened. They'd still be alive if I'd been more careful."

"You also made the potato salad?"

She had.

"Did you put botulism in the potato salad?" Bear continued.

"Of course not. There wasn't any in the potato salad." She appeared confused at the line of questioning Bear was taking.

"How about the coleslaw?" Bear asked.

"I made the potato salad, then the coleslaw, and last the green beans. It was the green beans that killed them. That's what I did wrong. I contaminated them and they're all dead and it's all my fault and I want to die."

I shot a sideways glance at Bear. I knew, but she didn't, that both the potato salad and green beans had been contaminated. The coleslaw had not. As a way to eliminate false confessions, the police had not released information about the potato salad. No doubt Janis Abbey was feeling terrible, but she wasn't the perpetrator.

Bear questioned her, going over the information from her earlier interview. Her story had not changed. He tucked his pen back into his shirt pocket and closed his notebook. "Miss Abbey, as much as I'd like to solve this case, I don't think you were responsible for those deaths. I can't tell you everything we know, but if everything you've told us is true—

"I told you the truth. I did!"

He gestured with his huge paw and she settled back. "And I believe you. Trust me, you are not responsible."

"Janis," I said. "Can I take you back to that weekend and ask a few questions? You may have already answered them all before . . ."

She rolled her head to face me. "Okay."

"How did you get the job?"

"I went to high school with one of the guys who worked there. He knew I'd worked private parties during the school year. You know, where you have to get dressed in a frumpy black uniform and walk around with plates of hors d'oeuvres and glasses of champagne. The pay's good. Free food. And the tips aren't bad."

"Was it what you expected?" I asked.

"The parties were fine . . . they were mostly outdoors. The kitchen work I don't much like. I should have noticed something was wrong. I can't sleep, thinking I've killed all those people." Tears carried the remaining mascara down her cheeks. "I keep dreaming of old men and women with their trusting eyes holding out their plates. And I served them death and smiled and wished them a great summer. I can't live with that." Her voice trailed off, choked by sobs.

"I know this is hard for you," I said. "But you may have seen something that will help us. Think back to the days before the picnic. What were the preparations?"

She rubbed a hand over her eyes. "We precook most of the food and heat it up shortly before a picnic starts. At the picnic, we use warming trays. I was on potato salad patrol—I must have made three billion gallons of potato salad for all the picnics. But one of the girls was sick. We divvied her stuff up and I got stuck making green beans and coleslaw for that picnic. They should never have let me make the green beans."

I ignored the last bit. "What happens to the food after it's made?"

"We keep everything in a walk-in refrigerator until it's time. Then we gather all the tagged items."

"Tagged items?"

"Each party has an ID—the date and an event letter. All food for a given event is kept together in the refrigerator. Napkins, plastic utensils, and such are labeled the same way. We prepack those and store them on the shelves. That way we don't forget anything when we go to the location."

"Who has access to the cold storage?" I asked.

"Everyone's in and out. Even the deliverymen know where to put their supplies."

"How do you know which code is for which picnic?"

"Events are listed on a white board near the refrigerator door." She turned onto her side. One of the instruments started beeping.

The nurse raced into the room, looked at the monitor, and ran her hand down the IV line. "You pinched the line when you moved. Make sure you keep your line flowing, dear." She patted Janis on the arm. "You let me know if these gentlemen stay too long." Pointing at us, she added, "She needs rest."

I waited for the nurse to leave. "Any of the staff or deliverymen have access to the green beans between when you put them in the refrigerator and when you took them out for the picnic?"

Looking up with tired red eyes, she asked, "You mean you think someone doctored the food after we made it?"

"Did you notice any new deliverymen or anyone who acted differently—hung around more than usual or made more trips to the cold storage?"

She stared at the ceiling, "You know, there was one guy on Saturday."

"Yes?"

"Well, I don't know," she said. "I remember him because he had to borrow a hand truck to deliver bread. The boss mentioned later that someone had delivered a bunch of extra rolls we hadn't ordered, and they were put in the wrong spot."

I didn't want the next question to appear more important than any others and paused before asking what the guy looked like.

"I don't know . . . he was cute, but I didn't see him very well. Kind of like your height. Not real tall like the detective and not too short. Older. You know, thirties, probably. His hair was super short. Not shaved, but close. Brown, I guess. He didn't have a mustache or beard or anything like that."

I glanced at Bear to make sure he was writing this all down. He was.

"Do you remember what he was wearing?"

"Jeans and a T-shirt. And sneakers."

"Any writing on the shirt?"

She closed her eyes. I could see movement under her eyelids. "I don't remember."

"How about the sneakers? Brand or color?"

"White, maybe?"

"Janis, if you saw him again, would you recognize him?"

Her eyes opened, but her face seemed to draw in on itself. "I only saw him the once and not for long. It was back in May . . . he was hot, but not *that* hot." The hint of a smile creased her face.

Bear cleared his throat and her gaze shifted toward him. "Miss Abbey," he said, "would you mind looking through some pictures we have to see if you can spot the guy?"

Smile gone, she started to tear up again. "You mean mug shots? I guess I could if it would help."

"One more question," I said. "Anyone besides this delivery guy seem at all unusual that weekend?"

"No sir, he's the only one I can think of."

We wished her a speedy recovery and walked to the elevator.

I pressed the down button. "Think she'll be any help?"

"We could luck out. Sometimes when they concentrate—"

A nurse in blue scrubs hurried down the hall. "You two, wait! She says there's one more thing."

Bear and I exchanged hopeful glances and hustled back.

"I'm sorry," she said. "I'd forgotten this until now. He had a tattoo on his back. Right above his butt. His shirt rode up when he bent over. It was really awesome. I'll draw it for you."

Bear gave her pen and paper. She depicted a Celtic cross.

"The outside lines are royal blue," she said. "But the interior ones of the cross . . ." She pointed with the pen. "Those are a forest green. And it had a piercing blue eye in the middle. It's looking right at you."

As I stared at the drawing, a buzz of excitement zipped through me. I had seen this cross before. Recently, but not as a tattoo. Bear continued to question Janis. I slumped into the chair and plugged my ears. Willpower and concentration didn't release the memory from its locked prison in my mind.

I knew it was important. I hoped I could exhume the memory.

THIRTEEN

AT THE TICK OF NINE o'clock Monday morning, I phoned Matthew Yeung at his office. He apologized for not calling back, but he hadn't gotten home Sunday night until after eleven.

Yes, Presser had been doing extracurricular work for a small insurance company. A number of TransOhio actuaries had similar side gigs and often did their work together after hours. Management ignored the possible conflict of interest, provided the work didn't use TransOhio computers. Matthew agreed to come over from work and look at the files.

"Can I switch gears," I said, "and ask you a quick question about retiree medical insurance? What's the cost of a typical policy?"

"I'm not an expert. It depends on what's covered and whether the person is Medicare eligible."

"It's a union plan. Assume it's got good coverage and a small deductible."

"Well, I don't know . . ."

"Make a wild guess. I'm not going to carve it in stone."

"Okay. It's expensive and getting worse . . . ten, fifteen grand for a couple under age sixty-five, depending on their age. Over sixty-five, it's a lot less. Medicare kicks in, so it's closer to four grand. Although it might be covering the Part B premium as well, so you can add that in. But costs are currently skyrocketing, especially drugs, so . . ."

I wedged the phone between my shoulder and ear, feeling the pull of muscles on the opposite side of my head. I rotated my hands like two tires spinning in the mud. He couldn't see my signals and continued to drive me crazy with several minutes of caveats. I understood Harry Truman's desire for a one-armed economist who couldn't say, "on the other hand . . ."

He finally exhausted his supply of exceptions and concluded that, based on the number of retirees who had died, Chillicothe Machine would save a couple hundred thousand bucks annually. Not huge for a corporation, but not chickenfeed, either.

Was the prejudiced Deb Holt correct about Chillicothe Machine's Japanese owners? Was saving money or defanging the union motive for the botulism murders? Maybe, but I wasn't ready to suggest it to Detective Wright.

◊◊◊

INGSTRAM RAVEL'S EMAILED SUMMARY ABOUT Appalachian Casualty and Life provided an early afternoon break from my unfruitful mining of Presser's computer. He outlined the corporate structure: James Nadler was one of three executive vice presidents, all of whom had joined Appalachian four or five years ago. They reported to the president, William A. Snyder, a thirty-two-year veteran of the company.

Appalachian's business was concentrated in the eastern half of the U.S., with the lion's share in Ohio, Pennsylvania, and West Virginia. They had recently developed more business with unions on the East Coast, a new, profitable niche. Ingstram's report provided details about Appalachian's financial state, including analyses from their competitors of Appalachian's strengths and weaknesses. Appalachian's performance suffered after its demutualization. Its assets and liabilities grew at about the same pace as the industry during the last five years, and they were profitable, but in decreasing amounts. An analysis of the various lines of business indicated that the group annuity business continued to disappoint with lower-than-expected profitability.

Ingstram summarized, "The company is a solid small insurance carrier. They've carved some successful niches, but overall have more weaknesses than in prior years. The stock was $15.25 on Friday's close, down from the $25.00 issue price." He promised to get detailed financial analyses and interviews with former executives.

How should I approach Mr. James Nadler, executive VP of Appalachian Casualty and Life? I had no facts to conclude he was involved in Presser's death. On the other hand, Presser's note to him about the irregularities was the only ripple—well, that and a little smut on his hard drive—on the otherwise smooth pond of Samuel Presser's life.

I called Appalachian and asked for Nadler. The switchboard put me through to his line, which rang once and automatically transferred. A voice picked up. "Mr. Nadler's office, Mimi speaking. How may I help you?"

Mimi's voice reminded me of a kindly grandmother. "May I speak to Mr. Nadler, please? This is Seamus McCree."

I answered her clarifying questions about why I was calling and waited on hold through nearly a minute of dead air before she transferred me.

"Mr. Nadler, I'm helping investigate Samuel Presser's death. Would now be a good time for me to pick your brain, or would you prefer tomorrow?"

"That was a real shock." He sighed. "I am embarrassed to say that I was really steamed at him because he blew off a meeting. Then I found out he was murdered. How can I help?"

I tried to place his mid-Atlantic accent—New Jersey? Pennsylvania? "How did you learn of his death?"

"When he didn't reschedule, I emailed him and later tried to call him at home. I eventually got his office number from an actuarial directory one of my associates had. I was all set to lay into him for unprofessional behavior when his assistant told me of his murder. I had to scramble to get someone else to do the work he was supposed to be doing."

I hoped for a catch in his voice or some little clue to indicate he was lying. No luck. I tried my dumb act. "What kind of work? I'm not an insurance expert."

"Only a qualified actuary can certify portions of our annual report, and for a number of years we've used people from TransOhio, usually newer Fellows. Until this year it's worked well."

"You said Presser missed a meeting. What was it about?"

"You know, he never really said. We rushed to pick up the pieces. His replacement saved the day."

"And Presser didn't alert you to any problems?"

"Just said he had something I should see. Do *you* know?"

Was I a dog baying at the moon, finding the brightest object in the night sky? Or a hound wandering through a swamp and thinking everything with an odor had to signify death? I knew this: however slender and weak the thread linking Presser's discovery and his murder, it was the only one I had. I planned to keep pulling it to see what unraveled.

"I don't," I said, "but I'll have someone look at his work."

"You'll let me know?"

"Sure," I said. *Maybe.*

◊◊◊

FROM DOWNSTAIRS, PADDY YELLED UP to my study, "He's here. I'll let him in." The chatter of their introductions wafted upstairs as I arranged all the papers and files. The clomping of two pairs of feet climbing the stairs announced their approach. Matthew's tie hung at half-mast; his collar unbuttoned and the sleeves of his white dress shirt rolled up.

Paddy apparently decided to play host and suggested pizzas. He phoned in an order for one vegetarian and another topped with cholesterol-laden meats.

Matthew recognized the red folder. While I recounted my conversation with Nadler, he looked through the index of computer files.

"Okay," he said. "As I suspected, all these exhibit files relate to the company's annual statement. But these other files—" He pointed to the list of Excel files that had confused me. "These are something else." He opened the huge Excel spreadsheet, clicking from spot to spot and tab to tab.

"Samuel performed an experience analysis," Matthew said. He indicated the file with annuitant names and dates of birth and death. "This is the raw data. And this"—he clicked to the next tab—"is where Samuel set up the exposures and deaths."

He must have seen my confusion. "So, follow this line. He determined for the five-year period of the study how many males Appalachian covered were age seventy at the beginning of each year—that's the exposures. And then he counted how many of those died during the year."

"The deaths," I said.

"Exactly, and on this tab, he did the same thing for females, because we know males die earlier than females so we need to keep them separate. You with me?"

"So far," I said.

"Here he compares the actual deaths to the expected rates for each age and sex. You can see the actual mortality—the rate of people dying—is lower than anticipated. That means they've been running losses."

"Wait," Paddy said. "I thought if people lived longer, that was good for insurance companies."

"True for life insurance, not for annuities. Those pay while people are alive, so living longer costs the company money. Early deaths produce actuarial gains for annuities. Insufficient deaths, like here, cause actuarial losses."

"How bad is it?" I asked.

He did a couple of calculations. "Their mortality is running ninety-seven percent of expected. Not a disaster since it's over a short period, but it's a bigger difference than you'd expect for group policies."

The doorbell chimed and Paddy rubbed his thumb over his fingers in the universal signal for "Give me money." Cash in hand, he thundered downstairs.

"Would this difference," I wondered aloud, "be big enough for Samuel to set up a special meeting with the company?"

"Not unless they specifically asked him to do the experience analysis, which I don't believe they did. I bet Samuel fooled with this stuff on his own time."

Paddy brought the pizzas, beers for Matthew and me, a Pepsi for himself, three plates, napkins, a jar of applesauce, and a large spoon. We divvied up the booty and I ladled applesauce over my pizza.

Matthew pointed. "Applesauce on pizza?"

"I did it as a kid. I even convinced my mother and sister, but when Paddy found out the rest of the world didn't see the appeal, he gave it up."

"Actually, it's not bad," Paddy said. "It gives you a hot and cold taste at the same time. Fortunately, he doesn't eat it that way out in public."

"Maybe some other time," Matthew said. Between bites of pizza and slurps of beer, he roamed Presser's spreadsheet. Paddy chowed down, and I concentrated on eating and staying out of Matthew's way until an idea appeared from the ether.

"Matthew," I said. "Is George F. Proudt in that data?"

Bingo! Several hits, all in the Excel files. He opened the largest file, the one with more than 8,500 rows. Proudt appeared in the column labeled "Annuitant Name," on row 6,077. Other columns were "DOB," "Begin Date," "DOD," "Amount," "Form," "Contingent Annuitant," "CDOB," and "CDOD."

"It's annuity information," Matthew said. "'DOB' is date of birth. 'Begin Date' is when the annuity started. 'DOD' is date of death. 'Amount' looks to be monthly given the range runs from ten thousand bucks down to something under seventy-five. 'Form' shows how their annuity is paid: just for their life or with a contingent annuitant—someone who receives payment after the annuitant dies—and the rest is the information about the person."

"Wait a minute," I said. "It's got Proudt's death in 2005. The death certificate said 2002."

Paddy and I explained to Matthew the death certificate Presser had ordered from Oklahoma. "Do you think this experience study was why he asked for confirmation?"

"How could he know?" Matthew mused. "Let me see the other files this guy Proudt is in."

One file was an alphabetical listing of twenty-four names. Another listing looked like a subset of the huge file and contained people with dates of death in 2005.

"Looks like he was specifically evaluating people who died in 2005." I said.

Matthew looked at his watch. "Whoa, it's late. I need to make some phone calls at home. Can I take a copy of these files with me?"

"Sure," I said. "Paddy, what's on this USB flash drive?"

"The one in the laptop? That's not ours. That's from Skyler."

I must have showed my confusion because he continued, "When she brought over her computer, the flash drive was in it. It contains backup to Samuel's Quicken program and a bunch of Word documents. I kept it, figuring you'd want to look at those files."

"And you didn't think to mention that?"

He shrugged. "I thought it was obvious. I'll get a spare from my room."

While waiting for Paddy, I asked Matthew whether he knew Samuel had porn on his computer. He claimed not to, but avoided eye contact and pretended not to hear my follow-up, "You sure you didn't know about it?"

Paddy copied the Excel files onto a flash drive. We brought the remains of dinner downstairs and saw Matthew to the door. He promised he'd continue working this evening after he made his phone calls and would let me know if he found anything.

Watching Matthew walk away, I had the uneasy feeling he had known about the pornography collection. Had Skyler? Was it common knowledge or a norm with their group, and consequently Matthew had not considered it an issue? But then, why lie when confronted? And if he had lied about that, what else had he lied about?

Or had I misread him? Sure would be nice to have a bullshit detector.

If wishes were horses, beggars would ride, my mother would say. Time to study the newly discovered—at least to me—files on the USB drive.

The Word files contained mostly correspondence, much of it related to an improperly charged item on his Visa card. It took Presser four months and ten letters to get it corrected—the charge was $14.32.

I should have started with the most recent file. On May 25, Presser wrote a letter to the Oklahoma State Department of Health, Division of Vital Records.

Dear Sir or Madam:

Based on my conversation with Ms. Vicki Simpson yesterday, I am writing to request the death certificate for Mr. George F. Proudt.

To the best of my knowledge, I am unrelated to the deceased. I need this certificate to resolve a disparity between Social Security published records and those of Appalachian Casualty and Life that I discovered as part of an actuarial review I am performing for that company. The Social Security death database shows that Mr. Proudt died in Oklahoma City on February 26, 2002. However, Appalachian Casualty and Life records show the year of death as 2005.

Enclosed is a certified check for $10. Your quickest response is appreciated as I am operating under a deadline.

Thank you for your assistance,

Samuel W. Presser, FSA

Presser was correct: he was under a deadline, but not the one he anticipated. He wrote the letter less than two weeks before his murder. This letter would have saved me time had Paddy let me know we had these files to look through, but it didn't answer the question why Presser had even wondered about the year of death. Were there conflicting data on the material Mimi Collier had sent him from Appalachian? If so, why didn't he straighten it out with her? Why did he even think to make the comparison to the Social Security database?

I redid the search for files with Proudt included, hoping something would click. I soon realized the alphabetical list of twenty-four people was a subset of the longer group of people listed as dying in 2005. Why the subset? Had they all died in 2002? To easily check someone on the Social

Security death database, I wanted a name without many matches. James Petrosky looked promising. Three records came up: one died in 1968, another in 1976, and the third in 2002. The birth date for the third matched the Appalachian database.

Second person: Vincent Antonovitch. Again, Social Security showed his death in 2002. This was no longer a coincidence.

I started to phone Matthew Yeung but disconnected before it rang. What did I know about him? I was nearly certain he had lied about the porn. What else was he lying about? Would I get straight answers from him?

Upon reflection, I decided the only way to be sure of Matthew was to ask questions and evaluate his answers. I called and told him I felt strongly that the file with the twenty-four names was key to unlocking whatever Presser had been working on. I wasn't going to sleep until I heard from him.

I verified that Social Security had all twenty-four with 2002 dates of death. It could be a coding problem—maybe a remnant of the Y2K bugs all insurance companies had to fix. I tried to remain calm and consider innocuous reasons for the data errors. I checked my watch for the twenty-seventh time—only quarter to ten.

I paced, looked out the window, tapped on the windowsill with my thumbs, and repeated the sequence. *Crap. Only five till.*

Finally, the phone rang.

"This is Matthew. I think I found Samuel's problem."

"And?"

"The twenty-four people were all single life annuities, and I discovered that according to Appalachian's records, no annuitant with a single life annuity died in 2002, 2003, or 2004."

"That's unusual?" I asked.

"Impossible."

Impossible? Matthew hedged everything. "While you were working, I checked the names on the list. According to Social Security, all twenty-four died in 2002. Maybe it's a recording error?"

"A recording error would generate extra deaths in some earlier or later years. In 2005, only the twenty-four you gave me were listed. That might explain the 2002 deaths, but then where are the 2003 and 2004—or even the 2005 deaths, for that matter." He paused and I let him think. "Here's the real kicker. Almost all the mortality variance we talked about is attributable to the life annuity people. I found no significant variance for any other option."

"Meaning what?"

"It's so unlikely, Samuel may have decided to report it."

"Life annuities are the ones where the annuity ends when the person dies," I said. "The other kinds pay some kind of death benefit. Right?"

"Correct."

I performed a silent fist pump. "What if someone gamed the system to continue payments for three extra years? It would only work if no one else was expecting any money."

"So you'd use life annuities," he said. "I see where you're going. If you try to subvert joint and survivor payments, the beneficiary would be expecting them, so that doesn't work. You've got a devious mind, Seamus, but it can't succeed. Every system has checks and balances, and confirmations would catch anything like that."

"Matthew, when it comes to money, anything's possible. Can you guess how much three years of payments for those twenty-four people was?"

I listened to the phone's low hum and the chattering in my head. Had I come up with a reason for someone to silence Samuel Presser? Or, as Matthew Yeung suggested, had I used my fertile imagination to invent a crime no one had committed?

"Eight hundred thousand dollars," he said.

"Now we're talking."

"And that's only for those twenty-four. Remember, we can't find any recorded deaths in 2003 or 2004 and the only ones in 2005 are the ones you think actually belong to 2002. If they had the same average pension . . ." Tapping fingers sounded in the pause. "Oh man—two point five million plus, and probably still counting."

I whistled. "This could explain why their group actuarial business hasn't been particularly profitable over the last few years. What about last year and this year?"

"It wouldn't be in the data yet. But I'm telling you, Seamus, there's got to be some other explanation."

"You're probably right," I said, although I was thinking just the opposite. "But to be safe, let's assume I'm right. You must not, under any circumstances, tell anyone about this. Not your mother, not Skyler, no one. Understand? . . . You there?"

I could barely make out his response: "We could get killed."

FOURTEEN

AIR CONDITIONERS HUMMED LIKE CICADAS in Georgia's August heat. He was so not a Southern boy. How did people stand it down here before A/C? Sweat tacked the camouflage suit to him. He hated feeling the damp cloth plastered against his skin. He could smell the rain and wished it would come. Being soaked by fresh rain was infinitely preferable to drowning in his own sweat. *Fine.* He'd had his one-minute personal bitch session. Now that was finished, he had to concentrate if he was going to come out alive.

The heavy overcast was a blessing. After procuring the stepladder from the garage, he had everything he needed. Even an owl would have had difficulty hearing him as he carted the borrowed stepladder to the basement door. Picking the lock was even easier this time. He stationed the ladder by the furnace and rocked it to make sure the legs were steady. A sudden lurch at the wrong time and the Grim Reaper would harvest the Happy Reaper—not how he planned to end his days among the quick.

He slipped off the backpack, settled it on the floor away from anything that could snag, and opened all the compartments. From three rungs up the ladder, he unscrewed the duct fasteners with quick and practiced motions.

He closed his eyes and reviewed his photographic memory for the steps.

One: wire the counter.

It required less time than he'd allotted to rig the counter to the furnace ignition and run the wires up into the duct.

Two: switch from work gloves to impermeable gloves.

He also removed a gas mask from his backpack and put it on. Now came the hardest part. It had taken more than thirty practice tries with salt and water before he could consistently construct the apparatus without spilling water or dumping salt into it.

Three: center and secure bowl.

He finished and held his hands out in front of him. Rock solid. He performed a shoulder roll and massaged his neck.

Four: gently pour liquid from glass bottle into bowl. No splashing! Stopper bottle. Return bottle to foam-lined container.

He stopped pouring as a drop of sweat snailed down his back, settling at his waist. Concentration restored, he finished the pour.

Five: attach paper box over bowl.

Six: attach metal tip from counter mechanism to paper box.

He adjusted the final position of the tip, allowing it to pierce the top of the box's side by no more than two or three millimeters.

Seven: fill paper box with chemicals.

Was it his imagination, or was the humidity causing the chemicals to clump the tiniest bit? *Careful. Careful. Careful. Do not fill past line.* His mouth was horribly dry—nerves, he thought. He held his hands out in front of him again. He couldn't afford any waver now. Extra weight could cause the box to shift. He was holding his breath. Counterproductive. Breathe in. Breathe out. Tap ever so gently. *Well done, sir. Well done.*

Eight: reattach duct.

All fasteners replaced. As long as he did not knock the furnace with the ladder, he was safe. He backed down one final time and carefully moved the ladder into the room, away from the furnace. The danger over, he removed his mask and gloves and stored them in his backpack. He again donned work gloves, zipped each compartment of the backpack, and double-checked to make sure nothing could fall out during his departure.

Using the penlight, he scanned the entire room for anything out of place, anything to suggest he had been there. He would take the ladder with him; otherwise everything looked peachy. He eased his pack onto his shoulders, grabbed the ladder, and walked outside, shutting the door behind him.

Outside, the air conditioners still hummed, battling the hot, fetid air. He waited pressed against the basement door, listening and watching, mentally whistling five full repetitions of the *Jeopardy!* theme.

Happy Reaper indeed. He could picture the headlines across the world. *USA Today*, *Times* on both coasts, BBC, and more. Many more. And the millions of dollars he would earn wasn't too shabby, either.

Farmers' Almanac called for a cool autumn. He needed the heating season to commence, and then he'd be big time. Everyone would know his work.

FIFTEEN

TUESDAY MORNING I ROSE WITH the sun and put in eight miles of roadwork at my expected marathon pace. Around the five-mile mark I devised a great plan for learning more about Appalachian Casualty and Life.

The expression *strike while the iron is hot* exists for a reason. After showering, eating a leisurely breakfast, and twiddling my thumbs until I could call Appalachian, I was no longer so sure I had a terrific idea.

Since I had come up with nothing better, I dialed Appalachian's main number and told the operator I needed to report an annuitant's death.

"Thank you," she said. "I'll put you through to operations." The phone rang and rang, transferred itself, rang more. "Operations, Nadler speaking," a voice answered.

I disconnected.

Now wasn't *that* interesting? The same person Presser was meeting to discuss a problem, which I was nearly certain had to do with the misreporting of Appalachian's single life annuitant deaths, was the person to whom those deaths would be reported.

Time to dig deeper into Mr. Nadler's background.

I called Ingstram Ravel at CIG and described what we had discovered and my suspicions. "I'm keen on the idea, Seamus. But Matthew Yeung is correct—your theory has holes. An administrative cockup, some problem they didn't catch, seems more likely to me. Where's the money? Don't you Yanks have some kind of tax reporting? What happened to the tax forms?"

"I don't know any of that stuff," I said. "I had CIG hire all you smart guys so you can tell me. While you're doing your magic and getting me the full scoop on James Nadler, would you ask our U.S. insurance experts about how someone could pull it off?"

"Aye aye, Cap'n Bligh."

That pulled me up short. "Am I a tyrant, Ingstram?"

"Focused, I would say. Most people don't know William Bligh became one of our rear admirals, praised in battle by Nelson himself."

While I waited for Ingstram's research, I worked the Appalachian data. Starting with the oldest single annuitant, I searched the Social Security death database for someone who had died, but was still "alive" according to Appalachian's records.

Joseph Drucker fit the bill. Ninety-two years old and alive on Appalachian's records, Social Security had him dying in 2005. Whatever began in 2002 was still going on.

◊◊◊

DESPITE—OR MAYBE AS A result of—his Captain Bligh crack, Ingstram Ravel called me with the information early evening his time, my midafternoon.

"Nadler was born in Brooklyn in 1960 to a schoolteacher and a carpenter," he reported. "Honored in *Who's Who of High School Students* and attended NYU while living at home. He graduated summa cum laude with a bachelor's degree in mathematics."

"Ancient history," I said. "What about his work life?"

"Started at MetLife in their actuarial department but moved to operations. He switched to Mutual Benefit in Newark. While there, he completed his MBA at NYU at night. Rose to assistant vice president. They folded and he returned to MetLife until he took the VP operations job with Appalachian five years ago. Last year he was promoted to executive vice president."

"Family?"

"Married Hanna Franks at twenty-five. No children. Excellent credit. The Nadlers have done very well for themselves since they moved to Chillicothe. Their net worth is in the millions of U.S. dollars, up from roughly a hundred thousand five years ago."

"That's more than quite well."

"Their checking account has an average balance of thirty-five hundred dollars. Early each month the balance spikes to more than fifty thousand, then quickly resumes normal levels. We don't have a bead yet on the source of those funds."

"If Nadler controls the expired single life annuities, moving the money through his checking account doesn't seem bright."

Ingstram's long-distance laughter sounded tinny. "People have done stranger things. They didn't increase their net worth more than tenfold based solely on his salary, which is under a hundred grand. His parents are dead. I have people checking on his inheritance. Maybe there's a trust fund payout?"

"Every question answered leads to five new ones."

He blew out a long stream of air. "Righto. We'll keep on it, but we've got some other cases besides yours . . ."

"I hear you, Ingstram. Thanks for letting me jump the line."

Nothing in the report changed Nadler's suspect status. The bank account was interesting, and a court order could shed light on the large transactions. Time to rattle Nadler's cage while Ingstram's crew kept digging.

Since Appalachian was located in Ross County, I toyed with asking Detective Wright along to show a badge and increase the startle factor. This was, however, a Cincinnati case, and getting another jurisdiction involved could be a bit dicey, politics being what they are. I suspected one police force would typically alert the other when they were going to be in the area, and since I figured my relationship with Bear was still like walking on eggshells, I should play nice.

The more I thought about it, the more I warmed to the idea of telling him I'd be in town for a CPD case. The implication was that if Cincinnati used me, I must be good, and little ol' Chillicothe should be happy they got me. Well, maybe I was engaged in a bit of wishful thinking, but I had nothing to lose and perhaps some credibility to gain.

Besides, I wanted to pin Bear down about what he'd learned from reinterviewing the caterer's employees. Maybe they had a better description of the mysterious bread vendor. If I was really lucky and caught him in a good mood, maybe he'd give me access to the information from Phoenix on the murder of Chillicothe Machine's former CEO.

I called Nadler and got his assistant, Mimi. She stalled, I cajoled, the final result being I had a half-hour appointment with Nadler at two o'clock the following afternoon. I caught Bear moments later. He agreed to meet me beforehand for lunch at Sue's to, as he put it, "hash a few things out."

◊◊◊

I DISCOVERED ON THE TRIP to Chillicothe the next day that singing along with Bruce Springsteen made my foot heavier. It took twenty minutes less than I'd allowed, and I'd been darned lucky I hadn't passed any speed traps. Charlene saw me coming in the door and rushed over.

"You here to see Bear?"

"I'm supposed to meet him around noon."

"Great. I'll put you in his booth."

"He has his own booth? I know bars where the regulars have their own stools with their names on brass plates, but—"

"It's nothing like that." She tucked a strand of blond hair under her red bandanna. "He likes to be close to the door and this is the closest booth in my section."

"And he always chooses your section?"

A faint blush appeared underneath her makeup and she broke off eye contact. "Here we are," she said. "Can I get you something while you're waiting?"

"A Diet Dr Pepper and, if you're not too busy, some conversation."

"Look, hon, this ain't no Starbucks with Bengal Spice tea and Diet Peppers. We got the real deal—slim guy like you can afford the calories."

She brought two sets of service and a tall Pepper. After preparing the table she slipped into the seat opposite me. "If someone comes in, I'll have to leave."

"I take it you've known Bear awhile?"

"Sure. We were in the same high school class. I was a cheerleader. He was our star athlete—a four-letter man."

"Four? I thought you could only play three sports a year."

"During winter they let him wrestle and play basketball. He practiced wrestling with the coach before school and played hoops after. As a freshman, he was already six six."

"What was his best sport?"

"He loved football—offense and defense. He played defensive end and no one could stop him rushing the passer. On offense, he was a tight end. He loved to block on runs and he had soft hands for passes. And he could run once he caught the ball. Listen to me. Rah rah rye for Chillicothe High."

"I can see the pom-poms now."

Her eyes crinkled when she laughed. "Senior year some punk clipped him and blew out his knee. The big schools weren't interested anymore. Mount Union still wanted him and he played on their first Division III national championship team. He got one pro linebacker tryout, but he wasn't fast enough."

"It's tough to crack the pros. Did he go straight to working for the sheriff?"

"What's with the twenty questions?" She had been leaning in to talk, but now she sat back, arms across her chest.

"Look, Charlene." I opened my hands on the table to show I had nothing to hide. "Bear and I got off to kind of a rocky start. I hoped if I knew more about him I'd have a better chance to get on his good side. I don't want you to feel like I'm prying or anything."

The smile returned to her face. "He started working at a brokerage firm in town. Didn't like it. Thought he'd be helping people. Everyone loves and trusts Bear, and the company used him to sell whatever was best for New York. Bear couldn't do that."

"I know exactly what you mean." That's something we have in common.

"He eventually quit and worked construction. Soon he was closing the bars every night. He was well down the road to Drunkville when the sheriff sat him down and read him the riot act before offering him a job on the force. It saved him. He's been doing AA for ten years now."

I thought of my own misspent youth and smiled. "Cops can be persuasive. I got a free nose job from one who decided I needed straightening out."

"It gives you character." She made a big show of batting her lashes. "Otherwise, you'd just be another pretty face with your curly black locks and your steely blue eyes." More eyelash batting. "What happened?"

"Very funny. The short version is I was running with the wrong crowd. The cop was my father's best friend. He found out I was in a gang fight and caught me on the street one night. Beat the crap out of me. Told me my old man would rather see me dead than a gangbanger."

"Wow. What did your father do?"

"He was also a cop, but he'd been killed on the job. I doubt he would have objected."

"I'm sorry."

I waved away her concern. "I learned a good lesson. And, as you say, it gives me character. Bear married?"

"Speak of the devil." She pointed behind me.

He occupied the doorway. Charlene got up quickly and the faint blush reappeared on her cheeks. She brushed back an imagined loose hair with her right hand and pulled her order pad from her apron pocket. As Bear slid into his seat, she asked if he wanted coffee.

He nodded and reached for the menu while Charlene fetched the pot. He shot me a glance over the top of the menu. "Whatcha talking about?"

"Charlene was telling me about your playing days. Do you get a ring for a national football championship?"

He laughed and his eyes brightened. "No, but I still have my Purple Raiders letter blazer, and it's nice to see the trophies when I return to Mount. We were the beginning. We won the Ohio Athletic Conference championship my freshman year, lost it the next year. That sucked. Then the following year we started the OAC championship streak that hasn't ended. Nothing's ever been sweeter than our National Championship win over Rowan my senior year. What else did Charlene gab about?"

"Not much, we weren't talking for long."

"Uh-huh." His eyes scanned the menu. Charlene returned with Bear's coffee. "Is your split-pea soup what's stinking up the joint?"

"Hush your mouth." Charlene flicked her fingers at him.

Bear turned to me, grinning broadly. "It's even better than it smells."

We both ordered bowls of the soup. He added a steak sandwich.

This was going fairly well, I thought. I wondered when the few things we needed to hash out were going to come up. Maybe they wouldn't if I didn't bring them up?

The soup steamed my glasses as I wafted its hinted herbal scent toward my nose. Made me wonder about its taste, but Bear was right. The soup was delicious: thick and, despite containing several chunks of ham, not salty.

When Charlene stopped by to find out if we were okay, I asked about the scent. She returned with an answer from the cook. Marjoram. I wondered if Paddy would have known.

Since we were talking anyway, I asked Bear about the caterer interviews. Turned out several people remembered the bread guy, but their descriptions were all over the lot. No one else had seen the Celtic cross tattoo.

"How about the murder of the ex-CEO of Chillicothe Machine?" I asked.

"The Phoenix police don't see a link. He was killed in bed while his wife slept in the next room. The area's had a rash of robberies recently. They're thinking robbery gone wrong. Nothing taken. Figure the old guy woke up and the robber panicked, stabbed him, and fled. I'm supposed to get the file today."

"When can I get a copy?"

"I'll let you know if there's anything interesting. Have you gotten any further with the Chillicothe Machine retiree medical costs being the motive? That really seems hokey, but . . ." He held out his arms, huge hands up—hands that could swallow a football. "But I guess anything's possible, especially since we haven't come up with anything better."

He brought his hands together in a mini-thunderclap. "But I still don't get it. Aren't all the hospital costs going to run them more money?"

Bear was channeling Thor with his size and mini-thunderclaps, and I had to try to channel Matthew Yeung. "It's a long game. First year does cost them money, but from then on they make quite a bit, I think."

Bear pushed his empty bowl aside and leaned in. "I suppose it's possible. Japanese companies do seem to take a longer-term approach than U.S. firms with their emphasis on each quarter's earnings. But let's say you're right. How did they contract this out? How would anyone go about doing that? Speaking of the Japanese, I had to calm Sheriff Lyons down when he got a couple of complaints about you and a verbal confrontation at Lefty's?"

"I—"

"No explanation necessary or wanted. I'm just letting you know that since I had to smooth things out with Lyons, we're now even with him. We aren't like New York or even Cincinnati. Everybody knows everybody here and everything eventually gets to the sheriff. Keep that in mind."

I made soothing noises, thanking him and the like, all the while wondering what subtext I was missing.

"You didn't really tell me what Cincinnati wants from us country yokels."

I should have anticipated it, and I would in the future, but I hadn't. I resorted to the greater power theory. "I guess you'll need to talk with Lieutenant Hastings."

"She's homicide. This isn't related to our botulism murders, is it?"

"Not in the least."

Was it? Presser's murder had occurred only a week or so after the Memorial Day picnic murders, and the victims had connections with Appalachian Casualty and Life. A resonant thrum set up in my chest.

SIXTEEN

APPALACHIAN CASUALTY AND LIFE WAS originally in Chillicothe proper, but had moved to a semirural setting north of the city, past the hospital. The perky receptionist called Nadler's office, had me sign in, and gave me a visitor's badge.

A woman in her late fifties walked through the double glass doors. She had a slight limp, a precursor to future hip problems that would worsen if she didn't lose weight. The clicks of her low heels on the faux marble floor echoed in the lobby. She looked like a librarian, glasses dangling from her neck, her auburn hair wrapped into a bun. A three-inch calla lily pin decorated her lapel. Her mouth was wide, which she emphasized with a broad swath of red lipstick. Her nose was slightly off-kilter and above it were two vibrant green eyes.

"Mr. McCree."

I knew the voice from the phone.

"I'm Mimi Collier. I'll take you to Mr. Nadler's office. He'll only be a minute."

We walked through a rabbit's warren of corridors to the operations center on the lower level. Identical cubicles symmetrically lined the passageway leading to an office at the far end. An evergreen scent from a plug-in diffuser attempted to cover a musty smell. In the cubes, young women stared intently at papers clipped to the right of their computer monitors on hangman's arms. Other than the tapping of fingers on keyboards and an occasional throat clear, the room was silent and depressing.

Mimi opened Nadler's door and indicated I should sit in one of the visitor chairs opposite the walnut veneer desk. After offering me something to drink, which I declined, she left, shutting the door behind her.

I snooped before Nadler arrived. Paintings of racing sailboats decorated one wall. A nautical map of Long Island Sound decorated the wall behind his desk. Against the opposite wall sat a large bookcase filled with binders. Mounted above it in pride of place were a walleye and a large-mouthed bass.

Clear glass covered his desk. Under the glass were several family photos. The largest was a wedding picture of the couple stuffing cake into each other's mouths—never my favorite part of weddings, I suppose because I never liked the idea of anyone shoving things down my throat. That attitude might illustrate why he was still married and I was not. Another photo portrayed a dozen ten- or eleven-year-olds listening attentively to his wife reading a book.

His Dilbert cartoon screensaver surprised me. It seemed inconsistent with being a boss. Other than the monitor, his desktop was clear. Behind, on a closed file cabinet under the Long Island Sound map, sat two decoys. Nadler's arrival caught me examining the smooth surface of the carved canvasback. Its weight surprised me—could have been used for a doorstop.

He was dressed in gray pinstripes, white shirt, and repp tie. The thousand-dollar European-cut suit fit his lithe frame well. In his lapel was a gold pin with the company's logo. I could have shaved in the luster of his highly polished wingtips—probably Allen Edmonds at four hundred dollars a pair. His face and hands were deeply tanned and his fingernails shone with a clear polish. Pale blue eyes drifting to gray mirrored his suit.

"You must be Seamus McCree." We shook hands. "I'm Jim Nadler. Careful with the ducks."

"They're beautifully done and look old."

"My dad gave them to me shortly before he passed on."

"I take it you like sailing?" I said.

"What gave you your first clue? Actually, I like racing. I'm not much of a pleasure sailor. Unless I'm trying to beat another boat, I find it boring."

"Did you race in the East?"

"I crewed. Didn't have a boat. Now I keep two on Lake Erie. One sleeps eight, the other's strictly for two-man racing. We go up most weekends if the weather's okay. Now, what can I help you with?"

At his hint, I sat. "As I mentioned on the phone, I'm looking into Samuel Presser's murder. How did you end up hiring him?"

"Before we went public we had a couple of actuaries on staff. Once we became a stock company—that is, once we had to worry about our stock price and quarterly earnings—the company had a big layoff. Overnight, we went from plush to lean. We've hired out the actuarial work ever since. This was the first time we used Presser. He was recommended by the gal who had done the work the last couple of years."

"Did Presser indicate he'd discovered an error?"

"As I said on the phone, he was not forthcoming about why he wanted to see me. Do *you* know?"

I had prepared myself for this moment. "I'm not at all sure, Jim. Notes I found in his files indicate he was concentrating on the group annuity product." I paid careful attention to his reaction.

He tilted his chair and gazed over my head at the stuffed fish. "Group annuity business? The product hasn't changed in years. Anything more in his notes?"

"Not really. Something about adverse mortality experience." I smiled. "I had to have someone explain that to me."

"I understand we've had some losses there, but nothing serious. The company I worked for in New Jersey made a big bet on real estate that didn't pan out, but here our investments are in bonds and have performed as expected."

"If Presser had found something amiss with your group annuity product, any guess what it could be?"

"No clue. Given the work he was doing, maybe something to do with the allocation of expenses." He paused and sighted over my head again. "That's the only thing I can think of, but I really don't know."

Innocent or a good liar? He had taken several seconds before answering a couple questions, but otherwise his responses were immediate and he made reasonable eye contact. I sensed no nervousness.

"I'm groping in the dark," I said. "Following any clue no matter how unlikely. Out of curiosity, who knew Presser had scheduled the mystery meeting with you?"

"Let's see . . . My assistant, Mimi—she handles my calendar." He paused. "I may have mentioned it at the executive committee meeting in my weekly update on the status of our annual report. I guess that's it. You don't think whatever he planned to talk with me about is somehow connected to his murder, do you?"

I tilted my head slightly in response.

His jaw clenched. "Preposterous. No one at Appalachian could have had anything to do with his death. Frankly, I can't imagine anything Presser could have uncovered that could justify it."

I could imagine many reasons, but I gave him a reassuring nod and changed tacks. "I wonder if you could check something for me. Do you have access to annuitant records?"

He interlocked his fingers behind his head and again leaned back in the chair. "Sure, although depending on what you want, I may not be able to provide it. Confidentiality . . ."

"Understood. George F. Proudt had an annuity with you folks. What can you tell me about him?"

"You happen to have his Social Security number? It's much easier to access the records that way."

I checked my notes and gave it to him. He pulled a keyboard from under his desk and rotated his chair to peer at the monitor. He proceeded to tap and mouse-click his way to finding Proudt. "Deceased. What do you want?

"Whatever's there." I figured he might limit his answers to my questions if I asked for specifics.

"Let's see." His finger scrolled the screen. "Born October 3, 1930, and died February 26, 2005. He had a life annuity with us—part of a group annuity contract. His payment was $755.82 a month. Direct deposited. He didn't have optional tax withholding. Anything else?"

"Address?"

"Post office box in Las Vegas." He wrote it down on a slip of paper and handed it to me.

I asked about Joseph Drucker, an Appalachian annuitant who Social Security indicated had died in 2005.

"There he is, still alive." He peered at the screen. "Old codger—ninety-two. Can't tell you much more. Any others?"

"No, thanks. But if you find any irregularities, no matter how small they may seem, please give me a call." I handed him my card.

"What is it with these two guys?"

"You've confirmed that your information exactly matches what Presser's records show. I'm not at all certain what he thought was going on." *Liar, liar, pants on fire. At least give him a crumb.* "It seemed to revolve around the single life annuities. If you do find anything . . ."

"I'll let you know," he said. "Mimi will take you to the receptionist." He buzzed her in.

Had he lied to me as I had lied to him? I hadn't visibly rattled him. I had the empty feeling I might be barking up the wrong tree, but annuitant deaths were reported to his department, and he was at the top of that food chain.

◊◊◊

WHILE I'D BEEN TALKING WITH Nadler, clouds had rolled in. The storm started with a jab of drizzle, followed by a left-right combination of high winds and driving rain, making it a two-hands-on-the-steering-wheel trip home. I was thankful for the Infiniti's low profile, but I would have preferred the four-wheel-drive traction of the Expedition.

Paddy's car was gone from my driveway, allowing me to park closer to the door. I sprinted from the car to the porch. For all the good running did me, I could have walked and not been any wetter. My shoulders were tense from the drive home, and I thought about taking a hot shower but decided a glass of wine would do a better job of avoiding an oncoming headache.

Cheech and Chong descended the staircase with soft thuds as they hopped from step to step. They weaved between my legs, rubbing against my pants and purring at the head scratches I provided while I dripped on the floor. Who knew cats could work as well as a glass of wine to reduce tension?

The kittens followed me back upstairs to change and then into the kitchen, perhaps hoping for an early dinner. Paddy had left a note covering the piles of bills and junk mail he had stacked neatly on the table. I threw the junk into the trash, poured a glass of merlot, and read the note.

Dad, I'm at a friend's to work on our strategy for the Magic tournament. Matthew Yeung wants you to call him either at work or home. Detective Wright said to call his cell—something about Phoenix. I'll be late. Could you please feed the cats?

Maybe the cats knew about the note and didn't love me after all. I'd make them wait until dinnertime to show them who was boss.

I eeny-meenied my way to deciding to call Matthew at work before calling Bear.

"I tracked down the woman who did the Appalachian work before Samuel," he said. "She's on maternity leave—landed a seven-pounder last month."

Matthew clearly hadn't experienced a delivery.

"Mr. Nadler called her for another recommendation. That's how she learned about Samuel's death. What a way to find out. Anyway, she ended up agreeing to do the work herself. No experience analysis and she said everything looked fine."

I settled with the portable phone into an easy chair and sipped the wine. "I've confirmed Appalachian's records still show the incorrect death dates, but I didn't tell him what we'd found."

"Why not?"

"Something's hinky. It just didn't seem like the right time."

"It needs fixed before the next monthly checks go out. You can't delay long—they've got a bunch of work to do."

I mentally stumbled over the regionalism *needs fixed* and didn't respond.

"In fact, I may even have a professional obligation to tell them. I'll have to look into that."

"Let me know if you're required to say something. Otherwise, I'd prefer to keep it between us for a few days."

We signed off. As I dialed Bear's number I grumbled to myself about a kid who would lie to me about Presser's porn, but had to rat me out to an insurance company because of his professional responsibilities. I still wasn't sure I quite trusted him. The call hadn't even started ringing before I realized Matthew was right: one way or the other, I was on borrowed time with the Appalachian information.

"Two things," Bear said. "How did your meeting at Appalachian go?"

How did he know? "You follow me?" He didn't answer, which I took for a yes. "I was able to confirm a couple of facts for the Cincinnati Police."

"Anything I need to know?" he asked.

"I don't believe so, but I'll let CPD be the judge. You said two things?"

"Yeah. You need to work harder on getting the skinny on Chillicothe Machine. These murders revolve around them. I got the file from

Phoenix," Wright rumbled on an iffy cell phone connection that sounded as though it might cut out at any moment. "This wasn't a robber who got caught in the act. Framington was killed in bed."

"We already knew that."

"But with a single stab wound, and get this . . . the killer wiped the blade off on the sheets before he left. Sound like some scared burglar to you?"

"I agree with your assessment."

"Well, that's good to hear." He cleared his throat. "I saved the best for last. They found a business card stuck in Framington's Bible. The wife's never seen it before. On the front it says 'Results Guaranteed.'"

"Stuck in his Bible?" I waved my hands, signaling him to get on with it.

"In the middle of the book of Matthew. No address. No phone number."

I continued waving my hands, but I sounded calm. "And?"

"The clincher's on the back—a Celtic cross—a ringer for the one Janis Abbey drew. Even the colors match, and it's got that eye in the middle."

"Really! Like the bread delivery guy? You talk with the Phoenix cops yet?"

"They've never run across the Celtic cross stuff. They'll keep me informed of any developments."

Electricity tingled up my spine. The Celtic cross linked the botulism murders of thirty-eight at the union retirees' picnic and a cold-blooded knifing of the former CEO. *Wait a minute. The book of Matthew? It couldn't have anything to do with Matthew Yeung, could it?*

Bear had continued talking, and I interrupted whatever he was saying. "Any significance about the book of Matthew?"

Over the line I heard a rustle of papers. "Creepy. Phoenix thinks the killer was highlighting a verse about not being afraid of those who kill the body but cannot kill the soul. Like the killer's saying it doesn't matter what he did."

So not a reference to Matthew Yeung. Good. "Can you send me a copy of the file?"

"No need. I already told you everything. Clearly someone has it out for Chillicothe Machine. I've got a meeting with Sheriff Lyons to determine how much to tell their CEO, Elkin, and what, if anything, to release to the press."

Why were they, whoever *they* were, targeting Chillicothe Machine's retirees? I tried to explore that train of thought with Bear, but he seemed lost in his own concerns about his upcoming meeting with the sheriff. After he clicked off, I reached for the glass of wine—empty.

I hated waiting for other people, but there was nothing I could do to speed Ingstram Ravel's search for more info on Appalachian, and dynamite wasn't going to move Bear faster than he wanted to go. If those doors were closed, it was up to me to open another one. I'd bring Lt. Hastings up to speed. Could I convince her to get a court order to look at Appalachian's books? Only one way to find out.

SEVENTEEN

HASTINGS CHOSE TO MEET THE next day at 11:47 for an early lunch at the Clifton Skyline Chili. When Paddy heard the arrangements, he asked to come along. I wasn't sure why he seemed so interested, but he already knew much of what I had discovered. Besides, if I said no, the sneak would probably look at my notes while I was gone. Like father, like son. As a bonus, it would encourage him to switch from nocturnal to diurnal again, allowing me more time with him, which I wasn't getting with his weird hours. The two had met before and I figured, why not; the more heads the better.

My glasses fogged as we walked through Skyline's door. The A/C was blasting, but it still felt warm and humid. Their chili was an acquired taste for me—a regional dish unrelated to the real chili I knew before coming to Cincinnati. The base layer consisted of spaghetti, which was topped with your choice of cheese, red beans, onions, and the sweet chocolaty-cinnamon sauce that made it unique. The number of toppings you chose determined the number of "ways" you ordered.

I ate a four-way-no-onions. Paddy's four-way was without the sauce, which, since the sauce was the key ingredient in Skyline chili, he had to explain twice to the waitress. She finally understood he was vegetarian and he couldn't eat the sauce because it had meat. Hastings ordered two Cheese Coneys. Our order arrived pronto.

We spoke softly to prevent anyone from overhearing us. I told Hastings what I had discovered and what I still needed to know about Presser's murder. She asked clarifying questions, mostly around the whole annuity business, which was new to her. By the time I had painted the picture, Skyline was crowded and noisy. We were done eating and needed to vacate our table. Hastings suggested ice cream at Graeter's to complete the dining experience. I held my hand behind my back in a twist-my-arm gesture. She mimed cuffing me, which Paddy thought hysterical. We left

Skyline's cinnamon steam, walked up Ludlow past the Esquire Theater, and added ourselves to the ever-present Graeter's line.

Hastings and I got double scoops in a cup. I chose raspberry chocolate chip, with pieces of chocolate larger than some candy bars. She picked black cherry. Paddy figured his tongue was faster than the melting power of the sun and ordered a waffle cone with the ice cream flavor of the month—coconut. Between bites, Hastings asked what I thought the next steps were.

"Two things. First, peek at Nadler's bank records to understand the large inflows. Second, follow the trail of Appalachian annuity checks for the dead people. We might find Nadler's accomplices, if he has any."

"I hate to deflate your balloon, Seamus, but I'm going to stick it with a large pin called reality. You weave a nice story. I believe it might be true. Me believing and a judge believing are two different things. No way we can sell that proposition to a judge. He'd say we were fishing."

"Picky, picky, picky. How can I make the case strong enough without alerting people that we're onto them?"

Paddy broke from his race with the drips. "Dad, what makes you think Nadler doesn't already know? If he's half as smart as Ingstram Ravel thinks, he's already put Presser's death and your questions about the annuitants together. He knows you're onto something, and with the two guys you had him look up, he can figure out what—assuming he is involved."

Hastings scoured her cup with the plastic spoon and smacked her lips after cleaning the spoon. "I finally figured out why you brought your son with you. He's the brains of the operation and you're the front. The kid's right, Seamus. If Nadler's your guy, the cat's out of the bag."

"And Dad, if Nadler had Presser killed, what's to prevent him from putting a contract on you?"

I can read a balance sheet with the best of them. I'm not bad at working with and around people to get information. It had never occurred to me that either of those activities could make someone want to kill me. I used a mouth stuffed with a chocolate chunk as an excuse to remain silent.

"Nothing," Hastings said. "But if they succeed, we'll have no problem getting those court orders." Paddy swatted her on the arm, but she was laughing so hard she didn't react to the assault. "Actually, Seamus, Patrick's right. You might have poked a beehive."

"But," I said through my ice cream headache, "he only has my phone number."

"Big deal," Paddy said. "Any idiot can spend two minutes on the Internet and find an address from a phone number."

True. I've done it often enough myself to know any idiot could. They both stared at me. I am neutron-star dense sometimes. Then the light blinded me. With Paddy home, I needed to worry about *his* safety. "Since I've already alerted Nadler, what do you think about stepping up the pressure? What if I tell him my theory and see how he reacts—making sure he knows I've already reported everything to the police?"

"What if he runs?" Paddy asked.

"Again, no problem getting our court orders," Hastings said. "I think you should meet Nadler pronto. Say you couldn't tell him anything until you met with me, and now you can."

"I know a detective in the Ross County sheriff's department from another case I'm working on. Any reason to get him involved?"

"A request would need to come through me. I'll think about it, but you know, Seamus, I have no idea if you're really onto something, or if you've taken gossamer threads and manufactured a spider's web to capture our imaginations."

I smiled at her ease in lightening the conversation. "Gossamer threads—how poetic."

"Yeah, it's one of the vocabulary words I memorized for the SATs and it stuck. Don't interrupt when I'm thanking you. You've done some great work where we had nothing. We still might not have anything, but I want you to know I appreciate what you've done." To Paddy she said, "Patrick, your dad's a great thinker, but sometimes he's naïve and forgets to keep his head down. Make sure he does, okay? At least until we run this to ground."

We finished our goodbyes and Hastings headed downtown. Paddy and I walked home.

"Hey, Dad, we've got our plans now for the Magic tournament in Chicago this weekend. We nailed our team strategy yesterday and we've got a place to stay."

"What tournament? What are you talking about?"

"I told you yesterday that's what I was working on . . . in my note."

What note? I searched my memory. I knew Paddy played Magic: The Gathering—a fantasy-based card game, a variation on the Dungeons & Dragons theme. "I don't remember anything about it. Give me some details. Who, what, where, when, and how?"

Paddy stopped. I felt his eyes bore into me and I faced around into a blinding sun.

"You still think I'm some six-year-old. I could just go—"

"But you're not—"

"When I'm at college, you have no clue where I go or what I do or who I do it with. I wasn't asking permission."

"But you're not at college, you're here." The words were a reaction. A moment later, my slower brain concluded I'd picked the wrong fight at the wrong time.

He planted his feet slightly wider than his hips, thrust out his crew-developed chest, and locked his eyes onto mine. He was a Marines poster without the uniform.

"You sound just like the Jerk. Mom should have kept you and saved the aggravation." He stalked off.

"Wait," I called. Time for me to retreat. "Worrying is parental habit. Let's start again. When's the tournament?"

He turned around, but didn't come closer. "Starts tomorrow evening. Goes well into Sunday. We'd probably stay until Monday."

I consciously softened my voice. "Hastings got me thinking. Until I meet Nadler, maybe it'd be good if you weren't home. If your mom knew I was endangering you, she'd have my head."

His tension released. "No reason she has to know."

"Maybe you should stay with a friend tonight and leave for the tourney from there?"

"What?" His voice rocketed. "Now you want to get rid of me?"

Can't I say anything right?

"Look, Dad, it's got to be safer with two of us home tonight than just one. We'll be fine after your meeting with Nadler. Besides"—he flashed his I-know-I've-won grin—"we've got guard cats in the house."

I snorted at the picture of Cheech and Chong winding between my legs. Guard cats, indeed. "Okay, we'll go home and stay in. You do your tournament. I still need to know the details, though. Call me when you get there and when you're ready to come home. By then I'll know better where we are with Nadler, and we can decide what's safe."

"Deal."

It felt more like a cease-fire.

◊◊◊

ON HER DRIVE DOWNTOWN, HASTINGS must have changed her mind— or she lied to me. Didn't much matter which, the upshot was she called Detective Wright and asked if he would accompany me whenever I could meet with Nadler at Appalachian. I was on the phone with Bear so long I ended up with hot ear by the time I finished giving him the details about the Presser case and answering his questions. He reluctantly offered Friday morning or anytime on Monday for the Nadler meeting.

I called Nadler, but ended up with Mimi Collier.

"I need to meet with Jim as soon as possible. When tomorrow does he have a half-hour slot?"

"Tomorrow's a vacation day. A big regatta on Lake Erie. Let's see." The rustle of flipping pages filled the void. "On Monday he's open from three on. Shall I pencil you in for three?"

Later than I wanted, but it would do.

"Can I tell him what this is in reference to? He'll need to know before he says yes. I'll call you Monday morning and confirm."

This was my chance to make a safety play. "We've uncovered some possible improprieties at Appalachian. Please let him know Detective Wright of the Ross County Sheriff's Office is fully briefed and will be accompanying me." The scratching of Mimi's pen came down the line.

"Can I give him any more information? Improprieties sounds serious. He's not in trouble, is he?"

"Oh no. Nothing like that. We need his help in a police investigation."

EIGHTEEN

"WE'VE GOT A NEW PROBLEM," the muffled voice said. He paused the message and opened a fresh notepad. At the top of the page, he wrote "Chillicothe" and the date and time.

Thinks he's so clever. As though talking through a handkerchief hid his identity. How dumb can you get? Before he accepted a job from anyone, he thoroughly vetted them.

He replayed the message. "A private dick working with the local fuzz is asking questions we don't want answered. Without this guy, they don't have a clue. Twenty-five large, same as the last time. Name's Seamus McCree. Lives in Cincinnati . . ."

He recorded the details: home address, phone number, and description. McCree would be in Chillicothe on Monday for an afternoon meeting at Appalachian. Time was of the essence.

He sauntered to his balcony overlooking the blue-green of the Caribbean. The salty air helped focus his mind. His inclination was to decline. People who acted in fear rarely made good decisions, and even through his handkerchief, this guy sounded fearful.

Below, several gulls squabbled over the remains of a fish, the squawks crescendoing until one gull grabbed the prize and flew off. One good thing about his occupation: he didn't have to work with others.

This guy might be overreacting, or he might be correct. His client knew nothing more about the Happy Reaper than how to contact him, and that was easy to close down. If this guy was caught before he paid off on the Georgia job, the Happy Reaper would end up stiffed seven figures. That was a serious issue. He could consider dealing with McCree as an insurance policy—one he'd be paid to execute.

Whistling the *Mister Rogers' Neighborhood* theme song, he went inside, retrieved his Cincinnati map, and spread it on the dining room table. He compared McCree's address on McAlpin and the site of the earlier hit on Milton. After referencing the scale, he decided the two and a half miles' separation was sufficient to avoid anyone connecting the two places. As to logistics, Cincinnati was centrally located between the Columbus, Indianapolis, Lexington, and Louisville airports. Last time he had flown into Louisville. This time he'd pick Indy, rent a car, and two hours later arrive in Cincy with no one the wiser.

The more he thought about it, the more comfortable he felt with the insurance aspect of this hit. It would be the last job he'd take from this guy, even if he came up with another million-dollar assignment. The risks were growing too large.

He checked weather reports on his computer. A major storm system would bring rain and thunderstorms to the Ohio River Valley through Monday. In the southeast they predicted an early cold snap for late next week when a high-pressure system brought Canadian air all the way down to northern Florida.

The timing couldn't be better. Take care of McCree, then a few nights dropping below fifty in Georgia and nighty-night penguins, hello fat bank account.

After that, the guy with the handkerchief could stuff it in a dark place.

Nineteen

WHEN I ARRIVED AT SUE'S Home Cooking shortly before noon on Monday, Bear was ensconced in his booth, reading *USA Today*, a steaming cup of coffee wafting its slightly acrid scent into the air.

Charlene followed me to the table with a Dr Pepper in hand. "Usual drink for you, good-lookin'?"

"Good-looking?" I flashed a big smile. "You can serve anything you want."

She set the drink in front of me and gave my shoulder a squeeze. Her hand was strong and warm, and she left it there for a moment before taking our orders.

"I see you brought your Expedition today," Bear said. "You expecting to haul off a bunch of files or something?"

"I had my son take my other car to Chicago for the weekend because his is a piece of junk, and it's one less thing I need to worry about." I handed him the outline I had written for my "presentation" to Appalachian's Jim Nadler, along with a list of items I wanted Bear to request. While he looked at the list, I wondered for the umpteenth time how Paddy had done at the tournament and when he could safely come home.

Charlene delivered our meals with a flourish. I again noticed the pedometer on her hip, and asked if she was into the ten-thousand-steps-a-day craze.

"Honey, sitting on my bum all day is not my issue. I agreed to run/walk a half marathon with a girlfriend. You need anything else? I got people coming in." She bustled off.

"Interesting," Bear said, looking past my shoulder. "Wonder what they're doing here in the middle of the day?"

I spotted Charlene greeting the redheaded Deb Holt and a trio of green-shirted guys. Holt saw us gaping at her, pointed the guys to their table, and marched over.

Bear moved to stand but she stopped him. "Keep your seat. You know I'm not a lady to stand for. McCree, right? You got any answers yet?"

I recalled my conversation with Robert Rand about the complaint and felt my mouth go dry. "We're working on it."

"Like I told you before, I already figured out the reason. Our negotiating team"—she tilted her head toward the table of green shirts— "had our first bargaining session the other day. Japs want to take away our retiree medical benefits. That's a strike issue. By the way, I hear our former CEO got bumped off and TV's doing a special tonight."

Wright and I traded looks—the special was news to us. What would the exposure do to Chillicothe Machine?

"Those Japs are gonna find out we won't roll over and play dead. Hope you get the bastards soon. Our negotiations'll go smoother if they're all in jail." She marched away.

"You know about her dad?" Bear asked.

"No, what?" I returned to eating.

"He was a Japanese POW in World War Two for three years. He's still alive and never talks about it, but Deb sure has a bug about anything Japanese."

"I noticed."

"That reminds me," Bear said. "You carrying?"

I stopped with a spoonful of soup halfway to my mouth. "That reminds you?"

"Whatever. I was thinking about the old-time strikes around here. They got pretty violent, and in case we run into trouble I want to know whether I have to worry about being shot by you."

"I don't own guns," I said. "What are you thinking? Deb Holt poisoned the people as a negotiating tactic? Or Jim Nadler is going to come gunning for us?"

"Just asking. You never know."

◊◊◊

I SPOKE TO THE APPALACHIAN receptionist through the circle in the glass partition. "Jim Nadler, please. We're a tad early for our appointment. I'm Seamus McCree and this is Detective Wright."

The receptionist picked up her phone and dialed. Her half of the conversation wasn't what I expected. She graced us with a smile. "Will you gentlemen please have a seat? Miss Collier will be out to see you in a minute."

Mimi Collier, her face pinched into a frown, strode through the French doors. The glasses around her neck swung from side to side as she rushed in. Her limp was accentuated, her heels pounding the floor with a syncopated beat.

"I am so sorry. Mr. Nadler was called away from the office at the last minute. I tried to catch you, Mr. McCree, but I guess you'd already left home." She wheezed from her speedy trip.

"When will he be back?" I asked.

"Late. Mr. Nadler asked me to express his sincere apologies. He can come into the office at seven tomorrow morning. Otherwise, the rest of his Tuesday is already crammed. I am so sorry for this inconvenience. Are you sure there's nothing I can do in the meantime to help you folks? We're all concerned about the possible impropriety you mentioned, Mr. McCree."

"I'm afraid it's Mr. Nadler we need to speak with." I glanced at Bear. He tipped his head in assent. "Okay, tomorrow at seven."

"Thank you so much. Mr. Nadler will be here to let you in."

A brief downpour had passed through while we were inside, and steam rose from the parking lot in swirling curlicues.

"That sucks," I said. "I wonder if he really had something come up or if he's avoiding us. I guess I'm staying in town tonight. Got any suggestions?"

"You like history, right? A couple of nice B and Bs in the historic district serve great breakfasts—probably not early enough, though. Otherwise, we have the typical brand names. You want something inexpensive, the Christopher Inn isn't far from here."

"Cheap is fine. I'm traveling light. All I brought was my running stuff. Weather permitting, I'd planned on putting in seven miles on the way home."

"You're skinny enough to be a runner. You training for something or just a fitness freak?"

"Thought I'd see if I could do a marathon."

He shook his head. "Guy's got to be pretty desperate if he's running a marathon just to see if he can."

◊◊◊

I CHECKED INTO THE CHRISTOPHER Inn and, in case Nadler's plans changed, called Mimi Collier to tell her where I was staying. She'd leave him a note. I checked messages on my cell phone. One: Paddy was staying in Chicago—actually with a friend in Evanston—for another day, and I should give him a call. He had some important information for me, and I'd never guess whom he'd met. I stood by the window to get good reception and dialed his cell phone from memory. Someone answered, burning my ear in rapid-fire Spanish.

Must have dialed the wrong number. I looked it up in my address book. Right number, I must have misdialed. Transposition is my middle name. No answer. *What's up with that?* I left a message: "Tag."

It would have been a perfect time to review the Phoenix file, but I couldn't reach Wright to get it. The Weather Channel claimed only a 30 percent chance of thunderstorms. I changed into running shorts and a cow T-shirt Paddy had given me from Save-a-Bovine-Today Foundation, or some such. The tattooed desk clerk didn't know of any good places to run, but when I asked about parks, she suggested the Great Seal State Park.

The iffy weather must have kept everyone else away because the park roads were empty while I jogged. I startled a doe and spotted fawn, slowed down to watch a red fox with something small in its mouth cross the road in front of me, and from deep in the woods heard the cackling call of a pileated woodpecker—Woody Woodpecker's model. With a couple of miles to go, the skies opened up and drenched me in seconds. The temperatures were still in the mideighties. With endorphins flooding my bloodstream and now cool from the rain, I felt euphoric, like when I had successfully played hooky. Best, I didn't worry about anything. If I hadn't needed to maintain my training schedule, I could have talked myself into continuing for more than the seven miles.

Showered and in street clothes, I headed to the pool to relax on a chaise, but boredom and chlorine's stench drove me out. I needed a book. The desk clerk pointed me to a Wal-Mart close by—not my idea of a bookstore, but beggars can't be choosers. I picked up a thriller and bought some toiletries.

As I crossed the lobby to get to my room, the desk clerk waved me down and handed me a message. Call Charlene at Sue's; she'd be there until five. *I still have ten minutes.* I loped to my room.

It took a while for her to come to the phone. "Well, hi there, Seamus. Bear told me you were staying tonight at the Christopher. I thought you might be lonely. How about dinner?"

Before I could respond, she added, "Dutch treat."

◊◊◊

I FOUND THE CAFÉ CHARLENE chose tucked among the chain restaurants up the road from the Christopher Inn. She had commandeered a booth at the far end of the dining room and was nursing a beer. I pointed to her glass and told the waitress I'd have the same.

My mother would probably have loved the place, a late-fifties time warp including piped-in Perry Como and ceiling fans pushing the air around in a way that made your skin think you weren't warm. We studied the plastic menus with slide-in tabs announcing the day's specials. Charlene chose the meatloaf platter, which included mashed potatoes, gravy, green beans, and fruit cocktail. I picked the ham slice in raisin sauce with a pineapple ring.

I wasn't sure why I'd accepted her invitation—probably harmless curiosity. The only two things I figured Charlene and I had in common were running, sort of, and, I guessed, a conflicted relationship with Bear.

The small talk about road races petered out quickly. While we waited for dinner to arrive I tried the second link. "Were you and Bear once an item?"

"That obvious, huh?"

A tear formed at the corner of her eye and I wished Mr. Tactful had chosen to talk about the weather. I handed her a napkin from the chrome dispenser.

"I'm sorry," she said. "You'd think after all this time I'd get over it."

"I didn't mean to pry." *And who am I fooling?*

"We get along fine. But Bear is so blamed stubborn." She dabbed away the tear. "I never answered your question the other day about Bear being married."

What a dummy I am.

"We were engaged. We hadn't set a date, but I had his ring. That bitch went and ruined it all."

Her tears stopped and her face hardened.

116 | James M. Jackson

"Bear and I went steady in high school. When he went to college, we agreed we'd date other people. We saw each other on vacations, and every once in a while I'd get to Mount Union for a weekend."

Why has Charlene chosen me as her Miss Lonelyhearts?

"Bear finished college and got the stockbroker job. We were back to going steady. At Christmas, he finally proposed. We announced it to everyone on New Year's Eve. I was the happiest woman in the world. I really was. I loved Bear . . . I still do."

"Charlene, you don't need to—"

"We planned to get married in about eighteen months." Her face took on a dreamy quality. "Maybe June, maybe October. Those are the best months. Then bam, Bear hears from this bitch he went out with a few times in college. She tells him he fathered her child and she wants child support."

"Uh-oh."

"Bear admitted he'd slept with her a couple of times, but said he'd used protection. Anyway, based on the kid's birthday, he swore it couldn't be his."

"And you broke up?"

"Bear started drinking. She put him through hell, but the DNA test proved he wasn't the father."

I had no clue how I was supposed to respond to this. I chose silence and sympathetic nods. I knew how to do silence, and the sympathy was real.

"It hurt to find out about her, but we weren't engaged or anything when he and her . . . Well . . . I figured he was sleeping with some girls while he was at college. Those girls would throw themselves at him."

She grabbed another napkin from the dispenser.

"I told him I still loved him and still wanted to get married. I'd even get married sooner if he wanted. But no. He didn't 'deserve' me." She air-quoted *deserve*. "Couldn't face me, he said."

"I'm sorry, Charlene. If I had known I wouldn't have brought it up."

"No problem. Everybody local knows the story. I don't know what got into me tonight. Sorry I dumped on you."

The food arrived and we spent our time together chatting about our families and growing up. I picked up the tab. Lied about it being on my expense account so she'd let me pay.

I walked her to her car, all the while wondering what dinner had been about. She seemed to be a nice woman. She was still sweet on Bear. Was I supposed to pass on the information that she still wanted to be his wife? Who could understand emotions? I needed numbers to think about. At least there I had a fighting chance.

◊◊◊

BACK AT THE HOTEL, THE receptionist stopped me in the lobby. "You're a popular fella, Mr. McCree. Someone left this for you."

MC CREE, written with a black felt-tip pen, covered half the no. 10 envelope. Inside was a handwritten note.

I hear your looking into them retiree murders. I got the info you need, but you'll have to share the reward. I can't collect myself. I'm hiding from the cops. They'll arrest me if they see me. I'm willing to split the money 50/50. Follow the maps and drive down the access road to the parking area by Fitzhugh Crossing. Meet at 8:30 tonight. Come alone. I will be watching and listening and you wont see me if theres more than just you.

I'm serious as cancer. Want proof I know something? The stuff what made them folks sick was in the potatoe salad. The papers aint said that.

Sincerely yours,

Joe Fourier

PS if your late I will wait for 30 min.

Stapled to the note was a torn section of the official state map showing the route south from Chillicothe into the western edge of the Appalachians, and a grocery receipt with hand-sketched detail of the destination drawn on its back.

"Excuse me, miss. Did you see who left this?"

"Sorry, I was putting extra towels in the pool room. I found it lying on the counter."

"Was anyone else around who might have seen?"

Her forehead wrinkled. "Something wrong?"

I breathed deeply to put the brakes on my racing heart. "When did you find it?"

"An hour ago, maybe."

The clock at reception read a couple of minutes before seven. To get there in time, I'd have to race the sun. I ran to my room, called Bear's cell phone, and read him the note.

"You ever hear of this guy?"

"It's pronounced 'Foe-your,' not like the French math guy. Ever since Chillicothe Machine and the union put up some reward money we started getting crank calls. I'm surprised he didn't ask you to bring his half of the money with you. He skipped bail on a possession charge a couple of weeks ago. We all thought he and his girlfriend skedaddled. Your directions sound like it's in Pike County. I guess I should give their sheriff's department a jingle. Maybe they can find time to run by the area and pick him up if he happens to show. He's not the sharpest crayon in the box."

"But according to the note if he sees anyone we won't get the information."

"Don't be stupid, Seamus. The guy's a real loser—typical twenties stoner. He can't know anything. He's just looking for quick money to blow town or score some more weed."

"But he knew more than was in the paper about where you found the botulism. Maybe he does know something." I grabbed my long-sleeved shirt. "This Fourier been violent?"

Bear laughed. "He and his buddies are all peace, love, and rock and roll."

I locked the door behind me and rumbled down the stairs to avoid losing the call in the elevator.

"We agreed?" Bear said.

I realized I had not been paying attention. "Sorry, what did you say?"

What I took as an exasperated sigh came down the line. "I gotta call the Pike County guys. I'll see you in the morning, and we'll find out what Nadler has to say for himself."

I sat in the driver's seat of the Expedition and considered my conversation with Bear. This was probably a big waste of time, but I didn't have anything exciting—or even boring—to do until tomorrow morning's meet with Nadler, other than read a book. And this Joe Fourier knew something.

During the drive, the wind shifted directions and became gustier, pushing tendrils of high clouds across the sky. With a bit more clearing, I might see a good star display once I drove deeper into the country. Occasionally the wind rocked the Expedition, and I wished I were driving my low-to-the-ground Infiniti.

Fourier's directions were clear; the hand-drawn map led me to the top of the hill overlooking Fitzhugh Crossing. I pulled onto the berm, rolled down the windows, and surveyed the scene. A wash of oranges and reds smeared the western sky. The river lay about seventy-five feet below. A one-lane dirt road serpentined down in a series of switchbacks. To my left were the structural remains of a long-abandoned railroad trestle. On my right was nothing but open land.

The Expedition's clock read 8:23. Nothing moved on my side of the river or on the opposite bank. The first katydids chirped and twittering chimney swifts cruised the sky in search of insect prey before they lost their light. Swallows joined the chase with sorties from their perches on the railing.

I retrieved my handheld spotlight from the box of junk I stored in the back and shone it all around. No eye flashes. Nothing moving. Was Joe Fourier around or had the Pike cops shown up and scared him away? I thought to call Bear and learn if Fourier had been found. No cell signal.

Belatedly, I wondered how Joe Fourier had even known I was in Chillicothe, let alone staying at the Christopher Inn. Bear knew. Charlene knew—had she invited me to dinner to get me away from the motel? Were she and Fourier in cahoots? Who else even knew I was around?

Mimi Collier knew exactly where I was staying. She could have told Jim Nadler, but I had difficulty imagining how either of them had a connection to Fourier.

What did I know from the note? Someone was aware of botulism in both food items. Maybe Fourier had overheard something when he was in jail before he got bail? A sheriff's deputy could have said something or someone else in the jail could know something.

Whoa! The Jell-O finally stuck to the wall. Today, I had been in Chillicothe looking into Presser's death and the possible fraud at Appalachian. The note was about the Memorial Day botulism murders.

I mentally searched through all my conversations at Appalachian. Everything had been about Presser or about possible irregularities with annuities. Was there a link between Presser and the Chillicothe Machine killings? I couldn't see it. Either Charlene wasn't what she appeared to be, which would surprise the hell out of me, or the sheriff's department had a leak. A talk with Sheriff Lyons was in order.

With the time now past eight thirty, the dark was winning. The chimney swifts and swallows had disappeared. I sensed a bat flying and heard the *bzzt* of a distant nighthawk. I shifted the Expedition into four-by-four low and descended the narrow road to the parking area below.

Hugging the cliff side of the road, I didn't look at the drop-off. I had driven past the first curve and was about ten feet below the top when a thought arrived. Both Presser's killer and the Arizona murderer had stabbed their victims and cleaned the blade at the scene. There was a connection! I jerked the wheel to correct my drift toward the edge. The second switchback was a little tighter, but maybe only my chest felt tighter. The hairs on my neck started to prickle.

I crept into the third curve, now twenty feet down the hill. Okay, if the same murderer—

KRUMPFFFF.

The right side of the Expedition blew off the ground in a flash of orange heat. The SUV somersaulted down the hill, taking the direct route toward the water. Airbags deployed. Glass shattered. Metal ripped. I tried to stay loose and roll with the flow, but I'd been lousy at gymnastics and had no sense of where the vehicle and I were, other than alternating between being airborne and making brief, crunching, painful contact with the ground.

TWENTY

I AWOKE UPSIDE DOWN, HELD by my seatbelt in the constricted space that had once been the driver's compartment. I inhaled a shallow breath to avoid sucking in the stinking gasoline vapors. Even that caused my ribs to blaze in pain. Forcing my eyeballs right, left, up, and down, I experienced no lightning flashes, no swirling stars. Probably not a concussion.

Reaching across my lap with my left hand, I pressed the seat belt release—nothing. I pressed harder—still nothing. The damn mechanism must not be functioning. The third time I pressed hard with my ring and pinkie fingers while pulling with my thumb and forefinger. The belt recoiled across my hips and chest and I dropped to the ceiling. My neck screamed under my body weight. I slid my head sideways, relieving the strain.

Glasses. My glasses were not on my nose. No wonder I couldn't see clearly. I groped around my head and shoulders, hoping to locate them, but all I found were exhausted airbags, the smooth edges of imploded safety glass, and a surprise pool of cool liquid. *Why don't I wear contacts like the rest of the world?* I sniffed my fingers and discovered where the gasoline fumes were coming from.

Through a persistent ringing in my ears I caught the *plop, plop, plop* of a steady drip. Probably more gas adding to the pool near my head. I needed to get out before the gas caught fire. I pushed aside the airbags and checked the near side window opening. Too compacted to fit through. Escape would have to be through the windshield. I stretched my left hand to grab the steering wheel and gain leverage. A white flash shot behind my eyes. *Whoa, howdy!* I did not want to repeat that. I tried to replay the pain in slow motion to determine its source. Shoulder maybe? *Earth to self, get the hell out of here.*

I cautiously tried using my right hand and pulled myself laterally away from the driver's seat and rolled onto my back. The generalized pain lessened, but stabs of white fire pulsed from my left shoulder and radiated into my neck and head. I tested each leg. They moved, so I pushed further to the passenger side, scraping my butt along the ceiling—well, the floor now. I wormed my left leg free and rested it on the steering wheel. The heel of my right sneaker remained caught on something.

Trapped. My heart raced with a combination of claustrophobia and the realization that my clothes were wicking gasoline, making me a giant candle waiting for a light.

I wiggled back toward the driver's side to free my right leg. Each movement brought a fresh stab of pain from my shoulder and lower back. Sweat ran into my unfocused eyes. The damn sneaker was wedged tight. I reached down and felt around the shoe—pinned above the brake pedal, which I couldn't move.

I tried jerking my right leg while pulling the other way on the brake pedal. The sneaker remained frozen, but my heel lifted partly out of the shoe. Maybe I could wiggle my foot free. I untied the bow, loosened the lace, and pulled against the shoe. Bit by bit, I could feel the foot coming loose.

Until my knee contacted the dashboard.

All I needed was a little more space. I pressed the knee into the dashboard until I thought I might dislocate my kneecap. With a scream of pain and frustration I stopped.

I was becoming lightheaded from the fumes, and I was stuck like Brer Rabbit and his Tar Baby. Did Brer Rabbit get away from Brer Fox in the end? *Seamus!*

Pushing my knee against the dash again only let me know my pain receptors were fully engaged. I tried pushing the top of the sneaker with my good hand while I forced the heel backward. Nothing moved in this contortionist's concept of an isometric exercise. I counted to five and gave one last heave. My foot came free, slamming my knee into the dash.

I quickly removed the few pieces of glass standing sentry in the windshield frame and wiggled headfirst through the opening. *Hallelujah. Free at last, free at last.*

Not.

The hood rested on the ground, leaving a narrow gap between it and the earth on the right side. A large rock blocked any exit on the left. *Damn, damn, damn.*

The engine ticked as it cooled down, but gasoline continued to drip a steady tattoo. I pulled my head and shoulders through the windshield. Rotating my head, I realized a bush grew between the rock and the right front bumper. If I could remove the bush, I'd probably have space to crawl out.

I stretched forward to grasp the bush. Short by two hand-spans. Wiggling on my hips and using my legs to scooch like an inchworm, I kept at it, closing the gap a micrometer or two at a time.

Got it. Okay, hold my nose; suck in a deep breath. Pull.

The bush did not budge in the slightest.

I tried to break the branches; no go one-handed. Cut them off? Returning into the truck was harder than getting out; I had to drag myself in by my heels. I opened the center console, and everything dumped in a heap on the ceiling/floor. Sifting through the debris, I located the Swiss Army knife. This could take forever—if I had the time.

It did not take long to discover that Swiss Army knives cannot be opened with one hand. I pricked my finger several times before I found the saw blade. Ignoring the burning taste of gasoline, I used my teeth to work the blade partially out and pried it open against the ceiling.

I attacked the bush by feel. Every time the saw blade slipped, I had to insert the knife in the cut and start again. I was not setting any lumberjack records. Minutes later, I sawed through a branch, drank a mental toast to progress, and started on the next branch.

My sawing must have covered up the voices, because they sounded close when I next dropped the knife.

Rescuers! I nearly shouted for joy, until the darker side of my brain suggested Joe Fourier had come to make sure I was dead. Logical brain recognized the conundrum: if it was Fourier, I would need to play dead to live; if rescuers, I needed to call out to get their attention or possibly not survive. I needed to hear what they were saying to figure out who they were.

I held my breath and listened.

All I heard was the blasted drip.

◊◊◊

TIME VARIES. EINSTEIN PROVED INCREASED velocity slows time. What he didn't demonstrate, but I experienced while trapped in my ruined Expedition, was that without movement, time stops.

Infinitely later, I again heard a voice from the direction of the river. This time a woman's voice. I concentrated, slowed my breathing, and blocked out the pain.

Drip . . . drip . . . drip.

Yes, at least two people: one male, one female. Fourier and his girlfriend? Were they on the river? I held my breath and thought I heard over the katydids a paddle cut the water, and again. *Yes, on the river.* In the dark, I could barely see inches in front of me. Why would anyone be paddling on the river now?

Because they knew driving the road wasn't safe and water was the only other choice?

I nearly hit my head in reaction to hearing the canoe scrape onto shore. *Are they coming for me?*

Concentration lost, the *drip, drip, drip* again captured my attention. And the katydids seemed to increase in volume. Couldn't they put their sex lives on hold?

I could hear the pair's voices, but not words. I resumed sawing the branch. My only hope was to escape.

◊◊◊

MY ARM WANTED TO DROP off by the time I'd removed two more branches. The voices were still indistinct. I attacked the next branch but stopped when the woman's voice grew louder.

"I mean it. Something's up there."

I froze.

Mumbles. Followed by a clearer, "Then I'm going up myself, Jeff."

Jeff? Without further thought I screamed for help.

The girl shrieked. The guy said, "What the hell was that?" I rested my head on the earth in relief. With those reactions, they weren't Joe and girlfriend or any associate.

"I'm hurt. I need your help. Up the hill."

"We're coming," the male said.

They debated what to do and chose to dig out the entrapping bush. My legs were still wrapped in the passenger compartment. I inched toward the open space, unraveling my contorted body. Before I realized what the guy was doing, he grabbed my shoulders and pulled. I screamed.

Perhaps in getting out I caused a change in the Expedition's balance. Whatever the reason, I had no sooner attained a kneeling position than, with a shriek of twisting metal, the Expedition collapsed and sparks flew from something shorting out.

"Run!" the woman yelled. "It's gonna blow!"

A vision of burning Buddhist monks propelled me screaming down the hill and into the water. Behind me came a *thwomp* as the gas fumes ignited. While I crouched in the river to rinse my hair and thoroughly soak my clothes, a blurred version of the Expedition burned, billowing acrid smoke into the night.

I hurt all over. Sharp pain came from my left shoulder, which seemed somehow unstable. That arm tingled as though I had slept wrong on it. My nose throbbed. My abdomen felt as if I'd gone five rounds with a heavyweight boxer.

The fire burned down in less than ten minutes. Using the last of its light, I left the river and discovered, in addition to my other problems, a knee weeping blood from where I'd scraped it, and that I had twisted the ankle on the shoeless foot during my dash to the water.

I still couldn't see for crap and felt a bit woozy.

Jeff's voice cut through my haze. "Dislocated, not broken. I had one like it from football. It'll be fine once it's back in place. I'm Jeff Burroughs, by the way, and she's my girlfriend, Molly Fitzhugh. Has it happened before?"

I introduced myself and thanked them for getting me out. "Can you pop it back? That's what we did when I dislocated it playing soccer years ago."

"You want me to try? I know the theory, but I've never done it."

"Go ahead. If it doesn't work, I won't hold it against you. Then I need you guys to help me get the police."

"Man, I hope you're right." He grabbed my arm and rotated it.

I think I screamed. I know I wanted to. With a pop, the pain dropped from sharp to dull. I tried the shoulder out—it worked. I gathered my face into a grin. "Thanks, I needed that." My timing must have been off. He didn't even crack a smile.

"I'll start a fire," Molly said. "Get him your spare clothes."

Jeff handed me a shirt, pants, socks, and fleece jacket. "Here's an extra flashlight and a handful of aspirin," he said. "The clothes won't fit, but if you don't stay warm, hypothermia is gonna get you. It's supposed to get cold tonight."

I struggled with the flannel shirt and buttoned every other button in order to get it on. It still hurt to move my arm. The shirt looked ridiculous; the pants were even funnier. I couldn't button the waist and the legs were three inches short. I had to sit down to pull on socks, a warm wool-synthetic blend that immediately made me feel better. Using only my right hand, I draped the jacket over my shoulders as a cape.

Jeff retrieved a coil of rope from one of the two large packs sitting outside the canoe. He looped the rope around my waist and managed, through his laughter, to fashion a belt.

"Thanks," I said. "I feel better already." Which was only partly true. "And thanks for saving me. If you two hadn't shown up, I'm not sure I would've made it. I'm really grateful not to be the *late* Seamus McCree."

Molly reached into her shirt pocket and pulled out a pack of unfiltered Camels, offered me one, and lit hers after I declined. "I really shouldn't smoke, but I can't seem to kick the habit."

"I need to call the police," I said. "Do you have cell phones that work out here?"

Molly shook her head and took a drag. Through exhaled smoke, she said, "If no one showed up for your weenie roast, no one's coming. Never had cell service around here. We're miles from the nearest house, and it's too dark to try the river. We might run into a strainer and then we're drowned rats. Besides, if you aren't in shock already, you soon will be. We need to keep you warm. What happened? Did you miss a turn or something?"

Suddenly I had a strong desire to go to sleep. "Actually," I said, "I thought you might have tried to kill me."

"Kill you?" in unison.

I explained about the note and why I was here and how I thought someone must have mined the road and how when I heard them I thought Joe Fourier had returned to finish the job.

When I ran out of breath from my run-on sentence, Molly asked, "Are we in danger?"

"I think," Jeff said, "if someone were coming back, they'd already be here by now. You're working with the police?"

"Yeah. The note promised information about the botulism deaths in Chillicothe."

"What?" Molly's angry voice rang out. "Oh God," she said in a quieter voice. She folded like a rag doll onto the log. Jeff stood over her, his hand massaging her shoulder.

"Her grandfather died at that picnic."

Molly scrambled to her feet and ran up the hill. Jeff started to follow, but she yelled down, "Just leave me alone right now."

"I'm sorry I upset her," I said. "Why were you guys canoeing after dark?"

Jeff's shoulders drooped as he watched Molly slowly follow her flashlight up the road. "I'm heading to Chicago, Northwestern actually, to start my master's. I convinced Molly to take a few days and canoe this river she loves so much. We were late starting and then got a flat tire on the way to the put in. She grew up around here and really wanted to camp at this spot. In fact, a friend of Molly's lives not far from here. We can call from there. A road crosses the river about three miles downstream. It's only a couple of miles from there to the state road."

"The moon's bright. Can't we go once it's up?"

"We already passed a couple of downed trees—what Molly called strainers. Plus we have to run a decent rapid between here and there. You're starting to shiver. It's the shock. Molly and I can take watch on shifts. No one can sneak up on us with only the river and the road as ways to get here. We're as safe here as anywhere, and there's nothing the cops can do tonight anyway."

The clouds had cleared and stars graced the night sky, although I couldn't even make out the Milky Way without specs. Jeff found a level spot about thirty feet from the water's edge and set up a ground cloth and sleeping bag.

I crawled into the sleeping bag and Jeff retreated to the fire. I pulled the sleeping bag over my head and used my breath to warm up. Why did a doper want to kill me? And why sign his name if he was going to? That didn't make a lick of sense, although Bear had said he wasn't smart. But somehow he, or someone who controlled him, had figured out I was in Chillicothe, lured me here, and tried to kill me.

Crud. I needed to remember to notify the insurance company. Did my policy cover being blown up?

Assuming someone controlled Fourier, who was it? I had been worried Nadler might try to do me in, but I'd made sure he knew the police already had my information. Besides, my dealings with Nadler were about Presser; the note mentioned botulism.

Unless the two were connected.

I had to alert Paddy to stay away from home. At some point, whoever did this would find out I was still alive, and as we had already surmised, they could figure out where I lived.

That convinced me. I'd wait until Molly returned and then sneak off and walk to the house I had passed on the road. With moon and stars, even without glasses, I'd be able to see well enough to follow the main road without getting lost.

TWENTY-ONE

THE SMELL OF BACON AND eggs woke me. The sun was up. I'd obviously fallen asleep, defeating my intention of going for help. Before crawling out of the sleeping bag, I did an inventory of aches and pains. I felt like I'd been washed, wrung through an old-fashioned mangle, and tumble-dried. Only the soles of my feet didn't hurt.

Jeff arrived with my clothes. "You're awake," he said. "I have a present for you."

I thought he meant the clothes, but he handed me my glasses and four more aspirin. The world changed from Monet impression to Ansel Adams photograph, but with color.

"Molly found them on the hill. We soaked and washed your clothes and then cooked them over the fire."

This didn't seem possible. "How long have you been up?"

"We had a fire all night. Your clothes will be stiff and smoky, but I think you might prefer them to the fine fashion statement you make with mine."

I chuckled. Laughing hurt a completely new set of muscles, but it felt good. I sniffed my clothes. Sure enough, woodsmoke with a hint of underlying petrochemicals. The combination was unlikely to compete favorably with Chanel.

Molly joined us. "Seamus, I know we need to call the cops. Jeff has to pack the canoe and make sure everything is balanced. We don't want to end up swimming to the takeout. I have something to show you that I found this morning. Maybe it'll help you figure out who tried to kill you. But first, breakfast."

"Molly can track anything."

"Big overstatement. My grandfather taught me. At nine, I read Tom Brown's *The Tracker*." She grabbed the inside of her cheek with a crooked finger, stuck her tongue out, and crossed her eyes. "Hooked me. I've even managed to take a couple of courses at his school. I do okay, but I can't compare to full-time trackers. Wish I could."

"You've sparked my curiosity."

Molly shook her finger at me. "Eat first, then I'll show you."

Since I wasn't going to change her mind, I ate the bacon and fried eggs. The toast was crisp, served with strawberry jam from a single-serving restaurant container. I drank orange juice and declined the coffee. Everything tasted good. I hoped it augured well for the day.

Jeff put a big pot on the fire to boil water for dishes. Molly and I walked up the road. I was stiff, in socks and one sneaker, and the road wasn't exactly smooth. She bore a grimness I hadn't noticed before. With glasses, I could appreciate her slim, athletic build. She wasn't overmuscled, but all five foot four of her radiated energy.

The Expedition's carcass gave off the noisome New Jersey Turnpike stench of melted plastics and incinerated polymers. Molly veered off the road and onto the hill, where we reversed the path the SUV had taken in its descent. Scars showed where the Expedition had hit. Vehicle parts were scattered down the hill. I was grateful I had survived.

"I found your glasses there." She pointed to an area halfway between two open wounds on the hillside.

We returned to the side of the road. She walked in an uncomfortable-looking half crouch, scanning the area.

"This is it," she said, kneeling down and pointing to a spot in the road.

I caught up to her. "What?"

"Where he turned around. You can see he shuffled his feet and left toe marks here and here," she said, pointing with a stick. "And up there are a couple of really good prints, one going down and the other coming up."

I followed her pointed finger and tried to make sense of the various marks. She rose and walked uphill. I became distracted by a flotilla of barn swallows calling to each other in high-pitched chirps. Their split tails flared as they juked after early-morning bugs, bringing me a smile. At least some things don't change.

I should have been paying attention to where I was walking. I stubbed my big toe and pain shot from it to my shin. I focused my attention on following Molly's piston legs up the hill.

"It poured yesterday midafternoon," she said over her shoulder, "which was part of the reason Jeff and I were late taking off. We wanted to make sure the weather had cleared. These tracks came after the rain. If it'd been before, the rain would've obliterated them."

In many places, the Expedition had obscured the original footprints, but even I could easily follow those remaining. We crested the hill and, about twenty-five yards past the top, Molly stopped and pointed.

"The car made a three-point turn here. And this is where the footsteps going down originate."

"It looks like the returning footsteps keep going."

The footprints led us to a curve in the access road—a place an observer could spot trouble from any direction. The footsteps ended on the right side of the tire tracks.

"He got into the passenger seat. See how he shuffled his feet to open the door?"

As she gave specifics, I could picture the action she described. She moved across the road. "And look here. The driver must have been here awhile. See, six cigarette butts. He smokes unfiltered Camels. Like me, but my feet are much smaller and unlike this pig, I field-strip my butts." She closed one eye and squinted. "The passenger walks on the outside edges of his feet and he's a little pigeon-toed," Molly continued. "Shoes are about my size, but wider. I figure he's short, around my height but weighs more."

"And the driver?"

"A bigger shoe with a wider and deeper indentation. The lookout must weigh a hundred or a hundred and fifty pounds more than the first guy. That's a guess, but see how much deeper his prints are? He's a pacer . . . walks a box pattern, not a straight line. He's had shoes recently refurbished with Magic Feather Soft heels."

My face must have shown how dubious I was because she said, "See for yourself," and pointed to a print in the mud. "You can read it. And, until they clean it, his car's going to be muddy. One of the tires is a spare or a replacement. You can see all four tires—this one, the left rear, has a better tread than the others."

"Okay, what else did you want to show me?"

"That *was* the show, but I need to tell you something." Molly faced me but looked down at my feet. Her hands fluttered in circles at her sides. She gave her lips a quick lick. "This is really tough for me. This trip was supposed to get my mind off home. But now I'm madder than ever. I want to kick something so bad I could scream."

She reared back and booted a rock over the edge. "Jeff told you my granddad died. Grammy was with him. She's home from the hospital, but she's still weak."

"I am truly sorry for your loss."

Tears flowed down her cheeks. She didn't bother wiping them away. "I came home to help Mom care for Grammy. I feel so helpless and so angry. Jeff and Mom finally convinced me to spend a few days on the river. I love being outside. But I felt guilty leaving Mom all alone with Grammy. Then the river started to work its magic on me . . . I love Jeff . . . and I began to feel a bit more like myself, only sadder."

"I think I know what you're feeling, Molly."

"How could you?" A hardness entered her voice and her gaze rose from my shoes to my face. "Never mind. Everything happens for a reason. It's all part of God's plan. I was supposed to rescue you here and help you find whoever killed Granddad."

"I—"

"You can see I'm a good tracker. I have a crystal clear picture in my head of the guy who planted the bomb. If I ever see him walking down the street, I'll know he's the one."

"Well—"

"Seamus, don't say no. I can't get Granddad back, but I'd do anything to have those creeps pay for what they did."

"Feeling impotent is the worst. I lost my father. He was a Boston cop . . . killed on duty. The psychologists talk about people needing closure. We want it as fast as possible, and we want to make sure it sticks. They never found out who killed my father."

"That's terrible." She swiped at her tears. "Let's walk. I need to keep moving. How old were you?"

"Eleven. I have a scab, but it doesn't take much to get me bleeding."

It is nearly lunchtime on a cloudy and cool day for July in Boston. I'm racing my bicycle home from some summer enrichment class at the parochial school, probably trying to beat Patton's tanks or Jeb Stuart's cavalry. A stiff breeze rattles the leaves on our street. Panting like a dog, I wipe sweat from my forehead and lean the bike against the stoop. I don't see Uncle Mike towering over me from the porch of our South Boston home until he grunts my name. "Seamus." I look up. He's in uniform. His face is a thundercloud of anger. I stare at him, having no clue why he's furious at me. "Your father's dead," he blurts. "Killed in a hit-and-run." He's saying something about Mom, but I'm not hearing him. I'm fighting to be a man and not cry. My jaw starts to quiver, and I know Uncle Mike will think I'm weak. I jump on my bicycle and race away, my own keening wail chasing me down the road.

Molly touched my arm and returned me to the present. "Then maybe," she said, "you can understand why I need to do something."

"What we need to do is get the cops. Show them the tracks. That's important. Then . . . then, I don't honestly know what else you can do. I don't even know what I can do." Her shoulders slumped and she brushed away her tears with the backs of her hands. I felt like a bag of day-old crap. "I'm not telling you no. I'm saying I don't know. Okay?"

She shrugged. "We'd better get going. Jeff should have us packed." She headed toward the river. I followed, missing my father more than I had in years.

TWENTY-TWO

MOLLY TOOK THE STERN, JEFF the bow, and I was baggage in the middle. I tried to prioritize whom I needed to contact. I clearly had to report my stupidity to the police, but at least with Molly's tracking observations, we had some new clues. Where was Paddy? Was he home safe? Did Nadler show for his meeting with Bear and me this morning? What happened after my no-show? And last on the list, my insurance agent.

The current and their powerful strokes soon brought us to the takeout. We hauled the canoe onshore and stored it in the shadows under the bridge.

Jeff and Molly grabbed water bottles and we scrambled up the grassy bank to a gravel road. Molly pointed toward the sun. "Two miles east is the state road, and then we're golden."

My stiffness and playing Diddle Diddle Dumpling with one shoe off and one shoe on made me a sea anchor to their progress. We regrouped. Jeff stayed with me while Molly planned to hike to the intersection and either hitchhike or walk to her friend's house. I was not keen on the idea of Molly hitching, but she promised she'd only ride with someone she knew.

About an hour later, an ancient red Ford F-150 steamed down the road, rattling like a steel drum band, spitting gravel in its wake. Molly waved from the front seat. "Here's our ride." The truck made a U-turn and Molly hopped down.

"You're in the cab, Seamus. Jeff and I get the back."

Jeff boosted me into the truck. The driver was midfifties with dirty-blond hair tucked under a well-used Husqvarna cap. Molly and Jeff scrambled into the truck bed, pounded on the cab top, and off we went.

"Thanks for the lift," I said to the driver.

"No problem. Hardly out of my way, and I'd stop any day for someone as pretty as Molly."

"You know her?"

"Oh sure. Me and her daddy used to pal around all the time before he headed to Alaska to work driving rigs. I ain't seen him since."

"Did Molly grow up around here?"

"Her grandpappy owns a ton of land. I understand you was on some of it last night."

How did I miss the connection? "Fitzhugh Crossing?"

"They've owned the land pert near forever. Used to be a good ford until the army corps of so-called engineers went and spoiled it. Well, never mind . . ."

We pulled onto the state road, turned right, and shortly afterward made a left into the long driveway of a well-maintained white clapboard house with brightly colored flower boxes beneath each window. "Here's DeGroot's. Molly said you wanted to stop by here and make some calls. Pleasure meetin' ya, fella."

Jeff helped me from the truck. Molly ran to the door and gave it a shave-and-a-haircut-two-bits knock. After a moment, a silver-haired dumpling of a woman in a red-checked apron answered. "Molly!" she said, and enveloped the girl in a hug. "What brings you here? Let me look at you." She held Molly at arm's length. "Sarah's not around, you know. I was devastated to hear about your grandparents. How's your ma doing? Introduce me to your friends."

"Mrs. DeGroot, this is my boyfriend, Jeff Burroughs, and this is Seamus McCree. May we come in?"

"Sure, sure, dearie, anytime. Can I get you something to drink? How did you get here? Whose truck was out there? What are you doing out here? Are you hurt? Where's your shoe, young man?"

Everyone was talking at once, answering Mrs. DeGroot's questions while she asked more. Molly stuck two fingers in her mouth and blasted a shrill whistle. Made me jealous—I'd never learned how.

"I'm sorry, Mrs. DeGroot," Molly said. "There's been an accident up by the Crossing and Seamus needs to use your phone to make some calls. Okay?"

"Oh, goodness gracious me. Of course it's okay. Follow me. It's right in here on the wall. Oh my goodness, I hope no one was hurt. I didn't want to ask about your black eyes. Now what was that nice man's name who drove you here? Why did he run off and leave you?" Molly steered the still-questioning Mrs. DeGroot toward the front parlor and kicked the kitchen door shut behind her.

I called information to get the Ross County Sheriff's Office number. She provided it, and for an additional small charge, offered to put me through. Valuing time more than money right now, I told her to make the connection.

"Detective Wright, please. This is Seamus McCree."

"I'm sorry," the receptionist said. "He's not here right now. May I leave him a message or transfer your call to someone else?"

"It is really critical for me to talk with him. Can you please transfer me to his cell phone?"

"I'm afraid—"

"To serve and protect. Right now you will do both and earn my undying gratitude if you will please transfer this call. Tell him I made you do it if it protects you. It is quite urgent. Quite."

Two rings later, Wright picked up.

"Bear, this is Seamus. Did you miss me?"

"Where the hell are you?" He rumbled in a deep bass. "I couldn't decide whether to be worried or pissed."

"Worried. I'm okay, but someone tried to kill me last night."

"At your hotel?"

"Pike County—"

"Fourier tried to kill you?"

"Someone tried to blow me up with a road mine."

"A mine?" For the first time, his voice rose above rumble bass.

"Luckily it was set by an incompetent. Two kids found me. I'm at a Mrs. DeGroot's." I gave him the number off the phone.

"But you're okay, right?"

"Nothing time won't heal. Did Nadler make the meet?"

"Yeah, but without you, I didn't go through with it. We're tentatively set up again for tomorrow. He was fine, except for being steamed about your not showing."

"Okay, get into my room at the Christopher Inn. The message itself burned up in my Expedition, but—"

"Burned up?"

"Yeah, I'll give you the details later. Look, you need to get into my room and secure the envelope the note came in. It's on the bed. Get there before the maid cleans the room."

"I can't fucking believe you're so stupid to go off on your own. I thought you guys were supposed to be pros."

"Look, I called you before anyone. I'll need to talk with the Pike County sheriff to report my little mishap. I assume they didn't find Fourier or you would have heard about it. If you want to be in on the scene, do whatever interdepartmental stuff you need to do. Call me in fifteen. Then you can ream me out to your heart's content."

"Fine." Before he clicked off, his car siren screeched to life and his engine accelerated.

I called Paddy's cell phone and got a message: "We're sorry. This number is not in service. Please check the number you are calling and try again." I punched the buttons, making sure I didn't transpose any digits. Same result.

No one answered when I called home. My chest squeezed the air from my lungs. An anvil sat in my stomach. In a blast of fear I decided the Spanish speaker who had answered Paddy's cell phone must have stolen it from him. Was Paddy hurt? How could I check?

I tried calling my cell phone, screwed it up, did it right the second time, and punched in the codes for voicemail. Two messages. *Please let one of them be Paddy telling me he's okay.*

Message one was from Ingstram Ravel. I punched the "Save Message" key and tried the second.

"I wish," Paddy's message said, "that for once you'd keep your cell phone on. And charged. And with you. Then maybe I could get you when I need you. While we were downtown, some asshole stole my knapsack, which had my wallet and phone. Here's the number I'm calling from for whenever you actually get this message."

He gave me a number with an 847 area code—Chicago suburbs?

"I tried you before but since you didn't answer, I had to call Mom to get my credit card info from the fire box she keeps at home. Now she's pissed at me because I went to Chicago and she didn't know about it and pissed at you because you let me—but that's your problem. I've got enough of my own.

"I borrowed some money for gas and whatnot. I expect to get home late Tuesday night. And you never called me back when I told you I had important information. The thing just beeped. Call, will you?

I called the number he left. No answer. I left a message saying my cell phone didn't work. I'd try to call him later, but I didn't think he should stay at home. Could he please, please, please stay with friends until we sorted everything out?

Besides letting me play with her dog, my neighbor Mrs. Keenan had a key to my house. I called and asked her to please make sure the cats had plenty of food and water. She said she'd be happy to and would watch for Paddy's return.

Next was Robert Rand, to whom I recounted my mishap. Unlike Bear, he quietly took notes, evidenced by the scratching of a pen. "The fire destroyed my wallet," I concluded. "Could you please get me a new American Express card and wire money to Chillicothe in care of Detective Wright?"

"Why in the name of Beelzebub did you not give the note to the police and let them handle it?"

"They told me the guy was harmless and I thought maybe I could learn something." *Well heck, this isn't going well.* "I followed my instincts."

"Our mission is to work with the police—not by ourselves. You're supposed to observe and think, not pretend to be a field agent. I will not have any of our associates risking their necks with fool stunts. Am I clear?"

The depth of his anger stunned me. "Did you use a contraction?"

Silence. "How long do you think you were knocked out, Seamus?"

"What difference does it make? What about the money?"

"I will take care of your financial details. I ask about your health because if you were unconscious for any period of time you really should be checked by a neurologist. Do you know one in Cincinnati?"

"Robert, I still need to call the sheriff here and help them with their investigation. I feel fine, just sore."

"Call me after you *have* met with the local constabulary. I will need to call Ross County and make amends."

I had never seen or heard Rand that angry. Maybe I deserved it. Didn't matter. I wasn't about to tell him my plan, which included seeing Nadler tomorrow and continued with finding out who had tried to kill me.

I called the Pike County Sheriff's Department and had to hand the phone to Mrs. DeGroot for her to give directions to her house.

Bear called moments after we disconnected from the sheriff. "The envelope's on the way to the lab," he said. "We've removed your stuff from the room and I'm heading south. I've touched base with Pike County. Sheriff's officers were too busy last night to check for Fourier. What the hell were you thinking when—"

"We've already established that I screwed up—I paid the price. Let it go."

"Where the hell's this Fitzhugh Crossing? I can't find it on the map."

"Oh, and check out a strange connection with one of the botulism victims—Mr. Fitzhugh, he owns the land that was mined. See if you can find out who might have been mad at him or the family. And find out where his son is—worked in Alaska as a trucker."

"Huh?"

"Sorry, I didn't tell you my big aha moment. You and I were visiting Nadler about the Presser murder. The note referred to the botulism murders. Hold on, I'm getting Molly Fitzhugh. She'll give you directions."

We sat on the porch to await the Pike County officer. Mrs. DeGroot brought a pair of her husband's battered loafers for me. Too small. I was stuck with my single sneaker for a while longer.

The deputy arrived and we made introductions. I thanked Mrs. DeGroot for her help and promised to send her money for the phone calls. At Fitzhugh Crossing, we found several officers and a wrecker already on the scene. The cops interviewed the three of us separately. Molly walked them through her track analysis and joined Jeff and me at the top of the hill, where we'd been ordered to stay.

Bear arrived while they were winching up the remains of my Expedition and confabbed with the locals, who were ignoring us after our interviews.

Molly lit a smoke. "Seamus," she said. "I want to start looking for those two guys. I know I'd recognize the one guy from his size and walk."

Until Bear looked into the Fitzhugh clan, we needed to keep Molly away from the investigation. "Could be," I replied. "But right now we have no idea where to look. You and Jeff get one of the deputies to take you to your canoe and finish your trip. The peace and quiet will do you good. Give me your address and phone number. I promise I'll call on Thursday—that's when you'll be done, right?"

"But, Seamus—"

"No buts about it, Molly. You've told the police all you can. Some things they do better than anyone. We have to give them a chance. You know, they'll identify the explosive—"

"And so?"

"We wait. If you can help with something, I promise I'll let you know." I even performed the old cross-my-heart-and-hope-to-die routine. "It's the best I can do."

She stared at her feet and after crushing the cigarette made little circles on the ground with her left boot. She blew out smoke and said, "All right, Seamus. But if I don't hear from you Thursday morning . . ."

◊◊◊

ONCE BEAR STOPPED SULKING, HE tried to be helpful. He bought lunch on the return to Chillicothe and lent me money to buy new clothes, including sneakers. We tried for a replacement cell phone once we hit town, but without a credit card, it was no go. At each stop, I creaked out of his car and minced my way to the store. My injuries gave me insight into how I might feel in old age.

With the errands done, we stopped at the sheriff's office. The wired money had arrived and I repaid Bear. A note from American Express promised my new card tomorrow morning. The tech boys were done with my room at the Christopher Inn, so Bear signed for my stuff.

He gave me a box containing my running clothes, the toiletries, and the thriller I had bought at Wal-Mart.

"You aware Rand and I spoke?" he asked. "He was none too happy with you."

Which means I'm off the case.

"You can't stay at the Christopher," he said. "Or at any of our other motels."

"You've lost me."

"You and I have a meeting with Nadler tomorrow, and I don't have time to cart your ass to Cincinnati. You wanna take a taxi home? No. What you need is a place to stay here. Your observation that the note and your reason to visit Chillicothe are not obviously connected means someone is watching you, or—here's something for you and the Cincinnati police to consider—Presser's death is linked to the botulism murders. Regardless, whoever tried to kill you is still out there. Eventually, they'll find out you're not a stiff."

"I thought you or Rand or both of you would take me off the assignment."

"I told him I'd lock you in chains the next time you did something on your own, but that we were nowhere before you started working on this, and while I had no clue what was actually going on, the pot was boiling. Consider yourself on probation."

"Fine," I said. "Where do your street people live?"

"Funny. The attempt on you was in a remote spot. Maybe they wanted time before you were discovered. If those kids hadn't come along you might be buzzard food. And since you didn't wait—"

"Yeah, yeah. I'm not walking to Cincinnati today. You've eliminated hotels. What's the alternative, a B and B?"

"Charlene's. She has an extra room, and the killer won't find you there."

"Charlene's?"

"Sure. She likes you, and she could use the money—whatever you think's right. I already talked to her."

"Are you crazy?" I tamped my ire. "Charlene could have set me up. You are aware she called me to go to dinner last night, and the note was delivered while we were out."

"No fucking way. She's completely straight. There's not a bad bone in her body. That's where I'm taking you . . . unless you want to change your mind about walking home."

Was I being stupid again? Were Bear and Charlene mixed up with the botulism murders? *Nah. That's paranoid.* I could have insisted on a motel and he would have capitulated, but what would it get me other than an even more pissed-off Detective Albert Wright, who had been the one to keep me on the case?

He dropped me and my packages at Sue's Home Cooking, where I waited out Charlene's shift by sipping a Dr Pepper, blocking out the noise of the restaurant, and reading my book. She left later than normal because the cash register didn't tally. Finally, after a dozen minutes of imbalance, I reached into the till, hauled out the offending two bucks, and handed them to Charlene.

"Someone must have put tips into the register," I said. "How else could the register have too much cash?"

Charlene and her replacement tittered about my solution, but in the end decided to split the two bucks.

We parked in front of Charlene's house—a Cape Cod, tired around the edges, clad in banana-yellow aluminum siding complete with the brown spots. Her landscaping was strong on overgrown hostas and nearly dead lily of the valley. The front entrance spilled into the small but tidy living room and dining nook. The kitchen was down a narrow hall, which also spawned stairways leading to the second floor and the basement.

Charlene showed me the guest room upstairs. Potpourri on the nightstand made the room smell like fresh herbs. Her bedroom, with the door closed, and a full bath completed the second floor. She grabbed a set of towels from the linen closet and laid them on a rack. "You'll want to take a shower?"

"Sounds great. I really do appreciate your putting me up. I hope Bear didn't pressure you."

"It's no problem. What do you want for dinner? I'll cook, unless you think I might poison you, since blowing you up didn't work. Bear told me you thought I was a suspect."

"That's not exactly—"

"Do you always go beet red when you're embarrassed? We can talk about it during dinner."

TWENTY-THREE

CHARLENE WOKE ME AT SIX fifteen the next morning. My glasses were squished to my head, and a comforter covered my fully clothed body.

"Up and at 'em, sleepyhead. I bought you some Bengal Spice tea and I got Diet Pepper in the fridge in case you're one of those people who gets their caffeine from pop. Bear'll be here in thirty minutes to take you to your meeting."

My head felt disconnected, lagging six inches behind the rest of me. The book I'd been reading after my predinner shower had fallen to the floor, and I had slept through the night. I had a nagging feeling I was supposed to have done something the previous evening.

I showered, shaved, dressed, and was downstairs appeasing a growling stomach with Charlene's hotcakes in less than ten minutes. She'd warmed the faux maple syrup. It was thicker and sweeter than the real stuff, but got me thinking about winter morning breakfasts as a kid when Mom would banish the Cap'n Crunch and make pancakes that we drowned with Aunt Jemima.

I inhaled steam from the tea. "I could get used to this."

"Well, don't. Normally, I'm already at Sue's by this time, but I have a late shift today. Tomorrow you're on your own."

Bear arrived and poured a cup of coffee. "Charlene tells me you slept like a baby."

"Better than," Charlene said. "He didn't wake up in the night. You bring him back from your meeting. He needs to rest up. Any idea how long he'll be staying here?"

Bear drained his cup. "We'll see what happens. Time to boogie."

◊◊◊

NADLER MET US AT THE front entrance to Appalachian. The building was eerie with only exit signs lighting the way. The air fresheners were hard at work dumping orange blossom and mint scents into an air unstirred by human movement or A/C.

He showed us to chairs and offered cups of Starbucks wafting strong coffee odors. "They don't allow me to make the coffee around here—claim I make it like stew, and since I only drink one cup, they end up throwing away the rest of the pot."

Wright accepted a cup. I waved away the offer.

"What happened yesterday?" Nadler asked between sips. "Those are some shiners."

"Accident," I said. "Let me get right to it. I believe someone at Appalachian is committing fraud on a grand scale."

Nadler leaned forward, probably about to object. I held up my hand.

"It's a crafty scheme. Someone is keeping single life annuitants on your rolls after they die and absconding with fraudulent payments for three years. Then they record the death. Our back-of-the-envelope estimate is the theft runs to approximately two point five million dollars through last year."

"Oh my God." Nadler became ashen. "You have proof?" He stood and paced behind his desk.

"Remember I asked you to check your records for two annuitants? According to the Oklahoma State records, George Proudt died exactly three years earlier than your records show. And—"

"Input error?"

"Unlikely. Joseph Drucker, whom your records show as still living and receiving payments, died more than two years ago. We've done a detailed check. Your records show twenty-four people with single life annuities died in 2005. Social Security says they all died in 2002. This is fraud, not a mistake."

Nadler's face was devoid of color. "Two and a half million. No wonder we weren't making as much money as we thought we should."

"Jim," I said, "who has access to those records?"

"Everyone." He waved vaguely toward the darkened cubicles. He nervously spun his desk chair around until it careened into his desk with a *thunk* that seemed to startle him into sitting down. "But only supervisors can authorize changes. Clerks set them up for supervisor approval."

I looked him directly in the eyes. "How about you?"

His head snapped back as though I had slapped him. "You think I did this?" He turned to Bear. "Do I need to call an attorney?"

Bear now sat up and held his hands out in an open gesture. "If you want, we can go downtown and invite your lawyer. But really, Mr. Nadler, we aren't accusing you of anything. We need your help to verify Seamus's suppositions. Do you want to help?"

Nadler insisted he did and asked me, "What can I tell you?"

"Only supervisors and you can actually make the changes in the annuitant records? No other executives?"

"No one else . . . I suppose the guys in IT could. They have access to our whole network and can remotely take over any terminal and operate it." He placed his interlocked hands directly in front of him. His knuckles were white. A sheen of sweat glowed on his forehead. "I think that's it."

"How many people have been supervisors for at least five years?"

"Five years? Four of them. The fifth was promoted this summer."

"Jim, I'm curious," I continued. "You left New York with a lot less money than you have now. Where did it come from?"

His lips traced a faint smile. "Now I get it. You can check this out pretty easily. My wife's an author—children's fantasy. Not Harry Potter, but a very successful series. The royalties keep increasing. If we wanted, we could retire on them. They started shortly after we moved here."

There goes one perfectly good suspect.

Bear: "We'll check it out, Mr. Nadler. We'd like to work quietly to pin down who's been dipping into the honeypot. How's that sound?"

Nadler: "What's involved? We have an internal audit team we could use—"

Bear: "We want to limit the number of people to avoid chasing off the quarry. I could get a court order, but I'd prefer not to."

Nadler pulled a legal pad from his drawer and squared it in front of him. "What do you need?"

Bear ticked off the items on the list I had given him. "Verify payment continued for three extra years for the twenty-four folks who died in 2002, and we've got a few more recent deaths for you to check."

"No problem." Nadler noted it on his pad.

Me: "We want to know where those checks go. We'd like to see the endorsements."

"I don't know. We'll need accounting."

Bear: "Then we'll decide later how we get the info. We may choose to go directly to your bank."

Nadler jotted a note. "Okay. What else?"

We had run through the initial list.

Me: "The names of the four supervisors who have held their positions for five years and anyone on the IT staff who has access to the annuitant files—again, only those who have been here at least five years."

"That I can do now." He scribbled the four supervisor names and opened an employee directory to the IT department's page. He ran his finger down the list and jotted three more names on the pad.

Bear: "How did you know which IT guys to include?"

"Sequential employee numbers. Since I've been here five-plus years, I included anyone whose number was no more than fifty past mine. With our turnover, that should cover it."

I handed Nadler the list of resurrected annuitants. "When can you verify this information matches what's in your system?"

"I'll start as soon as you leave." He flipped a page on his calendar. "I've got a nine o'clock appointment, but it's only for an hour. So, this morning, maybe early afternoon, depending on interruptions."

Bear: "Great, Mr. Nadler. We really appreciate your assistance. This needs to stay between us for now. I don't want you telling anyone. This may have precipitated one murder, and I don't want there to be any more."

"Murder?"

Me: "This is the problem Samuel Presser planned to talk to you about."

Nadler turned so pale the blood vessels under his skin looked like a subway map. "I can't tell the executive committee? And the state insurance board? I don't know the rules, but I suspect we're supposed to notify them."

Bear rose and leaned all six feet eight inches in Nadler's direction. "No, that would not be a good thing to do, Mr. Nadler. Not good at all."

Bear turned away. Nadler was halfway out of his chair when Bear slowly rotated back.

"By the way, what forced you to postpone our Monday meeting?"

Nadler cranked his head back to look at Bear. "A client in Cleveland had concerns about our customer service."

"And you just found out about it?"

"It was supposed to be Ed Olson's meeting, but he had a conflict. Since the purpose was to discuss performance issues, he didn't want to reschedule and asked me to go."

Me: "What time did you get home?"

"I went straight home. Say, half past eight?"

Me: "Who else knew about your scheduled meeting with us?"

"I mentioned it in our executive committee meeting that morning. That's about it. Oh, and Mimi. She runs my calendar."

Me: "Tell me about Joe Fourier."

A puzzled expression settled over his face. "This another annuitant?"

Bear: "Give me a call at the sheriff's office once you have the information. Hey, and . . ." He shook his finger at Nadler. "Don't make any trips out of town until we verify your wife's writing income. I don't like to travel, and I would not be happy to have to chase you down."

Nadler's sweaty hand trembled as we shook our goodbyes. If rattling him was our intention, we had succeeded.

◊◊◊

BEAR FISHED A KEY FROM under Charlene's mat and let us into the kitchen, where we sat and divided the work. I'd get CIG folks to track down information on Nadler's wife, and I needed to get the additional data I'd requested on Appalachian from Ingstram Ravel, who, I remembered, had left me a message I hadn't listened to. Bear went off to research the Fitzhugh family: enemies, where Molly's father was, who benefited from the wills, and so on.

I settled into one of Charlene's overstuffed living room chairs and let my thoughts drift over the last couple of days. *Paddy!* I'd forgotten to call. He should be home, and he didn't have any way to contact me. I pulled myself out of the chair and shuffled to the phone in the kitchen.

With no cell phone, I figured I'd add the long-distance charges onto my room and board. Paddy answered with a sleepy "Hello?"

"Paddy, this is Dad. Are you okay?"

"I'm fine. Where the hell are you? Mrs. Keenan had to let me in last night and told me she'd fed the cats. What gives that you can't call your only son after he leaves multiple urgent messages? What's her name?"

"It's not like that, Paddy."

"Yeah?" His voice sounded suspicious. "Where are you?"

"Chillicothe, staying at the house of a friend who—"

"Yeah, what's the friend's name?"

"Charlene."

"Charlene what?"

I surveyed the trackless desert of my brain—no clue. I had never asked Charlene her last name.

"Paddy, it's not like what you're thinking."

"Yeah, what am I thinking? Oh never mind. Screw this. You and Mom were made for each other. You both care more about your love life than you ever did about me."

"Wait a minute—"

"No, you wait, Dad. I've been trying to get in touch with you for four days now. I tell you it's urgent and you're shacked up with some bimbo in Chillicothe whose last name you don't even know. I'm out of here."

"Now you wait a blasted minute, Patrick. Someone tried to kill me." *Crap. I didn't mean to tell him.* I eased my grip on the handset.

"What?!"

"Nothing. You're not talking to a ghost. Can you calm down long enough for me to ask my favors? Then if you want, you can still tell me where to go."

"You're the one who's yelling. So Lieutenant Hastings was right? Was it Nadler?"

"Probably not. I think it relates to the botulism murders. And speaking of not getting messages, didn't you get mine suggesting it might be dangerous to stay at home?"

"Because someone might still want to kill you?"

"Exactly."

"Well, they could have done it last night because I just crashed. I don't buy it, Dad. You're not here, what's the risk? What do you need me to do?"

"The Expedition's history and I need a car. Can you get a friend to drive my car out here and you drive yours? I have to stay at least until tomorrow. I'll spring for dinner, and I'd feel much better if you weren't home alone."

"Probably can't leave until after five. Everyone's working."

"No problem. Call me at this number once you know when you can leave. By then I'll have directions."

"You don't even know where you are?"

"I knew eventually you'd find out I'm not omniscient. I don't know Charlene's last name, I don't know where exactly she lives . . ."

"Yeah, right. What *do* you know? Never mind. What else do you want?"

"Can you pack some clothes, please? I'm not sure how long I'm going to be here."

"Anything else, Your Omniscience?"

"I don't think so. Thanks, Paddy. I appreciate it. I'll look for your call—"

"Wait! You'll never guess who I met in Chicago. Skyler Weaver. She was there protesting capital punishment at a big rally timed to coincide with the governor's appearance."

"Small world."

"Seeing her got me thinking about the missing insurance company money. We did a little research and ka-ching! The monthly annuities are direct deposited to a bank in Henderson, Nevada—each to its own account, but only temporarily. The money is then moved using an online bill paying service to a single account—this one in Las Vegas."

"How did you find—?"

"The owner is a Vivian Kennedy. Guess what? Vivian Kennedy's been dead for six years! She and her husband died in a car crash. And, surprise, surprise—Vivian Kennedy had an annuity at Appalachian Casualty and Life."

"Where did—"

"Whoever set up this whole deal is a woman! She stole Vivian Kennedy's ID, social security number and all. I checked this Vivian Kennedy out. She has a bunch of credit cards on which she periodically runs up huge balances. But she pays them off each month. Given we're talking Vegas, I'm thinking gambling with a capital *G*. She has a townhouse in a real nice area."

"How did you find this information, Paddy?"

"Internet."

"Too much detail—"

"Well, let's say we got some inside information."

"We? Hacking?"

"None of the companies had security worth a damn."

"Seamus Patrick McCree, I thought we agreed you'd never do that again. You could wind up in jail. And now I can't even use this material—a court would throw out the whole case in a minute."

"No way we get caught. Besides, you don't have to use the information per se. This gives you a big clue where to look. You want to catch your crook or what? You're supposed to be a great thinker—think along the right lines, ask the right questions and, poof, your pals come up with the real Vivian Kennedy. Besides, my friends have some new prospects to talk to about weaknesses in their computer security systems."

"That's how they prospect for business?"

"Sure. They never do any—"

"I don't want to know, Paddy. I just don't want to know. I appreciate your trying to help, but I don't approve of your methods. Let me tell you what we've *legally* discovered." I filled him in on our visit to Nadler earlier in the morning, along with a simplified version of my "accident."

"Some systems," he said, "put a tag on the electronic file to indicate when and by whom the file was changed. Maybe Appalachian's system uses similar technology."

"Excellent idea. I'll check it out. We'll talk again, Paddy. I'm still angry about your hacking, but you know I love you."

"I love you too, Dad. I'll call when I've found someone to drive out with me."

I slumped into the chair. Now what? Paddy had handed me a ton of valuable information. We would have come up with some of it anyway from the questions we asked Nadler, but the Vivian Kennedy stuff would not have been apparent. Of course, Paddy tracing the money to the fake Vivian Kennedy didn't mean the thief was female. A male could have an accomplice.

I didn't struggle long with my conscience. Paddy was right; I needed to ask the right questions. Furthermore, I had some information to compare with whatever Nadler told us. A little verification never hurt.

I telephoned Ingstram Ravel and had to explain why he needed to call me back at Charlene's number. I asked that he confirm the information I gave him on Nadler's wife and also asked him to check airline records for Nadler, the four supervisors, three IT guys, and Vivian Kennedy to determine if any of them made frequent trips from Columbus to Las Vegas. Before we were off the phone, Ingstram had already verified

Nadler's story about his wife. She was a fantasy author known worldwide—even I recognized her nom de plume.

I called Bear and passed on Paddy's suggestion about the annuity system containing tags to record who made changes. After requesting directions to Charlene's house, I fessed up to not knowing her last name. Worth—Charlene Worth. Paddy called back sooner than I had expected.

"I found a guy working construction," Paddy said.

"Great. Take US Fifty out of Cincy, and—"

"Fifty? Only snails travel that way. It's much faster to take the interstate up and cut across." He said he'd use his phone's GPS. Maybe when I replaced my phone I'd spring for a smart phone?

If only snails used US 50, why had Bear given me those directions?

Shortly before noon, Bear called to report Nadler had finished his research and wanted to meet at three. He'd pick me up.

◊◊◊

THE APPALACHIAN RECEPTIONIST HAD OUR visitor badges waiting when Bear and I arrived. Mimi, wearing a mauve pantsuit embellished with a gold-and-silver gecko pin, brought us to Nadler's office. At a slower pace, her limp was less pronounced.

"Gentlemen," Nadler greeted us as Mimi excused herself. "Please come in."

Bear and I sat. Staleness had replaced the smell of morning coffee. Nadler eased behind his desk, perspiration half-mooning his armpits.

"Unfortunately, everything Seamus suggested is correct," Nadler said. "We paid all twenty-four of the 2002 deaths exactly thirty-six months too long. Everything checks out. We've got a big problem. Here's the part I didn't want to tell you on the phone because I wasn't sure you'd believe me. All the overpayments use direct deposit."

Paddy was right. "Do you know where they go?" I asked.

"That's what really caught my attention. Our records capture the routing number and the account number. Are you familiar with those?"

Bear: "The routing one is the left-hand set of numbers preprinted on your checks?"

"Yeah. The deposits go to different accounts, as you'd expect, but all the accounts are at the same bank."

Bear: "What bank?"

"I don't know. I only have the routing number. I suppose there must be a way to find out—"

Me: "From the Internet."

Nadler: "Okay. Here's the other part. I checked all the single life annuities we paid this month. Sixty-four were direct deposited to that institution. They totaled slightly more than ninety grand. They're going to crucify me."

Me: "Jim, you've confirmed our suspicions. We'll still need to figure out who's doing it. Does your system tag changes with a who and when?"

"Detective Wright asked that when I spoke with him. We'll need one of our systems guys. I figured out how to do it without making anyone suspicious. You two could represent a company considering buying the system and checking it out with a current client."

I glanced at Bear, who looked dubious. "Good idea," I said. "Can we set it up now?"

Bear: "Chances are someone will recognize me. Say we're interested in the system and leave it there."

Obvious, now that he mentioned it. Was my brain still scrambled?

Nadler: "Have to be tomorrow at the earliest."

Me: "Can we try to schedule it now?"

Nadler: "When's good?"

Bear had only the afternoon free. Nadler checked his phone list and dialed. We heard him arrange a meeting for one o'clock tomorrow.

"Remember," Bear said, "don't breathe a word of this to anyone." He pointed at me. "You don't want to look like him."

Nadler: "The next payments go out the beginning of the month. That's only four days away. I'll have to do something before then."

TWENTY-FOUR

THE NEXT MORNING I AWOKE to a silent house. I felt creaky but mobile. My shoulder hurt less than the day before, and my black eyes had progressed to a greenish tinge. I showered, dressed, and drove my car, which Paddy and friend had delivered the previous evening, to a corner market.

The store wasn't big and candy bars and bags of chips occupied half of its display space. I bought *the* box of purportedly healthy packaged cereal, raisins, and a carton of milk, and prepared breakfast at Charlene's. I nuked a cup of the Bengal Spice tea and enjoyed sniffing it more than actually drinking it.

Following breakfast cleanup, I telephoned Molly. I didn't want that conversation hanging over my head. She launched into describing a variety of ways to find the short, slim guy who walked on the outsides of his feet, including—but not limited to—contacting all shoe stores, podiatrists, and chiropractors in the area; posting on the Internet; putting ads in the local newspapers; and, if all else failed, driving around town.

"I haven't heard anything about that part of the investigation," I said.

"I get it," she said, anger steaming her voice. "You're blowing me off. Fine. I'll do it myself."

"That could be dangerous. The police—"

A loud bang came over the line. She had slammed the phone down. I wondered whether in a few years kids brought up with only cell phones would be as clueless about what it meant to *slam down* a phone as kids now are that *dialing* a number had a physical meaning from rotary phone days. Progress. Speaking of phones, I needed to find a store and replace my cell phone.

Midmorning, Charlene's phone rang, interrupting my disjointed analysis of the case. I picked up with a "Hello." Silence. I hung up. I settled into the chair and the phone rang again. I grumbled, hobbled to the kitchen, and said my "Hello" again.

This time a wailing "Waaaaaaiiiiiiit" greeted me.

"Shite, Seamus," a British accent said. "Why did you hang up on me?"

"I'm sorry, Ingstram. I didn't hear anything and figured you were a telemarketer."

"Well right, but you get a bit of delay with a transatlantic call."

"I do occasionally hang up on friends."

"I'll take that as an apology. I've the information you requested."

"And judging from your voice, you're pleased with yourself. What have you got?"

"First, the bad news. I have nothing to add to what the police already told you about Joseph Fourier. Now, I was able to check the travel habits of your suspects. Nothing from Columbus. I expanded the search to Cincinnati . . ."

"And now I'm supposed to say, 'What did you uncover?'"

"Right, then. Well, only one of the nine has been to Las Vegas in the past year. Care to place a little wager on which one has been there twenty times?"

"Vivian Kennedy."

"Right you are, Seamus, but you'll never guess what else I found out about her."

"She's been dead for six years?"

"Bloody hell. Who told you?"

"Séance."

"Yes. Right, then. What don't you know?"

"Sorry I ruined your surprise, but you've confirmed my suspicions. Who is the new Vivian Kennedy?"

"Sorry old chap, no go there. The original Vivian Kennedy and her husband died in an automobile accident. The new Ms. Kennedy seems to have appeared about a year subsequent and she is interesting."

"How so?"

"All the big Vegas casinos know her. She carries a large line of credit, and she can be comped to a show or fancy dinner anywhere she wants."

"Comped?"

"Spend enough money at their tables and they pay for your room, meals, shows, whatever. This lady spends plenty. She dropped a quarter million bucks last year. Not bad for a stiff."

"Casinos have pictures of their high rollers, don't they?"

"Step ahead of you there. You want fax or email?"

"I can't handle either right now. Fax it to the Ross County Sheriff's Office, attention Detective Albert Wright. I'll ask him to bring it to lunch."

"Will do. I was about to email you the rest of the information you requested. Want a quick summary?"

Actually, I wanted a detailed summary.

"Appalachian's execs? President is William Snyder. Worked his whole life at Appalachian and engineered their transition from a mutual company to a stock company. You Yanks call it demutualization. Industry sources consider him competent, but not a real take-charge guy. Born and bred in mid-Ohio. When you read the full biography, you'll see he's bland at best. Scuttlebutt says he's waiting for the stock price to rise to cash out his options and retire."

"Wonder if he could be salting away some extra retirement dollars from the annuity scheme? He might know the ins and outs of the system."

"To steal an American expression, that's why they pay you the big bucks, Seamus. Their executive VP for finance is Edward P. Olson."

"I met him leaving Elkin's office at Chillicothe Machine with Chip Kincaid, the insurance broker I asked you about. Overweight. Had an unctuous handshake."

"Olson's been at Appalachian for five-plus years. Arrived from Noinu Insurance in New York following Appalachian's demutualization. Had a similar role at Noinu. They specialized in benefits for—"

"Union members. Spelled it backward."

"Aren't you the sharp tack in the box today? Marketing and sales also report to him. He's successfully introduced Appalachian into the union market, and expanded Appalachian's presence on the East Coast."

"And before?"

"Couldn't find bloody much. I tried the old recruiter's trick of getting references from former coworkers. I'm sure you're aware many of your US companies have policies forbidding everyone from providing information about past employees. Usually someone with a strong amiable trait wants to be helpful. These people were silent as the Rock of Gibraltar."

"You're a big help."

"Don't blow that big sigh at me, Seamus."

I hadn't realized I had shown my frustration. I needed to be more careful.

"Michael Schwartz heads legal, regulatory, and human resources. Grew up in Chillicothe, studied at Ohio State, and worked in Cincinnati at one of the large insurance companies. Obtained his law degree part-time from the Chase College of Law at Northern Kentucky University and joined Appalachian to replace the retiring incumbent."

"Wanted to come home?"

"Cheers. Wanted to raise his family near both sets of grandparents. The move to Appalachian was a big step up for the chap, and the jury is still out on whether he can cut the mustard."

"How long do they need? He's been there five years already."

"Right you are. I only report what they tell me. We contacted all three of the former executive VPs. Only the finance guy had been forced out. The stock was hammered after the demutualization because Appalachian missed their earnings target by a penny a share. Several members of the board were dissatisfied and forced Snyder to make the change. One of the board members recommended Olson."

"You know how analysts hate to be proved wrong."

"What? Oh right . . . you were one. It was a joke."

"Fell short—like the earnings."

"Moving right along. Nadler's predecessor in operations had planned to retire a year before he did, but agreed to help Appalachian through the demutualization. Chap had some gripes. Lost a battle to Snyder and the board about the level of staff reductions. Says they cut into muscle."

"And the former legal guy?"

"Well, yes. Since *I* don't excel at séances, I couldn't talk with him. Died from a stroke shortly after he retired. I spoke with his wife. Nice lady, but didn't know anything."

"Anyone else?"

"The last member of the executive committee is Arthur Jacobs, VP of plant and equipment. He's sixty-six and worked for Appalachian forty-eight years. Started part-time while in high school. He's responsible for the building, storage facilities, and equipment, other than IT. His bio is nondescript and frankly, Seamus, I didn't spend much time on him since he didn't seem to be in a position to commit the fraud."

"Fair enough."

"Two more quick things. Kobe Heavy Metal, Chillicothe Machine's parent, appears clean as a whistle, and hasn't had any problems, union or otherwise, anywhere else in the world. I'd say your worldwide conspiracy theory is dead."

"At best it was a long shot."

"Righto. Now, that chap Kincaid . . . how shall I say this? He's not dirty, but doesn't appear squeaky clean either."

"Assault and battery by handshake?"

"Pardon?"

"He tries to be a bone crusher."

"I see. The Ohio Department of Insurance has fined him twice for what appear to be recordkeeping problems. Had some arbitration with the NASD regarding sales of annuities. Might be sloppy recordkeeping, although I sense the hint of something more, but the records aren't available and the other parties involved won't comment."

"Interesting, but doesn't seem to tie into what we're working on."

"Anything else I can do for you, Seamus?"

"You've done great, Ingstram. I appreciate the information. Remember to fax the picture. I can't wait to see if I recognize Vivian Kennedy."

◊◊◊

BEAR TOOTED HIS HORN. I popped the question as I opened the car door. "You have the photograph?"

"What?"

"Faxed from CIG."

"Sorry, the clerks were complaining about a hundred-page fax on some court case tying up the machine. Yours must still be in line. Get in and tell me about it."

My report filled the drive to Sue's. Bear's booth had a hand-printed "Reserved" sign stuck on the table. I picked up the sign and examined the printing—not similar to the note left for me at the Christopher.

Charlene, arranging her red bandanna, hustled over, plucked the sign from my hand, and shoved it into her apron pocket. "I knew you were coming." We placed our orders and Charlene left to fill them. Bear put on a toothy smile.

"Okay, I'll bite," I said.

"Today's a day for ghosts," Bear said. "You have a reincarnated Vivian Kennedy. I have fingerprints of a man who died ten years ago."

"Those are old prints."

"No, dummy. New. They were on the 'meet me' note's envelope. Yours, the desk clerk's, and a ghost who left a partial index finger and a full thumbprint. One Eduardo Solonini, a New Jersey punk who died in a boating accident."

"Guess not. Not Fourier?"

"Maybe he wore gloves. You tell me why a dead midlevel crook in the New Jersey mob turns up in Chillicothe ten years later."

"Mug shot?"

"It's twenty years old. We've asked for something more recent, but since the guy has supposedly been dead for a decade, it'll take a while to search old case files. He had several arrests, but no convictions.

"According to a Jersey City cop I talked with, until the boating accident, Eduardo had lived a charmed life with witnesses recanting, never remembering in the first place, or becoming permanently cold and stiff before a trial. The closest they ever got to putting him away was a hung jury, which they didn't retry because Eduardo died shortly thereafter."

He handed me a folder with the mug shot. The guy was five ten according to the chart behind his head. Only a narrow separation prevented his dark eyebrows from meeting over a large, flat nose.

"This guy is skinny as a rail," I said. "Thinning hair. I wonder how much he has now." I looked at Bear. "You still look like the cat who ate the canary. Give."

"We lifted prints of a local loser named Thomas Moyer from the remains of the land mine. He's familiar to the department."

He handed me another mug shot, this time of an unshaven man about fifty-five whom life had not treated well. Deep-set eyes, untrimmed hair, sunken cheeks; he looked malnourished.

"We've had him mostly on drunk charges and petty theft," Bear continued. "He served time, but has no history of violence. In addition to our outstanding warrant for Joe Fourier, we've issued warrants for both these guys. Moyer wasn't at home, and who knows where home is for Solonini."

"Switching gears," I said, "any scoop on Molly and the rest of the Fitzhughs?"

"They're clear. Probate showed all the old man's money went to his wife. They had a joint will and at her demise, everything goes to Molly's mother. Her father gets exactly one dollar. According to a lawyer buddy, that prevents him from contesting the will. He's still in Alaska, living with some babe, logging now. Alibis all around. That's a dead end. Let's hope this meeting at Appalachian isn't another one."

◊◊◊

"YOU GUYS HERE AGAIN?" THE Appalachian receptionist gave me a broad smile and handed us visitor badges. "If I'd known, I would have redone my lipstick." She patted her lips. "Show up any more regularly and I'm going to have to get you permanent passes. You can find your way to Mr. Nadler's office?"

"We left bread crumbs," I said.

We passed Mimi's empty cubicle and entered Nadler's office. Nadler introduced a young man in cargo pants and a T-shirt. "Jesse Thompson's from IT. He's responsible for maintaining our annuity database functions."

The kid occupied Nadler's desk chair and didn't look up from the keyboard at Nadler's introduction. "Cool. Be with you in a nanosecond."

Nadler added a third chair between the two visitor chairs, and the three of us sat facing a second monitor placed on the desk.

"Okay, ready," Jesse said. "What aspects of security are you interested in? Password security? Network interface security? Transactional modification security?"

"If I understand correctly," I said, "we're interested in the security of the database itself, of limiting who can make changes and tracking them for audit purposes."

"Right. Cool. This has got a lock on that."

I really had only one question—who authorized the changes for the dead annuitants? I had to play the game, which meant watching Jesse demonstrate for half an hour how the system protected itself six ways to Sunday. I checked to see how Bear was doing: I think he was sleeping with his eyes open.

"Can we see tracking detail on a specific example?" I asked once Jesse came up for air. "How about someone who died?"

Nadler provided a social security number from his pad.

Jesse punched in the digits. "George F. Proudt. See, the second line shows he entered this system on February 14, 1995. We updated the whole system that month, so no way to tell when his record was entered into its predecessor."

"What are the following dates and notations?" I asked.

"When changes were made. The code tells us what the change was. Take this guy. Address changed in 2001. The next year all kinds of sh— stuff happened. I can look up the codes if you need 'em."

Me: "Nothing else until 2005?"

"Right you are, sir. On February 26, 2005, the annuitant died."

Me: "You mentioned earlier the system leaves a tag to indicate who approved the change?"

"The last column shows the—"

Nadler gasped. "That's my ID. I don't understand. I certainly didn't approve the entry."

Jesse: "This program doesn't lie. If it's your ID number, you authorized the change."

Nadler slapped the desk. "But I didn't, I tell you. I've never made modifications to the annuitant database. I don't even know how!"

Jesse nodded. "All it really means is someone was logged in using your ID."

Nadler: "My password's secure. I change it every time you guys tell me to."

Jesse: "It's a mystery to me, Mr. Nadler, but I'm sure the system's fine. You want to check someone else?"

Nadler gave him another social security number from the list of 2002 deaths.

Jesse: "James Petrosky. Hmm . . . That's funny. The recent changes have your ID. I don't know what to tell you, Mr. Nadler. We've tested the system, and I'm sure it works."

The veins at Nadler's temple throbbed. He slumped in his chair, rubbing his head, not making eye contact with anyone. I asked Jesse a couple of other general questions about the database software while he unplugged the monitor, loaded it on a cart, and wheeled it away.

Nadler glanced toward Bear. "I know this doesn't look good. But I'm not stupid. If I had done it, I sure wouldn't have invited you back to find my ID printed in bold and highlighted for the world to see."

Bear: "Maybe."

Me: "I don't think you did it, Jim." I wasn't actually sure, but I watched the TV shows. If Bear played the bad cop role, I'd be the good cop. "Let's assume you were set up. Who could figure out your password?"

"No one. I'm an amateur lepidopterist. My passwords are Latin species names for some of my favorite butterflies."

Me: "Do you write them down? Most people do."

"I don't."

Bear: "Who knows your Appalachian ID number?"

"Everyone. It's printed on the phone list."

Bear: "Which means we're still at the uncrackable password."

"Are you going to arrest me because I don't write my passwords down? I know I had nothing to do with it, but it sure doesn't look convincing."

Me: "Didn't you say IT could take over anyone's computer?"

"Yes, remotely."

I pulled out the list with the three IT names. "Any of these people act weird? Ask you strange questions? Hang around your group or date anyone in your group?"

Nadler: "IT people are all weird. I know you're trying to help . . ."

The uncomfortable silence of a windless fog settled into the room.

Bear spoke first. "Remember what I said about no sudden trips, Mr. Nadler? Don't think about it. We have some work to do to corroborate your story, but right now things aren't looking real good. Don't do anything stupid. Okay?"

We left Nadler slouched in his chair, hands folded in his lap, his eyes unfocused.

◊◊◊

BEAR POURED A CUP OF coffee from a sheriff's office pot that smelled closer to asphalt than the Starbucks Nadler had provided. The envelope with the Vivian Kennedy fax sat on his chair, presumably so it would not be lost in the stacks of paper covering his desk. He removed the fax from the envelope, glanced briefly at it, and handed it to me.

The blown-up picture of a middle-aged blonde wearing a cocktail dress was probably from an overhead observation camera. She was playing craps and had thrown the dice, causing the picture to be a bit fuzzy. Her mouth appeared a bit large for her face. Genetics or too much lipstick? Her plucked eyebrows formed two narrow arches over eyes heavy with mascara. Her nose canted slightly off-center.

Five bracelets dangled on her left arm, and she wore a ring on her right hand, none on her left. She seemed familiar, but I was not placing her. Something bothered me. I let my eyes drift across the picture, hoping they'd focus on an inconsistency or quirk. My gaze shifted from the woman to a corner of the picture where a dark cape hung over a nearby chair. Attached to the cape was a white calla lily pin.

I snapped fingers on both hands, causing Bear to startle. Grinning like a kid who discovered his stocking didn't hold the coal his father had predicted, I handed Bear the picture. "Do you see who I see?"

He studied it, looked up at me, studied it some more, and finally mirrored my grin. "She's wearing a blond wig and a gallon of makeup. Who would have thunk it?"

We'd have to get answers at Appalachian. Time to find out about annuity fraud, Presser's murder, and the attempt on my life.

TWENTY-FIVE

WE ARRIVED TO FIND NADLER'S office dark. At Mimi Collier's cubicle, Bear cleared his throat, startling her.

"Mr. Nadler wasn't feeling well and left shortly after your visit. Did you forget something?" She shifted her weight to get up.

"I'm sorry Mr. Nadler isn't here," Bear said. "Maybe you could help us?" He pointed to Nadler's office.

Mimi flipped the office light switch and the fluorescents hummed to life. Nadler's office still contained three guest chairs. Bear pointed to the one farthest from the door for Mimi. He shut the door behind us, and we pulled the chairs into a circle for a nice chat. I noticed Mimi had her gecko pin on today.

Bear handed Mimi the fax. "Do you recognize this person?"

She looked at it, and with a flat, calm voice said, "I'm sorry, I don't believe I know her." With trembling hands, she tried to return the fax to Bear, who didn't take it.

Bear: "No? Vivian Kennedy—picture's from Vegas, a couple years old. You sure you don't recognize her? Look again."

She looked, but her eyes were unfocused. "No . . . No, I'm sure I've never seen her."

Bear rose and stood over her, pointing down to the picture. "Now look carefully here." He tapped the fax. "On the chair. The cape. The pin."

Her vision tracked Bear's finger to the calla lily. She looked like a fragile doll as his massive presence dominated her. She shook her head, tears welling in her eyes, but she said nothing.

Bear took the fax from her. "You know, I don't think it's a good picture of you. The blond wig isn't as attractive as your real hair."

Mimi sobbed.

Bear did the Miranda thing and asked if she wanted to continue talking here or if she'd prefer to go downtown.

Me: "If we talk here, everyone will go home and they won't see you in handcuffs."

The combination of a towering Bear, his reading the Miranda rights, and the prospect of doing a perp walk in front of her associates were, I think, too much for Mimi. A hardened criminal would have suspected we had nothing and toughed it out. Mimi's response was like a cork popping from a shaken bottle of champagne. With the pressure released, her answers rushed out.

"I knew it wouldn't last," she said. "I was afraid of this day."

Me: "Tell me about it. How did you start?"

"Herbert was dying and needed a lung transplant, but we didn't have that kind of money and our medical plan didn't cover it. I don't know how it occurred to me. I guess an annuitant died and I got to thinking about what would happen if I didn't report the death and kept the payments."

"Herbert?"

"My late husband."

Bear took notes while I continued the questioning.

"How did you set up the bank accounts?" I was curious since normally you need ID and must appear in person.

She hesitated. "Do I have to tell you this? Can't I just confess? It's all my fault."

"I'm sorry," I said as sympathetically as I could, "but you do."

"My sister-in-law works for a bank. I gave her the information and she did the rest. She wanted her brother to live as much as I did."

"Did Herbert get the operation?"

"The wait was usually six months to a year. He only made it to the fifth month."

"I'm sorry, Mimi. That must have been tough on you."

Bear broke in. "What's your sister-in-law's name?"

"Peggy Collier. She returned to her maiden name after her divorce." She nervously fingered her brooch. "It was hard to see my husband slowly suffocating on a ventilator. Very hard. I can't tell you how depressed I became. So was Peggy. When he died, we needed to get away and decided to have a fling in Vegas. We stayed for two weeks at the Sands, saw all the shows, and had a wonderful time."

I asked why she had chosen the Vivian Kennedy persona.

"We knew it was risky to set up the account in our own names. I had processed the paperwork on Vivian Kennedy and knew she was about my age. With her social security number, I got some fake ID. Peggy knew somebody in Vegas. With ID, it was simple to set up a real bank account, get a driver's license. They send you plenty of credit cards in the mail."

"You started this whole thing to pay for your husband's lung transplant. Why didn't you stop?"

"We were going to, but then another month's checks arrived, and we decided we'd do a quick weekend in Vegas. You know, just one more time? Except this time I lost more than I had. I don't know how it happened, but all of a sudden, I owed about ten grand. So we kept things going.

"Peggy had been living in a real dump. She thought maybe we could have Vivian get a decent place to live, and when I retired I could join her there. Herbert's illness pretty much wiped out our savings. I guess we weren't very strong. One thing led to another, and . . ."

I let her collect herself before I continued. "Mimi, who else was in this with you?"

"No one besides Peggy and me."

"Mr. Nadler didn't know?"

"Why would he? Nobody figured out what we were doing."

"How'd you fix things at Appalachian? Didn't you need an accomplice?"

She sat up straight. "No, I figured it out myself. I couldn't have done it before the layoffs. Now it only takes one person to change the files, and there are no random follow-up reviews like we used to have. All in the name of efficiency." She gave a barking, contemptuous laugh. Fire briefly shone in her eyes but, like the laugh, was short-lived.

"How'd you game the system?"

"I already opened all the department mail. I started handling all single life annuitant deaths. They have no death benefits, see? So I wasn't stealing from anyone. I hid the paperwork, called Peggy, and gave her the name and social security number."

"So she could set up the bank account?"

"Yeah. Then I changed the payment system to direct deposit into the account Peggy set up. I changed the address to one of those private post offices. That way no one got the tax forms and stuff Appalachian sends out each year."

"You stole Nadler's password?"

Her face wrinkled in confusion.

"How did you arrange to have it appear that Mr. Nadler signed off on the changes?"

"You mean supervisor approval? I tried to steal people's passwords, but no one wrote them down 'cause IT made a big stink about that. One day, I realized I could sit at Mr. Nadler's desk while he was at lunch or in a long meeting. He never turns off his computer before he leaves. The Dilbert screensaver disappears with a space bar, so I just approved everything using his machine."

"What tipped you off that someone had started to figure it out?"

"Mr. Presser asked some questions and I wondered. But he died and that seemed the end of it. Until today."

"Who got the contract on Samuel Presser's life? You? Or Peggy, with her Las Vegas contacts?"

"What?" She sprang to her feet, knocking over the chair. "What are you saying? We never hired anyone to hurt Mr. Presser. Peggy didn't even know him. How could you ask such a thing? How could you even think such a thing?"

I could smell her fear. Her blouse had stained under her arms. "You expect me to believe that? You and Peggy steal gobs of money and this kid from Cincinnati starts asking questions about people whose annuity payments you were collecting. Presser sets up a meeting with Nadler to discuss a problem. You handle Nadler's calendar, so you know about it. Presser was going to blow the lid off your deal. So you made sure he didn't get to the meeting. Makes perfect sense."

"Perfect sense? You think I murdered someone and that makes perfect sense?" She was yelling loudly enough I wondered if people outside the office could hear her. "That's crazy! I may have taken some money, but I've never hurt anyone in my whole life. I don't know what you're insinuating, but I think you owe me an apology." She glared at me, an insulted Scarlett O'Hara.

At the silence, Bear looked up from his notes. I smiled at her and counted to ten.

"Mimi, please sit down. I'd love to believe you. Detective Wright would love to believe you. Look at me. Pretty sorry-looking, right? This is what happens to real people when you ask guys with broken noses to make a problem go away. I lived. Presser died. You tell me no one else knew? No one else benefited from your scheme? Who else would want to kill Samuel Presser?"

She righted the chair and collapsed onto it. Her chest heaved. I grabbed some tissues from the top of Nadler's file cabinet and handed them to her.

"Mimi, I think your scam was brilliant. Illegal, but really slick. Ohio's a capital punishment state. Detective Wright will find the link between you and the person who actually killed Presser, like we figured this out. Cooperate and he speaks a good word to the prosecutors, and you end up with jail time. I think it's barbaric, but if you don't help, they'll ask for your head."

Bear: "Now Seamus, calm down here. Maybe it's not as bad as that. Though I'm not saying yet it isn't, because, Mrs. Collier, it sure looks like you're the only one who had motive, and that's what juries look for. If someone's got a motive—and you have Las Vegas connections—getting a hitman—"

"You have to believe me. I never hurt anyone. I don't know why anyone would want to kill Mr. Presser, but you have to believe me. I did not do it. I didn't have anything to do with hurting you either, Mr. McCree. You two have got to believe me." She held her bowed head in both hands.

Bear nodded for me to continue.

Time for a different tack. "Let's forget about Presser for a second. Let's look at what happened to me."

She wiped her eyes and blew her nose.

"When did you tell Joe Fourier I was asking questions?"

She slowly shook her head. "I don't know any Joe Fourier. I left Mr. Nadler a note—just like you told me to."

"Who knew I was staying in Chillicothe Monday night? Detective Wright—he suggested it. You—I asked you to leave Mr. Nadler a note. Who else, Mimi? Is there someone else at Appalachian who doesn't want me snooping around? What about Mr. Nadler? He got your note."

"He didn't even get back to the office that night."

"How do you know?"

"He went straight home. And . . . And he called me on his cell phone sometime after five. He'd just left the meeting."

"You talked with him?"

"Voicemail gives you the time of the message."

"But you don't know he called from Cleveland?"

"Mr. Nadler would never do anything like that. Why would he? He's already rich."

"Not you. Not Jim Nadler. Who else knew? Who did you tell?"

"No one. I wrote up the note and put it on Mr. Nadler's desk. People are forever in and out of his office . . . the clerks . . . Mr. Olson and Mr. Snyder came down shortly before I left to find out if I had heard anything from Mr. Nadler yet about the client meeting . . . lots of people."

"Could any of the other clerks have the same scheme going?"

"No way. It would have to be a supervisor to get approval."

"Why? You aren't one."

"But I'd notice if someone else was using Mr. Nadler's office. It was only money, not worth killing for."

Talk about naive.

◊◊◊

ONCE BEAR'S BACKUP ARRIVED TO help transport Mimi Collier to the hoosegow, I split and cabbed over to Charlene's. The note on her kitchen table told me she was out with friends for dinner and bingo. Going out for dinner was too much hassle. I scrounged a couple of yogurts from Charlene's refrigerator and took them and a can of beer into the living room, where I settled into the stuffed chair I was beginning to think of as mine.

Note to self: after yogurt, beer tastes bitter. I was glad Paddy wasn't observing my version of a vegetarian diet.

I should have been celebrating a major success, but instead I twitched to make progress on three major issues: Presser's death, the botulism murders, and someone trying to kill me—related to the botulism murders, but deserving its own column.

Mimi Collier had mostly convinced me that she knew nothing of Presser's murder. I hadn't met her sister-in-law, Peggy Collier. Maybe Mimi had told Peggy that Presser was sniffing around, and Peggy hired out the hit without involving Mimi. Peggy *was* the one with Las Vegas contacts. But if not Peggy, then who and why?

The timing between Presser informing Appalachian he had issues to discuss and his murder seemed suspiciously close for coincidence. But coincidences do happen, and Lt. Hastings' postulated dyslexic hitman was still a possibility. I hated that idea.

The question is what can I do now? Ask Ingstram to check on the Collier sisters and look deeper at the Vivian Kennedy persona? The mantel clock had already sounded its tinny chime eight times, which meant it was after one a.m. in England. Tomorrow, then, as soon as I awoke. I noted on the pad to have Bear subpoena Vivian Kennedy's bank and credit card records to pin down exactly how much the Colliers had skimmed from Appalachian and where they spent their money. We'd need their personal finances as well. Hitmen do not take credit cards. If they'd hired a killer for Presser, somewhere there would be an unexplained cash withdrawal or purchase of diamonds or gold coins—something that wouldn't otherwise add up.

If Presser's death connected with Appalachian, and if Mimi and Peggy weren't responsible for the hitman, who was? If Mimi Collier had figured out the security hole, maybe someone else had spotted and copied her plan? Grasping at that straw, I added digging up information about the other people who could approve changes on the annuitant system to Ingstram's list.

What if a higher-up had stumbled onto Mimi Collier's swindle? If that person set up a similar scheme, they wouldn't want hers revealed because it might point to the new one. Could Nadler be involved, and would that mean Mimi was covering for him? Oh wait, that probably wouldn't work because Presser would have detailed more unexpected actuarial losses, and nothing in his notes indicated that.

I went to cross that possibility off the list, but stopped—it could have been recent and not shown up in Presser's study. *What a flipping maze.*

How about someone adding annuitants into the system? No way Presser could discover that, and maybe it didn't require supervisor approval. While adding a bunch of annuitants, a clerk could slip in a few extras and direct the payments. Did Appalachian have procedures to discover that?

If only I could look through Appalachian's financial records. Could we convince a court to allow such an expansive fishing trip? Probably not.

Bear could get a court order for the annuity records, but what if the other swindle wasn't in annuities? Maybe I could get Nadler to provide the information on the sly, or maybe the president would give his permission. I added it to the list without yet deciding how to go about it.

Now the botulism murders. The most likely scenario was that the delivery person with the Celtic cross introduced the bacteria. Probably the same person had killed Chillicothe Machine's former CEO. The link was the company. Who wanted to hurt the company?

Competitors, but the Chillicothe Machine incidents appeared unique in terms of the Japanese parent's situation. And I had no clue how to approach that possibility.

Deb Holt? She was upset with Chillicothe Machine and its takeover by the Japanese. Upset enough she'd kill her own union retirees to stir up the union? She didn't seem crazy; but crazy people often don't. On the day my Expedition blew up, she had seen me at Sue's with Bear. I added her to Ingstram's check-up list.

To my surprise, I found myself writing on my pad outside on the stoop. How had that happened? I must have gotten up to think. Across the street two kids chased fireflies in their yard. The katydids were cranking up for their nightly performance. Hard to believe so much nastiness was going on in such a quiet city. No stars tonight and it smelled like rain was coming.

Who was Eduardo Solonini, presumed dead for the last ten years? And how was the local loser, Thomas Moyer, involved? More names for Ingstram's list. Where was Joe Fourier?

I still had a nagging thought that something bigger was happening in Chillicothe—something linking Appalachian to the botulism murders. But what? Who?

Chip Kincaid? He did business with both Chillicothe Machine and Appalachian. I met him with Appalachian's finance and marketing guy, Olson, pitching retiree medical to Chillicothe Machine's CEO. He'd had a couple of scrapes with the insurance regulators, but I couldn't see any significant advantage to him from the botulism deaths.

Was I the only link between Presser's murder and the botulism attack?

Jeez, almost nine o'clock. Before it got any later, I wanted to make sure several folks heard of the Colliers' arrests from me rather than being surprised by the news. I used the new cell phone I had picked up earlier in the day.

I told Paddy we had exposed Vivian Kennedy and filled him in on the details. He was delighted his illicit information had helped solve the crime, and we nearly butted heads again on hacking, but both pulled back in time. The more I talked with Paddy about who had tried to do me in, the more I decided it must have been a Chillicothe local. Maybe by dumb bad luck someone connected with the botulism murders had seen me poking around Monday and decided I was getting too close to something.

"I'm uncomfortable about how safe our house is," I said.

"But if it's a local Chillicothe person," he said, "and they know you're still in Chillicothe, then being in Cincy is completely safe, at least until you come home. When *are* you coming home?"

"Maybe for the weekend? We'll talk before I leave here."

Paddy gave me Skyler Weaver's phone number. I pictured her hollow black eyes and, as the phone rang, worried how much I should tell her. What would be helpful and what would cause her more worry?

"How are you?" I asked to ease into the conversation.

"We missed you at choir practice," she said. "You know the piece, will you sing on Sunday?"

Oh yes, there was life outside of Chillicothe.

I told her we'd discovered the what and who behind the abnormalities Samuel had uncovered at Appalachian, but said it was premature to know if a connection existed between Samuel's murder and the embezzlement. Hopefully, we'd have more information soon, but no promises. I did not tell her about my mishaps and deflected her attempts to speculate. Time would tell.

Lt. Hastings was not in—no surprise this late. I kept my message short: I'd uncovered monetary theft, identity theft, fraud, tax evasion, and probably a bunch of federal banking crimes, but didn't have anything I could give her on the Presser murder.

Inside, Charlene's phone rang. I hurried to the kitchen. What the hell was her last name again? Well, never mind. "Charlene's residence, how may I help you?"

"Bear here. Mimi Collier and her lawyer are cooperating. Nevada State Police picked up Peggy Collier. Their two stories materially match, except each claims credit for the initial idea and says we should let the other one go. Makes you wanna cry."

"But nothing on Presser's murder?"

"I figure someone else for Presser."

"My conclusion exactly. We need to get a court order for all the banking records, and—"

"The Colliers kept immaculate records. When the Nevada troopers arrested Peggy Collier at Vivian Kennedy's townhouse, she showed them detailed banking records for Vivian Kennedy and documentation for each of the affected Appalachian annuitants. They even had a tickler file to remind Mimi when to change the Appalachian records from living to dead. The Nevada police will look through everything over the next couple of days. Got Vivian Kennedy's credit card records, too."

"Excellent. If they need help, I could fly out to—"

"Patience, Seamus, patience. They're fully capable and will get back to us. We'll need to work out who gets the Colliers first, assuming they plead guilty. The feds are going to want a piece of this as well. Sorting out jurisdiction takes time."

I found myself pacing around the kitchen. "Whatever. Any news on Moyer? Anything else on the Solonini guy?

"I'd tell you if we had—"

"I thought in all the excitement . . ."

He took a deep breath. "Didn't we just talk about patience? Look, thanks to you, we cracked a major fraud that no one knew anything about. We have that totally under control. You need to back off and let us do our job."

"Do I at least get to be there when you inform Appalachian?"

"I suppose you've earned that. I plan to meet Nadler first thing in the morning. I'll pick you up at Charlene's at, say, a quarter to nine. Now, I've still got work to do."

In other words, thanks for your help, Seamus, but we professionals are in charge now. *Don't call us, we'll call you.* As he had with the search for Moyer and Solonini, the guys who'd tried to blow me up, I figured he would freeze me out of anything else on the Colliers.

My mother would disapprove of making calls after ten p.m. I wouldn't tell her.

"Molly, this is Seamus McCree. You free tomorrow? I have a bit of news to share and maybe the two of us can do a little sleuthing."

"I've got time now," she said.

"Sorry, but it has to be tomorrow.

"I'm supposed to take Jeff to the Columbus airport in the morning. Do I need to find him a ride or can this wait until the afternoon?"

Given my morning meeting with Appalachian, we agreed on Sue's Home Cooking for a late lunch. I planned to introduce Molly to Charlene, guaranteeing Bear would soon hear that I had met with Molly. The next move would be up to him.

TWENTY-SIX

HE DROVE PAST MCCREE'S PLACE on McAlpin, comparing on the ground what he had anticipated from the Internet's satellite and walk-the-street views. The houses were grouped close together, which was not ideal, but the target's redbrick Victorian sat across the street from the Rawson Woods Bird Preserve—open to the public by appointment only, ha ha. That naturally wild area ran into Edgewood Grove Park, which bordered Mt. Storm Park. Behind the house was a bit of a wooded ravine. All those trees were favorable. Very favorable indeed.

He found off-street parking in a grouping of apartment buildings near McAlpin's intersection with Lafayette. Backing the rental between two parked cars, he waited for a passing car before he got out and slipped across the street and into the woods. He waited for his eyes to adjust to the starless night. The air carried a hint of peppermint—he guessed it was from the Mill Creek Valley. He could feel the air's moisture on his face. The weatherman was right: there would be rain tomorrow. Nearby, small animals skittered across the leaf mold. The yips of coyotes elicited the hoots of a great horned owl. Those natural sounds made it unlikely anyone else was in the woods that night.

Pupils now fully dilated, he moved deeper into the woods, placing his steps to avoid any sticks that would snap loudly. Once he was far enough in to be invisible, he flipped the red filter on his headlamp into position and engaged the LEDs. A deer startled at his appearance and crashed away through the woods. Before long he was sitting high in an ancient blue ash tree with a clear view of McCree's place.

A couple hours later—he didn't bother consulting his watch—the lights in the house clicked off one by one. He had spotted only one person inside, but did not get a good look. Others might be around; impossible to be certain. A well-worn Civic sat in the driveway. Were the subject's registered vehicles, an Expedition and an Infiniti, parked in the garage?

He'd wait an hour and make his move.

TWENTY-SEVEN

IN NADLER'S OFFICE, I LET Bear lay out the story.

"You can knock me over with a feather," Nadler said. "Who would have guessed Mimi was a thief? Never showed money around here. The only thing she splurged on was her brooch collection."

"It appears they spent most of the money around Las Vegas," Bear said.

"I knew she visited a sister-in-law out there somewhere, but I never . . ."

Bear leaned in and Nadler physically shrank back. "We'd like your help figuring out if something else funny is going on."

"Funny?"

"Seamus doesn't think Mimi is the one who had Presser killed. He also doesn't think she had anything to do with his 'accident' on Monday. Does that make sense to you?"

"Yes, I guess . . . well, no, not really."

"Right, me too. I can see Seamus's point, but I can't figure out what someone else's motive might be. You know?"

"You don't think I was involved?"

"Were you?"

"Absolutely not!"

His reaction convinced me he had been shocked by Mimi's scheme. "You have to inform the state insurance department?" I asked.

"After I tell the executive committee and probably the board."

"And," I said, "the department is going to want to review your records with a fine-tooth comb. Can we look at them first?"

"That flushing sound you hear is my career going down the toilet. To let something like this happen on my watch . . ."

Bear gave me a little shoulder shrug and a hand signal seeming to say, *All yours, bud. Let's see what you can get.*

"Jim, those records could help solve a murder."

Nadler mumbled into his chest. "I should call an emergency executive committee meeting. I'll need to offer my resignation. I've got to cancel my crew for the regatta tonight."

I raised my voice enough to get Nadler's attention "Access to the records?"

"I have to ask Snyder. I don't know if he'll approve anything like that without the executive committee's input. You have anything else to ruin my life?"

Bear stood, casting a shadow on Nadler. "McCree and I will be available until Sheriff Lyons' eleven thirty press conference. I'd like for him to be able to report that Appalachian Casualty and Life is fully cooperating with the police. Think about it."

◊◊◊

SPRITZ FROM GRUMPY CLOUDS GREETED our exit from Appalachian. Bear waited until I had my seatbelt on before turning the key in the ignition. "I have stuff to do before the sheriff does his thing," he said. "How about I drop you off at Charlene's. That way you can pack up for your trip home and meet me at my office before the news conference. Think Nadler will get us access to the accounts?"

I wiped my glasses off on my shirttail. I got it: they wanted me as window dressing for Lyons' press conference and then I'd be dismissed. Now was not the time to tell them that their plans and my plans were not the same. "Nope. Might as well get your court order. Does the sheriff have any contacts with the state insurance agency, or whatever they're called?"

"No clue."

We pulled into Charlene's driveway. A flash of lightning had me counting one-one-thousand, two-one-thousand. At six-one-thousand, the thunder rattled the car. "Gonna be a big one. Call if you hear from Nadler or Nevada."

Bear faced me. "You're giving up too easy. What's up?"

◊◊◊

CHARLENE SPOTTED ME BEFORE I had my second drenched foot inside the entrance to Sue's Home Cooking. "Bear joining you?"

"Not this time. I'm meeting someone else. Maybe you know her, Molly Fitzhugh?"

Her headshake indicated she was not familiar with the name.

"Thanks for putting me up—and putting up with me." I slipped her a folded wad of bills to cover three nights' stay, and extra for the food and phone calls, rounded up to the next hundred bucks. This would be an interesting expense account.

She shoved the money into her pocket without looking at it and escorted me to what I recognized as Bear's booth. Without asking she brought a Dr Pepper.

"I'll wait to order," I said. "Did you add a Noah's Ark special to the menu?"

"You could try the Trucker's Dinner. It's got enough calories to last you forty days and forty nights. Did you come from the big news conference? We watched the little portable in the kitchen."

"Left that for Bear. Any surprises?"

"You guys didn't tell me they stole millions. Apparently the insurance department has opened an investigation." She looked toward the front. "Your date? Pretty, but a little young, isn't she?"

Molly was shaking off a dripping umbrella. Her cutoff tank top revealed a toned midriff. I waved her over. As she settled in I asked, "Jeff get off okay?"

"Right before the storm blew in. Security was a nightmare. You never know with all the new routines they keep thinking up."

Charlene interrupted, "You want a minute for the menus?"

"I know what I want," Molly said. "BLT on light toast and water. Thanks." She flashed a smile at Charlene.

"And I'll have the chicken pot pie special."

Charlene jotted on her pad and headed toward the kitchen.

"What's up? I could hardly sleep last night. And no, it didn't have anything to do with it being my last night with Jeff for a while. I can read that smile."

I laughed. I hadn't realized I was that transparent. She had not caught the press conference or the news summary. During lunch, I filled her in on the goings-on at Appalachian and the double life of Mimi Collier. She hardly said a word until I finished the tale.

"How's this fit with someone trying to blow you up?"

"No clue. If we could find Thomas Moyer or Eduardo Solonini or even Joe Fourier, we might understand the link." I bent forward and lowered my voice. "You game for a little extracurricular activity, which may not be entirely kosher?"

Molly leaned in close enough our heads nearly knocked. "Like what?"

"The cops have stopped by Moyer's place a couple of times and not found anyone home. Wright and I were going to visit yesterday, but with the Collier excitement, that didn't happen. I thought Moyer's garage might happen to be open, and if his car is there we could see what kind of tires he has. Or something like that."

"I assume Detective Wright doesn't know about this?"

"Charlene and he talk regularly. I'm guessing he'll soon know we met."

"Why? Are they like . . . an item?"

"They should be, but they're stuck in the past—a story for another time."

We agreed to take her truck since parking my car in front of Thomas Moyer's place might be asking for one of Ross County's finest to investigate.

The truck was old, but with surprisingly little rust. There were no running boards so I had to hoist myself into the cab and plop onto the cracked bench seat. A small fissure graced the windshield in front of me. A hole in the dash outlined where the radio should have been and behind the seat was a locked gun rack with a rifle and shotgun.

"Your truck?"

"Granddad's. Used it mostly on the farm for hunting and stuff. Grammy let me bring it up here to have some wheels."

Neither of us had a detailed map of the area. We found one at a drugstore, where we also purchased two pairs of cheap work gloves.

Moyer's street was one of a whole neighborhood that had seen better days. At my direction, Molly parked in the driveway. We didn't want neighbors to think we were sneaking around. We jogged to the front stoop and mounted the concrete steps, being careful not to touch the wrought iron railing, which was so rusty it would have trouble supporting a butterfly. Huddling under a narrow overhang, we looked in the side window. Dark. The doorbell sported a hand-lettered piece of duct tape reading "Knock." We did—several times—no answer.

I opened the mail slot in the door with my car keys and peered in. A pyramid of mail covered the floor. I caught a whiff of something rank. The A/C clearly was not on.

We eased off the stoop and quick-walked to the attached one-car garage, stepping around the lake forming at the end of the downspout. Locked. Squishing around the side, we found a window painted black and nailed shut. We slipped into the postage-stamp backyard.

I handed Molly a pair of gloves and pulled on mine. Good fortune smiled upon us in the form of an unlocked back door to the garage. From inside, the rain pounding on the roof sounded like a muffled snare drum. With the solitary window painted black, and with the sky nearly as dark, light from the rear door was insufficient to determine if Moyer had a mat on which we could wipe our shoes. I flicked the light switch. A miniature sun flared from a dangling bare bulb.

No doormat. A battered 1980s Toyota Corolla—rust held together by a lack of ambition to crumble—occupied most of the garage.

"Check the tires," I said, "and see if they match the pattern you saw at the Crossing. I doubt it. If this heap had been out there, we would've seen some pieces, what with the bumps in the road."

Molly inspected the left rear tread. "No way. This one's bald." She looked at the others. "These neither. The ones at the Crossing had more tread."

The garage was a sty. Old batteries filled one corner. A broken stepladder, tools, curtain rods, cinder blocks, and trash I had no desire to touch cluttered nooks and crannies. A pair of muddy work boots sat by the cement steps into the house.

Molly touched my arm lightly and pointed to the boots. "What do you see, Seamus?"

"They're muddy and left by the back door."

She walked to the boots, pointing. "Right, but look at the boots. What do you see?"

"They're small . . ."

"And worn down on the outside of the tread. He's the one. He's the guy who set the land mine at the Crossing."

At my touch to check the door, it cracked open, but I had to force it with my right shoulder to slip through. Even though I used my right shoulder, the impact sent a spasm of pain radiating down my left side. I was getting tired of feeling sore.

The unmistakable smell of decaying animal met me.

"I think I know why no one has seen Moyer. Stay here, Molly. I'll be right back."

I squeezed through the door, pushing against towels stuffed into the door crack. Dishes overflowed the sink in the small kitchen. A thin layer of grease and dirt preserved every surface. An open jar of peanut butter with a bread knife sticking in it sat on the counter next to a half-eaten chocolate pudding with a spoon lying nearby. A line of ants bustled from the window across the sink to the pudding.

The eat-in kitchen table had two chairs, one tucked neatly underneath and the other pulled out as though someone had only moments before arisen. A half-filled coffee mug sat where a righty would have placed it.

A narrow hallway led to the front door with the pile of mail in front of it. To the left was a living room; to the right, a staircase to the second floor. I walked toward the pile of mail by the front door and heard footsteps behind me.

"I thought I told you to stay out."

"No way I'm staying in that garage by myself."

"Just go to the truck, will you? I shouldn't be here and you *really* shouldn't be here."

"Where you go, I go."

Here I am, breaking every rule in the book, and I've brought someone who doesn't even know what the rules are. "All right. Don't touch anything. We're screwing up evidence by walking in here. We're dripping water everywhere. They're going to know someone was here. Follow exactly in my footsteps. Let's go."

We'd been whispering. I suppose we already knew we were in a morgue. The body was sprawled facedown on the living room floor, a bloody hole in the rear of his skull. Blood and tissue splattered the opposite wall. Congealed blood stained the yellow-orange shag carpet. Molly gagged and I backed us out pronto. Three or four days in the August heat were sufficient to accelerate the decomposition process.

Molly held it together and followed me out. We closed the garage door behind us, leaving it unlatched, and hustled around the house and into Molly's truck. I gulped fresh air while Molly grabbed the steering wheel with both hands and did the same.

Once Molly recovered, she drove to the highway and found a pay phone at a convenience store. She put on gloves, dialed 911, reported a murder at Moyer's address, disconnected before the police officer could ask any questions, and drove off.

"You like bowling, Seamus?"

"Been years since my son and I last went. Why?"

"I was thinking of a place that serves drinks, where we can talk without being overheard, and where I can get rid of some anger."

"Not a place I would have thought of, but sure. I'm still kind of stiff."

"Worried I'll beat you?"

"We need to ditch these gloves. Is there a Goodwill box around?"

Molly executed a U-turn, and after dumping the gloves, remained on secondary streets to a bowling alley near the Christopher Inn. She waited for traffic to clear and hung a left into an underused parking lot.

The lady behind the counter had a bowling shirt with "Jocko" embroidered above her ample chest. A local garage and towing service advertised on her substantial back. She reeked of cigarette smoke, and I wondered if she smoked outside or had a secret spot inside.

We gave Jocko our shoe sizes and received our red-and-white bowling shoes as a trade for our own. She assigned us to lane six, which was close to the bar and away from the only other bowlers, a group of high school kids.

We put on our shoes and left our stuff at our assigned lane while we scouted for balls. We met at the bar with our chosen weapons. I paid for a draft beer and Molly's Seven and Seven on the rocks while she and Jocko smoked outside.

When Molly finally returned to the lane, I insisted she bowl first since I needed to recover from lugging the bowling balls and the drinks from the bar.

"You just want the advantage of going last. It won't matter."

She used a smooth three-step delivery to release the ball, then followed through and held her position like a Greek statue. Transfixed by her pose, I thought Jeff was a lucky guy, and I was glad we weren't playing for money. Her ball hit the floor with a thump, curved into the pocket; ten pins lifted and fell together in a solid strike.

"You're up. Don't let the pressure get you."

Which, of course, it did. I pulled the ball past the head pin to the Brooklyn side, clearing off half the pins. On my second shot, I hit the head pin, but left the five pin standing.

Molly had drained half her drink.

"You okay?" I asked. "Wish you hadn't gone with me?"

"I was thinking about Granddad. Wondering if Moyer had helped kill him. Thinking maybe Moyer got what he deserved, or maybe he got off too easily."

She bowled her second frame: nine pins and a pickup. She was up eleven pins in the first and had already marked in the second. "Do you think he had something to do with the botulism killings?"

"I don't know, Molly. No one described anyone like him at the picnic or around the caterer. So far the only clue we have is one suspicious event at the caterer's, which involved a person much younger than Moyer."

I managed a spare. Molly applauded my success.

"I know I asked you this before," she said, "but do you have any idea why someone might have wanted to kill all those people at the picnic?"

"Not really. You?"

"Maybe someone only wanted to kill one person, and there were a lot of extra people who got hurt just to cover up who was the intended victim. Or maybe it's a local crazy who decided to make their own terrorist attack."

"Those types like to claim credit or threaten more mayhem. Hasn't happened."

"Okay, so not a local crazy."

"Deb Holt—you know her?"

"She's big in the union, right? I remember Granddad talking about her."

"Right. She thinks the Japanese are responsible, either to break the union or reduce their retiree medical costs."

"But you don't?"

"It's possible. Hell, anything's possible. The Japanese don't necessarily like the union, but they have them in Japan, and they don't go around trying to exterminate the members. No, I don't think it's union busting."

"Besides," Molly said, "Chillicothe Machine's retiree medical costs must have skyrocketed with all the expenses. I know what it's costing for Grammy. Although a lot isn't covered by the medical plan."

"Actually, the insurance company's the one getting hammered. In the end, Chillicothe Machine will have lower costs because there are fewer retirees."

"But you're still not buying it?"

"The company's making decent money and we're talking a huge conglomerate. The retiree medical savings aren't enough to make killing all those people worthwhile."

I was behind twenty-four pins in the sixth frame and needed some luck in a hurry.

"Molly, what did your granddad do at Chillicothe Machine?"

"He was a foreman on one of their lines. He retired with an unreduced eighty-five point pension at age fifty-five."

"Eighty-five point pension?"

"Granddad explained it to me. He was trying to convince me to get a union job because of the benefits. Their pension plan provides for a full pension if you're at least fifty-five and your age and service totals at least eighty-five years. No reduction for retiring before sixty-five. Actually, they provide a supplement until age sixty-two, when social security kicks in. Of course, Granddad had been retired for close to twenty years."

With strikes by me in both the eighth and ninth frames, our scores were close. The tenth frame would be the decider. A familiar twitch in my brain indicated I was close to putting something together. What was it?

Molly finished with a 172.

I needed a strong spare followed by a big pin count to catch her. I scored nine on the first ball, with the eight pin rocking, but refusing to fall. I cleared my mind and visualized my ball rolling inevitably into the eight pin, clearing the alley. I utilized my standard seven-step approach and laid the ball down on its mark. The eight pin disappeared with a satisfying *thwump*.

The pins automatically racked and settled on the floor. I needed eight to win. Seven would tie. Two deep breaths steadied me and cleared my mind. Taking a smooth approach, I laid the ball on my mark. With the ball's release, my mind sent a flash of understanding, aborting my follow-through. The ball slipped to the right and clipped three pins—a 168.

Molly whooped and hollered. I didn't care. I had a theory to check out with an insurance broker.

TWENTY-EIGHT

KINCAID WAS IN. HIS ASSISTANT ushered us into his office. "Seamus McCree, how are you, buddy? And who's the lovely lady?"

This time his handshake was firm, but not overly so. I introduced Molly, and we all sat down in the stargazer-perfumed office.

"Chip," I said. "I'm trying to remember something you told me about Chillicothe Machine. Did you get the medical contract changed yet?"

He put on a frowny face. "It's such an obvious move, but they're taking their sweet time. These days, large contracts need to go to Japan for approval. I'm just twiddling my thumbs."

"Too bad. Did you tell me the last new business you had with Chillicothe Machine was to help them terminate their pension plan?"

He pulled at his ear. "Terminate . . . no. Some Columbus consulting firm did the actual plan termination. That was for the nonunion plan. I helped them buy annuities for both union and nonunion retirees. There a problem?"

Why was Kincaid always asking about problems? "And they bought annuities from Appalachian Casualty and Life?"

"Yeah, good memory. I guess you heard about that broad . . . Oh, sorry, miss—that woman who stole all the money from Appalachian, huh? No worry. Annuities are insured by the state if they can't cover them."

He blathered some more, but I was already heading in a different direction.

◊◊◊

WE WALKED TO MOLLY'S TRUCK in silence. She didn't crank the ignition. "What was that about?"

"We've been trying to figure out who benefited from the picnic. If people die sooner than expected, their pensions pay less than expected, and whoever issued the annuities gets the windfall. Insurance companies call it an actuarial gain. What if someone poisoned the food at the picnic because they wanted to create a profit from those early deaths?"

"So not Chillicothe Machine." She raised her view to the roof. "Appalachian Casualty and Life?"

"Exactly. And let's say someone heard a few days after the fatal picnic that Presser was coming to discuss something disturbing about Appalachian's annuity business."

"But that was about the Colliers stealing money."

"We don't think anyone at Appalachian knew why Presser set up the meeting. Mimi Collier feared it was about her, but she didn't know. It's possible the person responsible for the botulism murders heard about the meeting, figured Presser had stumbled onto them, and had Presser killed. Then they tried to kill me because I showed up in Chillicothe asking questions about both Presser and botulism."

"I see what you're saying. Where to now?"

"Let's pick up my car. I need to be in Cincy for the weekend and get out of the way of the sheriff's department for a little bit."

"You coming back?" She keyed the ignition and the truck rumbled to life.

"Count on it. I'm waiting on more research from CIG and I need the Ross County Sheriff's Office to do their forensic work on Moyer. There's a time to push and a time to appear to back off. That's what I want to do now."

She pulled from the parking lot onto the street. "Appear to back off?"

"I want whoever is behind this to forget about me and concentrate on what the insurance investigators will uncover. I want him to worry about what the cops will find out about Thomas Moyer. I want to be the least of his problems."

"But you're not giving up, are you?"

"In war, direct attacks on a fortified enemy don't usually work. Great generals win through a combination of indirect action and superior intelligence. I don't mean by being smarter, I mean by having a greater understanding of the other side's position."

"I'm being dense. Meaning what?"

"If I'm right about this, our bad guy strikes out without knowing all the facts. Presser was murdered for finding out something about Appalachian Casualty and Life. What Presser knew wasn't really a danger to the murderer, only to the Colliers. The attempt on me had to be pretty spur of the moment. And Moyer is dead. This guy's solution is to clean up loose ends by killing them."

"You sure you're not just trying to avoid getting killed?"

I chuckled. "That is an important side benefit of my strategy. My plan is to allow the cops to do a frontal assault to find Moyer's murderer. It will be great if they succeed. Meanwhile, shunted-to-the-side Seamus will be digging up more info about this Solonini guy. He managed to fake his death ten years ago. Is he still mobbed up? How can we get him to trip himself up?"

"Got it. What can I do?"

"Right now, nothing. I promise I'll keep you informed. I have a feeling we'll be seeing each other soon."

Traffic caused her to wait to turn into the Sue's Home Cooking parking lot. She pointed to my car. "What's wrong?" Molly scooted across the highway through a gap in the oncoming traffic.

My car had two pancaked tires on the right side. A piece of notebook paper wrapped in clear plastic stuck out from the gap between the passenger door and the frame. Without unwrapping it, I could read the felt-tip pen block letters: "DON'T COME BACK. NEXT TIME THE HOLES ARE IN YOU."

"Why are you laughing?" Molly asked.

I read her the note. "How do they expect me to leave town if they disable my vehicle? Points off the exam for not thinking this through." A quick inspection confirmed slit sidewalls had ruined the tires.

Molly frowned. "You don't seem to be taking it too hard. I'd be madder than all hell."

"This plays right into the plan. This asshole's gonna think he's driven me off. Plus, now I know for sure someone else is involved. Guess I need to get this baby towed. Know anyone?"

"Jocko's shirt advertised Fred's Garage and Towing."

One of the reasons I've liked smaller cities and towns is their phone books don't grow legs and walk away from pay phones. Fred's number was in the directory sitting next to the phone in Sue's Home Cooking. While I waited for the hook, I left a message for Bear about the note and slashed tires and asked him to meet me at the nearby tire center. If he was tied up, I'd drop the note off before I headed home.

Considering our extracurricular activities earlier in the day, I thought it would be better if Molly vamoosed before I met Bear again. She parted with a "Keep in touch."

I pitied the guy with the tow truck having to work in the pouring rain, but he was quick. He exchanged the one good front tire for the flat rear, winched the front off the ground, and hauled the car to the tire store. They took less than an hour to fix me up. Bear hadn't shown—I figured he was probably at the Moyer murder site.

Holding the still-wrapped note with tweezers from my Swiss Army knife, I delivered it to Ross County sheriff headquarters. A deputy placed it into an evidence bag and insisted I file a report. I humored him, even though as far as I was concerned we were wasting time. I planned for the vandal to go down for crimes a lot worse than slashing tires and leaving threatening notes.

◊◊◊

I COULDN'T WAIT TO GET home. I felt the same anticipatory excitement as I did for the first snow. Cranking the volume on the local oldies station, I belted harmony all the way home. Too bad not all the songs had the same rhythm as the slapping windshield wipers.

Paddy greeted me at the door with a "Gee, Dad, you look really ugly. I hope it's not hereditary."

I shed my soaked coat in the entryway and, pretending I was going to ignore his dig, bent down to untie my equally soaked shoes. Then I popped up into a boxer's stance, causing Cheech and Chong to scatter. Putting a rasp in my voice, I said, "It might be if you keep it up."

Paddy rolled his eyes. "Got me scared. Because I wasn't sure when you'd get home, I made us big salads."

Over dinner salads, accompanied by a glass of wine for me and an illegal beer for him, I brought him up to date, leaving out my exploration of Moyer's house with Molly.

"Is Ingstram Ravel going to find anything useful?"

"We'll see. Sometimes the most inconsequential-seeming things end up being key. I can hope, but I really need to look at Appalachian's computer systems and records to figure out who the mystery person is. I might want your help."

"What do you expect to find?"

"You remember the ant farm you had in fourth or fifth grade?"

He gave me a quizzical look. "Yeah . . . and?"

"It's like that. The financial records are like the glass walls: they make everything transparent. Any business activity leaves accounting trails. You can see where people are currently working, where they worked in the past. It shows traces of abandoned work where the ant trails are partially caved in. You can anticipate where new trails are headed, even before the ants get there."

"And the ants don't know you're watching them," Paddy added. "I can picture your ant farm with an insurance company on top and people dressed in suits hurrying around with their briefcases. Unless you break the glass. Then they all escape, except for the ones that try to bite your hand as you pick them up."

"*That's* what happened to it. I always won—"

He pushed his chair away from the table, causing a screech. "You still suspect Nadler?"

"I've asked Ingstram to confirm with the publisher the amounts of Mrs. Nadler's book royalties. They're usually paid twice a year, not monthly. Nadler had all the opportunity in the world, but we've yet to catch him lying. I'd be amazed if he were involved with Mimi. But someone at Appalachian is doing something illegal—someone senior enough to cover his tracks well."

"But Dad, Mimi wasn't very senior and she pulled it off. You know, I forgot to tell you about last night. You missed all the excitement. Cops swarmed the neighborhood."

My heart went into overdrive. "What happened?"

"Alice kept barking at something outside in the middle of the night. Mrs. Keenan saw someone in our backyard and called her nephew, who's some big-shot cop. Patrol cars blocked the street. Looked like the McAlpin disco with all the red and blue flashers. They searched behind our houses and in the woods, but came up empty."

"We've pussyfooted around long enough," I said. "I need to get you out of here. Tomorrow morning you're driving to stay with your mother. I'm sorry if that's uncomfortable, but given what's happened in Chillicothe, some guy sneaking around in our backyard worries me a lot."

"I am not driving all the way to New Jersey just to turn right around and drive right back a few days later for fall semester."

"Can you leave for school now?"

"Dorms don't open for a week. And you're going where?"

Good question. Rand had suggested I head to my place in Michigan's Upper Peninsula. It would be a great time of year with few mosquitoes and the lake still warm for swimming. However, I wanted to be closer than a dozen hours from Chillicothe.

He didn't wait for me to answer. "Now I get it," he said. "I'm supposed to run like a scared chicken, but you stay here like a stubborn bull?"

"Not the analogy I would have chosen, but yes. I'm in the middle, but I'm not risking you."

"Not good enough, Dad. For one thing, without my help you wouldn't have an investigation to be in the middle of. Second thing, if it's safe enough for you to stay in this house, it's safe enough for me." He crossed his arms and widened his stance.

I stepped into his space. "Not gonna happen, Paddy. If I need to, I'll call Hastings and have her take you into protective custody." *Could I? Would I?* "Don't make me do it."

"You're acting just like the Jerk. Ordering me around. Not asking my opinion. I'm not some little kid, you know."

I did not want to globalize our argument. "I do know. You are my only child, and I don't want anything to happen to you. Do I need to call the cops?"

He puffed his lower lip over his upper one, creating a ridiculous face that almost made me laugh.

"I'll make you a deal," he said. "Classes start in about a week."

"You can't stay—"

"Stop interrupting." He thrust out his chin, I supposed daring me to interrupt again. When I didn't, he continued. "Fly me to Boston. I'll hang at Uncle Mike's, go with him to see Grandma at Sugarbush, catch a Sox game, and fly back in time to pack and drive to school. But you have to promise you'll leave too."

Hell, I'd fly him to Australia if that was what it took. This was better than my original plan; I could fly him out tonight and not have to wait until morning. I counted to ten while appearing to contemplate his offer. "If Uncle Mike's good on having you, I'm good on sending you."

I left him to call Uncle Mike while I raced barefoot up the steps to check schedules on the computer and get him on a flight. The cats followed me into the room and both settled on my lap, little massage machines purring up a storm.

I had forgotten it was Labor Day weekend. Coach was booked solid. Everybody and his proverbial brother had met Delta's premier status qualifications by the end of summer and they were all trying to use their upgrades. No hope for it but to purchase a first class seat on the last flight of the day. I got him a return flight shortly before classes began.

Paddy burst into the office. "Uncle Mike says you should come. He says it's been too long since you've visited your mother."

I pictured my mother. This time of year she'd be sitting outside, soaking in the sun, reading some weighty tome or *Paris Review*. On rare days, she put her book down and smoked a cigarette while you held a one-way conversation. On bad days, she provided no indication she knew you were there. She had not spoken for more than twenty years, and I always came away from visits with a splitting headache and a feeling of failure.

"Can't. I'm committed to choir on Sunday."

"What"—he pointed to my lapful of fur—"are we going to do with the cats while we're away?"

"Mrs. Keenan loves cats."

"Good idea. Where are you going to stay?"

Who said I was leaving?

TWENTY-NINE

HE PARKED HIS CAR IN the same apartment parking lot as he had the previous night, which had worked out well. When that cursed dog had spotted him checking out McCree's house and a posse of cops flocked to the area, he had been able to work his way down the ravine and reach his car with no one the wiser.

Tonight he positioned himself in the woods well behind the residence, allowing him to approach using the house itself as a visual block to the yappy critter and its presumably nosy or nervous owner. Plus, he could see into the target's rear bedroom. Without the wind, the mosquitoes were annoying. He'd rather kill them one by one as they landed than put up with the smell of DEET.

Shortly after dark, he heard footsteps reverberating on a wooden front porch. This house? Now he wished he were still in the woods facing the front. He might have had an easy shot.

From the far side of the house came, "You'll arrive after I've gone to bed." Male. Baritone. "How about you only call if there's a problem."

"Sounds like a plan," a more youthful voice said.

"Did you call your mother and let her know?"

"I'll do it once I clear security."

Two car doors slammed. A car engine started and the transmission clunked into gear. The vehicle splashed through puddles, stopped, and then drove away.

Putting the pieces together, the Happy Reaper figured the second person was McCree's son. He was flying somewhere and McCree was taking him to the airport.

Which meant McCree would be back.

Which meant he could finish this job tonight, get away from this stinking wet weather, and relax under blue Caribbean skies.

THIRTY

PADDY HAD BLACKMAILED ME AT the airport, making me promise that if he got on the plane I would sleep that night at the Cincinnatian, my favorite hotel in the city. I hadn't said anything about the day. Driving home Saturday morning I picked up a few things at the grocery store. A flashing message light indicated someone had called in my absence. I figured Paddy was checking to see if I had spent the night in a hotel as I promised.

I would have lost the bet. It was Bear. I put away cold cuts and a baguette and stuck some sodas in the fridge before calling him.

"Why didn't you call me last night?" he growled. "I was getting worried something else had happened to you."

"Worried? Sorry. I—"

"Look. Moyer showed up dead in his house."

Academy Award time. "Really? What happened?"

"Single shot in the head, which no neighbor heard. Mail on the floor suggests TOD between mail delivery on Monday and Tuesday. Seems he was a Vietnam vet and knew all about land mines. Boots and a spade in his garage had fresh dirt, which forensics will no doubt match with soil from Fitzhugh Crossing."

"Forensic confirmation will be when?"

"It's likely he was the small guy who tried to blow you up. Down on his luck. A decent mechanic. Made good money, but apparently drank and gambled most of it away. Word on the street says he owed a bundle to the local numbers racket."

It was like he was reading from notes. "So you think—"

"Found only Moyer's prints in the house, although some areas were wiped clean. His car didn't leave the tire prints at Fitzhugh Crossing. My guess is Moyer set the mine and the heavy guy bumped him off."

"Did you ever get any more dope on Solonini?"

"We're still waiting for more recent information. Anyway, on Moyer. Some woman tipped us off from a phone booth. We've got two possible witnesses, but they're away for the long weekend. Neighbor across the street from Moyer reported an old truck in the driveway early yesterday afternoon. Wasn't there for long. She didn't know make or model or even the exact time. Two guys. One short, one tall—kinda like Mutt and Jeff. They were definitely inside the house. Left wet footprints."

My stomach was roiling at the thought that two witnesses might have seen Molly make the call. My voice remained normal, I think. "Sounds like you've got your work cut out on this one."

"Sheriff Lyons wasn't pleased when you didn't show up at the press conference."

"Molly Fitzhugh was in town and called me. We met at Sue's for lunch."

"I heard you were there."

Aha, he'd been fishing. Glad I brought Molly up before he did. "Then, she decided bowling would be good physical therapy. We bowled some, had a drink, and then we discovered the flat tires and the note."

"Long time between lunch and when you showed up with the evidence."

Fishing for whether Molly and I had been at Moyer's? "Anything on the note?"

"No prints. Forensics may test the ink and compare the writing to the envelope you got at the Christopher Inn. What's your next step?"

"Lots of fun stuff. I need to get a new driver's license, file the insurance claim. All that crap when you lose your wallet."

"I meant, was there anything else you were planning on doing about these botulism murders?"

"CIG's checking on a bunch of people for me. I figure I'm in your way until we get permission to look at Appalachian's books."

"Our court order only applies to areas from which the Colliers were embezzling, and we got that covered. Neither Collier can make bail. Vivian Kennedy had all the assets and she's not doing business anymore. If I need you, this is still the number to call?"

As in, *Are you staying in Cincinnati?* I saw no reason to tell him my plans. "You know I'm not happy about being shut out like this."

His booming laugh caused me to pull the phone away from my ear. "At least you're honest."

I'm glad you think so.

THIRTY-ONE

ON SATURDAY AFTERNOON, HE HAD discovered McCree was home.
Maybe with his son gone McCree had stayed overnight at a girlfriend's?
He decided on a different approach, retrieved his car from the apartment
parking lot, and parked on McAlpin a few doors down from McCree's
house. The overcast skies spritzed and drizzled, which was enough to kill
all pedestrian traffic. To prevent the car from fogging he cracked the
windows. Cars driving by didn't slow down or appear to pay any
attention to him reading the Gideons Bible he'd borrowed from the
hotel.

His heart pumped a bit faster when he saw a police car crawl down the
wet road toward him. He ducked below the window line and waited until
the car squished by.

His wish for McCree to stay home was dashed when the target strolled
from his house in the early evening and unlocked his car. McCree
cranked the Infiniti's engine. Because exhaust fumes in the cool air might
draw McCree's attention to him, he didn't want to start his rental until
McCree had gone by. Once the Infiniti passed, he turned the car on and
waited for three more cars before he could make a U-turn.

Ahead, McCree continued through the Lafayette intersection. One of
the cars between them waited to make a left into the apartments where he
had earlier parked, allowing McCree to drive out of sight. "Come on," he
muttered. "*Andele. Andele.*"

The guy turned, emitting a cloud of smoky hot oil. Driving through
the stench, he followed two cars to the intersection of Lafayette and
Ludlow. Looking left then right, he caught sight on the right of the
Infiniti with its left blinker on. To stay a Happy Reaper, he needed some
luck to catch McCree.

The first of the two cars cleared the intersection, leaving one car
between him and McCree, who now made his left.

Eventually, the other car in front of him crept right; he followed on the guy's bumper, revving his engine to try to hurry the guy. As they approached the stoplight it changed to yellow.

"Run it," he commanded.

The dweeb in front of him was the one guy in a million who thought yellow meant *caution* instead of *speed up*. The Happy Reaper slammed on his brakes to avoid hitting the asshole. He didn't think McCree had made the immediate right onto I-75 North—he would have seen McCree change the signal from left to right or caught the tail end of the gray car. Was he heading south toward downtown? Across the river to Kentucky? Picking up his son at the airport?

He drummed his thumbs on the steering wheel. While the light was against him, no cars had followed McCree onto Central Parkway; he still had a shot at catching up. The light changed to green. On Central he pulled into the yellow-painted divider and zipped past the dweeb. That earned him a honked horn and flipped middle finger. Tough shit.

He'd bet McCree was heading for I-75 South. He saw Frisch's around the bend and wondered if McCree was going for fast food. He slowed as he passed the parking lot, peering left, looking for the gray Infiniti or McCree walking toward the door. Nothing.

He caught the light at Hopple, and had a moment of panic after he had committed to the turn when he saw a small dark car pulling into the White Castle across the way, but realized it was some American box, not the sleeker Infiniti. He blasted across the overpass, took the right-hand ramp with squealing tires, held the car steady, and merged onto I-75.

Right behind a cop car going fifty-five fucking miles an hour.

◊◊◊

WHEN HE'D DECIDED MCCREE WAS not coming home for the night, he had set his phone alarm for five a.m. and kicked back in McCree's lounger in the library.

Four hours sleep was not enough, but it had to do. He could sleep all he wanted once he finished off McCree. He now sat against the front wall where he would not be seen as McCree mounted the porch steps, even if McCree peered in the side windows next to the door. His muscles ached enough from the night in the lounger that he considered rooting around in the bathroom for a pain reliever. He should have stretched.

From outside he heard the crunch of tires as an automobile drove into the driveway. McCree? The engine revved and the car drove up to the house and stopped with the barely perceptible squeal of brakes soon to need new pads. He unsheathed the knife and slid into the dark corner to await McCree's arrival.

The automobile door opened and closed with a solid *thunk*. He waited to hear the double chirp from the car to signify McCree had locked it, but either he left it unlocked or the car predated the technology. What he heard instead was whistling. Sounded like a hymn. Yes, "Old Hundredth." When had Catholic-raised McCree learned a Protestant hymn?

The music trailed away from the house as McCree whistled a second verse, this time the bass part. McCree was walking down the driveway. Picking up a newspaper? Piece of trash? Was he walking somewhere? The Happy Reaper eased to the side window and glimpsed McCree as he turned right on McAlpin. Once again McCree had eluded his trap. Remaining in the house longer was taking an avoidable risk. He sheathed the knife, slung the backpack over his shoulder, and left by the kitchen door.

The cursed neighbor's dog was out and gave one woof, but apparently lost interest once the Happy Reaper moved between McCree's house and the neighbor's on the other side. He walked purposefully toward the front of the house to the sidewalk and proceeded to trail McCree. He found himself humming "Old Hundredth" while thinking of the doxology he had learned at his mother's knee: "Praise God from whom all blessings flow."

He had no plan other than to track McCree as an exercise to keep in practice. They hung a right on Middleton, left on Wood, and through a wonderful wrought iron gate into what he recognized from driving the area must be a back entrance to the Fairview-Clifton German Language School. He remained by the gate until McCree moved past an abandoned stone building at the near edge of the property.

The windows in the building were missing; he stepped inside and watched McCree cut through a fence into the parking lot for St. John's Unitarian Universalist Church and enter through its back door. Even with plentiful airflow, the building smelled dank, but it provided excellent cover with a clear sight line a hundred meters down the hill into the school parking lot, through which McCree would return.

He made himself comfortable, posed with a book. Should anyone spot him, he'd be another graduate student from the University of Cincinnati. The church and school parking lots filled up, and by eleven everyone was inside. Change in plans. This spot would do nicely.

Assuming an hour-long church service, McCree should come out noonish. That allowed time to grab a bite from one of the stores on Ludlow and return in time for the big event.

◊◊◊

HE SAUNTERED BACK INTO THE stone building at a quarter of twelve. The sun burned fiercely in an Aztec sky. Without the hint of a cooling wind, a trickle of sweat stained an exclamation mark on the front of his T-shirt. He would be glad to get out of this place, although it was not going to be the last thing he ever did.

It required less than a minute to remove the rifle parts from his backpack and assemble them. After the shot, he'd break down and store the gun. By the time people figured out what had happened, he would have skedaddled through the wrought iron gate. He'd collect his car and be on his way to the airport well before the cops arrived.

His patience and skills would soon be rewarded. Today would close the McCree contract, and, if he could believe the weather forecast, next weekend should be cool enough to give the blood sisters their ticket to heaven.

At seventeen minutes past the hour, the first group of parishioners left the Unitarian church. Service must have run long. He closed his eyes, inhaled slowly and fully, and visualized a bull's-eye on McCree's chest.

THIRTY-TWO

THE CHOIR SANG BOBBY MCFERRIN'S contemporary version of the twenty-third psalm for the anthem, part of a service celebrating the many facets of God. The harmony consisted of magnificent open chords contrasting with dissonances, all reverberating in the sonority of the sanctuary. Soft dynamics enhanced the sound, which was lucky for me since singing loudly hurt my chest. At the end of the piece, the choir director kept his hand raised and the congregation absorbed the silence without a single cough. In that silence, I temporarily felt whole.

We closed the service with the Unitarian version of the doxology, which I had been humming and whistling earlier in the day. My hope was to escape as soon as the service ended and avoid questions I didn't really want to answer.

Didn't happen. The curious surrounded me, wanting the scoop on my injuries. By the second telling, I had the story down pat about how I'd rolled the Expedition and came out with only bruises. Skyler Weaver lingered at the edge of the crowd. I hoped my eyes told her not to question my story. Something worked because she veered away from the group.

As I was leaving by the back door, an arm slipped into mine, causing me to startle.

Skyler said, "Let me give you a lift home, sailor."

"I can walk fine, but thanks."

"Actually, I want to talk with you. I know you like to walk, but I don't want to have to walk back here to get my car." She tugged at my arm, causing a twinge of pain I tried not to show.

"Okay, I get the picture. 'No' isn't one of my choices."

"I knew you were a wise man, Seamus."

We made our way through the church and left by the front door near where Skyler had parked her car.

"How do you like the Prius?"

"It's great, but I didn't grab you for a test drive. Fact is, I'm feeling really bad about what I've gotten you into. I couldn't live with myself if you were seriously injured. I'd like you to drop it. I wanted to know why Samuel was killed, but I never intended to endanger you."

I waited until we were out of eavesdropping range. "What makes you think I'm in danger?"

"Look at you. Your rollover story was touching, but you lied through your teeth. Paddy told me what happened to the man who tried to kill you. And Friday, someone slashed your tires. If they know your car, they have your license plate, and from that, they can easily get your address, and—"

Paddy was talking with Skyler? "The Cincinnati police have already stepped up patrols near my house. In fact, they practically strip-searched the neighborhood late Thursday night because a neighbor's dog barked. I'm fine here. I've discovered Samuel was correct in his suspicions about something funny at Appalachian Casualty and Life, but I still haven't found his killer."

"Strip-searched the neighborhood? You are so full of it. I did not intend to put you in harm's way. If I'd known, I never would have asked for your help."

Why didn't I choose to tell her I was staying at the Cincinnatian because Paddy and I had come to a similar conclusion? "Look, Skyler, I appreciate your concern. I'm a big boy. I would have taken the assignment even if I had known all the risks. All the king's horses and all the king's men can't keep me away."

"It's 'All the king's horses and all the king's men couldn't put Humpty together again.' You should listen to your inner fears." She pulled to the curb in front of my house.

"Whatever. The point is I'm finishing what I started. The police are working hard with the evidence we've gathered. Samuel's information allowed us to uncover a huge theft. I'm confident we'll catch the people responsible for his murder. I hopped out. "Thanks for the lift. Everything will be fine."

I closed the front door behind me and stopped in the entryway. The house smelled . . . different. I tried to chase the scent. Sweet? Fresh? The harder I tried, the quicker it disappeared, but it was there.

And it was foreign.

◊◊◊

I AWOKE MONDAY MORNING FEELING antsy. As nice as the Cincinnatian was, I hated feeling imprisoned. After spooking myself at home and leaving for the hotel room as soon as I'd packed more clothes, I had spent the remainder of the day dropping further into a funk. The more I reviewed my notes and thought about the last few days, the more I became convinced somebody knew a whole lot about me, and I knew nothing about them. To win this war, I needed to flush the hunter and let him hear hounds baying on his trail.

Easier contemplated than done.

The Brits don't celebrate our Labor Day, and late afternoon, evening for him, Ingstram Ravel called. He and his group had once again performed miracles developing information on Peggy Collier, Appalachian's operations supervisors, and the IT folks.

Nadler's story checked out again. Ingstram had determined how much Hanna Franks Nadler made on her books, including a Hollywood option. At Hanna's request, her agent spread out payment of her semi-annual royalties over the six months; a bit weird, but it did explain the monthly deposits that brought their account balance over fifty grand each month. Ingstram also confirmed Nadler's cell phone had indeed called Mimi Collier's work number at 5:18 last Monday evening. Before the call disconnected, the primary cell tower had switched, indicating Nadler was traveling south from Cleveland.

That snuffed my lingering doubts about Nadler.

Thomas Moyer had not always been a loser. Several of Moyer's Vietnam buddies claimed he was a genius with explosives of all kinds. They unanimously agreed that if Moyer wanted to blow up a car, the car would be demolished. His biggest flaw was he didn't like orders. In fact, the more he was under someone's thumb, the more likely he would rebel.

Moyer was into the numbers racket to the tune of about ten large. I figured he had paid his debt in full.

Next, Ingstram talked about Deb Holt, the union treasurer. "She comes from a long line of union leaders. She's an only child and Popsy and Mumsy brought her to the union hall from the time she was in nappies. Her grandfather was an early leader in coal. Those were rough times, with killing on both sides from what they say. Her father was Second World War navy, captured by the Japanese and kept prisoner for three years. Besides a Purple Heart, he received a Silver Star with clusters. He was not treated well in the camps."

"She's certainly not friendly to the Japanese."

"Seamus, we are a long way from the union violence of the early coal days."

"I know. She'd have to be crazy. If she idolized her father—"

"Holt doesn't have a rap sheet. We found no documented psychological problems. You're barking up the wrong tree. I saved the most interesting for last."

"You sly dog, you."

"Eduardo Solonini. Most files on him were closed following his supposed death. We tracked down an old Jersey City cop who never bought the accident and kept his files. Solonini's sobriquet was 'Used Car Eddie.'"

"What's that supposed to mean?"

"He could sell anything to anybody. Listened carefully and got you what you really wanted. Always a good deal. He was the fair-haired kid of some big boys in Jersey who were moving into legit operations. Supposed to be grooming him to be a bigwig in a legit concern, except it wouldn't be legit. It would be under the boys' thumbs."

"An insurance company?"

"Didn't say. Solonini went to NYU night school for several years. He disappeared a couple of months after graduating with his MBA."

We batted stuff around for a couple more minutes before giving up, none the wiser. I needed to get access to Appalachian's financials to put the financial equivalent of their ant farm trails under a magnifying glass. Or I needed to shatter the ant farm and watch the ants scatter. Maybe one of them would give himself away by where he ran.

The realization of how I could threaten Appalachian with just such a shattering event arrived fully formed.

◊◊◊

AT THE TICK OF EIGHT thirty Tuesday morning, I stopped pacing around the hotel room, took a deep breath, and called the editor of the *Cincinnati Business Courier*. My first year in Cincinnati, I wrote several articles from a former analyst's perspective that the *Courier* published. The series was a hit and every once in a while, I still gave them ideas for a story.

"You know about the doings at Appalachian Casualty and Life?" I asked.

"Saw a blurb about some embezzlement."

"Off the record, I think something else is amiss. I'm working with the Ross County Sheriff's Office looking into it. We really need to see Appalachian's books and they're providing only the legally required minimum."

He swallowed and the clunk of a mug meeting the tabletop came over the line. "This has what to do with me?"

"I want to use the paper's name to try to pry out the information. If they don't voluntarily provide the records we want, I'll give you an inside exposé of the lax controls at Appalachian. With the implication that more trouble is expected."

His chair squeaked. I could picture him: his head would be craned back to contemplate the ceiling tile stained with generations of smoke. In the ensuing silence, I imagined his brain cells firing. "Would you deliver the goods?"

"Absolutely."

"We'd love to have that story, but I don't think I can allow you to drag our name into whatever you're really trying to do. You could try *Columbus Business First* given the geography, but they'll probably feel the same way. If you do write the story and we can confirm it, we'd certainly print it."

Next call, Jim Nadler.

"How are things?" I asked.

"I worked all weekend with one of our accountants. We know the extent of Mimi Collier's embezzlement—over $2.6 million through the end of last year and in excess of $3.3 million now. We've spent a lot of time making sure no other schemes are out there. I made a rush deal with a group to check for deaths—we should do it periodically anyway—make sure no one is still signing Uncle Albert's name on checks after he died. We're clean."

"That's good news, and I take it you're still employed."

"For now."

"Any luck convincing your president to voluntarily open the books for the sheriff's department?"

"Snyder decided the insurance department review was sufficient."

"I'd like to take a crack at him. Would you be willing to conference call me in to him? I know you've tried hard, but maybe an interested outsider can persuade him."

"I can't imagine what else you think you're going to find, but eventually everything will come out. The sooner we clear everything up, the better. Here goes—I'm putting you on hold."

Following the click was an eternity of silence before another click.

"Everyone there?" Nadler asked.

We both said we were.

"Seamus, I have Bill Snyder, our president, on the line. I have another call to take." Nadler clicked off.

Not what I'd expected. "Mr. Snyder, Appalachian has another rotten apple in addition to Mimi Collier. I think we can figure out who from your computer and financial systems. I know you don't legally have to provide complete access to the police, but I believe it is in your best interest to do so."

"Mr. McCree, I've listened to the arguments for and against. We are cooperating with the Ohio Department of Insurance in their investigation. That process should uncover any other problems. As Mr. Nadler informed you, we have spent the last seventy-two hours doing an extensive audit of the annuity department and found no other problems."

My next words gave me pause, but what choice did I have? If this backfired it would all be on me. "I know the business journals and how they work. Unless you head them off at the pass, they're going to investigate Appalachian and write a negative story. They'll talk to disgruntled employees and former employees. They'll find people familiar with the specifics of how your staff reductions eliminated necessary security checks. They'll highlight Appalachian's unwillingness to voluntarily provide information to the police. They'll speculate whether you are hiding something."

"Is that a threat, Mr. McCree?"

"What will your shareholders and policyholders think of such an article? Particularly if it is picked up by other publications? Fully cooperating with the police now eliminates a major reason for the press to be interested in the story."

No response, but no dial tone. I paced around the desk sending acceptance vibes down the phone line.

"The executive committee has already made their decision," he said. "If you think you can convince them with this—and I use the term loosely—*information* of yours, fine. We have a meeting scheduled this afternoon at two. I'll give you five minutes."

I called Nadler. "See you at the executive committee meeting. Whom do I need to convince?"

"Snyder will go with a majority and we were split evenly before. Jacobs, he's plant and equipment, agrees with me about being completely open. Olson, finance and marketing, has been the strongest advocate for not opening up. He says if you let the camel's nose under the tent, soon all you'll smell is camel piss. I think the swing vote is Michael Schwartz. He's focused on the purely legal point of what we *must* do rather than what we *should* do.

"And, the Street doesn't like what it's hearing. Our stock dropped three dollars on the opening this morning. Our executive group is feeling the pain now—all our stock options are underwater. You might work that into your presentation."

Now I was flying solo, running on fumes and without a parachute. Still better than spending any more time cooped up in the hotel room.

◊◊◊

ON THE WAY HOME FROM the Cincinnatian, I waffled on whether to wear a blue or gray pinstripe suit. When I reached into the closet, I pulled out the gray. The lightweight wool would project a sense of power without making them feel like I was trying to cram something down their throats, which is how one or more of them might react to blue pinstripes.

I removed a light blue oxford shirt with French cuffs from its dry cleaning bag and paired it with a maroon silk tie showing the slightest hint of a pattern. It required three tries before I tied the Windsor knot exactly as I wanted. From cloth dust covers, I retrieved highly polished black wingtips and used a metal shoehorn from the bedside table to slip them on.

Checking in the mirror, I approved the uniform. I could walk into any boardroom in America and not get a second glance—other than for my multihued face, still recovering from the Expedition's demise.

If Appalachian gave me immediate permission to look through their records, I wanted to be prepared to stay in Chillicothe for a night. I optimistically added my running gear to the change of clothes I tossed into a duffel. I hadn't been able to run yet, but my legs were feeling less sore. A short, slow effort might get me back into training mode, although I had a feeling my planned marathon would need to be postponed.

That thought put me into something of a foul mood. I popped Vivaldi's *Four Seasons* into the car's CD player to set a different tone. I deliberately chose the US 50 route to Chillicothe and spent the trip planning my five minutes before the executive committee. I mentally rehearsed my presentation and tried to devise answers for any questions I anticipated. Pulling into the parking lot, I crushed a breath mint between my molars, each crunch bringing a blast of peppermint. I breathed into my hand and quickly sniffed: pure freshness.

If all it took was logic and fresh breath, I was a guaranteed success. Time for a reality check.

THIRTY-THREE

MIDMORNING TUESDAY HE SPOTTED MCCREE'S car in the driveway. Heat shimmered off the hood, meaning McCree had recently arrived. He drove around the block and then parked on the street. Before he could decide what his best alternative was, a suited McCree solved the problem for him by tossing a briefcase and duffel into the backseat and driving off.

McCree's route headed toward Chillicothe. Patience and planning, he reminded himself, made the difference between his success and others' failures. Near misses were minor frustrations when you succeeded in the end. Sunday had been frustrating. He'd waited in ambush for an hour after the service was over. McCree had obviously left church by a different exit. By the time the Happy Reaper had walked back to McCree's house, the Infiniti was gone. That night he waited in the woods behind McCree's house until nearly midnight before retreating to the Cincinnatian, where he relaxed with a long shower and hydrated his skin with their lotion—even though it did smell a bit prissy.

On Monday he swapped out rentals on the off chance some Nancy Drew wannabe had noticed his car. He drove past McCree's place throughout the day and evening with the new ride. No car in the driveway.

Now none of that mattered; McCree was in his sights. As he followed, he studied the route for an ideal place to ambush him on his return. He might experience another temporary setback if McCree remained in Chillicothe proper. But he was nothing if not patient.

He found an ideal location a few miles outside of Chillicothe. When McCree entered town, the Happy Reaper turned around. He bought food at a convenience store, parked the car a mile away, and hiked back along the river. If someone saw him from the highway, he might appear to be a birdwatcher looking through binoculars. They wouldn't be able to see his long gun, which he'd save for McCree's return.

If McCree did not drive past by dinnertime, he'd wait until dark and then cruise the motel parking lots for his car. Patience and preparation and "Results Guaranteed."

THIRTY-FOUR

APPALACHIAN'S RECEPTIONIST MET ME WITH a "Wow, you sure clean up nicely . . . except for your face." She placed her elbows on the desk in front of her, rested her chin on her fists, and batted her eyelashes. "If I ask, are you going to tell me, 'You should have seen the other guy'?"

I batted my eyes back at her, earning her grin. "Hardly. The other guy was a steering wheel. Would you be so kind as to tell me where the two o'clock executive committee meeting is?"

She called Snyder's assistant to collect me. I chatted with the receptionist. She'd been "totally blown away" by Mimi Collier's theft. Employees were shocked, she said, but mostly dismayed because the company-match portion of their 401(k) plan was invested in company stock. The stock price had dropped to under twelve dollars. I sympathized and made a minor adjustment to my prepared remarks.

A middle-aged woman in a severe blue suit with an expression to match retrieved me from the reception area and escorted me to conference room A. She opened the door, looked toward the gentleman at the head of the table, and said, "Mr. Snyder, here is Mr. McCree."

The setup was not ideal; I couldn't look at everyone at the same time. The two people I hadn't met besides Snyder flanked him. Age differentiated them. Schwartz, sporting a classic comb-over, sat on Snyder's left. Jacobs, who looked like he would be more comfortable in overalls than a suit, was on his right. Nadler sat next to Schwartz. Olson occupied the opposite end of the table from Snyder.

I chose to stand in the gap between Olson and Jacobs where I was directly opposite Schwartz, the one I had to convince. From there I saw Snyder and Nadler well. Jacobs was only partially visible. I ignored Olson, since according to Nadler he wasn't going to change his mind. Best to stand above him and visually diminish his importance in the debate.

Snyder indicated with a wave that I should begin. I addressed my comments directly to Schwartz, with occasional eye checks on the others. "Appalachian is in a tight spot. I understand the instinct to protect yourself by following the letter of the law on what material you must make available to the Ross County Sheriff's Office. However, that approach misses the broader picture of how best to protect the organization. I was a Wall Street analyst for a number of years. I understand what has happened and how it will impact your stock."

Schwartz shifted in his seat, which I anticipated was preparatory to interrupting. I didn't give him the chance.

"Today, the stock has already lost twenty percent and is sitting around twelve dollars. That's tough for all your shareholders, but especially your employees, since they are counting on their 401(k)s for retirement. If you continue your current course, I estimate your stock will drop another thirty to forty percent within a month. Once it drops into the seven-fifty-to-eight-dollar range, value investors will come in and stabilize the price."

Snyder's face matched the dull gray of his hair. Schwartz was taking copious notes.

"Why will this happen? Because over the next few weeks all the press about Appalachian will be either negative or speculative about what else is wrong. The rating agencies will put you on credit watch. A.M. Best may lower your rating.

"Eventually, if nothing else like the Collier situation comes to light, the stock will rebound to reasonable valuation levels . . . in two or three years. The stigma will last that long."

Having gained their full attention, I brightened my demeanor to offer them a different and better resolution to their problem. "On the other hand, if Appalachian is aggressively transparent, the slide will likely stop and may even reverse."

Snyder asked, "Meaning what?"

"Put out a press release to trumpet that not only is Appalachian cooperating with the state insurance department, but effective immediately, you are voluntarily providing the police complete access to your records. Hire an independent accounting firm to review all operational areas. Promise to publish results as soon as they are available. You may be able to get a clean bill of health before the rating agencies can act. Certainly it will give them pause."

"That's bullshit," Olson said. "Between the money we'll recover and our insurance, we're getting back most of our loss from the Collier theft. People should be buying, not selling. Stock's a bargain."

"Mention the recovery and insurance as an afterthought," I said. "Facts have little to do with the Street's reaction. It's all about perception. You need to stop the shorts right now with a clear demonstration that you aren't hiding anything and will quickly root out any other problems. Be assured, the facts will all eventually come out. Your task as the leaders of Appalachian is to manage expectations and make it riskier for the shorts."

Nadler winked what I assumed was approval. Schwartz continued taking notes. Jacobs raised his hand and craned his neck to look up at me. "What are shorts?"

"Most people buy stock in hopes the price will rise. Shorts make money if the stock falls. They borrow shares and sell them. When the price drops they buy the stock back and pocket the difference."

"They're parasites," Snyder said.

"And what I am suggesting is for you to inoculate Appalachian against them."

I looked from person to person, ending at Olson, whose pad was blank. The strange pattern of his hair caught my attention—hair plugs. From the front, back, or side his hair looked natural. From directly above, the effect was off.

"Thank you, Mr. McCree," Snyder said. "My assistant will call you with our decision."

I had hoped to remain for the discussion, to counter whatever arguments were against my plan and bolster those that supported it. I stalled by writing my cell phone number on a business card that I gave to Snyder. But they maintained silence until I left the room.

As the door clicked behind me, Olson said, "If he's so smart, why isn't he rich?"

◊◊◊

I LUCKED OUT AND CAUGHT Bear in his cubicle, which stank of stale air and burnt coffee. I considered removing my suit coat, but settled for loosening my tie. Clearing off the visitor's chair, I plunked down and told him of my meeting with the executive committee.

He stared at me with troubled eyes. "With what happened to you and your car the last time you were here, you got some balls, Seamus. Or the accident scrambled your brains. They going to do it?"

"I'm not optimistic. They didn't let me stay for the discussion, and Snyder planned to have his assistant call, rather than calling himself. What's new on the Moyer murder?"

"Hold that thought. The coffee has worked its way through the system. I've got to use the facilities."

While he was gone, I read the papers on his desk, which were upside down to me. I'd learned this trick during my bank stock analyst days. Amazing what executives would leave uncovered under the assumption I couldn't read it. Nothing interesting this time.

"That's better." Bear's chair groaned as he settled into it. "The killer was about a foot behind Moyer when he popped the sucker. We're pretty sure Mutt and Jeff broke in. The place had been searched, but we have no idea what was taken. Maybe nothing. Money lay on top of his bedroom bureau, and a gold wedding ring sat in a drawer."

"The dirt on the shovel match?"

"And on his boots. Now that kind of dirt isn't unique, but the shoe prints also matched."

A whoosh of air surprised me as the A/C kicked on. I pitched my voice louder. "I think Moyer tried to avoid killing me. Everyone says he was skilled, and I suspect you have to work at it to plant a mine at an angle like he did."

After seconds, the A/C stopped and the room reverted to uncomfortably warm.

"You're lucky he was a boozer. Used an M15 pressure-operated blast mine. Kind used to blow up tanks. We found his print on a piece of the pressure plate. A bunch were stolen a couple of years ago from a National Guard depot. Probably one of them. Oh, and Joe Fourier turned himself in. He claims, and I kinda think he's telling the truth, that someone framed him in the note to you. We'll see, but since he's behind bars until his trial, we know where to find him."

My cell phone rang. A local number.

Snyder introduced himself. "I wanted to call and personally thank you for your presentation," he said. "We're working on a press release. I know you wanted to start this afternoon, but I think it will work better if you start tomorrow morning—say, eight thirty?"

I thanked him, rang off, and pumped my hand in a victory salute.

"Congratulations, Seamus," Bear said. "Magic. Hope it's worth it. Now what?"

"I have faith I'll figure something out. I'll go home tonight, come back first thing tomorrow, and plan to stay a couple of days. Then I need to get home to meet my son and get him off to college."

"You staying with Charlene again?"

"I don't think I need to. Besides, if someone tries to follow up on their threat, I don't want to involve her. It'll be safer where people are around. You want to join me at Appalachian tomorrow?"

"I don't think that's a good idea."

"Why? I thought you wanted to learn how I did things."

"I meant staying at a motel. What am I going to learn at Appalachian? I'm starting to think you pull everything out of your ass."

He leaned both arms on his desk and stared at me. "Which reminds me. When we were talking to Nadler, how did you know the Colliers were taking the money to Nevada? And how did you find the picture of Mimi posing as Vivian Kennedy?"

Oh crap, I must have slipped with Paddy's information. A bead of sweat trickled down my cheek. "CIG maintains extensive networks, and they worked." I forced myself into a winning smile and made a measured retreat before he asked any more questions.

◊◊◊

GIVEN I HAD NOTHING TO look forward to in Cincinnati, I again chose Route 50 instead of the quicker way home using I-71 that Paddy had suggested. Paddy would undoubtedly joke it had more to do with old dogs and new tricks than conscious choice. Thinking about Paddy got me wondering what he was up to in Boston. I'd call him this evening and find out.

I slid *The Very Best of Fleetwood Mac* into the player and began wailing away with Stevie Nicks on "Dreams." Something whapped the driver's side rear window, exploding the glass. I slammed on the brakes. At a second thud, I floored the accelerator, fought against the pushback, and tucked tight against the steering wheel to present a smaller target.

The whine of the engine and pulsing of the wind drowned out whatever insanities I was yelling at whoever was trying to kill me. I was struggling to control the speeding car from that scrunched position. I sat up and checked the rearview mirror. No one was following. I eased my speed from ninety-five to ten miles over the speed limit and tried to sort out what had happened. Someone had shot out the window. I had anticipated that appearing before the executive committee might blow smoke into the hornet's nest, but I hadn't expected such a quick or violent reaction. I lowered the rear passenger-side window a bit and the pulsing wind stopped.

Whoever had ambushed me could still be trying to catch up. *Get off Route 50.* With no one coming in either direction, I swung right on Lower Twin Road and sped toward Wilmington. From there, I could reach Cincinnati on I-71.

Lower Twin Road took me through South Salem to OH-41, where I turned right toward Greenfield. In Greenfield, I picked up decent cell phone coverage. I needed a plan and pulled off to the side of the road. My hands shook so hard I struggled to hold the cell phone steady enough to dial. But who to call? 911? There was no emergency now. Bear, then, although I wasn't looking forward to the hassle and hoped he wouldn't answer. He did and I told him of the attempt.

"I'm fine," I concluded.

"Where are you now?"

Why was that his first question? Was he somehow involved? I clicked off the cell phone and drove. Whom should I trust? Even paranoid people are sometimes right.

Spotting a Ramada Inn outside Wilmington helped me realize I was stressed and tired and needed to stop. Since I was returning to Chillicothe tomorrow, I could stay here and save myself a couple hours' driving.

I checked in and grabbed a bite to eat, but my stomach roiled in protest and the fish I'd ordered tasted like cardboard. The thought of cardboard forced me to consider covering my broken window. The convenience shop clerk in the hotel found a box and lent me a magic marker.

Picking out the rest of the safety glass took patience. With my Swiss army knife I shaped a cardboard window. In block-letter printing I wrote, "NO RADIO." I smiled, remembering the probable urban myth about a guy who made a similar sign and the next morning found his temporary window on the driver's seat with the words "Just checking" added.

If only *my* problem was a thief with a sense of humor. I needed to figure out who was gunning for me. The only people who knew of my trip to Chillicothe were the members of Appalachian's executive committee. And Bear. Surely he hadn't had time to set up an ambush. Unless he did it when he left for the men's room? Was he crooked?

THIRTY-FIVE

MIDNIGHT, LOOSENING KNOTTED MUSCLES IN a steaming shower in his Cincinnatian room found him whistling snatches from *Jesus Christ Superstar* and pondering what had spooked McCree.

Instead of the thirty-five or forty miles an hour he had expected, McCree must have been doing ninety on the straightaway before fishtailing around the curve he had planned to use for the ambush.

Where was McCree now? The kid's car was still parked in the Clifton driveway, but no one was home.

There had to be an explanation. Tomorrow morning he'd ping his Chillicothe contact for insight into McCree's movements. This was taking a lot longer than he had anticipated, but sometimes shit happened.

THIRTY-SIX

SLEEP BROUGHT ME A CHASE dream. Two choppers were hunting me, probing the dark with searchlights. I climbed into the crotch of an ancient elm and pressed my back into its rough bark, pretending to be part of the tree. The lights passed by me several times. From the distance came the deep baying of bloodhounds mixed with higher-pitched beagle calls. The dogs were a long way off, but they would find me. I woke up sweating.

Since I'd brought my running gear, I did an early-morning slog—slower even than a jog, but a step toward full recovery. No helicopters or bloodhounds trailed me. No strange looks from passersby.

I tried to increase speed but the pain was too much. Clearly, I would not be ready to run in the marathon. That realization felt like a crushing pressure on my shoulders. I had put so much training time in. The marathon was to be my challenge—and my reward when I finally finished. Gradually, the vibrations from the steady beat of my feet slapping the pavement soothed me. I had an immediate mission. I should concentrate on what I could do, not what I couldn't. I was good with that and ready to *carpe* this *diem*.

As long as the day didn't decide to seize me.

◊◊◊

I ARRIVED AT THE ROSS County Sheriff's Office without incident and steeled myself for a verbal attack that didn't come. Bear poured himself coffee and me water. He asked why I hadn't answered my cell phone after we'd been disconnected. I fessed up to my paranoia. He nodded as though this happened all the time. I changed the subject.

"It's someone on the executive committee," I said.

"Because?"

"Who knew Presser was coming to tell Jim Nadler some disturbing news?"

"Nadler, Collier, the executive committee, and anyone they told." He laid on a crooked smile. "As for who knew you were coming? Add me and subtract Collier. She was in jail, unless she has an accomplice, who—"

"She didn't have anything to do with Presser's death. You already agreed, and killing me now isn't going to help her."

"Okay, not Collier."

"And Nadler keeps checking out, leaving the rest of the executive committee. I can't imagine it's Arthur Jacobs. He doesn't have enough spunk to arrange murders."

"You never know," Bear said. "And don't forget about all their administrative assistants and worker bees. Could be anyone."

"Olson and Snyder, and possibly Schwartz, have the most to gain if the stock goes up. I don't think it's Snyder because he could have stonewalled us and not let me meet the executive committee."

"Smart people know how to make misdirection plays."

"Never mind. Talking to you is like talking to a black hole—ideas go in and nothing comes out."

He yawned. "You're stretching and hoping. You got no clue, Seamus."

"Fine. Let's interview each of them and find out where they were late yesterday afternoon. Someone was on a hill taking pot shots at me."

"First, do you know where you were ambushed?"

"I tried to find it on my way back this morning. No luck."

"For someone as smart as you're supposed to be, you get yourself in an awful lot of pickles. You're with me for now, since the boys are processing your car. But here's how it's going to go, Seamus. You're going to do your financial records thing that you're so het up about. I'll talk with the suspects. *¿Comprende?*"

◊◊◊

BEAR AND I SPLIT AT the reception area and I found Snyder in his office. He thanked me for my presentation, which had allowed him to take charge and "do the right thing" by making full disclosure.

"What did you do after you talked to me?" I felt the tiniest pinprick of guilt. Once again I was getting ahead of Bear's plans. *Oh well.*

"Jim Nadler and I discussed the proposed operations audit until five or so. Then I was on the phone with various members of the board until nearly midnight. You might be interested to know that they all thought your analysis made sense. Thank you for making the extra effort."

A knuckle rapped at the door three times and at Snyder's command to "Come in," Jesse Thompson from IT walked in. Snyder checked his wristwatch. "Right on time."

I got up and shook Jesse's hand. "Good to see you again." His hand was damp. Nerves?

"Oh good," Snyder said, "You've met. Jesse seemed perfect because he worked in finance before joining IT and has an understanding of our reports. I've authorized him to print out anything you want. Either of you have questions?"

We looked at each other and both shook our heads. Following an awkward moment where no one knew what to say, Jesse and I departed for his work area. Away from Snyder's assistant's hearing, Jesse leaned toward me and said in a low voice, "Mr. Snyder is a nice guy, but I get nervous around any of the execs."

"I know it sounds trite, but if you remember that he puts his pants on one leg at a time it helps." I smiled at a memory. "Although when I tried the same trick when I met George Bush, it didn't help much."

His eyes grew as large as LP phonograph records. "You met the president?"

"Not the current one," I said. "His father, in the last year of his presidency. This your area?"

We had stopped at a cubicle in the bowels of the building with a Nerf ball hoop attached to the far wall above a to-do list with half the items crossed out.

"Cubicle, sweet cubicle," he said.

I requested complete information on any Chillicothe Machine annuitants with a status change during the year. He hunched over his keyboard typing commands while I peered over his shoulder.

"ANALYZING DATA" flashed on his screen like a traffic light, repeating a red-green-yellow sequence. He waved his hands in circles trying to hurry the program. Jesse's constant movement had the effect of making me conscious of each passing second. Finally, a whir from a distant printer announced success, and he retrieved a printout, the type magnifying-glass small.

"Perfect," I said. "I also want detailed budget information. What have you got?"

Bear tracked me down as I was deciding with Jesse which accounting reports would help and which would be of marginal value in understanding Appalachian's business during the last three years.

"Either I leave you here for the day or we need to leave now."

"It will take me a good long while to print these all out," Jesse said. "I can messenger them to you when they're done."

"To me," Bear said. "At the sheriff's office. That way we can log them in. Make it official."

From the corner of my eye, I tried to gauge what was going on in his mind. No clue. I stuffed the annuity information into my briefcase—I had immediate plans on how to use it—and left with Bear.

Once outside, I questioned Bear about what he had discovered. Nadler had confirmed he and Snyder had met until well after I had been ambushed. Michael Schwartz claimed he'd been meeting with outside counsel on a separate issue. Bear would verify with the lawyers. Olson was out for the day at client meetings, but according to his administrative assistant, he had not returned to his office from the executive committee meeting, and no, he hadn't told her where he went. Happened all the time, she said. Bear had also verified Jacobs' whereabouts.

"Olson was the one totally against letting us look at the financials," I said.

"Your car should be processed," he said. "Maybe you should have a glass place fix your window. I'll deliver the accounting junk to you once we get it. Where are you staying?"

In other words, I was dismissed.

Which suited me fine.

◊◊◊

THE KNOCK AT MY DOOR in the Christopher Inn rattled the walls. I peered through the peephole: Bear.

I accepted the proffered thick manila folder. "I figured you'd send a minion."

"I am the minion. What are you looking for?"

"I don't really know. If anything shifty is going on and it's recorded in the company books, it'll probably show up as a big change in a budget line from one year to the next or as a significant budget variance. That's where I'll start." I gestured toward the room's chair, but he remained standing by the door, forcing me to look up to maintain eye contact.

"Any guess how much Appalachian made because of the Chillicothe Machine murders?"

"That's in here?" He pointed to the manila folder I had placed on the table.

"Nope, but I have not been idle. Chip Kincaid told me Appalachian sold the annuities for the Chillicothe Machine retirees. Jesse Thompson, the IT kid, printed out this year's status changes for their union retirees, which included those who died from the botulism."

Bear leaned against the door and frowned. "Why didn't you tell me this?"

"I didn't have answers. Now I do. While I was waiting for this stuff, I gave the information to an actuary friend of Presser's who estimated Appalachian had a tidy actuarial gain, including the death of the former Chillicothe Machine CEO, of $5.6 million." I waggled my hand. "Give or take."

"Actuarial gain means profit?"

"Comes to twenty-eight cents a share in earnings. My source tells me it would be reflected at the end of the fiscal year."

"If that is the motive, who wins?"

"All stockholders, because the price of the stock would go up once the earnings were reported. Those with options are the big winners because they're leveraged."

"I think I understand, but give me a simple example."

"Okay, two guys. First one, a stockholder, owns a hundred shares that sell for ten bucks a share. It's worth—"

"A thousand."

"Next day the price goes up two dollars, or twenty percent, to twelve dollars a share."

"Hundred shares are now worth $1,200. Made $200."

"Right. Mr. Exec has options to buy a thousand shares at nine bucks a share. If he exercised the option before the stock price change, he'd pay $9,000. Then he sells the shares at $10 a share and clears $10,000. So the option is worth—"

"Got it. They both have investments with starting values of $1,000."

"Exactly. If he doesn't exercise the options and the next day the stock goes up two bucks, he can still buy the shares for $9,000."

Bear's face lit up. "But now he sells them for $12,000 and earns $3,000, making a $2,000 profit."

"The stockholder makes $200 and the executive makes $2,000. That's leverage."

Bear paced the room with heavy footsteps. "I see the theory, but it doesn't exactly point to anyone in particular. Unless you have some other inside information you're withholding."

"No, but all roads lead to Appalachian. Hopefully, the budget data will shed some light." Time to shift the focus from me to him before he resumed questioning me about my sources. "I've been meaning to ask, did you get the complete Phoenix police file on the ex-CEO's murder?"

"I told you already. There's nothing in there. Keep me informed of what you find. I don't want any more surprises."

I considered the last statement more an aspirational goal than a command.

With Bear gone, I sorted through the papers and looked for something odd or peculiar, an unexplained difference between what was budgeted and actually spent, an income variance, anything unusual. I eventually found it.

The total marketing budget had a substantial, but plausible, increase for the current year. The detailed budget showed most of the change was in a new category, "Consultant." All the other marketing line items had increased between 1 and 3 percent. That meant the "consultant" had not been included in any of the other budget lines the previous year, otherwise that line would have shown a decrease.

The $2.5 million for consultants had been budgeted evenly throughout the year. Could be a fixed contract agreed to before the year began, or they didn't know the timing and smoothed it out. Variance reports provided the answer. The first payment was $50,000 in May, followed by $25,000 in June, $270,000 in July, and $70,000 in August, totaling $415,000.

I pounced on the phone and jabbed Jesse Thompson's number. Voicemail. I flicked a glance at the microwave's clock: already seven thirty. I had not only worked through dinner, I had converted the room into an ice chest and until now hadn't realized I was hungry and cold.

And antsy. With tomorrow would come answers. And those could not come too soon.

THIRTY-SEVEN

THE APPALACHIAN RECEPTIONIST YAWNED AT my arrival. "Jesse Thompson left a note on my desk to let me know you were coming. You must be a morning person. Wish I could be one. Your papers are filled out. Just need your John Hancock."

"Thanks," I said, "but where's my reserved spot?"

She giggled and fanned herself with a manila folder. "I'll see what I can do. Here's Jesse."

◊◊◊

JESSE POINTED TO A LEANING stack of papers on the floor and suggested I use the empty cubicle opposite his. In no time I had figured out their accounting structure. All payments in the "Consultant" line were to Marketing Assurance Associates. Single payments in May and June. July and August each had two payments.

I asked if Jesse could determine who had approved the payments and the payee's address. It wouldn't be a problem, he said, but he had to get the file from accounting. He returned empty-handed. "Missing."

He tapped his keyboard and gave me a "That's interesting . . ." More taps while I waited in suspense. He relaxed in his chair and pointed to his monitor. "We're in luck. Another check for $10,000 to Marketing Assurance Associates is in the current batch. Here's the imprint— Cayman Islands."

"Wire transfer?"

"Yep. This is a copy of the confirm. Shows the bank transit and account numbers. We send one copy and keep another in that file I can't locate, along with the signed approval form. Only Mr. Olson can approve payments greater than $5,000 for marketing. They also require approval by either the controller or the president."

"You can't tell from this which of them approved it?"

"You need the paper file. We plan to have the whole thing go digital, but it hasn't happened yet. I'll send out an APB email to everyone in accounting about the file. Someone probably forgot to sign it out."

"That happen often?"

He shrugged. "Not supposed to . . ." He cleared his throat. "What's so interesting about this Marketing Assurance Associates?"

"I don't need it immediately," I said, "but could you verify that they're a new vendor for Appalachian this year? I'm going to see if I can catch Mr. Olson and Mr. Snyder before I leave. I suggest you keep this all to yourself. Mr. Snyder has a lot of confidence in you."

I packed the material, including a screen print of the confirmation statement, into an empty box. CIG could track down the bank. Even knowing the bank might not help; security in the Cayman Islands was tight.

Neither Snyder nor Olson was around. My enthusiasm for the day was slipping. I needed Jesse to find that file.

◊◊◊

THE CALL FROM CIG ARRIVED midmorning. No go on owner of the Marketing Assurance Associates' Cayman Islands account. Unhappy at the state of limbo I was in, I searched the radio for something I wanted to listen to and caught Sibelius's *Finlandia*. When even the stirring music couldn't lift my mood, I knew I was in trouble.

The only way I have ever been able to put the kibosh on the beginnings of depression was to be active, preferably outside. Trying again to find the ambush site would fit the bill. Perhaps if I approached it from the same direction I had been driving, I'd have a better chance of spotting it.

When I reached Bear by phone to apprise him of my meeting results and brainstorm, he asked about what I had found in the files.

"A curiosity," I said, making my voice light, "but nothing yet to report. I missed Olson and Snyder. Olson's out for a death in the family and won't be back until next week. Snyder might get back this afternoon from a meeting in Cincinnati. I have messages in to both of them. I'll know more once they call, but everything's pointing to Olson with a collaborator or two."

"Yeah, like everything pointed to Nadler earlier," Bear replied. "And look how that turned out. Remember, anyone could have made a phone call to set up the latest attack on you."

I was surprised he didn't delve into what else I had learned, and I didn't want to give him an opportunity to remember he had questioned my sources about the Colliers. I offered my brainstorm about approaching the ambush site from the direction I had driven and asked if he wanted to accompany me.

"We already canvassed the area and didn't find squat. Now, what—"

"Sorry," I said. "Got a call coming in."

I disconnected. If Bear wasn't going to help, I knew someone who would.

◊◊◊

MOLLY PICKED ME UP IN the beat-up truck. We drove through town before heading west on US 50. Several miles out, we rounded a curve, revealing a cemetery. My body tensed in recognition. "Stop!"

Molly slammed on the brakes and pulled into a private driveway immediately beyond the cemetery. The driveway crossed a culvert and proceeded to the house. "Up there." I pointed toward a dirt lane that forked right from the driveway and paralleled Route 50.

Molly pulled onto the dirt lane and was out of the truck like a borzoi on the trail of a wolf, yelling about a car having been here since the last rain. She indicated where the car had pulled into the side lane, an access road to power lines cutting across the hayfield, and turned around. The ground was too hard for any clear tire tracks. Molly pointed at bent grass, slight scuffs, and other signs of passing invisible to me as I followed in her wake.

I spun around 360 degrees and concurred that the ambusher had found a great spot for a turkey shoot: up on the hill with a clear view of the highway, and people weren't likely to notice anything as they drove by.

I caught up to Molly at a scuffed area where even I could see someone had spent time pacing. Several partial footprints molded the fine dust covering. She pointed, then reached down and picked up several small bits of paper. "Remains of a cigarette. Either it's unfiltered or he removed the filter. The guy at the Crossing smoked unfiltered Camels. Same guy?"

Molly squatted and inspected the dirt. She pointed again and said, "Tobacco. Can forensic guys figure out what kind?"

"I'm sure they can," I said. "I guess I better call Bear."

Who was not thrilled by my discovery. "Don't touch a fucking thing. I'll be out with a team."

While I waited for the police, I called Jim Nadler to determine who on the executive committee smoked and what. He had to put me on hold to call one of the other smokers at Appalachian. They were smoke-free inside and congregated together outside. Jacobs smoked Kools. Olson smoked unfiltered Camels, and only one other guy in the entire company smoked unfiltered—some kid got off on English Ovals.

"Sounds like it's time to apply thumbscrews to this Olson guy," Molly said.

With Molly, I wasn't sure whether the statement was figurative.

Bear and a couple of Ross County deputies arrived with camcorder, camera, and other gear and planted red flags wherever Molly pointed something out. I pulled Bear aside and told him about Olson's smoking habit.

"I'll stop by his house once we're done here and see if he's in," Bear said. "Assuming he is the one, he's dangerous to your health, Seamus. Stay safe. Make yourself scarce."

Molly motioned me to her and indicated, sotto voce, that her welcome was finished. She offered to take me to my car at the Christopher Inn. I told Bear we were off. He waved acknowledgment.

No sooner had we moved away from the deputies than Molly asked, "Who's this Olson guy?"

"VP at Appalachian. My current theory points to him, but until we talk to him, it's only a theory. Worse, he's supposedly not going to return until next week—assuming he hasn't flown the coop."

"If he has?"

"Once we know who and why, it's the cops' job and I'm done. It's a beautiful day and the temperature's only in the seventies. I need to take a long walk somewhere and let my thoughts percolate."

"Didn't you hear Detective Wright tell you to 'stay safe' and 'make yourself scarce'?"

"Who knows where Olson is? All I need is a place where no one expects me to go."

"I think you're crazy. That's not what he meant."

"Whatever. I agree I can't go home, but I'm not staying cooped up in some motel all day—at night's bad enough."

Her sigh would have done any Irish mother proud. "Ever hear of Fort Hill?"

I shook my head.

"It's this cool state park. It has a museum, but in September, it's only open on weekends. It's got earthen mounds made by the Hopewell Indians—I don't know—two thousand years ago or something like that. It's really a neat place, and on a weekday like this, the trails are often deserted. I'd love to show you the area."

"Where is it?"

"Not far. Continue out US Fifty toward Cincinnati and head south on State Forty-One. A sign points you to the park. I want to go home and make sure Mom and Grammy don't need help. I'll grab a camera. One of my favorite places is a spot where boulders overhang the creek."

"How long are you going to be? Should I follow you home?"

"You need to get lunch, right? I'll meet you there. If you get there before me, pick a trail and head out. It'll give me some good tracking practice. And that way, if I have to help at home, I won't hold you up. You'll remember this place forever."

Right she was.

◊◊◊

ON THE WAY TO THE park I grabbed a takeout sandwich and scarfed it down. Molly's directions brought me to a mile-long access road for Fort Hill. The driveway passed the museum, a modern-looking structure on my right, crossed a creek and dumped me into a parking lot. I chose a spot halfway down in front of a wooden sign illustrating the park trails. Slipping the car key off its ring, I locked my wallet, cell phone, and house keys into the glove compartment.

A trail immediately ahead climbed steeply uphill toward the fort area. Too obvious. I walked down the parking lot and took a trail toward Baker's Fork Creek. Although it hadn't rained in two or three days, the beginning of the trail was sloppy, mostly slick grass interspersed with muddy patches. To make it harder for Molly, I kept to the grass to avoid making obvious tracks and meandered along the trail. I hadn't been gone long when tires crunching on the gravel announced Molly's arrival. Not wanting her to see me, I ducked low and quickened my pace. An opening through the multiflora roses beckoned to the right. Dead end; I retraced my steps.

Soon I entered the shade of the woods and the temperature dropped several degrees. The trail stepped up three or four feet and leveled off, overlooking and following Baker's Fork Creek. Dawdling was easy. This was a pretty place for a contemplative walk. I expected Molly to catch up before long unless she'd taken the wrong trail, in which case who knew how long it would be before we met. I stopped and inhaled the mature scent of early autumn woods and watched tree shadows tango in the slight breeze.

The hill steepened on my left and became one wall of a gorge. Carolina chickadees chased each other overhead with *dee-dee-dees*; a nuthatch joined the excitement with its *ank-anks*. Undulating over the stream, a red-bellied woodpecker gave its shrill flight call before landing twenty-five feet up the trunk of a large beech tree.

I continued on the path, periodically wondering what was keeping Molly. The woodpecker's beech tree guarded a flat section up from the creek bank. I bent down to examine the bottom of the beech where an animal had chewed the bark. A loud crack interrupted my study of teeth striations. A bullet smacked into the tree above my head.

Funny how a sound or a smell can bring an old memory so clearly to mind. The shot's sound was the same as my memory of target practicing on my grandfather's farm. With paper targets on thick boards nailed to a big chestnut tree, I had used his .22 rifle to shoot out the bull's-eye.

The second shot creased my thigh, bringing with it the sting of iodine on an open wound.

I scrambled to the other side of the tree. Rustling sounds indicated the shooter was working his way down the hill to my right. I needed to move. Up ahead, the creek undercut outcroppings of Silurian dolomite. I ran down the trail, and where the path curved left, away from the creek, I dropped to my belly and slithered to the bank, slipping into the chilling water.

Initially crawling on all fours, I switched to a walk, my upper body floating in the deeper water while my feet, weighted down by sneakers, pushed off the streambed. My heart was hammering in my chest. As my lips tingled and I became light-headed, I realized my panting threatened hyperventilation.

I flipped onto my back, took a deep breath to try to settle, and scanned the area where I had heard my assailant coming down the hill. The current pulled me toward an outcropping—a useless hiding place, exposed to view by the creek's bend. I floated past it and checked out the next one—much better. The creek ran straight and undercut the bank by four or five feet, with only about two feet of space between the water level and the bottom of the overhanging dolomite.

I sucked in air, ducked underwater, and breaststroked my way under the rock. The creek had narrowed, increasing the force of the current. My outer left thigh reminded me of squash-ball strikes that stung at the edge and throbbed in the middle. The deeper breaths and swimming cleared my mind.

"You can run, but you can't hide, McCree." The strident male voice came from my right. "I know you're hit. I can see the blood by the tree. I'm following the spots, and in case you're wondering, your car has flat tires. Shame it's those two new ones. You're mine, sucker. I got all day and all night. Brought my nightscope."

I could hear him, but from my shelter I couldn't tell where he was. I checked my leg to determine if I was bleeding enough for him to follow my trail. Impossible to tell in the turbulence. He sounded a bit winded, though, and he was a lousy shot. Hope sprang eternal.

"This is like shooting dogs in a dump. They can only hide for so long. Well looky here. McCree decided to take a little dip. Ready or not, here I come."

Answering the question whether he could follow my trail.

"Did I mention I brought a box of a hundred shells?" he yelled. "Looking to do a little target practice, and I was bored of the range."

From the sound, I figured he was still on the bank and close to the first overhang.

"Tell me, McCree, is your curiosity worth dying for? I hope so, 'cause that's what's gonna happen today."

The current pulled at my legs. I shifted position to take pressure off my left leg—not one of my brighter moves. Setting that leg down, I slipped on slick creek-bottom rock. I slapped the water to maintain balance.

"Gotcha, you bastard." He sent two shots skipping across the water.

From where he stood, his angle wasn't going to work; but with the water only belly deep, he could hop in and walk right to me. I edged to the far side of the dolomite. *Damn!* The bank on the near side of the rock gently sloped into the water. On the opposite side, the bank was chin high and straight up. No escape there. *I'll be a duck in a shooting gallery if I try to get across the creek.*

Two choices. One: sit still and hope he decided I wasn't under the rock. Two quick shots ricocheted off the stone not two feet from where I had been. Okay, second alternative.

Taking a deep breath, I ducked under the water and swam. In high school, we'd had a contest to see who could swim the farthest underwater on a single breath. In the twenty-five-yard pool, I had made it to the end and about halfway back. I didn't do nearly as well with sneakers, a pained leg, leftover aches from my trouble at Fitzhugh Crossing, and a strong desire to surface without spouting like a whale.

Looking back, I judged I had swum only thirty feet. I slipped back under the water and submarined thirty feet more. Another outcropping stood before the next bend. I might be able to sneak out of the water behind it and make a dash.

I began to gather hope. Slide under the water—take twelve strokes— glide out—breathe—repeat. The rifle cracked two more times; ricochets zinged behind me. He thought I was still hiding under the rock. Two or three more iterations and I'd be up to the next bend and its shielding rock.

The friggin' kingfisher ratted me out.

Normally, I loved belted kingfishers. They often fished from overhanging branches on rivers and lakes, becoming plummeting flashes of blue and white in their dives. Flying from perch to perch, they called attention to themselves with loud rasping calls. They didn't have much patience with interlopers and flew at the sight of a canoeist or, in this case, a swimming mammal. The kingfisher's call and flash must have caught my stalker's attention.

I surfaced and two bullets smacked the water a few inches to my left. I dove with only a partial breath. Minds are funny, or at least mine is. It offered the picture of Davy Crockett, played by Fess Parker, using hollow reeds to breathe underwater. No reeds here.

The searing pain in my lungs brought me to the present. I needed air and I needed it right now. I muscled through two more strokes, surfaced, gulped air, and heard the rifle crack. I dove under the water and strained to get past the next big rock, succeeded, and burst to the surface, gasping. I couldn't hear anything over the rasp of my breathing and the roar of blood rushing through me.

Past the rock, the creek widened into a noisy riffle too shallow for swimming.

Beached.

The boulder provided temporary shelter and the creek would cover any noise. I slipped out of the water, crouched next to the boulder, and checked my leg. It wept blood from a deep, wide scratch. Not a problem.

The path I had been on earlier, and which my hunter was probably still on, wound around the boulder and continued down the riverbank. I could try to outrun him, or I could jump him here, using the boulder and the sharp bend in the path to shield my ambush.

Get a weapon. Rocks? Only boulders or pebbles, nothing usable. A broken limb protruded from the bank into the water, solid enough to make a reasonable stave. I leaned against the boulder for support and lifted the branch above my head, planning to smash my stalker when he came around the corner.

The riffle became my enemy, drowning out my attacker's movement. I tried to convert the creek into transparent background noise and concentrate on any sound other than the water. It didn't work. My arms grew tired; I rested the still-upraised branch against the boulder to lessen the weight.

The only person who knew I was coming here was Molly. I had not been aware of anyone following my car and, if they had, where had they picked me up? Come to think of it, I had been equally certain Molly was on my side. Maybe not.

A twig broke close by.

Then silence.

I concentrated intently on hearing something, anything. At the stalker's appearance, my breath involuntarily imploded and I froze.

My mind operated a slow-motion camera. Muscle memory of splitting gnarly yellow birch at my camp in the Upper Peninsula kicked in. I rose onto my toes and slammed the limb down.

My breath had startled him, and he faced me while retreating a step. His foot slipped on the upward curve of the path, throwing his weight away from me. His eyes, hooded by a straight line of eyebrow, were all pupil, staring into mine. His mouth, half-open with an exclamation I never heard, expectorated saliva in a thin mist. His rifle barrel swung toward me like the turret of a tank.

I tracked the downward arc of the branch, inexorably accelerating toward his head, missing, slamming into his shoulder. His slip had saved him and doomed me. The branch's momentum smashed it into the ground, pulling me off balance.

He spun around with the blow and now fully faced me, his body registering pain and fury, but his eyes . . . his eyes were smiling.

I desperately looked for an escape route.

He took a step back and pointed the rifle directly at my chest. "Nice try, McCree, but that crap only works in the movies."

I have no recollection of hearing the shot.

THIRTY-EIGHT

MOLLY STOOD BESIDE ME LOOKING down at Olson. "He'll live. Meat and lard is all he lost. I missed the shoulder bone."

"Sit up, Olson," I said.

"Fuck you."

Molly gave him a solid kick in his side. Olson and I both gasped. "Sit up when the man says sit up. Next one's in your nuts."

He rolled onto his good arm, pushed into a sitting position, draped his legs over a gently sloping rock, and eased back against the wide tree.

"Molly, a million times, thanks."

"Look at his boots, Seamus. Magic Feather Soft heels. He's a fat slob who leaves deep prints. I was tracking and saw someone else had followed you, but it's a public park, so no big deal until I spotted his print in that muddy patch before you went into the woods. I raced to the truck and traded my camera for Granddad's rifle. I'm sorry I got here so late."

"Believe me, you're forgiven." I put on my smiley voice and focused on Olson. "How did you find me?"

"You're a dead man, McCree. You too, bitch. Nobody shoots me and gets away with it."

Molly: "Why is he trying to kill you?"

"Afraid I'd figure out his game. He's behind the botulism. Ordered Presser killed. Probably killed Thomas Moyer."

Olson: "You got nothing. I wasn't even in the state on Memorial Day. All I know is I'm going to sue your ass for shooting me, bitch. And you'll be a dead man shortly, McCree. Very shortly."

Molly leveled her gun at Olson. "He killed Granddad?"

"Not personally. I'm sure he didn't personally kill Samuel Presser, either. He's the paymaster."

"You got nothing. You're blowing smoke."

Me: "We found out about Marketing Assurance Associates."

He pursed his lips and blinked twice. "What the fuck you talking about, McCree? Your head's so far up your ass you're eating shit. You got nothing."

Molly: "Will he get the death penalty?"

"I don't know. Maybe. Why?"

"I keep seeing my granddad and grammy and then this garbage." She spat at Olson and hit his cheek. "Maybe he doesn't have to be found for a while."

I thought a flicker of fear crossed Olson's eyes.

"Molly, you can't kill him."

"How about I give him time to consider fully what pain really means before I turn him over to the cops. Take him to Granddad's hunting camp. Nobody would find us there. It could take a long time for that fat lard to starve, but I'll bet it wouldn't take long before gangrene'd set in."

Olson kept glancing my way, his face troubled by tics. I didn't think Molly said it to make him nervous, but she was doing a good job of it.

Me: "Can't do it. You might like to, and he deserves it, but I can't let you."

Molly lowered her gun, resting the butt on the ground. "I suppose you're right. I don't want you to be, but I guess you are. Still, if you weren't here, I think I'd hurt this guy. I mean really hurt this guy."

She probably would. "Olson, what are you getting out of it?"

"Get me to a hospital before I get really pissed."

I stared down at his hair plugs and tried one more guess. "And Molly? I forgot to mention Mr. Olson is actually Eduardo Solonini."

His eyes bugged out; his face became puce. He couldn't speak. He hissed.

"You seem to have lost your executive language and dropped back into the sewer. Better treat me nice, Olson, because if I walk away you may have to piss in a bag for the rest of your life. I'm the only thing standing between you and immediate justice."

I ignored Olson and faced Molly. "What's the easiest way out of—"

Molly sprang to her left, grabbed her rifle by the barrel, and in a single smooth motion slammed the rifle butt down smashing skin and bones against the rock. Olson screamed, stopped long enough to suck air, and screamed again. He held his right hand before his face and stared at three crushed fingers.

"Knife in his boot. He was going for it."

I pinned Olson's right leg with one hand and pulled out a throwing knife, which he had partially extracted from a sheath sewn inside his boot. Cool to the touch, I drew its edge across my fingernail. Razor sharp. This was several leagues better than my gang knife in South Boston.

Through her sobs Molly said, "I busted . . . the stock . . . on Granddad's gun." I wrapped her in my arms, thought about what I could say, and opted for silence.

Olson rocked back and forth, his screams becoming moans. He was entering a state of shock. Time to move.

From behind, I lifted Olson to a standing position facing the tree and patted him down. He had a half pack of Camel unfiltered cigarettes in his breast pocket. His other pockets were empty except for car keys. I collected his rifle and cartridge bag from the ground.

"Start walking," I said.

"Up yours."

"Your other choice is I go for the police and Molly stays with you. Alone."

He walked.

I recalled driving past a "Welcome to Highland County" sign. The nearest hospital was in Chillicothe and I didn't want to have to deal with another police department if I could avoid it. I was sure I was breaking some law, but I decided the most expedient approach was to get Olson to the hospital and sort out the jurisdictional stuff from the relative safety of Ross County.

Only our three vehicles were in the lot, and Olson had lied about flattening my tires. Since I didn't want to disturb any evidence in Olson's car, and I didn't want the three of us sharing Molly's bench seat, we needed my car for the trip. If Molly drove, Olson and I could be in the back.

I belted him in on the passenger side to make it hard for him to get to Molly in the front if he tried anything. She stored the guns and ammo in the trunk and adjusted the driver's seat to fit her. I retrieved my wallet and cell phone and hooked the car key back on the ring before tossing it to her. I walked around the car and buckled myself in behind her, holding Olson's knife in my left hand, away from him but handy if needed. He and I were still oozing blood, but shock made him docile, or at least appear to be.

We were soon in Ross County and I called Bear. With the exception of one "unfuckingbelievable," he listened in silence. When I finished, he produced an exaggerated sigh. Couldn't I just stay in Ross County if people were going to kill me? A deputy would meet us shortly and accompany us until we met the ambulance. He would contact the Highland County Sheriff's Office.

How had I been so oblivious that I didn't see Olson following me? My right knee bounced, burning off excess energy and fear.

The first deputy reached us outside Bainbridge. Pulling his patrol car in front of us, he engaged his flashers and we picked up speed. Past Bourneville, we pulled to the side of the road to transfer Olson to the approaching ambulance. Officers in the accompanying patrol cars came out with guns drawn. Once they saw what shape Olson was in, they holstered them and watched the paramedics strap him on a gurney and place him in the ambulance. One officer went with Olson. The others secured the guns and ammo from the trunk and stored Olson's knife in an evidence bag.

"Leave your car here," a cop said to me. "We'll pick it up later. We're supposed to take you two in for your statements."

"Isn't it too late to worry about us colluding on a story?" I said.

My cop frowned. "Are you saying you've already colluded?"

Being a wise-ass generally has more to do with the ass part than the wise. I shut up before I dug any more holes for Molly or myself.

◊◊◊

AT HEADQUARTERS, TWO OFFICERS REMOVED Molly to one room while Bear and Sheriff Lyons escorted me to another. I had dried out, except for my sneakers, which squished at every step. I followed the sheriff's Vitalis into a small interrogation room that stank of sweat and fear. They grilled me on the details of what had happened at Fort Hill.

Once they finished taking my statement, they both left. I assumed they were checking my version against Molly's. Ten minutes later, Bear returned.

"Your stories mostly match. Not that we didn't believe you, but you know—"

"You had to make sure. What's next?"

"We're getting search warrants for Olson's house and office. His car is already on a hook and heading in. It took some effort to straighten out the jurisdictions."

"Olson was clearly nonplussed at my mention of Marketing Assurance Associates. I'm guessing it's the conduit he used to pay off the killer. The file with the approval forms is missing from Appalachian. Olson may have stolen it. Because either the president or controller approved the invoices, one of them may be involved. Olson seems too rash to be the brains."

An officer brought Molly to us. "We'll find out," Bear said. "While these gentlemen take you to the park to compare your statements with the physical evidence, we'd like to have forensics process your car, Seamus. Assuming you have no objections?"

"Do you have any special deals, like the third time I get a free oil change?"

"Highland County is not happy with your departing the scene of the crimes," Bear said. "My suggestion? Can the humor."

◊◊◊

OFFICERS HAD CLOSED THE PARK to keep the public out. Molly showed the deputies where she had spotted Olson's heel print. She found the shell casings from Olson's first two shots. The deputies dug a slug out of the beech tree and found the one that had scraped my leg buried in the dirt. In all, they found twelve .22 casings.

The deputies made a cast of Olson's heel print, captured video and still shots of each evidence location, and spent extra time around the area where Olson was shot. I didn't watch them scrape pieces of Olson off rocks and catalog them in evidence bags. I could hear the crack of Molly's rifle butt slamming into Olson's hand and his scream reverberating in the gorge. Once a beautiful spot—maybe even the one Molly had in mind to take her picture—it would now haunt my memory.

Once done, we caravanned to headquarters, where Bear waited, wrapped in a big smile.

"Goldmine at Olson's house. One of our guys was suspicious about a newly painted closet wall and found a safe hidden behind it. Got a freshly cleaned snub-nose thirty-eight. We sent it to the lab to test it against the slug that killed Moyer. Be sweet if it matched. We found draft copies of the note you got at the Christopher Inn from Joe Fourier. They seem to match Olson's handwriting. I figure he read about Fourier in the paper and used the name and excuse to set you up."

Bear turned to Molly. "They'll be looking at Olson's car more thoroughly, but a preliminary comparison of the tire track cast from Fitzhugh Crossing shows a match to Olson's tires. And he has a fresh tire on—"

"The left rear wheel," Molly finished.

"Right . . . I mean, exactly. We need to process Molly's truck. We found a transmitter on your car, Seamus. Highland says Olson's car had the receiver. Pretty sophisticated. He knew exactly where you were."

"How did you miss the transmitter before?"

He rose to his full height, expanded his chest, and looked as though he would like to squash me like a noisome bug. "Must have put it on after we looked at your car."

Sure. I needed to return to my normal sequence of think first, speak second. I was apparently reacting to shock as well. "You do his office yet?"

"Sheriff Lyons and I thought you might help with what we should be looking for. We've got a deputy waiting with Jesse Thompson."

"I'd love to go. I need to take Molly home since Highland impounded her truck."

"I'll have an officer run her home. You can come with me."

"Go, Seamus," Molly said. "I want them all. I want them for killing Granddad and hurting Grammy. Don't worry about me." Molly touched Bear's arm. "Any idea when they'll get my truck back to me?"

"Well, no," he said. "I think the bigger question, really, is whether or not they're going to charge you two. That's why we need to get Seamus's help now. We can't use him if he's been arrested."

THIRTY-NINE

I WAS THE FIRST ONE to step into Olson's office and caught a hint of cigarettes. *I guess if you're willing to kill someone, sneaking a smoke in the office is small potatoes.* Bear went through Olson's desk drawers, looked behind books, felt under shelves, checked under the credenza, poked up the ceiling tiles—and found nothing. He left Jesse Thompson and me to ransack Olson's computer. Jesse reset the password to grant me access.

The screen welcomed Ed Olson to the network. Each employee, Jesse informed me, had a secure area on the server to which only the individual and IT had access: the P directory.

I mouse-clicked the P directory. Empty. "Is that unusual?"

"They're never clean," Jesse said.

"Backups?"

"Nightly, with a full weekly, but it'll take a ton of time. I'll have to do it over the weekend when nothing's running."

I tried Olson's hard drive—only system files and standard program files.

"Jesse, do you have one of those utilities to restore deleted files?"

Lips a straight line, he shook his head.

"I know my son does. Is there a way to give him remote access to this machine?"

His eyes smiled, then his mouth. "Sure, we can do that." He bounced on his toes and rubbed his hands together.

I dialed Paddy on the speakerphone. He and Jesse figured out the protocols. In less than a quarter hour, Paddy was remotely controlling Olson's machine. Jesse and I watched the cursor move and the screen display resurrected files.

"Paddy, can you do a search for any files containing 'Marketing Assurance Associates' or 'MAA'?"

"No problemo," replied the speakerphone. Within two minutes, he had confirmed what I saw on the screen: "No matches."

"Try 'fifty thousand,'" I said, "with or without the comma."

One hit, an Excel file titled "Summary." Paddy opened it.

What	Amount	Total
Deposit on Contract	$50,000	$50,000
Pest Control	25,000	75,000
First count 28 (less 2 not ours less deposit)	210,000	285,000
Second count 35 (less 28 less 1 not ours)	60,000	345,000
Deposit on Contract # 2	50,000	395,000
Third count 37 (less 35)	20,000	415,000
Special Project	25,000	440,000
Pest Control #2	25,000	465,000
Fourth count 38 (less 37)	10,000	475,000

Paddy sent the file to the printer. I called Bear in. "This details the payments to Marketing Assurance Associates. How many died from the picnic?"

"You already know—thirty-eight."

"Right, and three didn't have annuity policies. You're looking at a record of the payments to the killer. The bastard was on a contingency basis at ten thousand a head."

Jesse plopped down in Olson's chair, squishing out the air in one whoosh. His mouth agape, eyes vacant.

"I don't follow you," Bear said. "Give me the 'Crime for Dummies' version."

"Okay. The deposit was to get the guy to do the work—fifty grand up front. The next payment was some time after twenty-eight had died. Two of them were not annuity holders or beneficiaries. The killer was paid based on twenty-six targeted deaths. That's two hundred and sixty thousand less the fifty paid up front."

"Two hundred and ten thousand. The next payment is seven deaths later and one was not an annuity person. Right?"

I gave him a thumbs-up.

"What's this 'Pest Control'?

"Contract for Presser?" I mused aloud. "Timing looks about right."

"Deposit number two means he's got another mass murder working?" Bear asked.

"That's my guess. He hasn't paid anything beyond the deposit. Maybe nothing's happened?"

"And the second Pest Control means he had a contract on someone else? Moyer?"

My neck hairs tightened. My vision blurred for a moment. I muted the speakerphone. "Not Moyer. I bet Olson did Moyer himself. I think it's me." Saying it made me feel better. "Bet the 'Special Project' was the Phoenix murder."

"Oh man, we gotta put the screws to Olson before someone gets to you."

"I'm more concerned about the next mass murder. We have to stop it."

Bear slammed his fist on the table. "How the hell are you going to do that? Oh God, I don't even want to think about another Chillicothe Machine deal."

While we spoke, the computer screen showed Paddy's efforts as he continued searching Olson's hard drive.

"Our best chance," I said, "is to make Olson's arrest known and imply without specificity that he's a suspect in masterminding the Memorial Day botulism murders. If we can get national media play, the person hired to do the next one may get cold feet, especially if he figures he isn't going to get paid."

"Maybe—"

"At the same time, we contact every company with an Appalachian group annuity and find out if they have any events where their retirees may get together. Have them postponed or canceled."

"That's a big chore.

"CIG can do it. Maybe we can use the Homeland Security apparatus to help us. Let's see if I can get the list from Nadler."

Jesse piped up from where he sat in Olson's chair. "I can run it from here."

I punched the speakerphone back on and thanked Paddy.

"Sorry, Dad. No contact information on Marketing Assurance Associates. You still picking me up at the airport tomorrow?"

A feeling of embarrassment flushed over me. In the excitement I had forgotten all about his picking up stuff from the house to take to school. What time was the flight? "I hope to be home, but things are breaking here. Maybe it's safer if you catch a cab—even better, I'll set up a limo for you, that way I can prepay. Remind me when your flight is coming in?"

I wrote down his flight details and immediately ordered the limo before I forgot. He logged off. Jesse used the computer to produce a list of companies, sorted by their number of annuitants, ranging from 519 to 2. Most of them were companies I had never heard of. Those with more than 300 annuitants were Extrusion Unlimited, Global Pressings, Sisters of the Transfigured Blood, Hocking Hills Trading, Chillicothe Machine, Cincinnati Castings, and Unterboten Express. Next to each contract was a contact person and phone number. Perfect.

Jesse slapped his forehead. "Wait right here. I should have thought of this before."

Bear and I traded glances and then continued reading the list.

"I got it," Jesse said, showing me a manila folder.

"The missing file?" I asked.

"Close. We've been testing a paperless system, and I wondered if any of those authorizations were part of the test. I found three. Hope they help."

Olson had approved all three. Snyder had countersigned.

The memo field held cryptic notes. The authorization reflected "Prepayment 5 days' work," and the $210,000 check note stated "Contingency payment for results." The label for the $25,000 check was "489 English Poet."

Presser's address was 489 Milton. Memo to self: pass info to Lt. Hastings.

With Bear shadowing me, I asked Olson's secretary about the payment authorization copies. She claimed never to have seen them or heard of Marketing Assurance Associates. To the best of her knowledge, they had never been on his calendar. Her face exhibited a quizzical expression as she flipped through the material again.

"I don't think these are Mr. Snyder's signatures," she said. She removed a folder from a file cabinet behind her, looked at its contents, tapped her finger on her lips, and placed the file on her desk where we could see it. "I know these are Mr. Snyder's. I was there when he signed them."

Bear and I made the comparison and concluded that while there were certain similarities, they appeared to be two different signatures. Bear confiscated the file to allow the experts to do their thing.

We left Jesse to shut down Olson's computer and hightailed it to Snyder's office. He wasn't in, but his assistant had multitudinous sample signatures. The ones on the payment authorizations were not his. Which didn't mean Snyder wasn't forging his own signature so he could deny responsibility.

I made a snap decision to beg forgiveness later rather than ask Rand's permission now. "Bear, do you have contacts with the local news media?"

"Yeah . . . why?"

"I want to be interviewed about my experience with Olson today and offer my speculations about the possible second mass murder. The sheriff, if he's asked to confirm, can refuse to comment on anything I say, since it's an active investigation."

"You don't like rules much, do you?" He shook his head, but at the same time picked up the phone.

"Hi, it's me, Bear. This isn't official . . . Yeah, exactly. I suggest you have a team in front of the north entrance to the hospital, underneath the pillars, in twenty minutes . . . I believe it'll be your six o'clock lead . . . Name's Seamus McCree . . . Lyons mentioned him at the club? . . . Hmm . . . Yeah, you can decide exclusive or not, but it won't be for long, and remember you didn't get this from me, and it isn't official . . . Thanks, bye."

He prodded me with a hard finger to the chest. "I just put my ass on the line. It better not come back in a sling."

◊◊◊

WE PARKED BY THE EMERGENCY room entrance. Bear went to find Olson. I followed the signs through the construction toward the north entrance. Television and radio were coordinating setting up mics, lights, and so forth while hospital personnel seemed to be simultaneously trying to figure out what was happening and appear nonchalant. A nurse pointed to my leg and asked if I needed assistance. I thanked her and said I was okay.

I walked to the woman giving orders and introduced myself. She wore a patterned blouse, pressed gray slacks, jacket, and pumps. Her long blond hair, parted in the middle, curved around her face like wide parentheses focusing attention on the pendant tastefully sitting at the open neck of her blouse.

She looked me over and beamed a sparkling smile. "Cindy Nelson. Oh, you look perfect, Seamus. What a sense of theater you have."

Her handshake was strong and dry. We agreed I would start by giving my short prepared remarks, then she would ask questions.

"Seamus, give me a hint what this is about? Why should I trust you?"

"You trust Detective Wright?"

Without hesitation she said, "Bear's always been straight."

"This is much larger than my being shot by the guy the cops arrested and brought here today. You'll be glad you came."

She shook her finger at me. "You're a naughty boy. I like that."

Cindy gave me a cue and I stepped to the mics, looked directly at the camera, and began. "My name is Seamus McCree. Today Mr. Edward Olson, who I understand is in police custody in this hospital, attempted to kill me. It is the third attempt on my life in the last two weeks. I suspect Mr. Olson, whose real name is probably Eduardo Solonini, also sponsored the first two attempts."

I was accustomed to microphones and speaking in an unnaturally formal way. What I hadn't experienced, however, were the surprisingly hot lights. I hoped I wasn't sweating. "Now, I'm a nice guy. Why would someone want to kill me?" I paused for effect.

"I have uncovered evidence implicating Mr. Olson in a despicable scheme to profit from the Chillicothe botulism murders, which killed thirty-eight."

Hospital staffers no longer made any pretense of ignoring us. People streamed into the crowd gathering underneath the covered area outside the entrance. Bear watched the proceedings, looking over everyone's head.

"I believe Mr. Olson is responsible for paying ten thousand dollars per death related to the Memorial Day mass murder. The police have this evidence and I have every confidence justice for these crimes will prevail. That information alone might be news, but I would not be standing here if it were all I knew or feared.

"I am here to ask your assistance in spreading the word. Mr. Olson and his conspirators may have planned a second attack directed at a large group of Appalachian Casualty and Life annuitants. Since Olson is in custody, those involved in a second attack will receive no further compensation, and therefore have no reason to carry out their plot.

"Appalachian Casualty and Life has been cooperating fully with the investigation. I will personally make sure all organizations with Appalachian annuity contracts are contacted. I have no details about where or when the attack is planned. Many lives and millions of dollars are at stake if these criminals are successful. If you in the media assist me in getting this message of concern out, together we may save some other community the heartbreak Chillicothe has felt because of the Memorial Day atrocity. Thank you. I will now take questions."

The camera panned to Cindy Nelson. "Mr. McCree, how did you come upon this information?"

"I have been assisting the Ross County Sheriff's Office with some aspects of the Memorial Day botulism murder investigation. I want to be clear. I am here on my own, not as a representative of any organization."

"You mentioned annuity contracts. Is that some kind of life insurance?"

"Thank you for the clarifying question. Annuities aren't life insurance. They are more like pension payments. Appalachian sells many types of contracts to both individuals and companies. The only types we are concerned about are annuities purchased by an organization for its employees, usually as part of a pension plan."

"If the police have this same evidence, Mr. McCree, why aren't they here with you?"

"I can only tell you why I am here. I wish to prevent a recurrence of the tragedy that struck Chillicothe. I am confident the police are doing everything within their power. I have been impressed with the efficiency of the Ross County Sheriff's Office, especially the corporate crime task force headed by Detective Albert Wright. Disseminating this information is a great service you can perform."

I relaxed and smiled to the camera. "And at the same time, the story will be good for your ratings."

"Do you believe this second attack will also involve botulism?"

"As the media have reported, terrorists can attack groups of people in many ways. Until we can root out the entire coterie, I think it is wise to postpone large gatherings of potentially targeted groups."

The questions and answers continued for about fifteen minutes before they wrapped in time to edit for their evening news. Cindy strode to me with her thousand-watt beam. "Splendid! You're taking a big risk, but I'd bet a dinner that you're our lead story, even if you did use a twenty-five-cent word like 'coterie' when 'group' would have done just as well. Speaking of dinner, what are you doing after our broadcast?"

I *was* hungry, but the only reason she'd want to have dinner with me was to dig deeper into my story. That was not in my best interest. Besides, Bear probably still wanted a piece of my time, and I needed to get out of my "wash and wear" clothes courtesy of the creek at Fort Hill. That would require fresh clothes from Cincinnati. With Pest Control #2 for $25,000 still floating out there, I would do well to stay at the Cincinnatian again.

I thanked her for her offer, but explained I had pressing work. Could I have a rain check?

One of the nurses dragged me off, insisting I have my leg properly attended. Bear waited until the emergency room had cleaned and bandaged my wound.

As we walked away from emergency, he said, "Quite a statement. What now?"

FORTY

BEAR AND I SCARFED DOWN Chinese and watched my performance on the TV in the sheriff's breakroom. With no reason to stick around after the show only to watch Bear do paperwork, I retrieved my car from the impound lot. I had sown; now I'd see what I reaped.

I was still in Chillicothe when I received a call from CNN. We tried using the cell phone, but the service kept cutting out. I found an outside phone at a service station to complete the interview. By the time I finished, three more calls had come in: NPR, one of the network morning shows, and a sputtering, fuming diatribe from a pissed president of Appalachian. William Snyder thought I was ruining his company. Half an hour later, he was speaking nonprofane English and had decided I had probably saved his company rather than destroyed it.

On my advice, he agreed to call his own news conference for tomorrow morning before markets opened. He would contact his directors tonight and convince them to approve a fund using the actuarial gains from the Memorial Day botulism deaths. The fund would pay for unreimbursed medical care and other losses caused by the crime.

I called back the news organizations and ultimately arranged a radio interview with NPR and an on-camera network appearance. Both would take place early the next morning in Cincinnati. While I was arranging those, Robert Rand left a message. I filled him in on recent events.

"Ross County faxed us the list of organizations with Appalachian group annuity contracts," Rand said. "We are already on it. I spent the better part of an hour engaged in conversation with Detective Wright about your recent mishaps. We agree you have been a tad casual about these attempts on your life. Consequently, I have engaged the services of a highly qualified bodyguard. Your coverage starts tonight."

"I don't need—"

"This is not up for discussion, Seamus. I was fortunate because the bodyguard and car were already in Cincinnati for personal business. They will be waiting for you at the Cincinnatian. She has already been by your place and packed your clothes for a few days."

His choice of words caught my attention. His *fortunate* would be my *lucky*. Then a disturbing thought raised its claw for attention. "She packed my clothes? How?"

"You once told me your neighbor with the dog had a key to your house. She let the bodyguard in and supervised. You are blessed to have someone as interested in your health as she is."

He's fortunate, I'm blessed. *How nice.* "You paying?"

"Of course, you penurious skeezicks. Have I ever scrimped on you? Besides, this has to be less expensive than the damage to your vehicles."

I had no clue what a skeezicks might be, but since it was combined with a fancy word for *stingy*, I didn't figure it for a compliment.

◊◊◊

CIG HAD ALREADY PAID MY reservation at the Cincinnatian. The desk clerk welcomed me back and handed me a room key and an envelope with a note. One of my suitcases sat inside the room, packed with whatever a bodyguard thought I should be wearing. It had been a long time since someone else had chosen my clothes for me, and I was not looking forward to the results.

The note probably presented perfect Palmer penmanship. I've joked that my hand can't keep up with my brain, resulting in the nearly illegible McCree scrawl. If handwriting was indicative of different styles, I had a feeling the bodyguard and I were going to be like oil and water. I read the note.

Rand hired me to protect you. Call my room once you get in, regardless of the time. Signed A, with a room number.

I wasn't doing anything until I had a long shower. Scented from the soap, muscles relaxed, fresh clothes—the selections seemed reasonable— and *voilà*, a new man. I dialed A's room and heard a phone ring next door.

A feminine voice answered with "This Seamus? I'm Abigail. Meet me in the lobby bar so we can talk about tomorrow."

"Okay. How will I know you?"

"I'll know you. Wait five minutes before you come down. I need to make sure the lobby is secure."

"That's ridiculous. This is the Cincinnatian."

"Which demonstrates clearly why you need a bodyguard. Five minutes."

◊◊◊

MY EYES NEEDED TO ADJUST to the dim barroom lighting before I saw an athletic brunette signaling me. I offered her my hand, which she shook without hesitation. Compared to Cindy Nelson's strong and dry handshake, this woman's was muscular. Subconsciously, I had expected an Amazon. She stood five eight or five nine in sandals. I guessed her age at thirty-five, plus or minus. Her caramel-colored eyes sucked me in. A logical part of my mind told me her pupils were large because of the lack of light. Other parts of me could not have cared less. Some bodyguard.

We sat alone in a corner where she could scan the bar and the main entrance. I pushed aside one of the russet throw pillows on the blue couch and settled in, placing us at a ninety-degree angle.

She ordered seltzer water; I chose the house cabernet. The server left and I requested her full name.

"Abigail Gwendolyn Hancock, but anything past Abigail is superfluous."

Her smile was broad, making me feel at ease. I thought maybe I'd like Abigail Gwendolyn Hancock despite her perfect penmanship.

"I've never had a bodyguard. What do I need to know?"

"Only one thing. If I tell you to do something, you do it immediately, without any thought, without any question. You will do it because if you don't, you may not have a chance to do anything else."

"I—"

"And Seamus, from what Robert Rand tells me, that one thing may be hard for you. I'm going to make it easy and not give you oodles of little rules, although they might be helpful. Just one. I say 'jump,' you immediately jump as high and far as those two legs can take you. Got it?"

I assented and patiently sipped my wine.

"A big Irish lad like you have any problems taking orders from a sweet little English girl like me?"

"Sweet little girl? I doubt it. I don't give a crap if you're the queen's handmaiden, provided you don't start talking about the glorious victories at Boyne and Aughrim."

"Whatever the hell they are."

I smiled. "Fine. What did you want to tell me that you don't want to sound like orders?"

"Very good, Seamus. Robert informed me you're intelligent in a productive way. Let me know your plans as soon as possible, and we can figure out together how to safely accomplish them. I go with you everywhere. I will be your chauffeur. We have a special car we'll use. I draw the line at the men's room—normally—but if need be, I will clear it before I let you in."

"And you step in front of bullets?"

"One more stupid question and I'll ring a large gong and cause you a nightlong headache. Hopefully, I prevent them coming your way. If someone gets a shot off, you had better hope they miss. In certain situations I will insist you wear a Kevlar vest—like the police use, but less bulky."

"Tuck me in at night?"

"You asked for it." She tapped her phone awake, pressed an app and in a moment our space was filled with a ringing gong.

It felt good to laugh.

"I will make sure your room is clear before you enter, but if you want someone between your sheets, you'll need to arrange that on your own. Any other adolescent questions, or can we talk about tomorrow?"

"No more questions, Miss Abigail. Please, let's talk about tomorrow."

Her whole body, except for her eyes, laughed along with me. She leaned in and poked my arm hard enough to give me a twinge. "Good boy, Seamus. We'll do fine."

I ordered another glass of wine and told her about tomorrow's plans. Afterward, I had to remain in the doorway while she checked to make sure there were no bombs under my bed or goons in the closet. She motioned me in and told me the connecting doors between our rooms were unlocked. I raised my eyebrows and she reached for her cell phone.

I raised my hand defensively. "No gong."

"It's a precaution, not an invitation. Keep in mind, Seamus, if you are correct about the second planned massacre, you have cost a killer millions of dollars."

FORTY-ONE

HE FINISHED HIS RUN WITH an all-out sprint that ended a block before the Cincinnatian. His panting covered a quick inhale when he spotted McCree standing in the lobby. What were the chances? Yet there he was, and nothing the Happy Reaper could do about it.

He walked toward reception, sweat dripping onto the hotel floor with miniature plops. Using the mirror behind the receptionist, he captured a mental picture of the woman with a commanding presence. Cop or bodyguard? Very attractive. He'd bet lots of people underestimated her—a mistake he would not make. He pretended to stretch and dilly-dallied long enough to discover the make and model of the car they were using. Armored, he decided, given how low it rode. That would make her a bodyguard.

Back in his room, he set the shower for hot. While it warmed up he tuned the radio to NPR to get the morning news and was stunned by McCree's interview. Two fucking days wasted when McCree blew by his ambush Tuesday afternoon. He could not believe Solonini's stupidity. He should have bailed out when the guy tried using a handkerchief to disguise himself. That was his mistake, which was minor compared to Solonini trying to do the job on McCree himself and screwing up everything. Everything! Including compromising a two-million-dollar job. Getting caught served the bastard right.

He paced, boxing the air in his frustration, too angry even to whistle. He stopped. Staring out the window, he let out a sigh. He was the Unhappy Reaper, and that was not right.

He stepped into the shower, grabbed his neck, and massaged corded muscles. *Don't physically react*, he told himself. *Analyze. You can't control what other people do, but you must control your own reaction.* He toweled off and contemplated the worst that would happen if Solonini spilled his guts. They could uncover the telephone drop, the next location, and a link between all the jobs, past and present. That was it. Bad, not terrible.

He dialed long distance and entered his own five-digit code, punched star and three digits, canceling the answering service.

He reminded himself that his luck was still holding. What were the chances McCree would end up hiding in his hotel? If he hadn't jogged after the night's surveillance at McCree's—well, *in* McCree's, to be more accurate—he would never have seen them.

Preparation meets luck.

Was McCree coming back? He called the switchboard and asked for Mr. McCree's room. Mr. McCree had checked out.

Where had they gone? Probably not to McCree's home; they wouldn't have stayed at the Cincinnatian if they thought his home was safe. Probably to Chillicothe. That's where the action was. Listening to media might point him in the correct direction. Right now, he needed sleep to rest and prepare for whatever opportunities arose.

He flicked on the Weather Channel and learned rain and cool were predicted for Atlanta this weekend. If it got cool enough, one hundred little clicks later . . .

Who didn't like a rainy night in Georgia? Especially a cool one.

Yes indeed. It wasn't really about the money, was it? He caught himself whistling "Something's Coming" from *West Side Story*. All right, he was the Happy Reaper once again. Time to wrap up loose ends.

FORTY-TWO

AT 4:20 A.M., THE CHIRPING ALARM had roused me. Too early, even for me, but I could fool myself if I converted the time to forty minutes before five. The morning went well. While Abigail was checking us out of the Cincinnatian, I paid the valets to take my car home after their shift ended. I must have been excessively generous because they sprinted away when Abigail asked them to bring her car. Or had it been because of how fetching she looked dressed in chauffeur black?

The NPR radio interview went off without a hitch. The second interview, at a television studio on top of Prospect Hill, took longer because they would edit it before airing. I never saw it, but the effect was what I wanted. Throughout the nation, people woke to my warning on TV and radio. Plus, since AP had picked up the story from the hospital interview, small blurbs appeared in many papers across the country.

Abigail and I met Bear at Sue's for breakfast. I made the introductions as Charlene poured coffee for the two of them. Bear pestered Abigail with a thousand questions about how different weapons affected the car's armor. I lost interest in their discussion. What fascinated me was watching Abigail. While she engaged with Bear in a detailed conversation, her eyes hawked the area, scrutinizing each car pulling into the lot and each customer entering Sue's. My eyes grew tired following hers.

"Find anything else on Olson?" I asked.

"As you guessed, his prints prove he's Solonini. His car had been wiped down, but we found one print of Moyer's on the passenger seat control switch."

"Did the tires match with the Fitzhugh Crossing prints?" I asked.

"Yeah. We've about nailed the coffin shut on Moyer's murder and trying to blow you up."

We agreed our priority for the day was to try to crack Solonini. Perhaps he'd go for a deal: name the killer and the next intended victims in exchange for life imprisonment rather than capital punishment. Until the ballistics report tied Moyer's death to Solonini's .38, we really didn't have anything other than circumstantial evidence. Solonini didn't need to know how weak our case was.

Before we talked with him, I wanted to spend more time on his computer. We also wanted to talk with Snyder. Although the payment authorization forms had a fake signature, it didn't mean he wasn't an accomplice.

"I'll drive us to Appalachian and then the hospital," Bear said.

"He goes with me," Abigail said.

Bear stretched to his full height and looked down his nose at her. "But I'm police."

Abigail smiled. "I promise not to speed."

◊◊◊

THE APPALACHIAN RECEPTIONIST GREETED US with a winsome smile. "New wheels and a chauffeur, Mr. McCree. Coming up in the world."

"I'm still looking for my private spot," I said.

She winked. "I'll put it on a higher priority. You know with that old thing you were driving, I wasn't sure I wanted it in front of our building."

"I am deeply hurt. You giving us passes so the laser beams don't get us or have you turned them off today?"

"You're a riot, Mr. McCree. It's safe . . . for now."

She waved us through and we walked to what I now thought of as Solonini's office. While we waited for Jesse to log me into the computer, Bear reinterviewed Olson's administrative assistant. Abigail parked herself in an empty cubicle and made phone calls, and I used my cell phone to answer more messages from the media. Had I opened Pandora's box?

Once logged in, I explored Olson's hard drive, which Paddy had completely restored. Paddy hadn't found references to Marketing Assurance Associates or MAA because Solonini stored those documents as JPEG files. I found copies of all the payment authorization forms for Marketing Assurance Associates.

The annotations for the Chillicothe Machine retiree murder payments were what I had expected. The note attached to the deposit for Contract #2 said "Habits." The Special Project was noted "11 Chukar Lane." I'd never seen one, but I could picture a chukar from my Peterson bird guide. Introduced to North America, the bird looked something like a bobwhite or members of the quail family.

My throat contracted at the notation on Pest Control #2, "Cincinnati shamus"—a wordplay on my profession and name. Solonini hadn't lied about one thing: he had put a contract on me.

Was Solonini's scheme to kill annuitants simply designed to make Appalachian more profitable? Or did the mob have plans to skim profits somehow? No answers here.

Abigail accompanied me to see Snyder while Bear continued to pore over files with Olson's assistant.

Snyder had reacted quickly. The board vote was not unanimous, but had overwhelmingly approved my suggestion to use the actuarial gains from the Memorial Day tragedy to fund victims' relief. Shortly after he learned (or claimed to learn, I had to remind myself) about the forged payment authorization forms, he asked for and received the controller's resignation—internal audit was his responsibility. Snyder brought the former CFO temporarily out of retirement to take control of the finances. He hosted a webcast before the markets opened to tell the analysts what steps Appalachian had taken. He had a call scheduled with the Ohio Department of Insurance for later in the day.

"I'm sorry for ranting at you last night," Snyder said.

I waved it off.

"I wasn't angry at you. I was pissed with everyone who had used Appalachian. Here I am. I've spent my whole life working here. I'm a few years from retirement, and I'll probably be fired."

Snyder didn't act like a suspect. We wished him luck and went to find Bear. He was still plowing through files. Abigail lounged on Olson's couch while I used his desk phone.

I was talking with NBC, explaining why I would not be flying to New York to be on their Sunday morning show, when Bear, with a Cheshire cat grin, burst into the office waving a piece of paper. I disconnected the phone call while I was talking so they'd assume a bad connection.

"Time to break Solonini."

◊◊◊

SOLONINI'S LAWYER WAS CHATTING WITH the deputy guarding the hospital room where Solonini was recovering from surgery on his hand. The lawyer, Bear, and I crowded into the room, leaving Abigail outside to cool her heels with the deputy.

Solonini was propped in bed, his left shoulder immobilized in a tight sling. His bandaged right hand lay on his lap. An IV dripped into his right arm. A cuff attached his ankle to the bed. At least he didn't have any of those beeping monitors that made me nervous. The place smelled of disinfectant, but I wasn't about to object to anything that killed germs in hospitals.

Bear muted the TV.

"What the fuck you doing? I pay for that." Solonini pointed at me. "And get that dead man McCree out of here."

"I'm Detective Wright. Are you threatening Mr. McCree?" Bear asked in his politest voice. "I'll happily add more charges to the ones I came here to discuss."

"I'm not discussing anything as long as that asshole is here. Get him out. Now!"

"Then this will be a one-way conversation."

Solonini raised another objection, but his lawyer gave him the cut-it sign and Solonini slumped against the pillows.

"Here are some facts I thought you and your counsel would find interesting. Fact one, your real name is Eduardo Paul Solonini. Your prints match those of a thug who supposedly died ten years ago.

"Two, we found a safe tucked behind some freshly painted drywall in your bedroom closet. Inside was a recently cleaned thirty-eight-caliber gun. And, miracles of miracles, the self-same Solonini's fingerprints were present on the weapon.

"Three, a bullet from that particular thirty-eight killed Thomas Moyer. One, two, three add up to the hot chair for you."

"I need to speak alone to my client," the lawyer said.

"Shush. I'm not asking questions, I'm providing information you need. You'll have plenty of time with your client."

The lawyer settled against the door.

"In addition, we know you authorized payments to Management Assurance Associates. We know that's how you paid for the botulism murders. We know you paid for the murder of Samuel Presser in Cincinnati. We know about Glen Framington, Chillicothe Machine's ex-CEO in Phoenix."

Solonini started to object with a string of curses having loosely to do with my parents being unmarried dogs. Bear cut him off and kept on talking.

"I'll be honest with you, counselor. We don't know who the contract killer is, and we'd like to. We'll leave you two to discuss these facts. Once you're finished talking, we'll have some questions."

While Bear presented the evidence and speculation to Solonini, I had one of those "oh crap" moments. I had been so concerned with Chillicothe, I'd neglected to keep the Cincinnati police updated about the Presser investigation. I sure didn't want Lieutenant Hastings hearing it from the news before she heard it from me. With Abigail trailing behind, I walked to the window of the unoccupied room next to Solonini's. A nurse passing by shooed me from the room, pointing toward the visitor's lounge.

Solonini's lawyer found us in the hall. "He wants to talk privately to Mr. McCree."

Abigail perceptibly stiffened. Bear said, "That's not the deal. I'm the one with questions."

Lieutenant Hastings will have to wait. "He's chained to a bed," I said, as much to myself as to Abigail and Bear. I motioned them away from the lawyer and whispered, "What's the harm? Maybe he'll say something he shouldn't."

Argument won, I entered Solonini's room and went on the offensive. "Marketing Assurance Associates is a phantom. Who did you pay?"

"I got only one thing to say to you, McCree, so listen good. The guy you want. His card says 'Results Guaranteed.' If I was you, I'd make sure my affairs are in order. You might even think of buying some extra life insurance."

I may have intellectually understood the concept of his hiring a hitman, but hearing the words "Results Guaranteed" triggered the feeling that I had forgotten something important. "What did you say?"

He laughed and fished around his bed for the magic wand that controlled everything in the room.

I wanted to regain the upper hand. "What organization are you targeting next? We know you paid a fifty-grand deposit. No one is going to benefit. If you watched the news instead of Nickelodeon, you'd know

Appalachian is applying the profit they earned off your botulism victims for charitable purposes. Your cohorts won't see dollar one."

"Guaranteed." He found the device and sound blasted from the TV.

◊◊◊

AWAY FROM SOLONINI'S LAWYER, I recounted the conversation. Abigail's face hardened as I repeated the line about guaranteed results. Bear worked his hands like he wanted to choke someone.

"Rand mentioned you had a cabin someplace remote?" Abigail said.

"I am not going."

Bear tag-teamed with Abigail to convince me I should take the threat seriously.

"Whatever," I concluded. "I am *not* running. I am *not* hiding. I *am* going to stop the next mass murder *any* way I can."

"I thought you were going to listen to your bodyguard," Abigail said.

"See if you can get Solonini to talk," I said to Bear. "I need to bring the Cincinnati police up to speed. Time's a-wasting."

◊◊◊

I WANTED FRESH AIR AND hauled a reluctant Abigail to the place of my impromptu news conference only yesterday afternoon. It seemed like ancient history. I breathed in deeply to try to settle myself and caught the scent of freshly mown grass. To the west, cumulus clouds were building toward a possible thunderstorm.

I lucked out and Lt. Hastings answered her phone. "I have all kinds of stuff on the Presser case, but I need to ask a favor. Can you detail a patrol car to meet Paddy? He's coming home to pick up his stuff and head to college. The hitman who killed Presser has a contract out on me and—"

"When is he arriving?" she asked.

I instinctively checked my watch, as though that would have the answer. Midafternoon already? I again had no recollection when his flight was coming in or what his schedule was. Mr. Scrambled Brain was not running on all cylinders. I disconnected from Hastings and called Paddy. It went directly to voicemail.

"Call me. It's urgent." My mouth was parched. I licked my lips. "Do not go home. I repeat, do not go home."

I called Hastings. "I left a message. I don't—"

"Slow down, Seamus. I've directed a patrol car to your house as a precaution. Now, back up to the beginning and tell me everything."

FORTY-THREE

BEAR HAD EXTRACTED NO INFORMATION from Solonini, and the three of us were again at the sheriff's office. Abigail was on the phone doing whatever. I badgered Bear about needing to nail down all of our suppositions about the connection between Solonini and Presser and the former CEO, Glen Framington. With a dramatic sigh, Bear pulled the Phoenix file from his drawer and tossed it to me. "Knock yourself out. I need to talk with the sheriff and DA about Solonini."

Framington's address was 11 Quail Lane; the chukar reference fit. I flipped through the rest of the file, moving from one photocopied page to the next. My eyes went blurry and then zeroed in on the words "Results Guaranteed" printed on one side of a business card. A Celtic cross decorated the other side.

I shook my head, wondering if I would have made the connection had Bear shown me the file when he first got it.

Again, Hastings actually answered her phone. "Find your son?"

"You didn't find him?"

"Patrol checked your house. His car is still there. They got a key from your neighbor, Mrs. Keenan, and checked around."

She'll give my key to anyone. "I'm guessing Paddy's in the air since I can't get him. Uncle Mike doesn't have a cell phone so when he's not at home he's incommunicado. I'm hoping he's driving home from Logan. Anyway, that's not why I'm calling. Do I remember seeing a business card stuck on the refrigerator in the pictures your guys took at Presser's place?"

"Weird-looking. A blue-and-green Celtic cross on one side and some slogan on the other. I can look it up. Why?"

"The killer left one like it at a Phoenix murder. A witness at the Chillicothe caterer saw a guy with the same cross on the small of his back. That's the link." I filled in the details. "One other thing ties in. Both times, the killer wiped his knife off at the scene."

Bear had returned while Hastings and I discussed the facts and missing pieces. I left the two of them to coordinate paperwork for Presser's murder. To keep my mind off Paddy, I called Robert Rand and checked on CIG's progress in contacting Appalachian's annuity contract holders.

Thus far, only two entities knew of any event in the next month at which retirees were likely to be gathered.

Unterboten Express retirees held a monthly meeting to discuss common issues, usually related to finances and investing. Thirty to forty attended. They canceled the September meeting.

The longtime CEO of Global Pressings was retiring at the end of the month, which entailed a company-wide celebration, including retirees. They had not yet canceled but assured Robert they would if we were still concerned closer to the scheduled date.

CIG staffers would finish the list before the day's end. They were already down to sponsors with fewer than fifty covered retirees. Something about the list was tickling at my brain, but I couldn't pull it to the front.

Still no word from Paddy. I caught myself gnawing on my lip and tasted blood. That was going to hurt for a while.

I next contacted Ingstram Ravel to tell him of my latest find and to stop his research on the various Appalachian folks. In appreciation for his superb work, I offered to buy him and his wife dinner at whatever top-notch restaurant was available, and I wanted him to extend the offer on my behalf to others who had lost weekends or evenings working on my rush projects. Have them send me the bills.

An idea popped into my head—not the one I'd been chasing. Solonini seemed to write things down, yet there had been no correspondence to the killer. Had Solonini called him? Where might he keep the number? We hadn't found an address book on him. Bear hadn't reported one at his home, and I didn't remember one in his office. Might he have used his office phone? I telephoned Jesse Thompson.

I couldn't see whom Solonini had called, Jesse said, because Appalachian's phone bill was not separated by extension. However, records of Solonini's company-reimbursed cell phone were part of his expense reports, and Appalachian used Outlook. Maybe the number I was looking for was stored in his Outlook address book.

Bear was still on the phone. I slipped him a note saying I was off to Appalachian and he should call me. Abigail parked in the same visitor's spot. Wind swirled dust devils around the parking lot. I cast a wary eye at the sky. The darkening clouds looked like they'd hold off for a few minutes.

The receptionist greeted us with "See, I saved the space for you!" I thanked her for her great kindness in the face of incredible statistical odds. Jesse was in the Olson/Solonini office, checking Solonini's Outlook address book.

"Do you know what you're looking for?" he asked.

"Let's try the obvious, Marketing Assurance Associates or MAA?"

He quickly scrolled to the "M" section. "Nope."

"How about 'Consultant' in the Cs?"

"Nope."

"Let me look through the names. Maybe something will hit me." The list was enormous. Marketing folks are great networkers, and he was no exception.

"You need anything else from me here?" Jesse asked. "If not, I'll try to find those old cell phone bills."

He left me at the mouse with Abigail standing by. Ten minutes later, I found an entry named Terminex. "Isn't the name of the exterminator people spelled with an 'ix' at the end? T-e-r-m-i-n-i-x?"

Abigail confirmed my recollection, so I dialed the number.

"Please enter your five-digit code," a computer voice answered.

Abigail scrolled down in Outlook to the note section. Five digits.

I punched them in.

"We're sorry, this service is no longer in operation," the voice said before switching to a rasping dial tone.

I shook my head at Abigail. "I'll bet this was it, but we're the proverbial day late and dollar short."

I paged Jesse to ask how he was doing obtaining the cell phone records. He had located details for the last three months, but was still working on finding earlier ones. They might be stored offsite. "Bring what you've got."

Solonini made a lot of calls. We each took a month's list and looked for the Terminex number. Jesse found one in early June. I found a call in late August. Abigail found two in late July. If we were correct, there should be one in April or May, which would have set up the botulism murders. The beginning of June fit for Presser's contract, July's dates correlated with the Phoenix murder and the second planned attack. The August date was when Solonini ordered the hired gun to take care of me.

The circumstantial evidence was piling up. Solonini was toast, but we had nothing on the hitman and nothing suggesting what group he had targeted. I had a quick flash of me hanging on the minute arm on some clock tower, trying to stop the clock from reaching the hour.

The figure on the clock tower changed to Paddy. *Where are you?*

◊◊◊

UNCLE MIKE FINALLY CALLED ME back and I felt immense relief that Paddy was indeed on a flight between Boston and Cincinnati. Should be getting in soon. I left Paddy one more message—not that it would change anything, but it made me feel like I was doing something. I considered asking Hastings to arrange for the airport police to waylay him, but discarded the thought. He always called back. I was probably overreacting anyway, and he might be really ticked off at me for "treating him like a kid."

Abigail and I were wearing a groove in the road between Appalachian and the sheriff's office. I needed to give Bear the phone records and our analysis. On the way, I cleared voicemail. No messages from anyone other than reporters. I willed Paddy to call.

He did at 3:17—not that I was paying attention to the time or anything. I excused myself from discussing the latest findings with Bear. As expected, Paddy told me I was, "being ridiculous" about my precautions, and if I couldn't remember his flight why hadn't I just called the limo service I'd arranged to pick him up?

Because I forgot. "Lieutenant Hastings is awaiting your call. She agreed to have a patrol car standing by while you get your stuff. It will only take you five minutes to pack your car and retrieve the cats. Be sure to thank Mrs. Keenan, and—"

"Daaad."

"Yes?"

"I will be so glad to get back to school, where parental units have no influence over my life. Fine. Give me the lieutenant's number."

I got him to cross his heart and hope to die, which had the effect of convincing me he would call Hastings and at the same time got him laughing.

"And call me when you arrive at school."

"Yes, your highness."

He disconnected. I felt light and free, energized by the reduced pressure of no longer worrying about him, the same feeling I had when I hiked in the mountains and removed my pack at the end of the day. With renewed enthusiasm I finished discussing everything with Bear, agreeing on what court orders the sheriff's office would request, and alerting CIG about what analysis we wanted with the phone records once we got them. We finished well after Chillicothe's Friday night rush hour.

I let Abigail do her chauffeur job and shield me with an umbrella until she loaded me into the back of the Mercedes. "Where are we shacking up tonight?"

"Ever hear of Glenlaurel in Rockbridge?"

"Honeymooner's hot spot—very romantic. I thought you didn't care."

◊◊◊

ON THE WAY TO THE Glenlaurel Inn we drove past the first circular barn I had ever seen. I received a little endorphin pop from seeing live what I had previously only read about. At Glenlaurel's entrance, Abigail told me to stay in the car while she confirmed our reservations. Since the rain was drumming on the roof, I didn't much mind. I again had to remain in the locked car while she checked our cottage. It reminded me of long-ago vacations with my sister and me locked in the car while Mom and Dad checked in. She eventually motioned me out.

"Impressive. Where am I sleeping?"

"Your choice of the two upstairs rooms. I'll take the one on the main floor."

We both decided a quick shower before dinner would be refreshing. I put on my most innocent expression and suggested we save water and shower together. She pretended not to hear, but I could tell she struggled to control her smile.

Just as well. I often do my best thinking while soaking under a warm spray. I'm sure Abigail would have distracted me. I was lathered with shampoo, reprising the bass part in McFerrin's Twenty-third Psalm, when the note for Deposit #2—"Habits"—suddenly made sense.

I rinsed my hair, toweled off sufficiently to slip on a pair of shorts, and dialed Robert Rand. I got his answering service and insisted they immediately get a message to him.

My cell phone rang three minutes later.

"The Sisters of the Transfigured Blood are the next targets," I said. "Many of their three hundred annuitants are probably congregated in their motherhouse."

"Georgia, somewhere. The nuns are not actually the recipients. The order receives the annuity payments to cover their living expenses and medical costs. The Mother Superior told me they had purchased the annuities to help assure there would be enough money to care for their aging sisters. They can't rely on new novitiates."

"Do all the religious live there?"

"They are a teaching society and have a special mission with Africa. Once they are no longer able to work, they mostly return to the motherhouse. Their dormitory includes a nursing wing and hospice center."

"This could happen anytime. Blow up the building or something at night, and he's got them all."

"Seamus, I apologize. I did not consider such a possibility. I had my assistant ask about special events. They have nothing planned until their quadrennial ingathering next year."

"I need to get down there and convince them to take precautions, maybe even leave for a while."

"I will contact them immediately and be in touch with you." He rang off before I could object.

Abigail rapped on the door. "You ready? We only have a few minutes before dinner."

"Come in. I was talking with Robert Rand. We're probably going to Georgia tomorrow."

"Georgia? What are we—Holy Christmas, Seamus, your front looks even worse than your face. And your leg's bleeding. Breathing must hurt. How did you get those ugly bruises?"

Until she mentioned it, I had felt fine. Now my leg ached and the deep breath I took to focus caused my ribs to twinge but good. "It's not bad. I reopened the leg when I removed the bandage in the shower. Haven't you seen seat belt stripes before?"

"You might consider contacting Boris Karloff to see if he has a movie part for you."

"He died a long time ago. I don't want to join him, thank you very much. Ever been to Georgia?"

"Get dressed and tell me about it at dinner."

◊◊◊

ABIGAIL HAD ARRANGED FOR A private table in the far corner of the St. Andrew's room, scented by smoke from the blazing fire. During the five-course dinner, highlighted by North Atlantic salmon, I filled Abigail in on my suspicions. She didn't think anyone related to the mob would be involved with killing nuns en masse. I groaned at the pun and disagreed. The mob itself probably wouldn't do anything like that, but if a lone wacko made the decision . . .

"How would you pull it off?" I asked.

"Got to follow his MO, not what I would do. I'd go with a team of four or five special-ops types. Right guys could probably kill most of the nuns while they were sleeping."

The thought disturbed my stomach, but I suspected she was right. Motherhouse security would not be tight. I had once organized a group of fellow Catholic school reprobates on a raid of our teachers' living quarters. Daredevils that we were, we short-sheeted a number of the sisters' beds. They suspected who the culprits were, but none of us ever confessed—to Mother Superior or the priest.

"He's used his knife for personal kills," she said, "but deployed botulism for the mass murder. They all eat from the same kitchen."

"Might not be as easy to gain access."

"True. He could plant explosives in the basement and collapse the building. Or use a truck with explosives, like the Oklahoma City bombing. You think he's acted alone. Unless he's a pilot, that rules out dropping a bomb."

The more she talked, the more I realized that even knowing where he would strike might not be enough to stop the guy.

◊◊◊

AFTER DINNER, I CHECKED MY cell phone. No message from Robert Rand. No message from Paddy. Despite my desire to stay up until Paddy called, I fell asleep early while pretending to read and awoke drenched in sweat from a nightmare in which I was about to have my throat slit by someone dressed in black with flaming red eyes shaped like Celtic crosses.

As soon as I put my glasses on, I checked my phone. Paddy had arrived safely. I carried my shoes in my hands and tried to softly walk downstairs. Before I got to the door a voice from the bedroom asked, "Where do you think you're going?"

"Since you won't let me run on the road," I said, "I'm going to walk in the woods. Isn't that why we came here, for the one hundred and forty acres of privacy?"

"Let me get dressed, I'll go with you."

"I won't get lost." I didn't wait for a reply and hurried out the door, slipping my shoes on once I got outside.

Everything was wet from last night's rain, but I didn't care. The ground smelled of leaf mold and blooming flowers—in other words, wonderful. I followed a footpath into the forest, up a stubby hill. From a rock overhang, I welcomed the sun's morning arrival, painting Ohio with slanting September light. With the sun up, I sat on a downed log facing east and unfocused my mind. My tension headache melted away amid the bird chatter and periodic *thunks* of acorns dropped from the oaks by squirrels.

A nascent plan formed. I hurried to the cottage and found Abigail pacing. She had dressed in jeans and a dark blue turtleneck, her hair pulled into a ponytail.

"Where have you been all this time?"

I described my spot in the woods. "I don't know where in Georgia the convent is," I said, "but if we catch the next flight to Atlanta we'll get a jump on getting there. I'll call Delta and get reservations. Cincinnati and Atlanta are two hubs. We shouldn't have any trouble getting a flight."

"Hold on. While you were out playing Boy Scout, I spoke with Rand. He already has a team on the ground at the convent in Andersonville."

"If we leave now, we can be down there midday. We can—"

"We're not going anywhere. Rand says you stay here. What are you going to do? He's got trained teams. They've even got sniffer dogs."

"I need to be there."

"You only think you do." She held her fingers a micrometer apart. "Look, I recently screwed up and let a killer come this close to getting my brother. I am taking no chances with you. Get it? Let's eat breakfast."

I spun on my heel and stormed out, slamming the door behind me. I was pissed to be out of the action. Abigail had the keys. And the control.

I had no choice. For now.

FORTY-FOUR

TAKING A PAGE FROM LT. Hastings' book, I timed my reentry for three minutes before eleven. Abigail glowered, her eyes darkened to deep brown with green flecks. She paced, lecturing me about her responsibilities for my safety and how I needed to cooperate. I tried to act contrite and might have been pulling it off until someone knocked at the door.

Abigail grabbed a semiautomatic from the small of her back, clicked off the safety, and held the gun behind her with her right hand. With her left, she opened the door.

"It's Molly Fitzhugh," I said. "Let her in and put your gun away."

Molly raised both hands and beamed me a bright smile. "Howdy, Seamus. Have you told the lady yet?" She eased past Abigail, who retreated to my side once she realized I knew the visitor.

"What the hell is going on?" Abigail asked. "Only Rand knew we were here." She spun toward me, her eyes flashing anger.

"Right. I called Molly and bought tickets to Georgia. The one thirty flight from Columbus arrives in Atlanta around three. From there, we hop a commuter to Columbus, Georgia. All these Columbuses are confusing, don't you think?

"Anyway, I bought you a ticket too . . . if you want to join us. Purely optional." I sounded a lot glibber than I felt. I had no idea how Abigail would react. Molly's price to spring me was to include her in the trip. Fair enough.

"You're not going anywhere," Abigail said. She ignored Molly completely and planted herself within an inch of me, anger rippling her muscles. She smelled of scented dryer sheets. "Rand ordered you out of circulation until this matter is cleared up. We're staying here."

I stepped away from her heat. "Unless you're going to risk kidnap charges, Miss Abigail no longer rules supreme. Molly has wheels. I have the tickets and a rental car once we get there. Your only choice is to join us or not."

"I should never have let you keep your cell phone." She exhaled a long sigh. "Fine. We can all go in the Mercedes. It's safer."

"You take the Mercedes," I said. "I'm going with Molly. I want to make sure I get to the airport. You'll find your ticket waiting at the counter."

In my face again, she poked one of the seat belt stripes with a hard finger, producing a blast of pain. "Damn it, Seamus. How the hell am I supposed to protect you if I don't have you under my control?" She stared at me with the piercing eyes of a peregrine falcon.

The scent of dryer sheets assailed me again. I wanted to lean down, kiss her eyes shut, and tell her to relax. I didn't dare. "Sorry," I said. "I'm getting my stuff. I'll be right back, Molly." I scooted up the stairs two at a time. A minute later, I returned and Abigail was on me again.

Had I thought this through? Did I know she would have to report this to Rand? Did I realize this would be a black mark on her career? Molly held the door open and I walked out and tossed my stuff into the beat-up truck with its cracked windshield. Since we were heading to the airport, the gun rack was empty.

◊◊◊

MY NOW YELLOW-GREEN-PURPLE EYES and noticeable limp targeted me for close, personal attention from airport security.

Abigail caught up to us in the waiting area shortly before boarding. She walked to Molly, leaned in, and whispered something in her ear. Molly tipped her head in my direction and smiled. What was that about?

Abigail sat down beside me, put her hand on my arm, and planted a quick kiss on my cheek. The warmth of her touch flowed through me. She had replaced the dryer sheet smell with what I guessed, based on the bottle I had seen in her toiletries, to be Chanel's Coco. If I recalled correctly, the ad copy called it mysterious, provocative, and sensuous. Perfect description.

Heat burned my face. "What was that for?" I asked.

"Just because." She flashed me a smile, gave my arm a squeeze, and occupied herself with a magazine.

A blare of static announced our flight. I should have thought ahead. Had Abigail cut a deal with security to prevent me from boarding?

◊◊◊

WHILE WE WAITED FOR THE commuter flight at Atlanta's Hartsfield-Jackson airport, my cell phone rang.

"I have excellent news," Robert Rand said. "We found the device at the convent."

"What convenient timing."

Five long seconds of silence preceded Robert's reply. "Your sarcasm indicates you do not believe me. I suppose that might be a logical response. I know how important trust is to you, Seamus. I am telling the truth. You can do nothing in Georgia. I want you to return to Glenlaurel."

Robert and Abigail could have cooked this up before we left. That would explain her docile approach. A kick of adrenaline prepared my body to fight. "Go ahead," I said. "I'm listening."

"You saved at least two hundred lives with your deduction. The device was in the main furnace duct. They heat with forced hot air. A counter kept track of how many times the furnace started. On the hundredth time, an electrical circuit would close, causing a metal tip to heat to about three hundred degrees Celsius. The tip touched a flash paper container filled with sodium cyanide. Once the flash paper burned, the sodium cyanide would fall into a glass container of sulfuric acid."

"Nazi showers," I said. "That's how they made hydrogen cyanide gas."

"Since the furnace would be on, the blowers would rapidly disseminate the gas to the convent rooms. They would all have died."

I held my elation in check. "Any evidence who did it?"

"Not yet. Teams are dusting everything. We will see what they find. Now you understand why you can do nothing here?"

I hesitated and gave a grudging "Probably."

"People are checking to make sure there are no other devices. Go to your retreat. Do you think you can arrange a TV crew to interview you about what we found?"

"What's your plan?"

"Assuming Abigail can find a safe way to do it, I would like you to follow up the police announcement of our news with your statement."

A bone for being a good boy and returning to my cage. "Why the publicity?"

"You scared the bejesus out of a lot of people . . . and rightly so. The public will need closure. If you do not provide it, the media will start looking for you, which we do not want. Set it for tomorrow afternoon. Please be prepared to discuss your ideas with me late tomorrow morning. All right?"

Heel, Seamus. Good dog.

Why was I reacting so negatively to being protected? I clearly needed it. More personal development to tackle in my spare time. Robert awaited my reply. "Thank you for letting me know. I'll call you around eleven tomorrow morning to discuss the press conference. I need to cancel flights and book new ones."

I broke the connection. I figured I owed Paddy an apology for my unilateral treatment. Well, maybe I wouldn't apologize, but I certainly could empathize, assuming he was willing to talk with me.

◊◊◊

WE ARRIVED BACK AT GLENLAUREL well past my bedtime. Abigail, in a spirit of goodwill, or to keep the conspirators under her watchful eye, invited Molly to spend the night in the spare bedroom. Molly preferred to return home.

After a fitful night's sleep, I snuck down the stairs, trying to slip from the house and not wake Abigail, but she again called from her room. I said I'd be in the woods.

I quieted my mind on the same log, dry this time, and embraced the awakening world, raucous in its celebration of daylight. Overnight, a feeling of dread had replaced the elated rush I had experienced from preventing the nuns' murder.

I had been laser focused on unraveling the who, what, and why of the various crimes; I had been in denial about my being the hired killer's other target. A light touch on my shoulder startled me out of my contemplation. Abigail settled onto the log next to me.

"Penny for your thoughts?" she asked.

"Probably overcompensation. I was considering what I should do about Solonini's hired killer."

"And?"

"And what?"

"Seamus, if I'd wanted to pull teeth, I would have been a dentist."

I matched her grin. "I'm not safe until he's caught. I haven't come up with anything I can do to speed up his identification and capture. That makes me mostly frustrated and frankly a bit worried."

"Reconsidering your cabin?"

Her surmise surprised me. "I was, but only because I need to regain a sense of balance. I feel off-kilter. The killer might not find me there, but he knows where I live in Cincinnati. Unless I go underground I can't hide forever."

"Maybe the police will find a print somewhere on the contraption at the convent."

"Want to make a small wager?"

"No. We can't both bet on the same side."

"Solonini, however, is not careful. I want to help Bear work on him. The phone number he used for the killer no longer works, but I wonder how Solonini found out about it. He may not know who this killer is, but if not, he can lead us to someone who does."

"With the plot against the nuns foiled," Abigail said, "all Solonini has to trade is the killer. It's his only chance of avoiding lethal injection."

"Who better than me to make that point?"

◊◊◊

CINDY NELSON, WITH HER PARENTHESES hairstyle puffed out in what Abigail later informed me was a "perfect blowout," met us at the Columbus studio for the taping. Abigail had insisted we go somewhere other than Chillicothe, and Cindy had made arrangements with her sister station.

A makeup artist subjected me to combing, brushing, and hair spray, which smelled like a high school chemistry experiment gone wrong. Twenty minutes later my black eyes didn't show and she pronounced me "purr-fect."

Cindy and I settled on couches a few minutes before the cameras rolled. Abigail remained off-camera, looking as comfortable as a gazelle dining with a pride of lions. "Who's the escort?" Cindy asked.

"Bodyguard."

"Now I know we should talk." She leaned in and whispered, "I'll be honest. This story could be my ticket out of here. Please, let's talk after?"

I tilted my head toward Abigail. "She makes an Azkaban guard look harmless."

Her makeup wrinkled. "Azkaban guard?"

"Not a Harry Potter fan, I guess. I'll keep it in mind when the timing is better. What's the latest with Solonini?"

"Had a second surgery on his hand for five hours yesterday. Going to ship him to the medical wing of the county jail tomorrow. Sheriff's holding a big press conference at the hospital before the transfer. I'll be covering it. You going to be there?"

Not if Abigail had her way, but it might be a good opportunity to interview Solonini, and lots of cops would be around for protection. I'd have to work on Abigail.

Cindy flashed her polished smile at Abigail. "How'd you qualify to be a bodyguard?"

"Secret Service, presidential detail."

"I smell a story," Cindy said. "Maybe we can all go out for a drink and talk about it."

Abigail's smile would have been perfect if the throbbing vein in her neck hadn't belied it. "The emphasis, Miss Nelson, is on the word 'secret.'"

Off set, a voice called, "Let's roll." Cindy became all newswoman. I was able to make the points Rand and I had agreed on and duck the areas we did not want to discuss, providing no information regarding our knowledge of the killer.

Walking to the parking lot, Cindy slipped her arm into mine, leaned her head in, and whispered, "You're very good at that, you know. When you don't need your protector anymore, please let's get together. I really could use your help to escape Dullsville."

◊◊◊

ABIGAIL PUT ON CHOPIN PIANO etudes for the return drive to Glenlaurel. She drove with two hands on the wheel, face forward. Had I pissed her off somehow? I sat in the back, oblivious to the rolling hills, trying to figure out an approach to allow me access to Solonini. Short of engaging the nuclear option of enlisting Molly again, all I could think of was to ask directly.

I cleared my throat and saw her gaze briefly flick to the rearview mirror. My mouth was as dry as when I first asked a girl out on a date. "I know this is childish, but I want to be there when they transfer Solonini. I want him to see I'm still alive and make sure he knows I was the one who figured out the nuns were his next victims."

"I don't know, Seamus. Might not be a good idea. As your bodyguard—"

"Whatever. I'll wear one of your magic vests if you're worried, but I have a gut feeling my showing up will trigger a big reaction. Solonini's our only link to the killer."

Abigail was silent until, miles later, she looked at me in the mirror. "You've already demonstrated your willingness to call Molly, and you probably sleep with your cell phone in your shorts so I can't get at it. Wipe that smirk off your face. I'll talk with Detective Wright. We'll figure something out."

FORTY-FIVE

THE HAPPY REAPER SAT ON the Cincinnatian sofa with a mug of tea warming his hand and stomach. He'd received a one-two punch of disappointment and the question was what to do about it. The over-the-fold story in *USA Today* felt like a whip kick in the solar plexus. Now he would never know how well his apparatus would work. At least the Georgia state police had called it diabolically ingenious. Then, in the kick-them-while-they're-down follow-up, McCree was all over the television with his interview. The bad news was McCree was the guy who had figured out about the nuns. The good news was they had finally connected the botulism attack with his two hits. At least his slogan, "Results Guaranteed," was receiving free advertising.

Between sips, he caught himself whistling McCartney's "Live and Let Die."

Okay, enough time mourning what was not to be. Time to focus on the remaining tasks. Eventually McCree would return home. His son had arrived by limo with a police escort, packed his car, and collected two cats from the next-door neighbor. That cleared the field of one annoyance. Now the game became hide-and-seek between McCree and himself.

Mail was piled up inside McCree's front door, indicating he had not been home. The TV interview in Columbus proved McCree was still involved in the investigation. The online version of the Chillicothe newspaper contained a filler story that the cops were moving Solonini—the major screw-up—from the hospital to the jail today. Put it all together and there was a good chance McCree would be in Chillicothe working with the local cops.

The more he meditated on Seamus McCree, the clearer it became that they had a lot in common. Smart, intuitive, dogged determination. If he were McCree, he'd be there when they hauled Solonini out for his perp walk. What better time to apply pressure to their only link to the murders?

Today would be a good day to halt McCree's progress.

ANT FARM | 277

◊◊◊

I ENVIED ABIGAIL HER MIRRORED sunglasses. I hadn't packed any and the sunlight about blinded me as we walked across the Adena Regional Medical Center parking lot. Not to mention that I was sweating rivers underneath the bulletproof vest. *Quit bitching, Seamus. You're here. That's what you wanted.*

The sheriff's voice boomed through a set of loudspeakers set up at the west entrance, but no one seemed to be listening. Abigail shepherded me to one side of the media frenzy. Cindy Nelson spotted us and marched over with cameraman in tow, gushed an intro about me saving hundreds of nuns.

I mumbled something circumspect about continuing to assist the Ross County Sheriff's Office in tying up loose ends. Cindy's bright smile faded at my unusable babble.

She licked her lips, shifting her stare between Abigail and me. Before her next question surfaced, Sheriff Lyons announced they were about to bring Solonini out. "Remember," Cindy said, "you promised to talk." She hurried away to regain a good vantage for filming the transfer.

I edged Abigail to a spot where we had a clearer view.

◊◊◊

HE HAD HIS SPOT. HE had his escape route. The raw meat of Solonini had drawn all the players like ants to a picnic. The Happy Reaper whistled Simon and Garfunkel's "59th Street Bridge Song"—his favorite when everything was "feeling groovy." McCree and his bodyguard were off to the side, the pretty TV reporter trying to talk to them. Sheriff Lyons held forth behind his podium. The overgrown Detective Wright, looking like he might be a descendant of the Praetorian Guard, starched at attention in the background. Soon, Solonini would join the circus and complete the scene.

Still no movement around the nearby state police building down below on Route 23. He scanned the surroundings looking for snipers or undercover cops or anything to indicate they had set a trap for him. Zip.

The crowds were a mixed blessing. They would help make his escape easier, but they made it difficult to get a clear line. He'd manage. He always did.

He followed Seamus in his scope. A worthy opponent, but all games must end.

◊◊◊

THE SHERIFF'S ENTOURAGE ROUNDED THE corner with Solonini. I involuntarily shuddered. Sheriff Lyons had his own sense of theater. Exiting the hospital, a guard unlocked Solonini's ankle from the wheelchair and helped him stand up. With each mincing step, Solonini rattled his leg chains. He looked fragile: a sling cradled his left arm, and an orange cast encased his right hand. A double chain surrounded his middle and attached to a harness wrapped around a deputy's waist.

The deputy stayed on Solonini's left and the broadly smiling sheriff chose the other side. Behind the three of them were three more deputies. Bear brought up the rear, overlooking the proceedings in front of him. I caught Bear's attention. He rolled his eyes, set a sheepish smile on his face, and motioned us to join him, which we did, slipping into the tail of the procession.

Solonini turned his head at our approach and mouthed the words "You're a dead man, McCree."

Abigail grabbed my arm in an iron vise and yanked me away from him. "Stay back and keep your head down. This is when it gets dangerous."

Cameras flashed and videotape rolled. Reporters called out questions to a sullen Solonini. The crowd, chanting "Death to murderers," waved handwritten signs and resisted police attempts to clear a path to the waiting vehicles.

I had come here to gloat, but was now sickened by the spectacle, and there was no escape.

◊◊◊

PELLUCID IMAGES MOVED IN THE scope while cops urged the crowd back and reporters scurried to secure positions for their photo op. His training allowed him to block out the increasing crowd noise.

The pushing and shoving was a blur, but not a distraction. He continued to focus on McCree, who remained mostly hidden by his bodyguard. The topmost fraction of McCree's head was visible. Positions would change once they brought out Solonini.

Movement. The crowd parted and the target appeared fully in the crosshairs. All he needed was one clean shot for game, set, match, and on to the next tourney. Easing his finger on the trigger, he slowed his breathing and ever so gently applied smooth pressure.

◊◊◊

THE PARTY MOVED FORWARD. SOLONINI'S chains clanked with each step.

Abigail yelled, "Shooter!"

◊◊◊

THE RIFLE'S RECOIL CARESSED HIS shoulder; the target keeled backward like a Kewpie doll in an amusement park. Screams from the hospital entrance caused everyone to stare toward the commotion. Collapsing the tripod, the Happy Reaper nonchalantly waved as if to someone in the far corner of the lot. Cops ducked behind cement planters, scrambling to release their weapons. Without waiting for a response to his wave, he walked briskly toward the outer road where his rental was parked, whistling "Heigh Ho!"

He sensed movement between the hospital and him. Casually glancing over his shoulder, he spotted two cops wrestling some schmuck to the ground. Another distraction. Thank you, crowd.

He had one more thing to do in Cincinnati before he could return his rental car and be finished with the assignment.

◊◊◊

ABIGAIL'S 135 POUNDS KNOCKED ME off my feet, cracking my elbow hard into the concrete. "Don't move!" she yelled in my ear. "Stay down and do not move!"

She crab-walked to attend to a downed hospital intern bleeding from the head. I caught sight of chain and visually followed its trail to Solonini, sprawled on the ground, blood everywhere. If he wasn't already dead, he soon would be.

I ignored the pandemonium around me and focused on the parking lot, where Abigail had been looking when she spotted the shooter. Legs blocked my view. I rolled over and squatted next to a pillar. From there I noticed a couple crouched next to a car, holding tightly to each other. Not them. Another person, a bit closer, was crawling backward toward a parked car. A possibility. Movement from the right caught my attention. Two cops wrestled someone to the ground.

In the distance behind the two cops a single individual speed-walked carrying . . . I stood on tiptoe to get a better view . . . carrying a tripod? *If he were a photographer, wouldn't he still be shooting—shooting—the shooter.*

I sprinted toward him as fast as my battered legs could take me, yelling, "There! There!" I dodged past two people in white coats running toward the bedlam behind me and stumbled when I caught the heel of my shoe on a low bush I hurdled. The guy shot a glance in my direction and picked up his pace. In front of him, a white SUV blinked its lights and sounded a "beep-beep." I modified my path to intercept the getaway vehicle.

Someone yelled, "Stop," and a surge of positive feelings warmed me. Someone other than me had noticed.

Next thing I knew I was on the ground and felt like I had stepped into a freezing-cold shower with every muscled tensed.

FORTY-SIX

I FELT OKAY, EXCEPT FOR the sore elbow where Abigail had driven me into the cement and the bruises from the tumble I had taken when the police Tasered me. Bear was waiting for us when Abigail and I made it to the sheriff's office. Another deputy shunted Abigail away to debrief her.

"I assume he's escaped?" I said to Bear once we were alone.

Bear reacted as though I had Tasered him.

"They thought you were an accomplice of the guy they had detained. They didn't recog—"

"I didn't mean it as an accusation," I said. "Fine. He's still loose. What do we know?"

"You didn't see the plate number and 'white SUV' doesn't exactly pin it down. By the time the deputies realized who you were and got your information out . . . We found this next to one of the oak trees at the end of the parking lot."

He handed me an evidence bag with a Celtic cross business card. I flipped it over: "Results Guaranteed."

"We'll dust it for prints," Bear said. "Eventually, he'll make a mistake. I wonder if he did this on his own or someone wanted to shut up Solonini. Did you recognize him? The guy is unbelievable. Parked on the road right behind the state police building. If only they had looked out their windows."

"When I first saw him I flashed back to a jogger Abigail and I saw at the Cincinnatian. The way he moved? I'd put him at midthirties, light hair. I'm guessing five ten or six feet. Looked like maybe he was carrying a surveyor's transit? Anyone else see him?"

"Nuh-uh," Bear said. "No survey crews were scheduled." He extracted my memories of seeing the jogger, got in touch with Lt. Hastings, and arranged for CPD to interview people at the Cincinnatian. They'd determine if the jogger had checked out, take a look at the guest room, and if he had a car there, find out what kind.

Sensing we'd been whipped, my energy drained and I zoned out. We could have nailed the guy if only I had concentrated on getting police attention and had them chase the guy rather than screwing it up myself.

My cell phone brought me to the present.

"Dad, did you ever pin down how they were going to benefit from the annuity murders?" Paddy asked.

I required several seconds to figure out what he meant. "Haven't had time. We've been a bit occupied here."

"I used the SEC records to check out your ideas about stock ownership." At my sharp intake of air, he added, "They're public, Dad. No insiders have been buying or selling, and the top shareholders are all fund families."

"I hear a 'but.'"

"But . . ." He paused. The kid had a sense for the dramatic. "But, Jesse gave me access to Appalachian's systems. Olson, Solonini, whatever you call him, swapped all his compensation for options, and so—"

"You mean Solonini converted his bonus to options?" Had Jesse knowingly given Paddy additional access to Appalachian's computer systems, or had Paddy opened a back door while we weren't looking? I decided applying the army's "don't ask, don't tell" policy to Paddy had some merit.

"No, Dad, I mean everything—bonus and base. He bet the farm, and—"

"They must be expensing it like regular salary, otherwise I would have seen the budget variance."

"Stop interrupting. One other executive did the same thing."

"Who?"

"Sure you don't want to interrupt some more?"

I really wanted to say something, but I refrained.

"James Nadler," he said. "Still, it doesn't prove anything . . . you still there?"

"I didn't want to interrupt."

"Well, that got me thinking, and I remembered you mentioned both Solonini and Nadler got their MBAs from NYU at night. Dad, they were in several classes together. They had to know each other."

"Anything else?" I asked.

"It smells funny."

Like Limburger cheese. I purposefully delayed telling Paddy about Solonini's murder and ended the call.

"You have time to check out a lead at Appalachian?"

Bear waved at the piles of paper in front of him. "What now?"

"Mind if Abigail and I go?"

"Be my guest. But let me know."

I found Abigail and filled her in. "Considering today's shenanigans," she said, "I'm convinced the only way I'll keep you alive is if we get to the bottom of this, but you're keeping your vest on. It doesn't do any good to put it on *after* someone shoots you."

◊◊◊

I SUSPECTED THE WARRIOR PERSONA Abigail projected had the effect of squelching any thoughts of flirting the Appalachian receptionist might have had. All business, she told us Nadler's whole department was in a meeting that should finish in half an hour.

Abigail wandered around Nadler's office, looking at pictures, checking out the ducks and fish. I sat in a visitor chair, closed my eyes, and wondered how to convert circumstantial evidence into proof. Nadler knew Solonini. They both traded all their cash compensation for options. If the stock price had risen because of the annuity murders, they would have reaped millions. Was Nadler the brains?

I got up and stared at the Dilbert screensaver. On a whim, I sat in his chair and ran a search for all documents containing "Samuel Presser," finding several uninteresting memos and a copy of Presser's contract. Searching the directory that contained those documents, I uncovered two versions of his replacement's contract. A PDF showed it was signed on June 12. I checked the properties of the original: author was Jim Nadler and date last modified was June 7.

Tilt. Game over.

I needed to call Matthew Yeung and confirm one thing. Nadler interrupted my dialing. I hit the "Alt" and "Esc" keys on the computer and waited until the screen shifted to one of his open documents before I left his chair. Abigail introduced herself and Nadler offered us something to drink.

"Where's the rest of your department?" I asked.

"Watching a movie on sexual harassment. I've already seen it."

"Did you hear what happened to Solonini?" I asked.

"Olson? No, what?"

I described the hospital scene. My stomach tightened, anticipating the part where Sheriff Lyons brought Solonini out in chains. I couldn't read his expression. Certainly curious, but not shocked at the resolution. "I understand both you and Solonini traded all your pay for options."

"Not one of my better decisions." He sighed deeply. "Ed convinced me the stock price would double within two years. Since my wife was doing so well, we didn't need my regular salary and it seemed like a savvy decision."

"Why didn't you mention you knew Solonini before you joined Appalachian?"

His pupils dilated and his nostrils flared. He nonchalantly settled into his chair. "He asked me not to. You can't imagine how shocked I was when I met him during my interviews. Of course, I knew him as Eddie Solonini. He took me aside and told me he'd legally changed his name because his brother had gotten into a lot of trouble. We'd gotten along okay at NYU. Even worked on a couple of case studies together."

"You didn't know he was mobbed up?"

"Mob?"

I let the silence build. From the corner of my eye I caught Abigail's glance in my direction. I kept my focus on Nadler.

"This whole terrible mess was because of the mob?" he asked.

"You told me you were mad at Samuel Presser because he missed your meeting, and you only found out about his death several days afterward."

"Sure. A day, maybe two."

"How do you explain the contract you prepared for Presser's replacement the day after Presser was killed? That's a full day *before* the newspaper published it and three days *before* your scheduled meeting with Presser."

"That's not what I said."

"I know, but it's what happened."

Everything seemed to slow down. I was aware of the artery pulsing in my neck. Abigail shifted forward in her chair.

Nadler laid clenched fists on the desk blotter. "I don't know what you think anymore. It's time for you to leave, Seamus."

"Check your computer. I have the contract pulled up," I said rising to my feet.

His eyes tracked my movement, but he waved a hand dismissively. "A typo. I'll get you the actual contract." He spun his chair around, stood and began sorting through the material behind his desk, lifting both decoys.

I sat down, waiting for his "proof."

"Ah. Here it is." He turned back and pointed a gun at my head. "Don't either of you move. You had to keep pushing and pushing and prying and probing, didn't you? Fucking Eddie. If he'd only left things alone, but he went and killed that kid and here we are. I didn't know it. He told me Presser wasn't going to fulfill the contract. He had inside info."

"What did—"

"Shut up! From here I can blow your head off and the vest you're wearing won't do a bit of good. If you help me out of here, we can all live. If I don't get away, you're dead."

I snuck a peek at Abigail. My stomach was doing gymnastics. I could smell my own fear. She looked like she was fresh from a massage.

"Abigail, you first. Walk around Seamus and stand at the door. If you get within six feet of me, I'll shoot Seamus. When she gets to the door, you"—waving the gun at me—"get up and walk in front of me. Once you exit the department, go right. And if either of you says anything, or tries anything or runs, Seamus is dead. Understood?"

Abigail got up and walked to the door. Nadler's arm was steady, the gun pointed at my head.

"Now you, Seamus. Nice and easy."

I got up. Anger replaced my fear. Anger at the death of so many innocent people. Anger at Nadler for holding a gun to my head. Anger at myself for forgetting to tell Paddy I loved him the last time we spoke. I looked to Abigail for a sign. Her face was inscrutable.

I walked to the door.

"Now through the cubicles. Seamus, give her two steps, then you start walking. Nice and regular and everybody stays alive."

I counted two steps and followed. Nadler followed what felt like two steps behind me, pointing the gun at my head. Abigail had said her job was to prevent bullets flying at me; she wouldn't stand in their way. Nadler had positioned me between himself and Abigail, essentially neutralizing her. I was on my own.

Was I fast enough to spin and grab his gun before he pulled the trigger? Probably not. Could I kick backward into his groin? Too far now; maybe when we exited the department he would get close enough. Even if I could, he might still have time to pull the trigger.

"Right at the hallway, Abigail. And remember, not a sound or Seamus dies."

Could I make a dash after I turned the corner?

"Seamus, you go straight ahead until your nose touches the other side of the hall. Then, when I tell you, go right."

Not that either. The gun must be getting heavy. I walked until my nose touched the musty wall covering. I sneezed away my cobwebs. I needed to try an old soccer move. Nadler entered the hallway and we proceeded in single file.

"Abigail, now make another right at the exit sign," Nadler said. He sounded in control, as though he'd done this a hundred times.

Abigail proceeded around the corner. I stepped forward with my left foot, threw my body backward and down, and windmilled my right foot past my head toward the gun.

My foot smashed into Nadler's nose, hurtling him into a wall. I broke my fall with my hands and rolled to a stand, twisting around to face him.

He was on his butt, his left hand held to his nose, blood and mucus streaming around his fingers. His gun was raised.

He pulled the trigger. *Click.* His eyes, confused, shifted to his gun.

I aimed a left-footed kick at the gun. The flash of a leg streaked by me. Abigail connected with Nadler's chin, leaving nothing for my foot to hit.

"Steel-toed shoes." She stood above the inert form. "I think these are yours." One by one, she dropped nine shells onto Nadler's chest.

"I hope he's the last of it," I said.

"There remains the minor issue of the 'Results Guaranteed' guy."

◊◊◊

WE HAD FINISHED WITH THE cops and were in the car heading to Cincinnati when Abigail again tried "A penny for your thoughts."

"Might be fair compensation this time," I said. "I'm wondering how many people would be alive if I had followed up on a comment Matthew Yeung made when he said the woman actuary was surprised when Nadler told her of Presser's death. If I had asked when Nadler called her, the whole thing would have been clear."

"It's easy to solve the puzzle once you know all the facts. You did figure it out. That's what counts."

Maybe. I blinked away the bright headlights from an oncoming car. I was developing a headache. "It occurs to me that if I recognized the shooter at the hospital as the jogger we saw at the Cincinnatian, he probably recognized me that morning."

"Probably so. Doesn't help us much. CPD fingerprint guys found nothing in his room there. But he was jogging around Cincinnati. Surely a surveillance camera someplace caught him. It's only a matter of time. Regardless, if you keep throwing yourself into danger, I can't protect you."

"Yeah, well, I still can't believe you didn't tell me Nadler had a gun hidden in the canvasback decoy. Or that you'd removed the bullets."

"A girl's got to have some secrets. I sure didn't expect you to try your David Beckham move. I thought it would be interesting to see if he talked, or where he took us."

"If I was any good I would have kicked the gun instead of nailing his nose. You know, I think the killer's been in my house. I smelled Cincinnatian moisturizing lotion in my foyer, but I couldn't place it. If I had, we could have caught him. "

"Stop beating yourself up. Without you, all the baddies would still be free."

"One still is."

"Close your eyes and listen to the music." She increased the volume on Hanson's lyrical Symphony no. 2. "We'll secure your home and go from there."

◊◊◊

I AGAIN HAD TO SIT in the car while Abigail checked out my house. I guess she looked for hiding people and exploding things and listening devices before she let me in. I followed the rank smell of rotting food to the kitchen. No one had emptied the trash. I pulled the bag from the container, cinched the top shut, and stopped on my way to the kitchen door.

A business card protruded from under the red public library magnet stuck to my refrigerator: a Celtic cross. On the other side: "Results Guaranteed."

He had been there. The trash bag slipped from my hand and hit the floor with a wet plop. Saying aloud that the killer had been in my house had not prepared me for my visceral reaction to proof of his presence there. A queasy feeling crept over me; moisture vanished from my mouth, and my tongue became the texture of sandpaper.

Abigail's response was to call Robert Rand. I cleaned up the mess on the floor and took the garbage out to the garage. The garage door stuck partway up. I kicked myself for not getting it fixed and gave the door a solid hip check. I set down the garbage and raised the door. A sharp prick at the back of my neck stopped my movement. My hands, extended above my head, still held the door. Behind me an upper Midwest accent said, "Turn around and you're dead."

I flashed to Presser's stiletto wounds and my butt involuntarily contracted.

"I could have had you at the hospital today, even if I had to take out your foxy bodyguard."

"I saw you." I immediately regretted sharing the information.

"Thought so. I've concluded we two are a lot alike, Seamus McCree. We're smart, we're dedicated. You probably guarantee your results, too. Look, my kills are clean. The guy never knows it's coming. That's part of my package. Somebody wants torture and stuff, they can find some cheap sick fuck. People pay me good money to do things right when they have a problem, and Solonini went and screwed it up by trying to do things himself. Here's the new deal—my apologies to FDR—I'm willing to take my chances with the cops, and I won't kill you. We're quits. But don't think that gives you a free pass to try to catch me."

The knife pricked deeper. Blood trickled down my back.

"If you keep looking for me, I'll still be a Happy Reaper because you won't get me. You'll be dead. Or maybe it's your son, Patrick, who'll be dead. Understand?"

My arms felt leaden, but I didn't dare bring them down. "How do I know you're telling the truth?" *Can I pull another David Beckham from this position?*

"I'm donating the twenty-five grand Solonini paid me for your hit to your favorite charity. Nature Conservancy, isn't it? Maybe Appalachian can even figure out how to take a tax deduction."

"What now?"

"Your trash stinks. You need to finish throwing it in the garbage can. You're a singer, right? Start singing your favorite song. No—I can't get "Old Hundredth" out of my head since I heard you whistling it. It's short. Whistle or sing if you want, let's say, four times through. I can tell by the sound if you face in my direction. If you do, you'll discover I'm expert with a nine-millimeter."

My throat tightened and I croaked out an "Okay." The knife's pressure decreased.

"Whatcha waiting for, maestro? Oh, and you really should get your garage door fixed. Someone could get hurt."

I licked my lips and started a wobbly whistle.

The knife disappeared from my neck. I picked up the garbage bag, caught a glimpse of New Balance sneakers behind me, and walked into the garage.

EPILOGUE

I ROCKED ON THE PORCH, enjoying the blazing colors of peak season on a late Indian summer afternoon. The weekend before Halloween was perfect for a celebratory party bringing together ten of us who had worked to take down Solonini. Earlier in the week, Abigail and I had gone to a local farm and bought ten pumpkins we had carved for decorations.

As usually happens, those who came the farthest arrived first. Bear, Charlene, and Molly carpooled from Chillicothe. Bear dressed as a football player and Charlene as a cheerleader. Molly wore a bloodhound costume and pretended she was at the wrong house. "Seamus, I didn't recognize you without black eyes." She let Charlene and Bear enter and then whispered to me that the two of them had been like high school sweethearts in the front seat. Charlene sat so close to Bear she left an imprint on his right side. Love was in the air.

"How's your grandmother doing?" I asked.

"Much better. The doctors think she can spend winter in Florida. And Mom's doing well now that we have a live-in nurse paid for by the fund set up by Appalachian Casualty and Life. Everyone still misses my grandfather, but we're getting on. Thanks for remembering."

Cindy Nelson arrived as a cowgirl, fancy-stepping her way up the driveway in a series of heel-stomping moves.

Paddy appeared next, having driven down from school for the shindig. He disappeared upstairs and came back down in costume: pressed shirt with cufflinks, repp tie, and one of my pinstripe suits, albeit with sneakers, since my shoes were too large for his feet.

Lt. Hastings appeared in a dress that looked like a phone booth. "It's a TARDIS dress," she said. "From *Doctor Who*." At my befuddlement, she explained the *Doctor Who* phenomenon and that TARDIS stood for "Time and Relative Dimension in Space." "Carrying a time-traveling machine with you is perfect for a homicide cop, don't you think?" She brushed my cheek with a kiss and I inhaled her now-signature lilac scent.

Matthew Yeung (a mad scientist) escorted Skyler Weaver (Dorothy from Oz) into the house. "Who are you supposed to be?" Matthew asked.

Paddy overheard the question and answered for me. "Doctor. He thinks he's a brain surgeon. That way he can figure out how people think. He's actually a proctologist because he keeps turning up assholes."

"Thank you for your expert commentary," I said.

"And I'm the dogcatcher," Abigail said as she joined the festivities. "Since Seamus wouldn't follow his bodyguard's instruction to stay put, I've resorted to nets and tranquilizer guns."

"I can stick him in a jail cell for you next time," Hastings said.

"I should have thought of that," Bear said.

Charlene gave me a playful hug, "Ah, Seamus. You know they pick on you because they all love you."

Once the laughter at my expense died down, Cindy stepped into the circle and addressed Hastings and Bear, who sat next to each other. "Off the record, how about an update, since everyone who knows the real story is here? What's happening with Nadler?"

"Unlike Seamus, he *is* in our jail," Bear said. "Lawyered up and refuses to speak, which would have been a bit difficult anyway since his jaw is wired shut. Good thing he pulled a gun on Seamus and Abigail because the only charges we have are related to the assault and kidnapping. Everything else is circumstantial."

"And the hired hitman?"

I perked up to see if I could learn anything.

"Cold trail, but not forgotten," Hastings said. "He's working his way up on the FBI's most wanted list. Someone knows something and eventually they'll talk. I know that's not what everyone wants to hear." She smiled at Skyler. "Sorry, dear, but that's true crime."

I asked if there were any further mob ties with Solonini.

Bear and Hastings looked at each other. Bear lost the mental coin flip. "We are not at liberty to say. I have a question. Charlene tells me that Seamus bought a bunch of Appalachian stock. Is it a good investment?"

"I'm not licensed to give investment advice," I said.

"Shay-mus," everyone groaned in unison.

"Okay, okay. I think it's equivalent to Warren Buffett buying GEICO. The stock's down under two bucks and it's probably a steal. But—and it's a big but—if I'm wrong, you could lose it all."

Paddy chirped, "Dad really believes in it. He bought a couple hundred thousand shares."

"Yeah, but I can—"

"Shay-mus."

"Caveat emptor," I said.

While Abigail filled wineglasses and replenished the cheese and crackers, I snuck upstairs and called Mrs. Keenan. Back downstairs, I clapped for attention. With all eyes on me, I situated Molly closest to the door, then reached underneath the dining room buffet and removed a large box wrapped in plain brown paper. "Hope you like it." At my request, Sheriff Lyons had delayed releasing Molly's rifle. A craftsman Bear knew in West Virginia had done a marvelous job repairing the broken stock. Molly unwrapped the box and tears filled her eyes.

The doorbell chimed. "Molly, you're closest. Can you get it?" She brushed away her tears, opened the door, and was lifted off her feet by Jeff's hug. My party preparations had included flying him down for the weekend from school, picking him up at the airport, and stashing him with Mrs. Keenan.

I ducked out to get more guacamole dip from the kitchen. Skyler Weaver blocked my return. Above her Dorothy outfit, her face had filled out and her eyes looked troubled, but no longer hollow.

I put the dish on the kitchen table and wiped my hands on the towel tossed over my shoulder. "What's up, Skyler?"

"That was nice what you did for Molly. I want to thank you again for everything you've done, and to apologize."

"For what?"

"For getting you involved, for risking your life, for endangering your family."

"Nothing to apologize for. If anything, I'm the one who owes you the apology. I still don't know who killed Samuel and, as you heard, the police aren't any closer to finding out."

"Nonsense, Seamus. Besides, you've forgotten what I asked you at the beginning. I asked you to find out *why* Samuel was killed. You did. And that's been a big relief." She grabbed my wrist with unexpected strength.

"And because of you, I know Samuel was a hero. If he hadn't found the problems at Appalachian, no one would have stopped those bastards before they killed two hundred nuns and who knows who else."

"Yes, but—"

"No buts. Would I like to have the killer caught? Whoever he is, he should be locked up and the key thrown away so he can't hurt anyone else. In Ohio, he would probably get the death penalty. You know how I feel about the death penalty." She blinked away tears. "I don't think I'm strong enough to face having to protest for the scum who killed Samuel. And yet, I think I would have to. I'm sorry Seamus, this isn't making any sense."

Tears rolled down her cheeks. I folded her into my arms and let her weep. Matthew Yeung came looking for her, grabbed several tissues, and led her to the back deck.

Abigail found me still standing in the kitchen, looking into space. Lifting slightly on her toes, she put her arms around me and pressed her body into mine. We shared a long, slow kiss, something we had been practicing since our last week at the cabin. It left me with a tingling spine.

Molly walked in. "Ooh la la. Come up for air, you two. Abigail, do you have the answer to your question from the airport?"

"What question?" I asked.

Abigail shook a finger at Molly. "No telling."

I pointed at Abigail. "Then you tell."

They traded eye messages and Abigail shrugged. "After your stunt getting Molly to take you to the airport, I told her you had some of the biggest cojones I had ever seen."

I was sorry I had asked, and felt my face start to heat up.

"And," Molly added, "I wondered if the rest of your parts came in the same size packaging." She raised her eyebrows at Abigail. "And—"

The phone saved me, but my face could have provided light and heat for a Parisian bordello. Molly laughed her way out.

Robert Rand was on the line. "I am sorry I could not be there, Seamus. Everything went well with Molly's gift?"

I assured him it had. I checked my watch. The catered food would arrive in another fifteen minutes. Everyone was enjoying themselves, but I felt incomplete. I ended the call with Rand and slipped upstairs to my study.

I opened my Internet browser and typed in "Celtic Cross Tattoo."

◊◊◊

THE HAPPY REAPER ENJOYED A late-night dinner at his favorite Cayman Islands beach restaurant and returned home to discover his computer beeping and flashing a message. He hit a key to silence the alarm and eliminate the flashing. He read the message.

Security Alert, Computer 15:FE:3G:29:0L:JD

He checked against his master list. "Seamus McCree, what naughty thing did you do?" He cued the keylogger program and extracted details from the spyware.

The program mirrored McCree's keystrokes and generated an alert whenever it detected any of a number of trigger phrases. The offense: "Celtic Cross Tattoo."

The Celtic cross was no secret; he featured it on his business card. Was the tattoo new information that Seamus had recently learned? Or after what—about six weeks?—had Seamus decided to break his half of the bargain? He followed the keystrokes and determined Seamus had found nothing. Only then did he realize he had been holding tension in his shoulders. Tension was not good; it could kill you.

He walked out onto his balcony and stared into the flawless Caribbean night.

Strike one, Seamus.

Acknowledgements

THIRTEEN YEARS BEFORE THE PUBLICATION of this novel I retired from my "day job" and gave myself permission to take six months to discover what I wanted to do for the rest of my life. The thing that kept bubbling to the top of my list was that I wanted to write. I loved reading mystery/suspense/thrillers, and it made sense to me to write the kind of book I like reading.

So I wrote and wrote and wrote and then offered my manuscript to two friends for their comments. That Carol Demarest and Gary Dickson remained my friends is testament not to the fine writing I presented them, but to their tact in telling me the book sucked. I had made every rookie mistake I could. The book had a slow start, a sagging middle, too many characters, an ending that was not particularly satisfying, too much backstory, cardboard characters, and on and on.

Then I made the most important decision of my writing life. I joined the Cincinnati Writers Project and participated in the Wednesday evening critique group. We met in the back room of Lenhardt's, a German restaurant now torn down as part of the renewal of areas around the University of Cincinnati. A chapter a week, I subjected that group to two early versions of *Ant Farm*. (Its working title at the time was *Actuarial Gains*—perfectly descriptive, but hardly something to generate book-buyer enthusiasm).

Under the tutelage of their red pens and verbal critiques I gradually learned how to write. My memory is bad and it's been a long time so I know I am missing people, but these folks were among those who patiently turned me from a scrawler of words into an author: Ryck Neube, who was president at the time; Ann Welsh; Jack Kerley; Judy Tracy; Marcia Eckstein; Mary Fitzpatrick; Karen George; Linda Arnest; Rob Schofield; and Woody Carsky-Wilson.

Despite their best efforts, and an agent who liked it, the story was not sufficiently well-written to justify publication. I filed it in the electronic version of a bottom drawer, called it my practice novel, and moved on to writing my contract bridge book, *One Trick at a Time: How to Start Winning at Bridge.* The Seamus McCree mysteries *Bad Policy* and *Cabin Fever* soon followed.

My life partner, Jan Rubens, periodically nudged me to reconsider *Ant Farm.* "It's a good story," she said. "It just needs work, and you're a better writer now." In the summer of 2014 I indulged her and read the last version of the manuscript. The story did have good bones. It needed a lot of work, but I thought that work would be fun.

Two people purchased the rights to name characters in charity auctions, and since this is the first book I've published since those events, their characters are included here. During the 2014 "Murder on the Menu," Deborah Holt donated her money and her name to the cause of the Friends of the Wetumpka Public Library (Wetumpka, Alabama). Martha Weaver won the auction at the Unitarian Universalist Church of Savannah and chose her granddaughter's name: Skyler Weaver.

After taking several months to rewrite the story, I sent it to my editor, Dr. Julie Spergel, for her eagle eye. Karen Phillips designed a book cover I love. And I received useful feedback from my beta readers, Judy Penz Sheluk, Nancy Ogreenc, Pat Dutson, and Rita Stull.

The team at Kindle Press made further improvements (and caught a few embarrassing remaining homonyms along the way). I offer my special thanks to Laura Cherkas and Caroline Carr.

This is a work of fiction and I have taken certain liberties with geographic and police entities and procedures in service of the story. In the end, whatever errors are present are mine, all mine.

James M. Jackson
Amasa, Michigan

James M. Jackson authors the Seamus McCree mystery series. ANT FARM (Spring 2015), a prequel to BAD POLICY (2013) and CABIN FEVER (2014), recently won a Kindle Scout nomination. Ebook published by Kindle Press; print from Wolf's Echo Press). BAD POLICY won the Evan Marshall Fiction Makeover Contest whose criteria were the freshness and commerciality of the story and quality of the writing. Jim has published an acclaimed book on contract bridge, ONE TRICK AT A TIME: *How to Start Winning at Bridge* (Master Point Press 2012), as well as numerous short stories and essays.

His website is http://jamesmjackson.com.

Turn the page to find out what trouble awaits Seamus when he returns home from what he thought was a routine business trip.

BAD POLICY

ONE

DRIVING UP MY STREET, A pillow calling my name, I spotted Cincinnati police vehicles collected near the top of the hill. My stomach clenched. An animated gathering of neighbors stood across the street from my house. With my Victorian's ancient wiring, I immediately thought of fire. Not that; no fire engines. I pulled to the curb behind a phalanx of cop cars blocking the street and approached an officer.

"What happened?" I asked, surprised either one of us could hear my words over the hammering of my heart.

"Other side of the street," he snarled and pointed to the gawkers.

"But this is my house."

"You live here? Hold on a sec. Hey Sarge," he yelled over his shoulder without taking his eyes off me. "Over here."

The sergeant gave me the once-over as he strode across the lawn, thumbs tucked into his belt.

"This guy claims he lives here," the patrolman said.

The sergeant held out his hand. "Got some ID?" To the patrolman he added, "Back to your post."

I dug through my wallet and handed him my license. "What happened?" I asked again.

He compared the license to my face. "Seamus McCree."

"It's pronounced 'Shay-mus,' not 'See-mus.'"

"Now you say it, the name rings a bell. Right address. We've got some questions for you. It would be better if we talked somewhere quiet. Any objections if we take a quick trip downtown? We'll give you a ride back. Frankly, I'm not sure when the crime scene guys will release your house. You should be thinking about a place you can stay tonight."

He gently took my arm and guided me to a cruiser, opened the back door, and ducked me in. We were moving by the time I realized that he had neatly removed me from my home and temporarily focused my attention on where I could stay rather than what was going on.

"Now can you tell me what happened?" I asked through the grill separating us.

"Sorry, we need to confirm a few things with you first."

My father had been a Boston police sergeant when he died. Even as tired as I was, I could interpret his answer: you're a suspect; we'll ask the questions.

The officer left me alone in an interrogation room smelling of burnt coffee and justified fear. I slipped off my suit coat and hung it over the back of the metal chair and loosened my tie. If the police had only wanted information, the questioning would have started immediately. Since I was cooling my heels in a room decorated with a table bolted to the floor, three chairs, and what I knew to be a one-way mirror, I was clearly a suspect. Standard interrogation procedures included keeping the subject off-balance. One approach was to use a sterile room away from familiar surroundings. With minimal furnishings and putrid green walls, this place fit the bill. Then they would add pressure by keeping him waiting alone in the silence.

Silence would not work on me. A thinker by nature, I thrived on solitude. Despite that, corded muscles grabbed my neck and shoulders, adding to the headache I'd had all day from lack of sleep and too much caffeine. My tension came from not knowing what had happened at my house combined with the knowledge that this interrogation room belonged to the Homicide Unit.